QUEEN OF THE SLAYERS

Buffy the Vampire Slayer™

Available from SIMON & SCHUSTER

QUEEN OF THE SLAYERS

Nancy Holder

**An original novel based on the hit television series
created by Joss Whedon**

SSE

SIMON SPOTLIGHT ENTERTAINMENT
NEW YORK LONDON TORONTO SYDNEY

This book is a work of fiction. Any references to historical events, real people, or real locales are used fictitiously. Other names, characters, places, and incidents are the product of the author's imagination, and any resemblance to actual events or locales or persons, living or dead, is entirely coincidental.

SSE

SIMON SPOTLIGHT ENTERTAINMENT

An imprint of Simon & Schuster Children's Publishing Division

1230 Avenue of the Americas, New York, New York 10020

™ & © 2005 Twentieth Century Fox Film Corporation. All rights reserved.

Manufactured in the United States of America

First Edition   10   9   8   7   6   5   4   3   2   1

Library of Congress Control Number 2004117774

ISBN 1-4169-0241-4

In memory of fallen warriors:
Marion Elise Jones
and
Karen Beth Ingle

And to their daughters and granddaughters:
Elise Jones, Leslie Jones Ackel, Anny Caya, Lucy Walker,
Sandra Morehouse, and Belle Holder,
Slayers all

ACKNOWLEDGMENTS

First and foremost, my gratitude to Joss Whedon, for thirteen seasons of wondrous television. My deep appreciation to Gail Berman, who brought *Buffy* to the box and held all calls except for her kids'. Thanks to David Greenwalt, Marti Noxon, David Fury, and Tim Minear, and to the staffs and crews of both *Angel* and *Buffy*. Thank you so much, David Fury, for supporting my book drive after the Scripps Ranch fire. David Boreanaz, you have always been so gracious, and I am grateful.

My appreciation for my Simon & Schuster family, past and present: Patrick Price, Lisa Clancy, Emily Westlake, Tricia Boczkowski, Amanda Berger, Lisa Gribbin, Liz Shiflett, Bethany Buck, and Micol Ostow. I owe Debbie Olshan at Fox so many "saves." Thank you. Howard Morhaim, you are King of the Agents, and I am lucky beyond measure to be your client. Thanks to friends and family, whose support means so much; and to the light of my life and queen of my heart, my darling daughter, Belle. I love you, Ya-Ya's.

And my thanks to Buffy herself, Sarah Michelle Gellar; may your life be the stuff of dreams.

Uneasy lies the head that wears a crown.
—*King Henry the Fourth, Part II*, William Shakespeare

QUEEN OF THE SLAYERS

PROLOGUE

Break in the sun till the sun breaks down,
And death shall have no dominion.
—*"And Death Shall Have No Dominion,"* Dylan Thomas

In the demonic places Hell hath fury.
And Hell hated Buffy Summers.

In dimensions across time and space, demons roared as the First Evil's legions of Turok-Han fell and the Sunnydale Hellmouth collapsed.

Buffy the Vampire Slayer had won.

It was impossible.

Inconceivable.

Unbearable.

A handful of human girls, a few men, and one half-breed champion—a vampire—annihilated the forces sent to break open the Hellmouth!

Runes and seers and oracles had foretold a different victory. After centuries of battling the champions of good, the floodgates would burst open; and the Old Ones in all their many guises would unstoppedly pour through, to wrest the world back from the domination of humanity. The humiliation of demonic exile would at last be lifted.

Now those hopes lay in ruins.

As the Hellmouth fell, demon lord after demon lord threw back his head and howled with rage at the indignity. Demon sorceresses turned their backs on their dark goddesses. Necromancers slaughtered their minions. Fortune-tellers died horribly. And very slowly.

Demons debated if they were doomed to stand idly by, for time and all eternity, while humanity desecrated what was rightfully theirs?

The frustration was unbearable. And worse, failure came again at the hands of the Slayer—the cursed, vile Slayer who had used her witch-woman, Willow Rosenberg, to trick them. Buffy, the Slayer who never stayed dead; the perpetual thorn in their side. Every demon that dwelled in darkness yearned for Buffy Summers's destruction; lusted for it the way lovers sigh and cling to each other.

As hells seethed and shattered, as tempers blew and minions suffered, the lords of evil began to hatch plots and dream of another night, another chance.

Buffy the Vampire Slayer was the cause of their defeat. She must be eradicated. True, she had shared her power to create other Slayers, but she was the apex. Once she was gone, all the others would crumble to dust in their fingers.

In every defeat lies opportunity.

New gods rise when old gods die. The time of the First Evil had come and gone. But there were other evils—hellgods and Old Ones and beings so terrifyingly void of good that they eclipsed the First, from which they had sprung.

Now they rubbed hooves and talons and hands together, appetites whetted, ambitions soaring.

The prize: the world.

The obstacle: Buffy the Vampire Slayer.

The goal: her final death.

CHAPTER ONE

Down, down, down into the darkness of the grave
Gently they go, the beautiful, the tender, the kind;
Quietly they go, the intelligent, the witty, the brave.
I know. But I do not approve. And I am not resigned.
—*"Dirge without Music," Edna St. Vincent Millay*

THE M⊙JAVE DESERT

It was finally, miraculously over.

Buffy Summers, the Vampire Slayer, stared out the window as the school bus bounced over the bumpy little off-road through the high desert. Giles had chosen to travel off the beaten track: The main highway was jammed with media racing to cover the story of the complete destruction of the town of Sunnydale. As they had sped away from town, news vans barreled past, trying to get around roadblocks set up by the California Highway Patrol. No one knew what had happened, or if it would happen again. The most sensible approach was to keep everyone well away from the disaster site.

The bus had rolled past the city limits as helicopters whirred like locusts overhead, swooping down for a look at the enormous sinkhole. The only explanation that made any sense was an earthquake, although the seismic readings reported by an earthquake preparedness agency in the Los Angeles basin were inconsistent with a quake of that magnitude.

A few grizzled desert residents told *The National Observer* they had seen a meteor coursing through the sky that landed smack-dab in the center of town. No tracking satellite confirmed it, but that didn't prevent the destruction of Sunnydale from becoming an urban legend: It was a comet; it was foreign nationals; it was the government.

No one would ever guess the real story, of course.

The place the Spanish settlers had called Boca del Infierno—the Mouth of Hell—was gone, swallowed whole. The gaping maw of the Hellmouth had devoured the town in one fatal chomp, rather than gnawing on a steady stream of victims, as it had for over a century.

We closed that sucker down.

But they would never be able to share why, and thus they had to stay well away from the limelight. Besides, there were Slayers all over the world now, and Buffy wasn't sure what that was going to mean. Would governments try to co-opt them? Study them? Control them?

I can't worry about all that now. We're safe, and we're mobile. And we've got wounded to tend to.

Protectively wedged between Buffy and the bus window, her sister, Dawn, drowsed against her shoulder, exhausted. The big battle had taken all Dawn had had to give, and more.

Thank you for sparing her, Buffy told the sky, the desert scrub, the Joshua trees of the high desert. *Thank you for sparing so many of us.*

The bus was quiet as the passengers nursed their injuries and tried to understand everything that had happened. Namely, that they had won, and that each of them was still alive. Considering the odds they had faced that morning in the basement of Sunnydale High, it was far more incredible than they could have ever imagined.

They had destroyed the Hellmouth. The thousands of Turok-Han—primal vampires sent by the First Evil to wipe out Buffy and all her Potentials—were history.

After the initial euphoria of victory, a weary joy had spread over those aboard the getaway bus, followed by the somber realization that very few of them had actually survived. There were fourteen people on the bus: Buffy, Dawn, Giles, Robin, Kennedy, Xander, Willow, Vi, Rona, Andrew, Faith, and three Slayers whose names Buffy couldn't remember. She was fairly certain one was named Leslie. There was that French one . . . Marie? She was almost positive it was Marie.

Faith would totally be on her case for not knowing. No need to worry; she was on her own case. She'd make sure she learned their names as soon as Dawn woke up.

Of three dozen Potentials, six had lived. Everywhere, heads drooped in mourning for lost comrades.

Anya had died defending Andrew. And Spike had died defending them all.

Spike . . .

Buffy's throat tightened; tears welled. Her throat was so constricted that she couldn't swallow the knot of grief lodged there, could barely breathe. Spike was dead. He had elected to stay in the Hellmouth cavern, bursting into flame, when maybe, just maybe, he could have left with her and still saved the world.

Nothing in it for him, no reason to do it except for love, or because it was the right thing to do, or both.

What urged him toward self-sacrifice? His soul?

His heart?

Why was she fated to lose the ones she loved best?

Oh, Spike . . .

Not all of them, she reminded herself as she fought to keep from breaking down. *I haven't lost all of them.* Many of their loved ones were elsewhere, and safe. Buffy wondered what had become of Clem, the floppy-eared demon who had sped away in his brand-new red VW Beetle days ago. She'd given him such a hard time for running out on her; now she was glad he had escaped.

And here was Xander in one of his trademark oversize plaid

shirts, dealing with his own grief, his profile concealing the black patch over his left eye—the eye Caleb had destroyed.

Willow sat a few seats behind in sparkly brown paisley, intoning a spell of healing as she moved her hands slowly over Robin Wood. The former principal was sprawled on the backseat. His red shirt was dark with his blood, and his eyes were a little glassy. But he was still alive.

Faith hunched beside Willow, her arms crossed over a bloody white shirt. Willow's hands glowed as she held them over Robin's deep gut wound, casting soft light on the other Slayer. The look on Faith's face touched Buffy to her core: It was raw emotion; total, naked fear.

I tried to kill her once, Buffy thought. *To save Angel. I gutted her like a fish. I put her in a coma, and we essentially left her for dead. But she came back to Sunnydale when I needed her most. And even when our situation looked hopeless, she stayed and fought. She could have left anytime she wanted. Same as Spike.*

Buffy felt another pang of grief. *Not the same. Not the same at all.*

Kennedy the Vampire Slayer was taking a turn at the wheel. Giles had needed a break. Everyone who could drive would take a turn. It was understood that Buffy was not on the roster. Not next, and not ever. There was no reason to tempt fate by putting her in the driver's seat of a vehicle with actual wheels and a motor.

Giles, seated behind Kennedy so that he could give her directions to the next winding, remote road, seemed to sense Buffy's despair. The Watcher turned his head, and their gazes met. His face softened with sorrow.

Then he got up and carefully threaded his way back toward her, passing Slayers as he approached. Buffy noted their instinctual reaction to him—the way they brightened slightly; the silent reassurance he gave them. She thought of battle-weary soldiers receiving a visit from their prince.

As he passed by Rona, the Slayer began to cry; he returned to her side and crouched down beside her, speaking to her quietly. He put his hand on her shoulder, and she nodded as he pulled a tissue from his trouser pocket. He handed it to her; she wiped her eyes and gave him a wobbly smile.

Vi reached out and touched his forearm, and he patted her hand. As he moved on, the redheaded Slayer got up and moved to sit with Rona, gathering the other girl in her arms and rocking her gently.

Then Giles reached Buffy and eased down into the seat in front of her. His clothes were ripped and bloody. Earlier in their journey she had seen him take a handkerchief to the scratches and dirt on his face; his glasses were perfectly clean, and there was something very reassuring in his efforts to stay tidy. It was very British of him, very Giles.

They shared a moment, Slayer and Watcher, mentor and student, survivor and survivor.

Two friends.

Then she could hold in her grief no longer. A tear coursed down Buffy's cheek.

"Spike died bravely," Giles said gently.

"He died," Buffy replied, her voice catching, "like a champion."

"Yes. I . . . perhaps I misjudged him." He pushed up his glasses.

"Ya think?" she said archly, but her feeble attempt at humor failed. Then she said, "Angel offered to wear that amulet, Giles. Would the same thing have happened to him? Maybe it would have been different. Or . . ." She trailed off.

"Buffy," he began.

She pressed shaky fingers against the gash in her forehead. "I don't know, Giles. I keep seeing it happen, over and over. Spike drew down the light, and the light killed the Hellmouth. I told him . . . I said . . ." She closed her eyes against the rush of emotion. She would not say it. Those words were between her and Spike, and no one else.

And Spike was gone.

"Are you blaming yourself?" he asked her, tilting his head to one side as he waited for her answer.

After thinking a moment, she shook her head. "No." She shook it again. "Maybe. I don't know." She lowered her hand to the wound she had been dealt in battle. "All I know is that he's dead."

"*You* were dead," Giles reminded her. His voice was gentle. "And where you were, it was warm, and welcoming. You knew you were loved, and that you had done well. And you wanted to stay there. You would have done so, if Willow hadn't brought you back."

Now the tears came. Freely. "Yes. And if he's there . . ."

"If he's there, we should be happy for him." But Giles's face was cast in shadowed sadness. She knew he was not grieving for Spike; he was grieving for her.

"Yes," she managed. "If he's there." She pulled Dawn close. Her sister was still fast asleep, and she looked like an angel.

"He died for others, Buffy," Giles said. "Fate generally deals kindly with . . . people . . . who do that."

"But before that, he *killed* others. *Lots* of others." She closed her mind to the stories Giles had told her about William the Bloody. Before he had changed, he had killed people just to piss her off.

"We can't know that he was forgiven. We can hope. Perhaps . . . pray. I do think miracles occur." He raised a brow. "After all, who would have dreamed Faith would be here with us?"

"I thought about that too," Buffy admitted. She turned and looked in the same direction as Giles—at Faith, who was wiping Robin's brow with a strip of torn T-shirt.

As if Faith sensed Buffy's gaze, her face hardened, and she said to Willow, "I still say we take him to a hospital."

"No," Robin murmured, half-lifting his head from the seat. "I want more miles between us and that pit."

Buffy agreed with that. She remembered reading an article—or had Xander told her about it?—about a giant fungus that grew beneath certain kinds of birch trees. It could span hundreds of miles—one of them was discovered in four different states—and it fed the trees' roots with vital nutrients. Aboveground, the fungus was invisible, but it was there in the depths, and it was necessary to the survival of the enormous birch forests.

If the Hellmouth was a parasitic tree . . . or an obliging fungus . . .

The Slayer sighed heavily. They had destroyed the Sunnydale Hellmouth. But that didn't mean that all the evil in the world had been eliminated.

It just meant that they had won Round One.

There were other Hellmouths—or at least one in Cleveland. Other battles. Other forces of darkness to keep at bay.

But I shared my power with the others. Let them take over. Let Faith take center stage.

Let me rest.

I have a sister to raise.

She was weary to her bones, although the adrenaline overdrive of battle still pulsated through her. Her Slayer's reflexes remained on high alert. She saw her wariness mirrored on the faces of the other Slayers on the bus—and felt another pang of loss as her mind's eye replayed the deaths of Amanda and Chao-Ahn.

You did not die in vain, she told the young girls' memories. *You each died a hero's death.*

That thought gave Buffy little peace. Death had walked beside her, a silent, stealthy companion, ever since she had been Chosen. For years she had gone to bed every night knowing that it might be the last time she saw a crescent moon outside her window; that she might never again feel the soft spring breeze on her cheek. That Xander and Willow would probably one day put roses on her grave, where she would stay; and that Angel . . .

She took a deep breath. She had outlived one of the two vampires who had loved her.

Of course Spike had been the one to die. Spike was brash and foolhardy, a creature of his passions. She felt a rush of longing as memories she rarely allowed into her mind replayed the journey she had walked with Spike. First enemies, then lovers, then finally, friends.

At the last, more than friends.

He had traveled to the ends of the earth to demand a soul—for her. He had known that would end him in so many ways, yet he had persisted.

In other times, he had despised Angel for being ensouled, despite Angel's soul having been forced upon him. Angel hadn't sought out a soul. It wasn't a choice. But Spike had not only asked for one; he had gone through hell to get it.

For love of Buffy the Vampire Slayer—a love that ultimately destroyed him.

Or had it saved him?

Giles patted her hand and said, "I am sincerely sorry for your loss, Buffy. I may not have approved of your relationship with Spike, or even understood it . . ." He trailed off, smiling bitterly. "I'm being dishonest. Of course I understood it. After I left Oxford, I adored the darkness. Its touch electrified me. And I was around your age when I went there. I reveled in rejecting all that was required of me. All that was 'good.'"

She nodded. He did understand.

Then she reached past Dawn and pressed her palm against the window, fanning out her fingers as if she were touching the blurring landscape of pines and sky. The sun was going down. The day was ending.

"We used to play a game called 'Anywhere but Here.' Willow and I. And sometimes Xander." She looked at him. "Is that where we're going?"

"Yes. Absolutely."

"Good," she told him.

He rose. "I'm going to see if Kennedy needs a break," he said. He swayed as the bus hit a pothole.

Buffy wondered if he was in any condition to drive, but she kept her thought to herself. As he turned to go, she said, "Giles? I . . . you trained me well. Thank you."

He shook his head. "You learned well, Buffy. A good student can learn from any teacher, though that teacher might be mediocre at best."

"A good student?" She made a show of preening, lifting her chin and squaring her shoulders. Her eyes glittered. "Hey, I *am* a good student. I just passed Advanced Apocalypse."

He inclined his head. "With flying colors."

"And extra credit for not dying."

"Indeed." A wash of youthful joy passed over his features, and she saw, as she did occasionally, the young man Giles once had been. "We did it, Buffy."

"We did it." She nuzzled Dawn. "We have done the impossible."

"That makes us mighty." He gazed at Dawn with a tender, protective expression. "I'm glad she's resting. She's been through so much." With that, he turned and moved slowly up the aisle toward the front of the bus. As before, hands reached out to him as he passed the new Slayers. He paused to speak to one young girl whose face was horribly bruised.

Then Buffy's attention was caught as the gleam from Willow's hands intensified, reflecting off the ceiling, and Robin murmured, "Oh. Yeah. That feels better."

"Good," Willow told him. Buffy craned her neck around to see her friend's face washed in a rosy glow. She was positively luminous, as if someone had brushed glitter makeup over her skin.

Andrew got up from his seat about midway down the bus, walked past Buffy, and stood in the aisle beside Willow. He stared in rapture as she worked on Robin and whispered, "Feel the force, Principal Wood. It surrounds and penetrates you." He turned to Willow and solemnly placed a hand on the crown of her head,

"Well done, young Wicca. The force is strong in this one."

"Oh, shut up," Faith snapped, but she was smiling at Robin. Andrew wasn't actually registering on her radar so much.

If only Willow could bring Spike back.

Buffy still couldn't quite accept that it was over. The legions of hideous Turok-Han had been wiped out by the supernova brightness of Spike's immolation. The Hellmouth had collapsed, taking the evil little town of Sunnydale down with it.

Her mother's image rose in her mind: Joyce, happily serving Thanksgiving dinner to Buffy and her friends. Buffy smiled. Then another image superimposed itself over that one: her mom—her mommy—lying dead on the couch, vacantly staring at Buffy as she came into the house. Joyce was buried in Happy Memories, one of Sunnydale's dozen cemeteries.

I won't be able to visit her grave, Buffy thought. *Who will bring her flowers? She loved pink roses. . . .*

And what about Jenny Calendar?

Giles's love, Jenny Calendar, was buried in Sunnydale, too, dead by Angel's hand after he lost his soul to the Gypsy curse forced on him by Jenny's people.

And Tara?

She was buried nearby; Xander had driven Willow out to Tara's grave. Tara was Willow's soul mate, shot by Warren when he had been aiming at Buffy. The loss had not taken Willow's soul, but it had temporarily stripped her of her humanity. If Xander hadn't gotten through to her, reminding her that he loved her, she would have ended the world.

And Anya . . . Xander's love. She, too, had been left behind, somewhere in the rubble of Sunnydale High, deep within the Hellmouth's maw. She had died a hero's death defending Andrew.

Mom. Jenny. Tara. Anya.

Buffy felt as if they were abandoning them, the beloved dead.

The Slayer closed her eyes against the pain, then opened them again as tears coursed down her cheeks. She was not one to wallow. She was one to take action.

I'll come back here someday, she vowed. *I'll bring them flowers and I'll let them know that we're all just fine.*

Because we will be. And we'll have normal lives.

Dawn stirred against her shoulder. Buffy breathed in the sweet scent of her sister's skin. She remembered that smell from Dawn's infancy, although she had never held Dawn when she was a baby. The Monks had given the Slayer a sister to love and protect, complete with false memories, when in reality Dawn had been a source of energy called the Key. But now Dawn was a real girl, and she and Buffy had long ago made peace with her past. As far as the Summers sisters were concerned, they were, and always had been, family.

Whatever it takes to give Dawn a normal life, I'll do it. We have a chance now. I'm not the only one who stands between the forces of darkness and the rest of the world.

I'm free.

Giles was standing in the aisle just behind Kennedy. He said, "Kennedy . . . look out!" at the same time that Kennedy screamed, "Oh, my God!"

Buffy tried to see around Giles; couldn't; the bus swerved hard to the left; the brakes squealed like a slaughtered animal. Buffy instinctively grabbed on to the seat ahead of her to stop her body from ramming against Dawn. The vehicle began to fishtail wildly as Kennedy lay on the horn.

Dawn jerked awake and cried, "Buffy, what's happening?" She began to stand up to see what was going on.

"Stay seated!" Buffy ordered her, cocooning Dawn so that her own back was pressed against the window. She tucked her sister's head under her chin while, around them, Slayers half-rose from their seats, shouting, yelling directions at Kennedy:

"Go left!"

"Slow down!"

"Straighten out!"

"Everyone stay in your seats!" Buffy shouted, but her voice was drowned out by the shouts of the others. She began to rise, then realized she should follow her own advice. Giles was up there, beside a battle-seasoned Slayer.

"You're going to hit her!" Giles cried, gesturing toward the wide front window.

"What is she *doing*? Get out of my way!" Kennedy yelled.

Giles reached over and pulled the wheel. The bus swerved hard to the left again. The stench of burning rubber burst into the air. Buffy held on tightly to her screaming sister, cradling her head against her shoulder. Then the right side of the bus raised from the ground; the bus was traveling on its left set of tires.

"Move to the right!" Buffy shouted to the others, thinking their combined weight could shift the bus's center of gravity back to the middle.

But it was too late. She braced herself for impact as the bus kept falling to the left. Dawn's fingers dug into her shoulders. "Oh, my God, we're going to crash!" Dawn cried.

The bus slammed against the tarmac in a kaleidoscope of screams and bodies, screeching metal, and shattering glass.

The window broke beneath Buffy's weight as she was thrown hard against it. Large shards of glass tore into her upper arm, but she barely felt them as she cocooned herself around Dawn.

The bus's momentum propelled it forward, sheering metal off the side with a horrible wrenching sound. Sparks arced. The bus kept sliding.

Chaos swirled around her; she cupped Dawn's head under her chin, shouting to be heard, "It's okay, Dawnie! It's going to be okay!"

"God, Robin! Don't you freakin' die!" Faith cried, and Buffy gritted her teeth, not loving how frantic the other woman sounded.

Willow's voice rose and fell in a new incantation, her voice jagged and frantic.

"I know CPR!" Xander yelled.

"Don't touch him!" Faith shouted.

Then the bus piled into something with the full force of a rocket launcher. The impact whipped Buffy's head back, and she held Dawn as if she had to keep her from flying off the Earth as her sister screamed again. Buffy heard another wail of metal as something detached from the bus.

Finally the bus lay still, a ticking sound keeping rhythm in the stunned chaos.

Someone was crying. Someone else was groaning. Buffy brushed Dawn's hair away from her eyes and searched her face. "Are you hurt?" she demanded. "Are you okay?"

Dawn looked dazed. "Yes. I'm fine." She waved a hand at the disaster site that was the bus. "Go. Help the others. I'm okay."

The distinctive smell of gasoline wafted through the shattered windows.

Oh, my God. The gas tank has been ruptured. Buffy looked away from Dawn and bellowed, "Everyone! Out of the bus! Help the injured out. *Now!*"

Buffy planted her feet in the shards of the window, helping Dawn to a standing position. A wide, deep gash bisected Rona's forehead; Vi's nose was bleeding. But both were moving under their own steam. Another girl with short, auburn hair had both her hands pressed over her eye. Beside her, another girl, dressed in a Sunnydale High School T-shirt, was trying to pull her hands away to examine the wound.

"Don't check injuries. Get out!" Buffy yelled.

The Slayers were already pulling together, finding their footing on the overturned bus, checking in with one another and seeing to the wounded.

At the front of the bus, Giles said to Kennedy, "Perhaps we can force the door open, by pushing . . . well, yes, like that," as Kennedy popped the door, which was now more like a hatch above her head. She sent it flying over the side of the bus.

Kennedy bellowed, "Out! Move it, Slayers!" to Vi and one of the Slayers whose name Buffy had forgotten. She made a handhold for Vi, who planted her boot in Kennedy's clasped hands, then hoisted herself up. She clambered out, then reached back in for the other Slayer's hand.

"Come on!" Giles shouted. "The gas could ignite at any moment!"

Dawn blinked at Buffy as Buffy clasped her heart-shaped face in her hands and said, "We have to get out of the bus. I'm going to take you to Giles. We have to crawl over the seats." She looked hard into Dawn's eyes. "Can you do that?"

But Dawn was staring at Buffy's arm. Her eyes widened, and she cried, "You're all mangled!"

"Dawn!" Buffy bellowed, clamping her palm over the worst of her cuts to stop the massive bleeding. "Crawl over the seats! *Now!*"

"Okay. Okay," Dawn said quickly. She pushed herself away from her big sister and gripped the top of the seat in front of theirs. Buffy maneuvered herself so that her feet were positioned flat against the broken window, which lay on top of the asphalt road; then she stood up, reaching out her hands to help her sister.

"Everyone else all right? Is Robin alive?" she called.

"Basically," Willow answered. She and Faith were hoisting Robin's limp body between them. The principal did not look basically alive to Buffy. He looked extremely unconscious. And too heavy for Willow to carry.

Andrew's head popped up like a prairie dog from between two seats; he raised his hand as if he were asking a question in class and said, "Um, I thought the dying part was over?"

Buffy didn't take the time to answer. The odor of gasoline was stronger. So not a good sign.

"C'mon, hurry up," she said tersely as she grabbed him and started pulling him behind herself and Dawn. The rows of seats were canted sideways like in a carnival fun house.

She looked back over her shoulder at Willow, Faith, and Robin. "Faith, can you handle it?" she asked.

"I'm five by five, B," Faith answered tersely. "What the hell happened? Junior forget to take driver's ed?"

Buffy herded Dawn and Andrew down the aisle, searching for Xander as she went. She didn't see him anywhere. "Xander?"

There was no answer.

Then she smelled thick, oily smoke, although she didn't see it. *Yet,* she told herself. *Where there's smoke, there's danger.*

From the front of the bus, Giles shouted, "Buffy, do hurry! The bus is on fire!"

"Oh, no!" Andrew wailed, his foot catching in the metal rungs of the seat. He fell forward; Buffy caught him by the scruff of his shirt and yanked him up.

He flailed like a marionette, the red motorcycle on his shirt undulating "We're gonna die! I *knew* it! I *knew* I wasn't supposed to survive the final battle! And now I'm being punished for tricking fate with an agonizing death!"

"Use the force, Andrew," Buffy gritted.

"Yeah. Use it to shut up," Faith said, threading herself under Robin's armpits, her hands clasped across his chest. Her dark hair hung in her eyes as she looked first at Buffy, then at the length of the bus she had yet to cover—and with Buffy, Dawn, and Andrew in her way. "Hurry up," Faith snapped at them.

"Excuse us, but we're going as fast as we can," Andrew replied, sounding miffed. "Some of us did not inherit the powers of the Slayers of the Vampyre, you know. If you hadn't noticed, there's sex discrimination involved."

"Hey. Girl here," Dawn snapped at him. "And I'm not a Slayer, either."

"True. But do I detect a certain bitterness about that, hmm?" he queried.

"Screw it," Faith muttered. She said to Willow, "We're going the other way."

"What other way?" Willow asked.

"This way. Here." Faith draped Robin over her, the way one might hand someone a large, rolled-up carpet. Willow bowed backward beneath his weight.

"Whoa," Willow said.

"Hold on." Faith lifted him back off her. Robin sagged in her arms as she executed an awesome sidekick at the rear window, pulverizing it into explosive drifts of powdery glass as she gave it a second kick, and a third.

Faith draped him firefighter style over her back and said to Willow, "You climb out first."

Buffy glanced at Dawn, who was managing to work herself toward the front of the bus. Then Giles hurried forward and grabbed her hands. He said to Buffy, "I've got her."

"Get him, too," Buffy said, hoisting Andrew up and over the next seat. "Go to Giles," she told him.

"I am, I am," Andrew assured her.

Buffy looked back at Willow, Faith, and Robin and threaded her way back to them. Then she said to Faith, "I'll hold on to him. You go out. Then I'll hand him down to you."

Faith looked dubious.

"Come on, Faith," Buffy gritted. "We're in a crisis situation here."

"Okay." Faith tenderly handed Robin over to Buffy. Buffy hoisted him over her back as Faith had done, while Faith turned to Willow and grabbed her forearm. "C'mon. Let's kick it."

Half-carrying, half-dragging Willow, Faith eased her through the empty window, knocking a few hanging shards of glass out of the window, then climbed out after her.

Buffy moved forward with Robin. *After this, I'll make sure no one else—*

There was a strange roar behind her as Andrew screamed her name. *"Buffy!"*

A tremendous burst of heat whooshed from the floor, scorching her feet. She heard nothing but a fierce thunder as she lurched forward. Flames erupted and shot along the side of the bus, then spewed from the floor.

I'm going to die after all, she thought.

I'm going to die like Spike.

CHAPTER TWO

And maybe there was a small part of Buffy that welcomed death in the fire on the bus. A voice whispering about rest and welcome; and the chance to see Spike again, and make good on the words she had spoken to him in his last moments on this earth. The ones he had not believed.

Maybe this fire was the literal baking of the cookie dough. . . .

But that couldn't be true. If she let herself die, Robin Wood would die, too, and maybe others. This was an emergency; lives were at stake; and she was the Slayer. The only time she got to die was in the line of duty.

Scarlet geysers rose up in front of her; intense heat buffeted behind her. She yelled, "Fire extinguisher! Now!"

She couldn't hear her own voice, or see anything but orange, crimson, and yellow flames. Sweat rolled down her face; blisters bubbled on her knuckles. The hair on her arms was singed.

The heat was intense. The pain was worse.

She forced herself to remain calm, though her instincts for self-preservation were screaming at her to flee. If she knew where escape lay, she would gladly go there.

I'm surrounded by Slayers, she reminded herself. *Someone's going to get us out of this. They won't let us go up.* . . .

Then, as if on cue, a figure burst through the flames, grabbed her, and threw a wet blanket over her head. She hastened to pull it over Robin's body. Then she let the figure guide her forward. Her eyes were seared with smoke. Her lips were cracking.

Her boots were burning off her feet.

Without warning, she was yanked to the side, and she began falling. She croaked, "Stop! You'll hurt Robin!"

She landed hard.

She must have blacked out; when she awoke, she realized the blanket was literally steaming on top of her. She threw it off. Smoke piled on top of her, on top of itself, like toxic and very dirty whipped cream. Then, all at once, the section directly in front of her thinned; there was just air, nicely transparent. Her heart skipped as she spotted a figure staggering about ten or fifteen feet away—it was hard to judge distance; she had no way to gauge depth—with one hand raised over its head. As if it had been shot, the figure jerked, stumbled, and collapsed.

"Robin?" she choked out.

Then the smoke rushed over Buffy, layers and layers of it, blinding her.

"Hey!" she shouted, darting forward, bending at the waist and waving her hands back and forth, searching for the other person. The smoke quickly overpowered her, filling her mouth and nose, her eyes and even her ears. Slayer powers, yes, but even she had limits. She began to hack badly; she retraced her steps and found the blanket. Though touching it burned her hands, she grabbed it up and threw it over her head again, hoping to use it as a filter to keep herself from suffocating. It was scratchy and rough, and where it touched her skin, it felt as if someone were sawing at her with a fingernail file.

She moved forward again, searching, trying to hear someone calling, or coughing, any indication that Robin was nearby. The fire engulfing the bus roared like a frenzied hellbeast, a tremendous, insatiable groaning that echoed through the smoke as the metal superheated and buckled. The stench of burning rubber was so thick that Buffy had to actually swallow it down to breathe. The odor hit her stomach and she coughed so hard, she felt something loosen in her throat. She doubled over, shuffling forward, still feeling with her hands for Robin Wood.

C'mon, c'mon, she begged him. *Help me find you.*

After a few seconds, a sharp wind flapped wildly at her blanket. She chanced raising up her makeshift hood and peered out, her eyes streaming with tears. Sure enough, the wind was carrying the smoke back away in the opposite direction. Through badly blurred vision, Buffy realized she was facing the bus—or what was left of it. A swirling blaze of orange, red, and yellow devoured the vehicle as if it were made of paper. She felt a terrible sense of finality. No one could still be alive in there.

She shivered. It was if the forces of evil had followed them out of town for one final, last-ditch effort to keep Buffy Summers from leaving the battlefield: *No one gets out of here alive. Especially not the Slayer . . .*

Buffy had no time to spend on such thoughts. She whirled and raced through the smoke, which, while thinner in the other direction, was still noxious. She coughed some more; then her heart lightened as she saw figures about twenty feet to her left: Giles, Rona, and Dawn.

"Dawnie," she rasped in a smoke-seared, raggedy voice. Then she stumbled over something soft and hit the ground on her knees. "Robin . . ."

She looked down, and though she had seen death many times, her heart lurched. It was one of the new Slayers, someone she had seen distinguish herself in battle and keep to herself on the bus. She looked to be about fifteen—the age when Buffy herself had been called—but Buffy couldn't remember if the girl had worn her black hair in a buzz cut, or if the fire had burned it away. She lay on her back, her neck canted at a fatal angle. Her left eye, horribly blood-shot, stared vacantly. Buffy touched her blistered cheek, easing her face toward herself. The other half of her face was charred and bloody. The eye was gone. . . .

Did you rescue me? Buffy silently asked her. She put her finger-tip on the lid of the bloodshot eye, closed it, and sat back on her haunches as she prepared to get up.

Out of the smoke, someone was crawling toward her, sobbing. It was Vi, looking shell-shocked as she reached Buffy's side, grab-bing the other girl's lifeless hand and pressing it against her cheek.

Buffy said, "What the hell happened?"

"There was a girl, running toward the bus," Vi murmured.

"And our *bus* fell over? Avoiding one pedestrian?"

Vi said nothing. "Are the others accounted for? Robin?"

"Buffy, Lisa's dead," Vi said, weeping. "She's *dead.*"

Buffy nodded and looked away, scanning her surroundings. "I know," Buffy told her. "But we have to get out of here. We have to find the others."

Vi pointed at the girl—Lisa. "But she—"

"You can't help her," Buffy said, grabbing her shoulders and locking her gaze with her. "But there may be others you *can* help. Who may be dying now."

Vi would not let go of the dead girl's hand, and it jerked in a macabre imitation of a handshake. Vi started to cry harder.

"No," Buffy admonished her. "You do not have the luxury of doing this, Vi. You're a Slayer. Let's go."

She took the dead girl's hand out of Vi's grip and placed it on the ground.

Then she stood up with Vi and eased her forward. Not for the first time, she wondered, *Have we done the right thing, giving them all the power? Their lives will be so different now. . . .*

It doesn't matter if it was right. It was the only chance we had. . . .

Dawn saw her and raced to her. "Buffy! Oh, God, you're alive!" Dawn burst into tears and threw her arms around her big sister. "I saw the bus go up, oh, Buffy . . ."

Buffy held her. "It's all right, Dawn. I'm fine. But we need to find the others."

"I thought we were safe," Dawn said, weeping. "I thought we would be okay now."

"I know," Buffy murmured, smoothing her hair. "I'll get you away from all this, Dawn. I'll take you somewhere. You will be safe. I promise you."

Dawn led Buffy over to Giles, and Rona. Andrew was there as well, throwing up. Rona was propped against a sign that read, NO GAS FOOD LODGING 100 MILES. She was holding her left arm, still in its white bandages. Scrubby pine trees and white sage bushes rustled in the hot wind behind her.

Giles stepped up to her. There was a deep cut above his forehead and his right cheek was puffy and mottled. He still had his glasses, and for the first time ever, she wondered how on earth he had managed to hold on to them through all his many trials and tribulations.

It was the sort of vague, errant thought that passes through most people's heads in times of crisis, and the fact that it occurred to her now told her that she was adjusting to the situation. Now that she had found Dawn, she was letting go of her singleness of purpose. That was all right. A good Slayer had to know when to focus on a single task, and when to spread her mental resources more evenly.

Buffy said to Giles, "It was one girl?"

"One girl," he confirmed. "The bus went out of control. Unexpectedly."

They shared a look. *We never outrun the evil.* "You do a head count?"

Giles nodded. "The fatality. Lisa. She's the only one, it appears."

"Good." Buffy nodded soberly. "Not that having a fatality is ever good."

"Yes, especially because she died saving you," Vi said hoarsely. Her mouth was pinched, her expression hard, her voice angry. "You don't even care."

Buffy understood Vi's high emotion. "Of course I care, Vi. You know I do."

Vi swallowed and pressed the hands against her eyes. "I know. I'm . . . I'm . . ." Her knees buckled and she retched hard, each contraction making her entire body jerk as if someone had run an electric current through her.

Rona put her hands around Vi, a mirror of their embrace on the bus. "Let's get you sat down," she said gently.

Footsteps sounded behind Buffy, and she turned to see Xander half-jogging, half-staggering toward her. His face was blackened, and he had wound a shredded T-shirt around the lower half of his face. His eye was bloodshot, like the dead girl's. He held out his hand and she thankfully took it, drawing him toward herself. He didn't speak; he was coughing hard.

As Xander held up a hand to indicate that he was not in danger of collapse, Buffy looked back to Giles. "I need to see Robin. And Willow and Faith."

He nodded. Buffy glanced down at Vi and Rona.

"We're good here," Rona said quietly.

"Okay." Buffy moved off, Giles, Dawn, and Xander following her.

Then Andrew caught up, saying, "I'm finished barfing."

"We're glad," Dawn told him.

He nodded seriously. "Me too."

Dawn kept hold of Buffy's hand as they walked back across the tarmac, the sisters circling the burning bus to reach the opposite side. Even on a less-traveled stretch of road, Buffy thought it was strange that no other cars had passed by. No one to call 911 on a cell phone, or stop and render aid. She had no sense of time, yet she hoped someone would happen by soon. Like in the next thirty seconds.

They reached Willow and Faith, both attending to Robin, who had regained a semblance of consciousness. Lying on the ground, he was the first to see Buffy, and he smiled faintly.

She smiled back. It was amazing that Robin had lived through all this, but Buffy didn't want to question that too closely. Robin alive was a gift. Given what they had been up against, every life was a gift.

Faith's back was to Buffy. The back of her white top had been burned away, and there was a mean burn mark between her shoulder blades. It looked like a scythe-shaped brand, and Buffy's stomach gave a little flip at the resemblance between it and the scythe that had proved to be the secret weapon of the Slayers, protected by the Guardians since the Shadow Men had created the First Slayer back in Africa.

Senaya, where are you now? Buffy silently asked her sister Slayer. They had called the First Slayer the Primitive; she had been frightening in her face paint and near-mindless obsession with killing. But she had had a name, which was Senaya, and she was the first to swallow the demon. *Are you asleep in time, on your bed of bones? Can you hear me? Can you give me some of your strength to help my people?*

Faith was holding Robin's hand. "I think he's going into shock. He's got a wicked strange look on his face."

"He's just smiling, Faith," Buffy told her.

"Huh. He doesn't do that much," Faith said anxiously.

Buffy met Robin's look. His grin became a grimace as pain caught hold of him.

Willow's forehead and cheeks were smudged with soot. She said to Buffy, "Hey. You okay?"

"Sure." Buffy gestured to Robin. "What about him?"

"Him's fine," Robin slurred as his lids fluttered.

Willow darted a surreptitious glance at Faith, who either had not heard the question or was ignoring it. "Oh," Willow said blandly, "he'll live." But the expression on the Wicca's face told Buffy that Willow wasn't certain of that.

Faith was no fool; she glared at Willow and said, "You are so full of crap. Of course he's going to live. Especially if we can get him to a hospital."

"We'll get to work on that," Buffy told her. She wondered if the driver of the next car that came by would cooperate willingly, or if they were actually going to have to commit a carjacking to transport Robin. Not that she would hesitate to just about anything short of homicide to ensure his safety.

Faith gestured toward more pines bordering that side of the road and said, "Kennedy ran after the idiot who caused this whole thing." As she stared back down at Robin, she added under her breath, "Good thing she went instead of me. Because if *I* found that girl . . ."

"Kennedy saw her through the windshield," Willow told Buffy, her tone a little anxious. "She said the girl was running from something. That she was scared."

"Did she make the bus crash?" Buffy asked the Wicca.

Willow shook her head. "I don't think so. I could be wrong."

"I'll give her something to be scared of," Faith bit off.

Despite her earlier musings on Faith's change of heart, there were occasional moments when Buffy was not so sure that the reformed Faith was the Faith who was going to stick around. This was one of those moments. Faith still had an awful lot of sharp edges; get too close and someone just might get hurt. Buffy knew that it was completely possible to fight on the side of good while you yourself walked in shadow. That was her own theme song pretty much. Seemed to her that the universe's favorite color was gray and the songs on its sound track were fast, frenetic, and over too soon.

Like a Slayer's lifespan, at least before Willow's juju womyn power thing.

"Do we have any water?" Buffy asked Giles.

"Unfortunately, no," Giles replied.

"We have nothing," Andrew said, sighing heavily. He put his hands on his hips and scanned the horizon. "And plenty of it. We're like Luke and Han on Toth, only it's not cold. All we have is our keen wits, which we must use to survive in this dismal outpost, while eluding the probes of the Empire." He looked heavenward.

"More likely we'll use our thumbs, to snag a ride to the next town," Xander informed him drily. "But as for the probes of the Empire . . ." He looked up at Buffy. "I'm seeing a big bad fire, a dead Slayer, and a bus that won't be going anywhere ever again. You think a few evil thingies survived the closure of the Hellmouth? And they arranged a going-away party for the Slayer and her Slayerettes? Maybe because they just couldn't stand the idea that you were going away and they would miss you ever so much?"

She made a face, wrinkling her nose. "Your alarming thoughts are my alarming thoughts, pretty much," she admitted.

"Oh, God," Andrew groaned. "So something evil made the bus crash? It started the fire? I thought it was over! I thought we were finished with fighting the Hellmouth. It's starting again!" He covered his mouth.

"Easy, barf boy," Xander soothed. "We all got A's today. We'll worry about the homework later, okay?" He snapped his fingers. "Oh, wait! No more homework! We graduated." He gestured to the bus. "Bus dead. Us, not so much."

"Except for Lisa," Buffy murmured.

"Yes." Xander grew serious again. "Except for Lisa."

"Payback," Andrew said, in a world-weary voice. "It's a bitch." He pointed at Buffy. "But we have to expect the gunslingers of evil to try to take her down. Everyone wants a crack at the fastest gun in the West. Like in *High Noon.*"

"I don't use guns, brain trust," Buffy snapped, sounding angrier than she intended. She turned to Giles. "Giles, *did* something evil start our bus on fire?"

"I haven't enough information to hazard a guess," Giles admitted. "However, it didn't start burning until it crashed."

"Buses don't catch on fire when they crash," Xander insisted, pointing in the direction of the blazing vehicle. "Well, they hardly ever do. They show that in the movies all the time because it's more interesting than real life. Like computers bursting into flames when there's something wrong with them. Doesn't happen. They just eat your blueprints and force you to buy things on eBay."

"Willow said there was smoke and flames when you guys stopped Willow's computer virus boyfriend Moloch," Dawn piped up.

Willow nodded earnestly.

Xander held up a finger. "Demon, not virus. Where there's smoke, there's a demon." He studied the bus with a grim expression. "Or not."

"The girl—" Giles began.

As if on cue, a shout of terror rang out from the direction of the pine trees.

"On it," Buffy announced, taking off. Her lungs were seared. It hurt to run, but she forced herself. She had gone about thirty feet when Faith raced up behind her, easily catching up.

Uh-oh, Buffy thought, but she didn't waste her breath suggesting Faith might prefer to stay behind. Breath was in fact hard to come by. Smoke inhalation was taking a toll, but she pumped her arms and legs as fast as she could, which was not speeding-bullet fast, but impressive nonetheless for someone who had not been born on the planet Krypton or was named Buttercup, Blossom, or Bubbles. Just Buffy.

Faith kept pace, then broke into a crazy-ass grin as she overtook Buffy and disappeared, crashing through the trees and leaving Buffy to negotiate the thick pine branches when they thwapped back into place as Faith barreled through.

The branches slapped Buffy's blistered skin. But the air in the woods was fresh, and the pine scent was welcome after the stench of the burning bus and charred flesh. It was a welcome relief simply to move, to feel her strength returning, her injuries beginning to heal.

She stopped a moment to get her bearings, panting as she draped forward, and pressed her palms against her thighs.

"Yo, B!" Faith's distant voice echoed against the tree trunks.

Then a second voice burst out with an almost animalistic scream, just a high, shrill wail of complete panic. Buffy said, "Faith, don't hurt anyone!"

There was another scream.

Buffy honed in on it; she ran between two towering evergreens and found herself moving into a clearing. Shadows loomed, bleaching the trees to a stale, dull gray.

On the other side of the clearing, the waning sun washed over the dark heads of Faith and Kennedy. They were hovering over a third person, who appeared to be kneeling.

As Buffy raced toward them, the figure dropped flat against the ground. She was a young woman with a strawberry-blond ponytail and dark eyebrows, and she began rolling around in a patch of mustard weeds. She was gibbering, spit coating her lips like fuzzy white lipstick. She wore jeans and a faded blue Old Navy sweatshirt; her arms were thrown over her head and she writhed crazily, as if she was on fire.

Faith and Kennedy both registered Buffy's arrival as they kept an eye on the girl. It was the first time since the accident that Buffy had seen Kennedy, and she was relieved to find that Willow's girlfriend appeared to be in good shape.

"What's wrong with *her*?" Buffy asked.

"She's an accident that didn't wait to happen," Faith answered. She waved her hand in a warning gesture. "And I wouldn't get too close, B. She's strong."

"Yeah," Kennedy chimed in, lifting her T-shirt to reveal four deep scratches across the left side of her rib cage.

"She did that?" Buffy asked in surprise, looking from the wound to the girl and back again.

Kennedy nodded. "She would have done worse if Faith hadn't shown. I think she was trying to rip my heart out."

Buffy glanced at Faith. "Did you hit her?"

"Only twice," Faith replied, distinctly unremorseful.

Cocking her head as she walked around the girl, Buffy caught a glimpse of her eyes. They were every bit as vacant as those of the dead Slayer who had saved Buffy's life.

"I don't think she's a firestarter," Faith said. "Or she'd have zapped us crispy by now."

"She's as wigged as we are," Buffy said. "It's okay," she told the girl. "You're safe." She glanced up at Faith and Kennedy. "Maybe she's a Slayer."

"I don't remember her from the battle at the Hellmouth," Kennedy said.

Faith shook her head. "I don't think she was there."

"That's what I'm saying," Buffy persisted. "Maybe she got her powers somewhere out here when Willow did the magicks. Then she just freaked out."

"It's an idea," Faith said.

"I think maybe it's the right one," Buffy replied.

"Or maybe you're seeing Slayers where there are just demons," Faith countered.

Kennedy moved her head back toward the highway. "I think she heard us coming and ran toward us, maybe for help. She didn't look like she was trying to be evil."

"And the rest is carnage," Faith finished. "Maybe all that happened is that Kennedy and Giles totally suck at group steering."

"Hey," Kennedy protested.

Buffy watched as the girl rolled around, whimpering. She remembered how it had been for her when Willow had called her back from the dead. How terrified she had been to find herself in her coffin; how disoriented and confused she'd felt as she had staggered from the graveyard into the streets of Sunnydale, hellishly illuminated by fire and the blurry gleam of demon motorcyclists.

"She's out of her mind," Buffy said sympathetically.

"Yeah, well, I'd like to put her out of my misery." At a look from Buffy, Faith gave her a bitter smile. "Just trying to work on my brilliant repartee, Buffy. Figure it's part of the Good Slayer arsenal. As opposed to the Bad Slayer arsenal, which is mostly just killing."

The girl then bucked and screamed, waving her hands and smacking at things none of the other three Slayers could see.

Faith drawled, "She's so active. And I'm so tired. Let's just put a saddle on her and ride her back to camp."

"Maybe Willow can get through to her," Kennedy ventured.

"One way to find out," Buffy said. "Let's try to restrain her. I'll take an arm."

"I'll take the other," Faith said.

"Here goes. We don't want to hurt her," Buffy reminded Faith.

"On the count of now," Faith said.

Buffy swooped down and wrapped her hands around the crazy girl's left arm. The girl batted at her, screaming like a banshee.

Faith gripped her other arm and together they brought the delirious girl to her feet. The girl kept screaming. Then she tried to kick Faith in the shins.

"It only gets better," Faith drawled. She shook her arm. "Hey! Stop it and shut up!"

"*Faith.*" Kennedy knit her brows. "She may be one of us. And she's obviously in pain. Psychic pain."

"Psychic pain can be a bitch," Faith added, sounding almost jaunty. "Take it from me. Going psycho? Total drag."

Kennedy smiled at the girl. She said, "It's okay. We're friends."

Something in her look or voice penetrated; the girl stopped screaming and stared at Kennedy.

"That's good," Kennedy urged. She smiled more brightly. "I'm Kennedy. What's your name?"

The girl remained mute. Tears streamed down her face as she fixed her eyes on Kennedy, as if the young, dark-haired Slayer was her lifeline to reality. Her lips trembled. Then she opened her mouth and said, "Wha . . . wha . . ."

"It's all right. You're among friends," Kennedy repeated.

"Officially, anyway," Faith muttered.

"We think you're a Slayer," Kennedy went on. "You're really strong, like an Amazon. We are too. We're warrior women."

"Like in a comic book," Faith added. "Or a TV show. A really weird TV show. Like the ones they shoot in New Zealand."

It was as if a switch went on. The girl's knees gave way, and she grabbed at Kennedy's hands, shrieking and looking around, her eyes darting left, right. "There was a monster! It was . . . it had a face . . . like a rat! Its eyes were glowing! And these *teeth*!"

She shuddered and fastened her gaze on Kennedy. "I ran away and hid all night. And then I . . . I thought I heard him behind me, and I started running. And I ran so *fast*. How could I do that? How could I run so fast? And then your bus was there, and I . . . I don't know why I kept running."

"Vamp," Buffy said to Faith and Kennedy. "Out here in the middle of nowhere."

"Or something else," Faith said. "Lots of things have rat faces. Look at Snyder."

"We destroyed the Hellmouth," Kennedy agreed. "That doesn't mean we got rid of all the evil for all time."

"Yeah. Whatever." Faith sounded sulky.

"Where are we going?" the girl asked anxiously. She scanned the sky. "It's getting dark!" she cried. "The monster will be back! Oh, God, it'll be back!"

"We'll save you from him," Kennedy assured her. "We're strong. We can kill him." She glanced around. "Maybe one of us should see what we can find."

"Let's get her back to camp first," Faith said. She added, "Can you set stuff on fire?"

"What?" The girl started struggling against Faith's and Buffy's grips on her arms. She was shaking as she threw back her head and said, "No! Please!"

"We'll get you home," Buffy assured her. "It's going to be all right. But for now, you'd better come with us."

"Where? Where are we going?" she wailed.

"Good question." Kennedy exhaled.

"You said you would tell me what's going on!" the girl cried, clearly misinterpreting Buffy's statement.

Kennedy smiled reassuringly and said, "Yes. We will. We'll explain everything once we get you calmed down."

The girl wiped her face and said, "Promise?" She looked from Kennedy, who nodded, to Buffy. Kennedy looked at Buffy as well. Their attention was on her; she understood that they were looking to her for the final word. The mantle of leadership still lay heavily across her shoulders. It was if she were wearing a badge that read, I'M A SLAYER. ASK ME HOW.

"Promise," Buffy said. Both Kennedy and the other girl visibly relaxed. Faith smirked at her.

"But I'm thinking now is not a good time to patrol for one

vamp," Buffy added. "We've got wounded. We should take care of them first, and come back later if we think we need to."

"Solid," Faith concurred.

Kennedy went ahead, and the girl said to Faith, "You're squeezing too tight."

"You gonna run?" Faith asked her.

"No," the girl said.

"Okay, then. I am." Faith let go of her and dashed on ahead. To get back to Robin, Buffy figured.

The girl held on tightly to Buffy's arm. She said, "The bus. I'm so sorry. I . . . I just . . . I lost my mind." She began to cry again. "Was anyone hurt?"

Buffy hesitated. Then she realized the girl would know soon enough what the full extent of the damage was. "Yes," Buffy said firmly. "Someone was killed."

"Oh, my God." The girl's knees buckled. "I'm sorry. I'm so sorry."

"It wasn't your fault," Kennedy said, her voice flat and angry. It was obvious from her tone that she thought it was.

"I . . ." The girl's breathing became rapid, shallow. Her eyes darted left and right.

"It's all right." Buffy stopped walking and looked at her squarely in the face. The girl's eyes widened. "It *wasn't* your fault. You were one person running on a road. Things happen. People die."

She could see that the girl was beginning to lose it again, so she moved her face closer to hers and said, "What's your name?"

The new Slayer swallowed hard. "Um, Britney. Most people call me Britney."

Buffy blinked. "At least it's not Bubbles. I'm Buffy. This is Kennedy."

"Hi," Britney murmured to Kennedy. "I'm so sorry I tried to hurt you. I was crazy. I—"

"It's all right," Kennedy cut in more warmly. She took a breath.

"It's easy to be crazy when you live in this crazy world." The left side of her mouth curved in a crooked smile. She held it for a moment, and then her face fell. Her eyes became hooded, and she looked beyond the trees, beyond the horizon. "We lost a lot of other sisters today," she said softly. "In a big battle."

At Britney's confused look, she added, "Slayers. Like you. I guess. Amazons. Y'know, warriors. Knights in shining armor." She gestured to Britney's clothing. "Or in Old Navy sweatshirts."

"I'm crazy," Britney murmured, touching her sweatshirt, then clasping it in both hands and giving it a twist. "I've lost it. Totally."

"No. You're good," Kennedy said, patting her arm. "You're fine."

"Why doesn't that make me feel better?" Britney asked. Her voice was plaintive. She looked very small in her sweatshirt, very young in her ponytail. Vulnerable, and defenseless against what she might come up against in the future.

Looks can be deceiving, Buffy reminded herself, picturing the slash marks on Kennedy's ribcage. *God, what if she had managed to seriously wound Kennedy? Willow's got her hands full with taking care of Robin. If someone hurt Kennedy, would she go all veiny and evil?*

"I've been having terrible nightmares," Britney went on. "Maybe . . . maybe what happened was a nightmare."

"Some girls have nightmares when they become Slayers," Kennedy said. "The dreams are mixed up with the memories of other Slayers."

Britney's forehead creased and she twisted her sweatshirt again, stumbling on a tree root and grabbing on to a branch.

"Easy," Kennedy said, giving her a steady hand.

"Thanks," Britney told her. "So, it's like a cult?"

Kennedy chuckled. "More like a secret girl-power organization. Like I said before. We're angels without halos. Or some guy named Charlie. Our guy is named Giles, but he's doesn't assign us missions or anything like that."

"Then what does he do?" Britney asked, falling into step beside Kennedy. Her nose was stuffy from the crying, and her eyes were very puffy.

"He trained me, after I moved to Sunnydale," Buffy explained. "And now he's like an adviser."

Kennedy gestured to Buffy. "Buffy is the main Slayer."

Buffy raised her brows. Kennedy had not been nearly so deferential toward her back when she was trying to rally them to go back to the vineyard to fight Caleb. During the fall of Sunnydale, Kennedy had been the force behind voting her out of office and installing Faith as their leader.

"And Faith, too," Kennedy added, gazing coolly at Buffy as if she had read her mind. "But Buffy was the Slayer first."

"Like the queen?" Britney asked, sounding awed. "The Amazons had a queen."

"I'm not the queen," Buffy cut in, waving her hand. "I'm just . . . the oldest one . . . that we know of." *Which raises an interesting question: Is there an age limit on Slayers now? Did some old ladies just become Slayers? What about baby girls? And girls who aren't even born yet?*

She said to Britney, "Where do you live? We'll get you home. Somehow." She looked back over her shoulder, scanning for signs of a house. She couldn't imagine that, if someone lived this close, they wouldn't have come running after the bus crash.

"No," Britney blurted. "I don't want to go home."

Her face clouded; she looked down at her hands and started picking at her cuticles. Buffy saw now that they were jagged and ripped. "My parents . . . well, I . . . I was running away when the rat monster came after me. I'd hitched a ride, and the guy who picked me up . . . he wasn't so nice, so I told him to stop the car and I got out."

She scraped a nail at its cuticle, drawing fresh blood. Buffy winced, more at the girl's emotional pain than at what she was doing to her hands.

"And he turned into rat guy?" Kennedy asked her.

"No. He came later." She sucked on her finger. Buffy noticed that there were rings under her eyes. She looked haggard. And her arms and legs were painfully thin.

Britney stopped walking and put both her hands on Buffy's forearm. She gazed up at the Slayer with pleading eyes and said, "*Please* don't take me back to my parents."

"Hey, it's okay. We won't," Kennedy assured her, either ignoring Buffy's pointed look at her or unaware that Buffy was sending her one.

"Thank you." Britney released Buffy and gave Kennedy a hug. "Thank you so much!"

Kennedy gave Britney's ponytail a playful tug.

Buffy said nothing.

She had nothing to say.

Finally the three stepped from the trees and crossed toward the others. Faith was still kneeling beside Robin. Willow had moved away. She was facing the highway with her arms outstretched. The sun was going down, casting Willow in a rosy hue not unlike that light cast by burning embers. She curled her arms slowly toward herself, then shifted her feet in fluid, graceful motions reminiscent of the tai chi forms Buffy used to perform with Angel, back at his mansion.

Giles and Xander were standing together, gesturing to the remains of the bus and to the road, and they both turned as they saw Buffy and the others.

"And here she is now. I give you Disaster Girl," Faith said acidly, gesturing to Britney.

"Hey, you can't blame her for the accident," Xander said. He scrutinized the unnerved newcomer. "Or maybe you can."

"There was a rat monster," she began. Buffy patted her shoulder.

"We think she's a Slayer, Xander," Buffy told him. "Her name is Britney. Looks like she got her powers, and then she didn't know what hit her."

"But we do. It was almost us," Xander riposted.

"Which brings us to another interesting question," Giles cut in, clearing his throat. "How many other Slayers are out there going mad because they don't know what's happened to them?"

"We're going to have to find and help them," Dawn told her sister.

"We already said we would," Buffy replied. "Willow said she can feel them all over the world, awakening."

"Yeah, and going bonkers," Xander drawled.

Faith sighed. "Well, guess we've still got jobs, eh, B? So much for the sleepovers and the shoe shopping."

Buffy nodded, daunted by the task. How many Slayers *did* exist now?

Then Britney's eyes widened and she pointed toward the road, where the setting sun framed Willow's head like a halo. She pointed.

"A car!" Britney shouted. "Coming to save us!"

"Or run us over," Andrew fretted, taking a step closer to Faith. He blinked rapidly at her, then took the same step away from her. "Maybe Death drives an Eldorado."

"That's not an Eldorado," Giles observed, squinting at the long, low-slung car. It was an old Chevy Impala. "And that certainly is not Death at the wheel."

Buffy and Britney drew back as the car squealed up next to them. The door opened, and an ornately tooled turquoise leather cowboy boot poked from beneath the door. It was connected to a pair of extremely tight boot-cut jeans wrapped around shapely thighs, which in turn belonged to a belt buckle that said, MEXICO LINDO. A skintight, spangled, Western-cut blouse decorated with fringes and cacti came next; and then a woman's face, made up so garishly that for a moment Buffy wondered if she was some kind of reanimated corpse trying to pass for a living human being—or possibly Christina Aguilerra.

Maybe she was fifty, but raven corkscrew curls tumbled to the

BUFFY THE VAMPIRE SLAYER

shoulders beneath a beige cowboy hat decorated with a rhinestone band and a trio of shocking pink feathers.

"Looks like y'all had a bit of a tip-over back yonder," she twanged, speaking to Giles.

"We did indeed," Giles replied for the group. "And we have wounded, one of whom needs to be taken to hospital. And . . . and a fatality."

She whistled. Then she spit a stream of tobacco that landed mere inches from Buffy's burned-up boots.

Ewww.

"Guess you need some help," she said to Giles. She whipped out a cell phone. "Where do we start?"

"I suppose you might want to call the authorities," Giles said. A trained ear—like Buffy's—could detect the merest hint of frustration in his voice.

"Ten-four, honey," the woman twanged. "We have a sheriff in these parts." She spit out more tobacco juice. "I got his office on speed dial." She depressed a button. "I'm Dixie Barnes."

"Rupert Giles," Giles replied.

"That's nice. Hey, Norell," she said into the phone. "Listen, honey. We got a situation out here. Yeah, buncha tourists. Bus accident."

Britney leaned close to Buffy. "Is she evil?" she whispered.

"Not sure yet," the Slayer replied.

CHAPTER THREE

I would rather live and love where death is king than
have eternal life where love is not.
—Robert G. Ingersoll

Dixie Barnes ferried some of the survivors in her Impala to her home, which turned out to be a motel called the Siesta. There was a main building consisting mostly of a lobby, and a detached ranch-style building with six rooms. Everything was scruffy and poorly maintained; above the tiled roof of the main building hung a faded neon sign featuring a man in a serape and a sombrero slumbering against a cactus.

Upon seeing it, Andrew whispered, "Mexico."

The Siesta wasn't getting much business; Dixie bustled around with a pile of dusty linens and a box of cracked little soaps. Vi and Andrew helped her get all six rooms ready while Dawn dozed against Rona and the others sat wearily in the lobby, spirits deflated, nerves on edge.

Those who had not ridden with Dixie had been transported by the local sheriff, one pewter-haired, mustached old boy named Norell Cruz, in his police car; and in his deputy's Jeep. His deputy was Stanislaus DeWitt, and he reminded Xander of David Arquette in the *Scream* movies. He seemed to have some sort of thing going on with Dixie Barnes, judging by the goo-goo eyes they exchanged as they loaded everybody up and got them to the Siesta. Plus, he helped get the rooms ready.

Faith and Buffy took Robin straight to the hospital in the ambulance that Cruz called to the scene of the bus accident.

Then Sheriff Cruz questioned each person in turn about the bus accident. In his khaki uniform and cowboy hat, a beer gut just barely contained by a large brass buckle, he was shocked that no one knew anything more about the dead girl than that her first name was Lisa. After all, she had been on their bus.

"I think you folks had better stick around until I get this cleared up," he ordered. "What with all the terrorist activity—"

"What terrorist activity?" Giles had asked, in his highly concerned Watcher voice. As if weirder things might have happened than the Hellmouth getting shut down for business.

The rotund peace officer narrowed his eyes and said, "Town of Sunnydale. Wiped off the map. Some folks think it was a meteor." He cocked his head. "You folks wouldn't be from Sunnydale, would you? In your . . . bus?"

Any identifying marks linking the charred bus to the Sunnydale Unified School District had been burned beyond recognition.

"We, ah," Giles had begun to stammer, in his British-y stammering way.

"Yes," Xander said, stepping up to the plate. "But it wasn't a meteor. It was . . . an earthquake. When it hit, and everything started shaking, we commandeered that bus and got as many survivors out as we could. Then we just drove like crazy. Because we were worried about the, ah, aftershocks." A lightbulb went off. "And that's why we don't know Lisa's last name. Because we just got everyone on the bus and . . . zoom."

Xander opened his eye wide and did his best to look a little stupid and very innocent. The look had served him well in the early grades; in the later ones, his reputation preceded him, and the look went the way of his *Jurassic Park* lunch box.

His average did not improve with the sheriff. The man squinted at Xander, then said to Giles, "Like I said, I need you people to stay put."

After that, the sheriff left. The girls finalized the rooming arrangements and went to bed. Giles left to fetch Buffy, with the understanding that Faith would be staying overnight at the hospital to tend to Robin.

Xander assumed sentry duty as they waited for Giles and Buffy to return from the hospital. Maybe that was ironic, he a one-eyed non-Slayer guy keeping watch over a bunch of superstrong girls, but he was too jacked up to sleep, anyway.

And besides, Dawn was among the girls, and he'd take a bullet for her any day of the week.

The desert temperature had plummeted, and all he had for warmth were his red plaid shirt and T-shirt beneath it. Next apocalypse, he was bringing a jacket. Also, some Doritos.

After a while, he got tired of walking the perimeter of the motel. He discovered a rocking chair stashed near a Dumpster and carried it to the porch. Both the porch and the rocker had seen better centuries. Nearly all of the chair's egg-yellow paint had worn off, and it squeaked like a rusty metal gate.

Xander had a bad feeling about all this. He was very unhappy that their flight from Sunnydale had resulted in further tragedy. And, in his opinion, they weren't far enough away from the Hellmouth.

So he'd decided to keep watch over his flock.

He rocked in the chair, wishing for a weapon. He thought about asking Dixie Barnes if she had some kind of six-shooter or something. Whatever she used to chase the revenuers away with ought to do just fine.

An owl hooted in the dark. Xander shivered in his shirt and

crossed his arms across his chest for warmth. He hurt, and he was hungry, but above all, now that the adrenaline had passed, he was lonely.

I ought to be doing my patented Snoopy happy dance. We freakin' survived. What more could I possibly ask for?

The image of his beautiful, crazy ex-demon-vengeance ex-fiancée rose in his mind. If she were standing right here, alive, would he ask her to marry him?

Yes, I would.

And we'd sing and dance and have babies.

After a time, he dozed. His dreams were strange, sliding from images of Anya to shrimp. And French fries. And dancing tacos.

When he awoke, Dawn was sitting on the porch at his feet, in a position like the guy in the neon sign. She had leaned her head against the porch post, and she was asleep. He watched her.

Then the hum of a motor alerted him that Giles and Buffy were back. He roused, stood, and walked to the edge of the porch, eager to hear the news about Robin. He liked the guy. Frankly, he liked that he had tried to kill Spike. Okay, immolation on Spike's part to save everybody, but Spike had tried to force himself on Buffy. Xander Harris forgave no one after they did something like that.

The car was a black shape in the darkness. The dome light came on as Buffy opened the passenger door and jumped out. She ran toward the porch. "Dawn!" she cried. "Oh, thank God!"

"What? Buffy!" Dawn cried, jerking awake. "What's wrong?"

Buffy and Giles both passed into the glow of the porch light. They had bought new clothes. Or stolen them: Both were wearing hospital scrubs.

Buffy swept Dawn into her arms as Giles said, "We tried to call. We have a problem."

Xander went on high alert. "I *knew* it," he said. "What's the what?"

"Where's Britney?" Buffy demanded, already heading toward the hotel rooms.

"She bunked with Vi, Rona, some others. Room 394. Fourth one from the lobby. Don't ask me why the triple digits."

Buffy took off in a dead heat.

Giles came abreast of Xander and began walking him and Dawn back up the porch steps. "We need to wake Ms. Barnes straightaway. Perhaps she has a rifle. . . ."

Dawn stared at him.

"What the hell is going on?" Xander demanded.

"While I was collecting Buffy, an ambulance pulled up. There were three people inside. Dead." Giles pushed open the lobby door. Xander swung through directly behind him.

"And?" he prodded. "Let me guess. Bus accident?"

"No. Ms. Barnes?" Giles shouted. He went around the reception counter, into what appeared to be a back room. "Oh, God."

Xander caught up with him.

Oh, my God.

"Dawn, stay back," Xander barked, blocking her view of the door as he waved her away.

"What is it?" Dawn asked, her voice shrill and anxious.

There was blood everywhere. A saggy queen-size bed was saturated with it; it was smeared on the walls, on the floor, on the *ceiling,* for God's sake. Xander had seen a lot of awful things in his day, but he had never seen anything like this. *Not even on late-night cable,* he thought, sickened.

"Seeing no body," he said to Giles.

"Body?" Dawn echoed querulously.

As Giles hurried through a doorway, Xander trailed after him. It was a bathroom, with a toilet and a pedestal sink, and a tub with claw feet.

A shower curtain was pulled across the tub.

No way, Xander thought as Giles reached for it.

He held his breath as the Watcher yanked it back.

Nothing. Untouched.

By unspoken agreement, they both ran out of the bathroom, through the bedroom, and back out to the lobby.

Dawn was sprawled on the couch in the lobby, doubling over and dry-heaving.

"You looked. I told you not to look," Xander said, crouching in front of her and taking her hands in his.

"No, you told me to stay back." She was trembling. "What . . . what *did* that? And where's my sister?"

"Finding her now," Xander promised.

Giles grabbed up a cell phone on the desk behind the counter. He punched in three numbers and said, "911? Yes, there's an emergency at the Siesta Motel. Immediately!"

Xander, Giles, and Dawn burst through the lobby door and down the steps just as the sheriff's car screeched to a stop. The sheriff jumped out, carrying a shotgun. Another uniformed man got out of the passenger side, unholstered a pistol, and aimed it straight at Xander.

"Freeze!" the man commanded him.

"Whoa," Xander said, coming to a full stop and raising his hands. "I'm good. I mean, I'm on the side of good."

Giles raised his hands as well and said to the sheriff, "We've just arrived. I made a call to 911. There's blood in Ms. Barnes's room. Buffy went on ahead—"

"You sent that *girl*?" the sheriff asked incredulously. He gave Giles a look of utter contempt. "Which room?"

Giles turned to Xander. "Which room did Britney go into?"

"Britney?" Xander echoed, bewildered.

"Room 394," Dawn informed him. "With Vi and Rona."

The sheriff turned to the other uniform and pointed to the low-slung building. "Go around," he ordered him. "There's no back door, but there are windows."

"Got it," the other officer said to the sheriff. He trotted in the opposite direction.

"You stay put," the sheriff ordered Xander and company as he took off toward the row of guest rooms.

As soon as the man's back was turned, Xander gestured for Dawn to stay behind. Then he bolted toward Room 394. Giles was right there with him. They struggled to keep up with the sheriff, but it had been a very long day.

Sheriff Cruz hissed at them, "*Stay back.* This is a dangerous situation."

Xander saw no sign of Buffy as they came abreast of Room 393. The door to 394 was still shut tight.

"We have friends in there," Giles argued.

"Then stay out of my way and let me do my job," the sheriff retorted.

"Everyone, get up!" Giles yelled.

"Stop that!" the sheriff yelled back. "All you'll do is make them panic!"

"All I'll do is save lives!" Giles retorted. "Vi! Rona! You're in danger! Andrew!"

"Giles, what the hell is going on?" Xander put on a burst of speed. The sheriff was hunched on one side of the door, a gun cocked and pointed up.

"Vi! Rona!" Giles yelled. "Get the bloody hell out of there!"

The sheriff yelled, "This is the sheriff. Open up!" He kicked the door open before anyone would have had a chance to respond.

Then the sheriff screamed.

"Christ," Giles breathed.

The two raced in after him.

As Faith stretched, she pressed her shoulders against the uncomfortable hospital chair and recrossed her legs at the ankles. Buffy and Giles had showered in Robin's bathroom and put on their fresh scrubs, but Faith would be damned if she'd leave Robin alone even that long.

She stank, and she hurt, and she was so hungry that even hospital food sounded like good eating. But Robin wouldn't be having hospital food tonight. He was on an IV drip, and they were pumping him with saline and morphine and a dozen different other things.

"It was a very close call," the ER doc told her after Robin had been admitted. "A few more minutes and . . ." He sighed and trailed off with a shake of his head and a tsk-tsk, obviously getting off on his own sense of drama. "Well, safe to say modern medicine saved the life of your friend." He took in Faith's appearance with a snooty grimace and added, "Street brawl? Turf war? Did you two 'get down' with his homeboys?"

Faith wanted to shove his sanctimonious face in. *We saved the world, you prick.*

Instead, she said, "Just keep thinking that way. It'll probably get you killed.

He waved her off. "Please. We see things like this all the time."

Oh, I'll just bet you do, she thought now as she watched Robin's monitors and anxiously studied the rise and fall of his chest. *If you knew what you were seeing, you'd be on your knees thanking me instead of passing judgment on the "homeboy" and me. Story of my life . . .*

But no. Story of the life of the old Faith. Angel had taught her different: *It's not how you feel, it's what you do. Atonement is about taking the chances that come along to do it differently.*

So she thanked the doctor and watched him saunter away to save other lives.

The squeak of shoes announced the night shift nurse, who glanced at all the monitors and examined the IV insertion in the back of Robin's hand before she smiled gently at Faith. She was wearing a scrub top decorated with little cat angels holding signs with sayings on them like YOU ARE LOVED. Her baggy hospital pants were a cheerful fuchsia. Her nametag read, ANGELA. Angela with angels. It was awful symbolic.

"He's going to be asleep for a while," she told her. "You could grab a bite to eat. Get a shower."

As if on cue, Faith's stomach growled. Angela pretended not to notice. She said, "Are you here alone, you two?"

Faith considered. "Kind of."

Angela hesitated, as if she was trying to make up her mind about something. Then she nodded to herself. "You're about my size," she said. "I have some extra street clothes in my car. I was taking them to the hospital consignment store. I'm about due for a break. You stay here and I'll go get them."

"That's okay. No big," Faith blurted, acutely uneasy. "I'm fine."

"I'll be right back."

She didn't wait for Faith's response, but turned around and hurried away. Faith said, "Huh," and crossed her arms. She tried to imagine herself in some little cutesy T-shirt with angelic teddy bears on it. Add some pants with an elastic waistband.

But that was not what Angela came back with.

A shower later, Faith was clad in to-die-for black leather pants and an olive green T-shirt. Also, a pair of black hiking boots that were just a little too big. Black socks too.

Angela beamed at her and handed her a paper lunch bag. Inside were a peanut butter and jelly sandwich swathed in plastic wrap, an apple, a bag of chips, and a beer.

Faith stared at the beer. "Get out."

The woman smiled at her, turned, and left.

In her hot new clothes, Faith sat down next to Robin, tore open the sandwich, and popped open the beer. *If I had mouthed off to that doc, I wouldn't be sitting here doing this.*

She raised her beer can. *Thanks, Angela.*

Thanks, Angel.

As Giles tore into the room after Sheriff Cruz, the room light clicked on. Xander clattered in directly behind him.

"Buffy?" Xander called. He ran to the window.

The sheriff was sprawled on his back with his hands clutched to his head. A bruise was forming on his forehead. Vi, with a sheet twisted around her torso, was bending over him in a pair of bikini underpants. Rona had hold of his gun, and it was pointed directly at his forehead. She lowered it as she saw Giles.

"It's all right," Giles said to the Slayers. "He's the sheriff."

"Where's Buffy?" Xander asked, turning from the window to face the others.

Buffy heard the shouting behind her, but she didn't stop running. The thing that had been Britney loped on ahead, transforming from the young girl into a savage monster as it skittered across the desert in the moonlight. Tufts of fur, fangs, talons—Buffy had only caught flashes of its altered appearance, more like fragmented impressions than a clear sighting. She had a pretty good idea it was some form of werewolf.

She had just about made it to Room 394 when Britney burst from the end of the building with a human head in her bloody hands. Actually, she was only partially Britney. She had grown— she was over six feet tall, and she had developed a hump on her back that had tore through the sweatshirt. Her exposed back was ridged, and tufts of hair stuck out like bristles. Her ears had elongated, and so had her profile. Her mouth was pulled up in a huge smile as long, sharp teeth jutted from her gums.

She—it—froze for an instant when she saw Buffy. Then she raced away from the building and into the desert night, in such a hurry that she dropped her grisly trophy.

The head hit the sand with a smack. Buffy glanced down at it as she gave chase. There was so much blood on it that Buffy couldn't see its features, but she could still tell that it was Deputy DeWitt.

No time for that now.

The Britney-monster faltered, falling forward. Buffy punched on the turbo. It was on its hands and knees, listing slightly to the right. Buffy was ten feet behind it.

The creature's arms extended, the limbs telescoping as they split the arms of the sweatshirt. The fingers expanded, hair sprouting on them, nails growing into long, black talons. It shrieked as if with pain, then scrabbled forward.

Almost a werewolf, but different.

Buffy had nearly caught up with it when it picked up speed and began to gallop away.

Her wounds were still tender; her throat burned. But the Slayer kept pace as the thing led her deeper into the desert. Past desert scrub and down into an arroyo, threading through a maze of Joshua trees and up onto a mesa, until she reached a tall rock formation that jutted out over a ravine—the creature appeared to have a final destination in mind.

Buffy followed up the rock formation, finding rough handholds and toeholds for balance, racing to catch the beast as it remained tantalizingly out of reach. Ahead, it threw its head back and howled a wolflike cry.

A chorus of howls answered it.

Moonlight bathed the beast as Buffy crested the summit. A semicircular rock formation served as a backdrop as it rose on its hind legs and faced her. It was now completely covered in hair, and its eyes were yellow and elongated. Its snout dripped mucus, and the teeth glistened with a dark substance. It looked like a werewolf despite its unusual humanlike stance. Buffy took that into quick consideration as she planned her attack. When werewolves transformed from human to wolf, they lost their sense of reason. They were savage predators, nothing more. Unnervingly, that didn't seem to be the case here. She could see cunning in its eyes.

I should have brought a weapon, Buffy thought. *There!* Seizing hold of a thick branch of deer weed extending from a crevice, she ripped it free. It wasn't much, but it was better than nothing.

She brandished it at the were-creature. "I don't know if you can understand me," she said to it, "but if you want to grunt a few words before I stab you through the heart with this thing—"

The monster chuckled. "With *that*?"

It *was* a pretty lame little stick. Nevertheless, the Slayer squared her shoulders and said, "Well, yeah."

It laughed.

Its laughter was joined by the others' laughter. Then a similar second creature emerged from behind the semicircle of rocks. And another, and another. Buffy counted five, all of them laughing as they stood up straight, towering above her. Her monster—if she could be so possessive—was by far the shortest of the group.

A gunshot echoed through the darkness. The bullet zinged inches away from her right knee. It was followed by a second as Buffy leaped behind the nearest boulder for cover. A third clipped rock as she poked her head out, quickly drawing it back in.

"Slayer." The voice was brutish and gruff, somewhere between a human voice and the growl of an animal. It mockingly laughed, appearing untroubled by the gunfire. "You thought *I* was a Slayer this morning. Welcomed me right into your circle. Performed no tests to see if I was what you thought I was."

Buffy frowned. "*You* said you were a Slayer. . . ." No. It had never said.

"*You* said," it retorted. "You assumed. Beware of such assumptions, girl."

"Thanks," she said tartly. "I'll put that on my not-to-do list."

"My kind is as old as the desert, Slayer. Older than you."

Hmm. "There's lots of stuff older than me."

"Than your kind. Slayers."

"Are you . . . older than a bread box?" Buffy quipped. "Let me guess. Shapeshifter?"

It didn't reply.

"And the rat-monster . . . made up? What was your problem earlier today? Did we catch you shapeshifting?"

Her only answer was silence. Buffy counted to ten, then looked around the boulder. Either the shapeshifter was hiding and getting ready to pounce, or it had left with all its chuckly pals to rip the heads off other girls and boys.

Option number three: They were surrounding her, and all of them were getting ready to pounce on just one ripe juicy Slayer.

Doesn't matter. 'Cuz I've got a . . . stick. She hefted the branch in her arm, and suddenly felt mortified for even threatening the monster with it. It was awfully puny. "Stupid stick," she muttered.

Then it occurred to her that if there were a bunch of those guys up there, there might be a bunch of those guys back at the hotel.

Dawn was down there, and the others, too. Some of them were Slayers. But some of them were not.

She stood experimentally, ready to do battle if that was the next item on the menu. When nothing rushed her, she hightailed it down the rock formation and raced back to the motel.

Wrapped in a blanket, Dawn stood on the porch with the gang and the sheriff. She was the first to spot Buffy and she threw down the blanket and leaped off the porch when she saw her. "Buffy!" she cried, opening up her arms as she ran to her.

They embraced tightly. Then Buffy took her hand and hurried back to the porch.

Dixie Barnes stepped from behind the sheriff. Her makeup was smeared from crying, and she looked like a killer clown. "You find the bastards who did it?"

Buffy glanced from her to Giles. The Watcher said, "It seems that Mr. DeWitt was a close personal friend of Ms. Barnes. She left to buy us something to eat at the convenience store down the road, and he decided to wait for her. In her room."

"It's Saturday night," Dixie moaned. "We had a standing date for Saturday night."

"Rain or shine," Andrew said sadly. "We have no reason to dispute her claim." He shook his head and lowered his gaze. "Except, perhaps, for the part where she said he was the best lover on Earth."

"It could have been me," Dixie whispered sotto voce. "It's like that movie *Signs*."

"Were you able to ID the perps?" Sheriff Cruz asked Buffy.

Buffy looked at Giles again, trying to let him know that it was *X-Files* time. Yes, she could ID the perps, but it probably wouldn't be a very good idea to do so. "Ah," she began.

Perhaps sensing the tension between them, the sheriff said to Giles, "Let's go through the whole thing again."

Giles ticked his attention to the man and cleared his throat. "As I mentioned, Buffy and I were visiting our friend in hospital. An ambulance arrived just as we were about to leave. According to the EMTs, the three victims in the ambulance had been savagely butchered. In fact, they mentioned they hadn't been able to sort out whose body parts belonged to whom," Giles said.

"They just flat out told you all this?" the sheriff asked incredulously.

"They were kind of telling everyone," Buffy offered. "They were pretty freaked out."

"Damned unprofessional," Andrew intoned. "However, juicy." When Buffy glared at him, he shifted and said, "In a completely icky way."

Xander raised a hand. "And?" he prompted Giles.

"And their names were Kenneth, Mary, and Britney Stevens," Giles replied as he regarded them all with grim satisfaction. When

Xander did not react, he continued: "Would you agree with me that Britney is a very unusual name?"

Andrew stared at him. "*That's* why you called him? Because that was a Britney and we have a Britney?"

"*Had* a Britney," Xander qualified. "She's AWOL." He gestured to the group. "Not here."

"There! You see?" Giles said triumphantly.

Dawn rolled her eyes. "Giles, Britney is, like, the most common name in America for girls," she said emphatically. "Now, if she'd had a really unusual name, like Faith—"

"Or 'Buffy,'" Xander cut in.

"Or . . . or Buffy, yes," Dawn continued, nodding and wagging her finger at Giles. "I'd be there with you on the coincidence page."

"Actually, my point is that it's *not* a coincidence." Giles pushed up his glasses. "However, it was the nature of the wounds that prompted us to rush back here—"

"Because the crime victim's name was the same as that girl's we found?" Andrew asked, getting it.

"What girl?" the sheriff asked sharply. "You found a girl? No one mentioned that to me before."

Uh-oh. Blurtation error. Buffy made a little *oops* face at Giles.

"You see, earlier today . . . ," Giles began.

"Wait a minute," Xander cut in. "You were already on your way here *before* Giles. You pulled up just as Giles got cut off. You knew something was up."

Dixie looked at the sheriff. "That right?"

"I tried to call, Dixie. Warn you. Couldn't get through."

Dixie nodded. "Damn shapeshifters," she muttered, letting fly a stream of tobacco off the porch.

Buffy and Giles mirrored each other's surprise.

"Did she change into something that looked like a wolf?" the sheriff prompted Buffy.

"Yes," she blurted, nodding, her eyes wide. "She did."

"And you sent her out after it?" the sheriff snapped at Giles. "What are you, some kinda girlie man?"

As Buffy moved into the lobby with Dawn at her side, Andrew shuffled around Vi and Rona. His hand was raised. "Excuse me? In England, they are called nancy-boys. No insult intended to the Nancys of the world."

The sheriff hitched up his trousers. His belt buckle gleamed in the porch light. "Whatever you call 'em, I can't believe you sent a little girl to do a grown man's job."

"Buffy's . . . older than she looks," Andrew ventured. At twin glares from Vi and Rona, he curled his hands together under his chest and said, "And stronger too. Don't let the, ah, slender nature of her form fool you."

Sheriff Cruz squinted at Andrew. "What the hell are you talking about, son? He on some kind of medication?" he asked Giles.

"Back to the shapeshifters," Buffy suggested.

"Actually, back to the fact that two 'girls' kicked your butt," Rona snapped at the sheriff. "And I'm one-armed and still dangerous, at the moment."

Buffy joined in the group smirk. The sheriff's face reddened.

"So," Giles said, and looked around the room. "Let's continue."

"Sheriff, you want a plug?" Dixie Barnes asked the sheriff as she honked her nose on a tissue.

The sheriff nodded, then made a gesture to encompass everyone in the lobby. Buffy counted the six new Slayers plus Vi and Rona. A tanned young guy dressed like the sheriff was interviewing Marie, the French Slayer. Everyone had their heads. That was good.

"Better get some for everybody," Sheriff Cruz added.

"*What?*" Dawn bleated.

"Shapeshifters hate tobacco," Dixie explained as she went behind the reception desk and pulled out an old-fashioned cigar box. "We think that's why it's sacred to the Indians. Only, DeWitt would never chew on account of his religious convictions." She blew into her tissue and stuffed it into the front pocket of her jeans as she opened the lid, revealing several metallic packages with colorful labels on them. "We got some Copenhagen, Apple Jack . . ."

"That's why you chew it?" Giles asked Dixie. "To ward off the shapeshifters?"

"Of course." She paused from her rummaging. "It's like garlic for vampires. Only that's a myth. There's no such thing as vampires."

"There's not?" Vi asked, all innocence.

"Nope." Dixie chuckled. "Who ever heard of such a thing?"

"Actually," Andrew began; at a look from Buffy, he made as if to zip his lip and throw away the key. "Actually, I do not know."

"We hadn't had any trouble from shapeshifters in almost a year," the sheriff told Giles. "We thought maybe they'd moved. Slim pickins around here anymore."

"Since the freeway got built, nigh on five years, they've slowed way down," Dixie said. She brought an aluminum pouch eye-level to Dawn's face and studied her, as if trying to match the proper brand to the Slayer's sister.

"I thought maybe you were a shapeshifter," Dixie said to Buffy.

"Me?" Buffy asked, wondering why she'd been singled out.

"Yeah. 'Cause you're shifty," Dixie told her. She chuckled. "Little humor there. I wondered about all of you, actually. But you didn't jump back when I spit back there on the road."

"No. We're far too polite," Andrew advised her. When she looked hard at him, he swallowed. "And also, we are definitely not shapeshifters."

"So the reason I was here at the same time you called is, I saw shadows loping across the desert, got to thinking about all the fresh meat at the Siesta. You folks. Saw some commotion, called for backup."

"Suspiciously good timing," Andrew mused.

"We couldn't exactly tell you about them," Dixie said. "You wouldn't have believed us."

"Perhaps not. But we can try to help you with them," Giles offered. "As you have, ah, already experienced firsthand, these girls are unusually strong."

"Things are not always as they seem," Andrew said sagely.

"Kung fu and self-defense classes are one thing," the sheriff announced. "Shapeshifters are another. First order of business is moving the whole passel of you out of here. You, too, Dixie. It's too dangerous."

She wiped her eyes again. "All right, Norell." She ripped open a package of chewing tobacco and passed it to Giles.

"This has been a very long day for all of us," Andrew said. "*We* fought . . ."

Every Slayer present turned and glared at him.

"An earthquake," Xander finished for him.

"Yes." Andrew's lids fluttered as he struggled to overcome his steady course toward the iceberg. "And the earthquake won. Just like in the song: 'I fought the . . . law, and the law won.' Except in our case . . ."

"In *your* case, the earth moved," Rona said drily.

"I'm going to put in some calls, get you folks moved," Sheriff Cruz announced as he whipped his cell phone from his pocket. "The casino has nice rooms. Don't it, Dixie?"

"Yeah, nice if you want to shoot porno movies," Kennedy murmured, waiting for Willow to come to bed. She wished she would hurry. She was beginning to doze off. "Willow?"

And then it hit her: Willow was delaying coming to bed.

And Kennedy knew why.

"Hey," Willow said.

Kennedy's beloved was wearing the fluffy white bathrobe of

the casino; a poker hand of three queens and two kings was embroidered over the left breast. The robe was enormous on Willow.

Kennedy gazed up at her, inhaling the piquant incense Willow had lit before the makeshift altar on top of the little refrigerator in their room. A six-inch-tall statue of the Goddess Kwan Yin gleamed by the light of the votive candle Willow was using in her nighttime ritual.

It was amazing what you could buy in a casino gift shop.

As Willow put one knee on the bed, Kennedy sat up, resting her weight on her hands as she gazed up at the young woman who had given her the power of the Slayer.

Time hung for a moment, giving room between heartbeats for her memories. Her lips tingled from Willow's very first kiss. Her ears caught Willow's breathless recitation of lines from a poem by Sappho, from the night before the big battle, as they gazed out the window at pitch-black Sunnydale:

> The stars about the lovely moon
> Fade back and vanish very soon,
> When, round and full, her silver face
> Swims into sight, and lights all space.

Resolutely, Kennedy took Willow's hands and brought her knuckles to her lips. She closed her eyes as she kissed each one, then cradled them beneath her chin. Her eyelashes moistened with tears that she didn't shed. "Willow," she began, wishing she didn't have to do this. Knowing that she did have to. Her heart was breaking.

"Oh, um, want some more orange juice?" Willow asked her, moving away and walking toward the refrigerator.

"Willow." Her voice was soft, but insistent.

Willow turned around. She folded her hands in front and smiled weakly at Kennedy.

Don't say anything, Kennedy told herself. *Willow's not going to bring it up. Why should you?*

She took a deep breath. "I saw her too."

Willow said nothing, only stared at her, and Kennedy had never felt more alone than at that moment.

Help me through this . . . don't put me through this. . . .

"When you went all goddess . . . I saw Tara gazing down at you. And I know you saw her too."

"Oh . . . ," Willow murmured.

"I think it took a while for you to process it. You were kind of high." Though her lips were trembling, Kennedy managed to grin at Willow. "Here's the thing, Willow. Maybe you are . . . were . . . in love with me."

"Are," Willow cut in, but the word was hollow. Kennedy heard it.

"She still has your heart." Kennedy cocked her head. "You had such a hard time letting her go. And I knew you did. I know you let her go, so I could have a place with you. But she came back. You know she's out there now. And I . . . I can't compete with a higher being."

"No . . . ," Willow pleaded, spreading her hands. "No, Kennedy. It was the magicks. . . ." She lowered her head and started to cry.

"I saw you all white-haired and glowing, and I thought maybe I'd died," Kennedy went on. "But I didn't die then. I'm dying now."

"Kennedy." Willow sniffled. She picked up the edge of her bathrobe and wiped her nose with it. "I do love you."

"Just . . . not like you love Tara." Kennedy grit her teeth. She wouldn't cry. That would only hurt Willow more. She had to stay strong because her sweet, dear girl wouldn't be able to stand seeing that much pain. Dear, sweet, beautiful Willow, with a heart as big as the moon.

I thought we would have a life together. Valentine's Days, our birthdays . . . we talked about going to Europe. We were going to have a handfasting ceremony with your coven back in England. And now that we have a shot at that—the Hellmouth's closed, and Sunnydale is gone . . .

Willow crossed to the black upholstered sofa in front of their TV and sank into the cushions.

"It's just . . . I know she's out there. Up there. She's still Tara. And . . . she still loves me."

"Then she wouldn't want you to go through life alone," Kennedy blurted. She bit her lower lip. "I didn't mean to say that."

"But you're right," Willow said hoarsely. "She doesn't want me to go through life alone."

And in that moment, for just one moment, Kennedy dared to hope. Her aching heart raced ahead to Willow rising from the couch and walking into her arms. Holding her close and whispering into her ear, "And I'm not alone. I'm with you."

But that was a mirage. There was no rain in the desert.

Kennedy said, "You're not alone. She's with you."

Willow picked up a couch pillow and bundled it into her lap. The tears were falling freely now. Willow was suffering, and there was no part of Kennedy that found any comfort in that.

So this is what true love is like.

It sucks.

She came to the couch and sat down beside Willow. The figure of Kwan Yin was posed with her hand in blessing.

She made her vow to Willow. Not the one she had written over and over in her head: *I, Kennedy, take you Willow, as my spouse . . . except in certain states and many countries of the world . . . but in the country of my heart, you are my beloved, always.*

No, this was a new vow.

"I won't leave you, Willow. We'll move on from here together. As friends. Very close, very dear friends. Comrades. Whatever comes next, I'll be there. I'll keep you safe, and I'll do everything I can to make it easy for you."

"Oh, Kennedy." Willow reached out a hand. Kennedy debated for a split second about taking it; then she closed her fingers around Willow's, and a surge of desperate longing washed through her. "Kennedy, I'm so sorry—"

"Don't," Kennedy said brokenly. "Don't try to let me down easy. I'm all right."

"I'm not," Willow murmured. She began to weep.

"It's all right," Kennedy said, putting her arms around Willow, holding her tightly. "It's all right."

"Yes, the rooms are nice, if you missed the Playboy Mansion during the disco era," Buffy said as she and Dawn lay on the black-and-gold velvet bedspread of their circular bed and stared at their reflections in the mirror suspended overhead. "I, for one, did not miss it at all."

They had taken hot baths with the hotel bath gel and shampoo. Now they were wrapped in fluffy white towels. Buffy's blisters were going down, and the gash in her forehead was beginning to close up. Her mangled arm was covered with bandages.

Dawn was bruised, and there were dark rings under her eyes.

Not their best looks.

"Our life just gets weirder and weirder," Dawn mused. "Now all the shapeshifters know about Slayers."

"Don't suppose it matters," Buffy replied, yawning and stretching. Dawn's big sister pointed her toes hard and spread her fingers. Her back arched off the bedspread, and she rolled her shoulders. "Maybe they knew about us before."

"I wonder why they attacked, when they've been so quiet. Maybe someone put them up to it. Someone who knew we had escaped from the Hellmouth." Dawn frowned at Buffy in the mirror. "Why couldn't they have all been destroyed with Sunnydale?

Is Andrew right? Will more evil beings come gunning for you? For us?"

"I'm hoping the evil beings need to recharge," Buffy told her. "Same as us," she added frankly. "We need some downtime. One thing I've learned from Faith is that Slayers can burn out if they don't have some fun."

"Want more cocktail weenies?" Dawn asked her. "Or barbecue potato chips? They're fattening and have no nutritional value. Eating them qualifies as fun."

"Get off that outlaw train, Dawn," Buffy said. "And could they have given us more food?"

The sheriff had explained the situation to the casino hotel's general manager. The man had miraculously known all about shapeshifters, and he was sympathetic to the plight of the motley busload of travelers. Although the dinner buffet was closed, he had assembled some impressive platters of food—fried chicken, cold cuts, salad, and rolls—and sent several to each room. Dawn had never dreamed that she would ever have more shrimp cocktail than she could possibly eat in one night, not to mention piles of chocolate chip cookies.

"I'm good," Buffy said. "But I might have some more cheesecake in a minute." She grinned at Dawn. "Or chocolate pudding. Or a cupcake."

"I couldn't eat another bite of anything. Not even Almond Roca." That was Dawn's totally favorite thing in the world.

Buffy rolled over on her stomach and rested her cheek on her black satin pillow. "The First is out. We've had a couple days off. Someone new needs a scary plan to take over the world. Hopefully, it'll take them some time to work on that."

"Hopefully," Dawn murmured, shifting her gaze from the mirror to her sister.

Buffy smoothed Dawn's hair. "My first priority now is taking care of you," she said, her touch gentle, her features soft. "Show you the good parts of the world. There are other Slayers now. It's not going to be Buffy saving the world 24/7 anymore."

Can that ever really happen?

"I hope so," Dawn said in a small voice.

"I *know* so," Buffy assured her. "Now go to sleep. Tomorrow we'll buy you some hot new fashions in the casino gift shop."

"Yay. A T-shirt with rhinestone dice," Dawn said, perking up at the notion of shopping. "Think I could find some gold lamé capris to go with it?"

Buffy didn't answer.

Dawn smiled lovingly at her softly snoring sister, and turned over in preparation for catching some z's of her own.

But rest proved to be elusive. Sunrise found her half-asleep; the other 50 percent was busy worrying and being scared.

Because something had occurred to Dawn that hadn't occurred to Buffy: Fighting vampires and averting the newest apocalypse *was* normal life for the Summers girls. And Dawn could imagine no other life. The bus accident. The shapeshifters. The fight and pain had followed them.

It's not going to change. I'll bet right now, someone's getting ready to hurt us.

Maybe kill us.

We're not vampires or hellgods.

We're not going to live forever.

CHAPTER FOUR

Kill a man, and you are an assassin. Kill millions of men, and you are a conqueror.
Kill everyone, and you are a god.
—Jean Rostand

AT THE CENTER OF THE WORLD

I am a God.

I cannot die.

Janus, Dread Lord of Latium, Holder of the Key, screamed and shook as he was made flesh within the molten core of the world.

The painful rebirth was an agony of unparalleled proportions. As he struggled to re-form his body, which he had lost during the teleportation, pain mastered him. Born in timelessness, seconds and minutes now weighed him down. A searing heat cauterized his wounds and kept him from dissolving into nothing more than a whispered invocation on human lips.

Janus, evoco vestram animam. Exaudi meam causam.
Carpe noctem pro consilio vestro. Veni, appare et nobis
monstra quod est infinita potestas.
Janus, I invoke your spirit. Hear my plea. Seize the night
for your own reason. Come, appear and show to us that

which is infinite power. Janus, Lord God of Chaos, demon, come!

He singlemindedly willed himself into solid form. And as he suffered, he hated Buffy the Vampire Slayer with his entire being. But Janus had an acolyte on this plane. Ethan Rayne, a skilled sorcerer with vast knowledge of the arcane, had opened portals for the hellgod, allowing his journey once more from his own dimension to this one. Janus was in fact pleased to be summoned; eager to spread mischief among Ethan's enemies—among them, particularly, the original Slayer and her friends.

Ethan was not the first to request Janus's favor.

The ancient Greeks had worshipped Janus as a god millennia before the birth of Ethan Rayne. Janus held sway as their chief god for centuries. The Greeks were very big on presenting him with nubile young virgins as a means to curry his favor, housing him in palatial temples and attending to his every desire.

Then it had all ended. History books suggested that the Greeks had turned to other gods—to a single god, in fact, forcing a new, more "modern" state religion on their conquered lands. As Janus's name no longer crossed their lips, and they stopped praying to him, and ceased worshipping him, his influence faded.

That was not entirely true.

GREECE, THE SECOND MILLENNIUM, BC

The rolling seas of crystalline blue; the hills dotted with olive trees. Whitewashed columns of marble; sunshine as yellow as wheat.

What was not to love?

"Save me, great Janus!" Pharmakos shrieked.

It was the Festival of the Sea, a rite that belonged to Neptune, God of the Sea. And Pharmakos belonged to Neptune as well. He was the sacrifice who would be torn to pieces by the masses, his flesh and bone tossed into the sea. Only then would Neptune be appeased for another year, quelling the sea storms and plying the fishermen's nets with fish.

Apparently Pharmakos hoped to elude this fate by seeking refuge in Janus's temple.

It was tempting to oblige him. The terrified lad was a perfect Greek youth: soulful eyes; lean and muscular; dark, curly ringlets held in place by a circlet of laurel leaves. Indeed, he had been chosen for sacrifice because he was such a perfect specimen of manhood. The gods loved to have the best.

Janus was a god.

He thought, *Why don't I keep this little morsel for myself?*

Janus's chief priest, who wore the wooden double-faced mask of the order, flung Pharmakos to his knees and snarled, "Silence! Hold your tongue and hide your face from the god!"

An interesting gyration, Janus thought, amused.

None of Janus's priests had ever seen *his* face. He sat behind a screen when they approached. If a mortal priest had ever worked up the nerve to sneak a look, all he would see was a version of a "regular guy," only taller and, well, two-headed.

The truth was that he attired himself in human form because it was easier than wearing his true form. So did all the other beings passing in this dimension as the gods of these people. They hailed from several dimensions, although a few—Venus and Hermes, for example—were actually from this plane.

He arrived in this dimension purely by accident. He had been traveling from his own hell dimension, en route to a secret meeting of ambitious hellgods plotting the downfall of the First Evil. But a strange force had yanked him from his path to Greece. The sensation had been like falling into a rushing river; he was swept along, then washed up beside the Temple of Zeus.

Later, he discovered that there was something called a Hellmouth located close to the site. Its arcane energy had seized him and pushed him through to this dimension. His misadventure proved to be a lucky thing: The First heard of the plot against them, and launched a surprise attack against the conspirators at the appointed rendezvous site. All of them were destroyed. Since Janus had never made it to the meeting, he escaped a hideous, brutal end.

No loss . . . and much gained: Janus would never underestimate the First again. For the time being, he would content himself at playing god over these foolish mortals.

"Great God Janus! I will be your loyal acolyte. I will serve you!" Pharmakos shouted. His curls bobbed. His forehead was beaded with sweat.

"You are pledged to Neptune, ungrateful dog," the priest said scornfully.

Easy for you to say, when no one is planning to strip your bones while you're alive, Janus thought.

Janus silently cleared one of his throats, then spoke in great, rumbling tones.

"Mortal, you have been chosen for a great honor. My brother Neptune will receive your soul. Your name will be blessed throughout all time."

What a crock. If this poor guy believes that, he deserves to die.

"No, it won't!" Pharmakos cried, raising his head. The look on his face was priceless: terror mixed with indignation. What cheek! He was arguing with a god! "I'll be forgotten before the year is over. This is a sham! We are thinking men, not primitive barbarians! Human sacrifice is an abomination committed only by lower men!"

How wrong he was. It was actually very common, and useful to boot: There was nothing like a human sacrifice to imbue a ritual with majesty. Having trouble getting the *populux* to listen to you? Hack someone up!

And how wrong *Janus* had been, to offer the brazen lad sanctuary. To this day, he had no idea why he had done it. To show his power that he could? He impulsively opened the man-size door in the screen the priests used to make offerings—burned animals, the occasional virginal maiden—and said to Pharmakos, "Enter."

Janus hadn't gauged the depth of insult this action would heap on Neptune—who, like him, was just a hellgod passing through. He had not realized at the time that, back in his own dimension, Neptune was considered something of an also-ran—pretty much a loser, actually. As a result, Neptune had an inferiority complex the size of the Colossus of Rhodes, and he took Janus's slight very personally. He swiftly declared war on Janus and his worshippers, delivered in the form of a fierce storm that wrecked the entire fishing fleet of Athens.

Whoops.

Janus tried to repair the damage. He personally tore Pharmakos apart and told his chief priest to hand-carry all his bloody little bits to Neptune's temple. So it was done, by twelve of his acolytes, each holding a small golden box against his chest. Janus assumed the acolytes were all a little put out with him; it was through his misdeed that they were in such big trouble with the entire population of Athens.

It was too little, too late. The Athenians started killing one another, then hiring mercenaries to up the violence factor. Blood ran in the aqueduct. The streets were slippery with decomposing body parts.

Still incredulous that Neptune had gotten them both so embroiled in the controversy, Janus suggested they meet alone at the Hellmouth, to discuss a resolution like reasonable demonic entities.

Neptune calmly agreed.

But then the God of the Sea showed up with a fighting force of ten thousand.

The cavern that contained the Hellmouth shook with the footfalls of twenty thousand sandaled feet as Neptune's men approached.

Swords and spears flashed in the light of the torches Janus had lit for the parley. The dozen or so dedicated acolytes who had accompanied him now prostrated themselves and begged him to save them.

Janus considered his situation. He was nothing if not practical. He had come to Greece on a fluke. He truly had no interest in battle.

So without saying so much as *"Efcharisto* for everything," he willed himself into his normal form, and stated his intentions to return to his home dimension.

Then he stepped into the Hellmouth, abandoning his shrieking worshippers, who had never seen his true appearance before. One face toward his escape route, the other glaring at them as if daring them to attack, he left them.

He successfully returned to his own dimension, but after Greece it was no longer pleasing to him. Compared to his adopted home, it was, literally, pure hell—a vast, seething landscape of hell-fires and brimstone. Janus's demons flayed the souls and bodies of damned beings. With their taloned hands, his minions scooped out their hearts and burned them before the sufferers' eyes—which they burned next.

And those were the lucky ones.

He tried to return to Greece, but he found that something had changed. His angry acolytes had apparently put up wards against him. They eventually managed to destroy the Athens Hellmouth. Then, to add insult to injury, Neptune hung around so long that he achieved lasting name recognition. The only lasting tribute Janus got was the dullest month of the year, cold and dull, only a few religions celebrating festivals the size and scope of December's haul of comfort and joy.

After perfumed nights discoursing with Plato and Aristotle, sipping fine Greek wine and cavorting with nymphs, the sheer monotony was enough to drive Janus mad. Whoever it was who said it was better to serve in heaven than to reign in hell . . . was only partially correct.

Things changed when Ethan Rayne chose Janus as his mag-ickal patron. As a young sorcerer, Ethan never realized that Janus was not a god native to the ancient Greeks, but his invocations and spells weakened the ancient wards and created portals through which Janus could work mischief in the dimension he had once enjoyed so very much. Had he been able to fully return, he would have wreaked instant havoc.

Unfortunately, less than thirty years later, Ethan had been cap-tured and locked away by Buffy Summers' lover. Janus was furious. Not only was he unable to commune with Ethan, he wasn't even certain where Ethan was. Ethan's voice had fallen silent, and Janus was beginning to wonder if the feisty sorcerer was dead.

Though Ethan had gone missing, his magicks had lingered. Before the fall of the Hellmouth, travel through Ethan's portals had been difficult, but it had not been painful. But now, the balance of good and evil had shifted, and it was a miserable experience.

My pain is the Slayer's fault.

Things were seriously out of phase. The Sunnydale Hell-mouth's closure was a serious problem, for not only did it prevent many species of demons from movement between various dimen-sions, but also the miasma of evil energy that had charged the earth at the source—the Hellmouth—had dissipated. The presence of evil was seriously weakened, the balance between good and evil badly compromised.

Demons in a hundred different hell dimensions raged at the girl who had dared do this to them. Hellfires blazed; gods roared with fury. Revenge was on the lips of any evil being that had lips. Dark landscapes flared with acid hatred; lakes boiled with the blood of the damned as devils dreamed of destroying the Slayer. Of being the one who would end her.

Buffy Summers had brought the forces of darkness to their knees.

She must suffer as no human had ever suffered before.

On this alone, every evil creature was agreed.

Few had possessed the imagination to think the unthinkable: that a mere human could thwart the First Evil. But she had.

Accustomed to the unpredictability of the human race, and well acquainted with tyrants, Janus had dared to wonder what would happen if Buffy prevailed. He had watched and observed, and he had planned his move should the First go down.

The first of his two chief allies shimmered into being beside him in the molten earth. It was purple-dark E'o, the many-headed, multiarmed goddess of destruction and rebirth who ruled her home dimension. A similar goddess was revered on Earth as the Hindu goddess Kali, and E'o had absorbed the vibratory thoughts of Kali's worshippers to facilitate her manifestation. In her green-and-black braids she wore a crown of skulls, and more of them hung around her neck. From her waist dangled severed arms. The golden, almond-shaped eye in the center of her forehead pulsed with purple membranes. Her fangs were long and shiny black, like the obsidian knives of the bloodthirsty Aztecs.

"We meet at last," Janus said to her, bowing low in his human form. "It is a joy to me."

They had never been able to see each other before, although of course Janus had researched both her and her dimension before approaching her to join his side. Until this moment, they had only transmitted messages through long, circuitous routes that could never be traced back to their original senders. With this meeting, they were taking the next big step toward their clandestine scheme to take over this dimension.

Her eye narrowed as she surveyed his human form. Janus wondered if she liked his appearance. Frankly, he lusted for her. She was bizarrely appealing, beautiful in a brutal, sensuous way he couldn't precisely understand. He wondered if she would care.

"It is a joy to me, as well," she finally replied. Her enunciation was low and breathy, more of a vibration in his ear than a voice.

They were speaking in English, the common language among demons from different dimensions. Once it had been Latin, and later, French. If the human race survived Janus's dominion, he would force them to learn the demonic language of his home world. Anyone caught speaking a human language would have their tongue ripped out.

"Where is our third?" E'o asked.

"He hasn't arrived yet," Janus replied.

She bared her fantastic black teeth. He had no idea if she was smiling or expressing her displeasure. Either was stunning.

"We chose this time," she said uneasily.

Displeasure, then.

"We'll wait a little while before we begin," he informed her, assuming his mantle as leader. He refrained from adding that it had been quite difficult for him to teleport, and perhaps Shri-Urth was having problems as well. He wanted to show no weakness before her. Though he wanted her, he would never trust her. He had survived all this time by never trusting anyone. He saw no benefit in changing that now.

The First Evil had terribly underestimated the power of the Slayer. Observing from his hell dimension, Janus had watched them make classic mistake after mistake—revealing their plans to her, giving her time to consider their moves—everything they had done reeking of arrogance. From the outset, he had feared them doomed to failure. So he had quietly worked behind the scenes, courting allies, laying out his own scheme.

As soon as the First fell, the trio—Janus, E'o, and their belated partner, Shri-Urth: the Legion of Three—had discreetly and ruthlessly assassinated rival demons and hellgods who also wished to destroy the Slayer and all her followers, break open the portals between their hell dimensions and the world of humans, and rule the human plane.

But existing in the human world was supremely difficult—at least as far as Janus was concerned. And he was quite worried about that. If the others learned of his predicament, would they still follow him?

E'o looked around herself. Their meeting room was a hexagram hewn from crystal, situated at the very center of the earth's core. It was the equivalent of the ancient secret place of the gods, the *atydion.* Janus wondered if the human race had grasped that the center of the earth was a locus of evil. That was why their racial memory contained so many references to a hell under the earth.

"I grow weary," E'o stated. Her snake hair wove and hissed. "I will depart if he doesn't appear in—"

The interior of the crystal plunged into darkness, then was lit with smoky crimson like the burning of a coal. Scarlet eyes glowed in the glowing, rippling illumination. The black silhouette of a cloaked figure slowly took form. It was topped with twin curled horns. From its cloak a hand appeared, gripping a staff topped with a cube of black crystal. Inside the crystal, an eye appeared. It was as large as the fist of a man, and it was the color of moss growing on the shadowed side of a gravestone.

Lord of a terrifying underworld, Shri-Urth had many manifestations; he had chosen to appear now as the human symbol of Death. Janus thought it interesting that all three of them had worn human-like guises to their first meeting.

"You are late," E'o said to Shri-Urth.

Shri-Urth remained silent. Then he glided forward in the darkness, paused, and collapsed.

Janus and E'o stayed where they were. Gods did not run to help other gods. It would speak of being lesser, and possibly humiliate Shri-Urth in the bargain. He had learned a lot since pissing off Neptune.

Using the staff, Shri-Urth pulled himself to his feet. Then he bowed low. His face was hidden by his caul. "I had difficulty arriving here," he admitted, his voice a papery whisper. "And I am having difficulty remaining."

There was another silence. The teeth of E'o's skull crown clattered as she lowered her head and said, with obvious reluctance, "I had difficulty as well."

Both looked at Janus. He cocked his head. "I see."

"You had no problem?" Shri-Urth rasped.

"No," Janus lied.

"Perhaps it is this venue," E'o ventured. "The central core of this dimension's physical location—"

"The traditional hell of many of their belief systems, and with good reason," Shri-Urth cut in. "Evil is most at home here." He raised his face, which remained a black shadow. Janus wondered if he had a face at all. "I attempted to teleport to other places when I realized I was having problems, and I experienced even greater difficulty."

Janus took that in. He noted that Shri-Urth had no hesitation to admitting a weakness, which usually bespoke strength. Additionally, the hellgod's English was better than his. In Greece, Janus had spoken Greek, of course. But, thanks to Ethan, he had been to this dimension many times since then, speaking English.

He must not allow his intimidation to show.

"It's because the Sunnydale Hellmouth was closed," Janus said.

"Because *she* closed it," E'o hissed. Her single eye darkened to a bronze color. Then, as Janus watched, two bulges appeared approximately two-thirds of the way from her chin, rising like bubbles to the surface. They flicked open, revealing two more eyes, these both a deep purple. Janus was fascinated.

"Yes, she closed it," Janus agreed. "But there's another Hellmouth. In Cleveland. I assume it will become quite active, if it hasn't already."

E'o again flashed her teeth. "That will keep the Slayer distracted."

Janus showed his as well. "Oh, I'm sure there will soon be plenty to keep her occupied. The forces of darkness are wild with fury at this humiliating defeat. If ever we needed a rallying point for our cause, the destruction of the Sunnydale Hellmouth is it."

"The Hellmouth is dead. Long live the Hellmouth," Shri-Urth intoned.

"Exactly," Janus said. He spread his arms. "Meanwhile, I'll see what can be done about the problems you two are having with—"

As if on cue, the figure of Shri-Urth began to flicker and fade. Within seconds, he disappeared altogether.

The other two waited. Shri-Urth did not reappear.

"So." E'o glared at Janus. Or, he thought she might be glaring at him. Her tone spoke of intense anger. "We cannot remain in this dimension with any predictability."

"It would appear so." He was careful not to apologize. "It's a minor inconvenience. We'll remedy it."

Her third eye pulsed. "Or . . . we could be two rather than three."

He suppressed a grin. Oh practical, blunt goddess! She stirred his blood. "I researched each of you thoroughly before I approached you. It is the combination of the three of us that will tip the balance in our favor. Our essences combine in a unique way that will set this world aflame. The humans will die, and we will finally reclaim this dimension for all demonkind, and reign over them all like the hellgods we are." He raised a hand. "But only if Shri-Urth's power is joined with ours: yours and mine. We two cannot hope to accomplish what the three of us can. We three must be one. An unholy trinity."

He spoke the truth. Janus had researched his chosen allies with great care; the combination of their natures would unravel the world.

He smiled at her. "Were that not so, I would be delighted to share my throne only with you."

She looked at him coolly. "*Your* throne?"

He didn't back down. "Yes. Mine."

A long silence passed between them. He assumed she was weighing her options. He didn't mind if her faith in him wavered. In the end she would see there was no other choice. She needed him as badly as he needed her; perhaps more so. His ambition was boundless. He would be the master here.

E'o huffed. "Very well. I'm not so naive as to believe I could do this without you."

"Good. Then we are agreed that I am the leader in this venture, and you and Shri-Urth will obey my orders."

"No. We are not," she said. "We will work together, and you will listen to us. You may have instigated this coup, but I am not your lackey."

"Of course." He inclined his head. This was one hellgoddess who would not be dominated. He was even more intrigued by her. "I concede your point."

"Excellent." Her voice was warm. Her face remained as wildly fierce as ever; slowly, her jaw opened, and a long, red tongue darted forward for just an instant, in a gesture reminiscent of a human woman seductively licking her lips.

Was she making a sexual overture? He hoped so. He realized that he had better learn more about her, and about Shri-Urth as well. He did not understand his allies as well as he'd thought he had.

"Janus," she said, his name a *hisss* like water on a superheated anvil.

"Yes, E'o?"

"I wish you to know—" Then she gasped and said, "Something is happening to me!"

She began to fade, just as Shri-Urth had.

"Send me a message to let me know you're all right," Janus called after her. "I'll begin working on the problem."

"I shall," E'o replied. Her voice was distant and muffled.

Then she disappeared altogether.

Damn it, Janus thought. What human philosopher was it who said problems are nothing more than opportunities?

If Janus ever found him, he'd tear the idiot to pieces, just as he had done to ol' Pharmakos, so very long ago.

Because problems . . . are problems.

CHAPTER FIVE

Die, v.: To stop sinning suddenly.
—Elbert Hubbard

Dressed in her fetching black leather gift, Faith lugged a gangling, wolflike carcass over her shoulder and dropped it with an unceremonious *fwap* on the desk of Sheriff Cruz. She stood back with her hands on her hips and smugly said, "That's the last one."

"Ooh, *felicidades,*" Andrew said approvingly. He was wearing a deputy badge and a ten-gallon hat.

"Thank God," Sheriff Cruz said, examining the pelt with his fingers, his face hard and angry. "Damn thing has fleas, just like the others."

Willow moaned softly. The witch's back was pressed against the wall hung with a rogue's gallery of wanted posters. Andrew felt a complex mixture of nostalgia for his own days as an outlaw, and relief that they were over.

He, Willow, Kennedy, and the sheriff had been waiting for the others in the sheriff's surprisingly spacious office. Faith was the first to show up, and she had brought quite a trophy with her. The sheriff's office was a typical frontier lawman's ops center: plain wooden desk; brick walls painted white; and a triple-decker set of file cabinets in avocado green, with an oak-framed picture of his wife and three kids on top.

Andrew turned to Willow, who had on some very attractive retro casino apparel: a black sleeveless mock turtleneck adorned with a sweet powder pink poodle with rhinestones for eyes; a pair of black capris; and gold lamé flats. She looked like a trashy Audrey Hepburn. As cute as she was, however, her facial features were all squashed together as if she were very nauseated.

"What is wrong, Wicca one?" Andrew queried.

Willow looked away from the dead monster on Sheriff Cruz's desk. "Oz . . ." Her voice was faint and strained.

Ah. The ex-boyfriend. Andrew had never met the infamous Oz.

"We've been over this," Faith said impatiently, grabbing the limbs of the creature hanging over the edges of the desk and folding them as if the entire body were something she had just taken out of the dryer. "Oz is a whole different species."

"He's a shapeshifter," Willow murmured, refusing to be comforted.

"Not per se," Andrew chimed in. "Although there are factions within furdom who would argue that there's not that much difference."

"These shapeshifters don't change back if you kill them when they're in animal form," Kennedy piped up, walking over to Willow. "If Oz got killed—if a *werewolf* is killed—he resumes human shape."

Andrew noted that she did not put her arms around the red-haired witch-woman. *Hmm, is there a rift in the Force?*

"Yeah, so?" Faith snapped.

Kennedy gazed at Faith coolly. "Meaning that they're different. We didn't just wipe out a nest of Oz's cousins. We killed animals that masqueraded as humans."

"Buffy didn't think that," Willow said. Indeed, the head Slayer had argued that the shapeshifters should be captured and locked up until a better solution was found. Faith insisted her solution was the better one. It had once again put the two champions at odds with each other.

They captured one of the creatures, and everyone had seen for themselves that they really were a form of animal that could only act human for a short time span. That whole crazy bit "Britney" had gone through on the day of the burning bus was part of their normal transformation process. They couldn't keep up the pretense of being human. That was why she had slaughtered Deputy DeWitt in Dixie Barnes's bedroom. She couldn't stop herself.

"They're like vampires, Willow," Andrew insisted. "They're not human. A true Scoob is quite able to stake vampires, no matter their appearance. Unless they are devilishly handsome. Then, upon occasion, a Slayer of the Vampyre is conflicted by the terrible allure of the demon lover, yes?" He tented his fingers and leaned back in his chair. As he did so, he lost his balance and nearly fell backward. His hat dropped over his eyes. It was a little on the largish side.

Faith snorted. Then she turned to Willow and said, "What, you'd rather leave these guys alone so they can rip apart more locals?"

The outer door to the building opened.

"Hello?" Robin called from the corridor.

"We're hunkered in the bunker, shootin' the breeze," Andrew let him know. He flashed a crooked smile at Sheriff Cruz. "A little law enforcement humor there to lighten the situation."

Sheriff Cruz frowned. "Sorry, I don't get it."

Robin walked in, a little slowly, because of his injuries. He was followed by Giles, also walking slowly, because of his age.

Giles looked at the dead shapeshifter, then over to Faith. "So, that's it? We are finished?" he asked briskly.

"Yes," Faith replied. She frowned. "And you're welcome." She leaned sideways, smiling at Robin. "You good?"

"Never better. Well, actually, I've been better." Robin smiled back at her. "But I'm good."

"Right. Thank you, Faith," Giles said.

She inclined her head.

Then Giles ticked his attention back to the sheriff. "So, as we discussed, we'll be leaving. We've appreciated your community's hospitality, but we have obligations. . . ."

Sheriff Cruz nodded. "Wish you could stay. We could use you around here, even without the shapeshifters. Got a lot of people up from the border trying to cross the desert. It's a race trying to locate them before they die of dehydration."

"Ah, *Mexico*," Andrew murmured. "Sweet *señoritas*, sweeter pineapple smoothies at the Siete Once. That's Seven-Eleven in Mexicoan," he informed them.

Giles chose to ignore the comment. "I'm sorry, but we can't. As I explained, we're needed elsewhere."

"Europe," Andrew said excitedly. "All those beautiful young Slayers, looking for guidance. Desperate for someone to explain to them the solemn duties of a Slayer of the Vampyre."

"Oh God, does he have to go with?" Faith groaned. She grabbed the back of the chair Andrew was sitting in and tipped it forward. "Out," she said blithely. She eased Robin into the chair. The handsome ex-principal smiled up at her. She shrugged as if to say, *Hey, no big, okay?*

Andrew was stricken. He turned to Giles. "You already said I could go," he reminded him.

"We're very shorthanded," Giles told Faith. "The Watchers have reassembled in London—"

"There's a plus," Faith grumbled.

"And they're trying to put the word out so that Slayers will hear what's happened and will come in. They all need training, and it's up to us to give them a hand. After all, it was through our efforts that they became Slayers. We have a responsibility toward them."

"Supergirls, Incorporated," Andrew mused. "It has a certain 'je ne sais quoi.'"

"Shut up," Faith ordered him. To Giles: "It was the Watchers who forced the Primitive to become the First Slayer."

"She has a name. It's Senaya," Willow said. She brushed her bangs out of her eyes as she steadfastly avoided the dead shape-shifter on the sheriff's desk. "Can we talk somewhere else?"

"Yeah," Faith said tensely, scratching her arm. "Just so we're clear, Giles: For the record, I don't like pimping out the new girls to the Watchers. I say we tell the Watchers to go to hell."

"Your concern is duly noted," Giles replied.

"My *concern*?" She threw back her hair like the wild she-goddess she was. "More like my total contempt."

She held out a hand to help Robin to his feet. But he stood on his own steam—*go, Principal Wood*—and led the way out of the office. Faith followed after, then Giles, then Willow.

Andrew was the last to leave. He hesitated, standing before the sheriff's desk, and mournfully placed his hand over his badge. He unpinned it and held it out to his superior. "It's been an honor," he said, all emotional.

Cruz blinked. "Keep it, kid. I've got a ton of 'em." He pulled open a drawer and got out the phone directory. "I'm going to have to get this place fumigated," he muttered to himself as he flipped through the pages.

Andrew smiled, thrilled at the big man's generosity. "I'll treasure it," he breathed.

"Good." Sheriff Cruz picked up the phone. "Yeah, this is Cruz. Fleas again, damn it."

• • •

Xander pulled up outside the Siesta Motel in Dixie Barnes's Chevy Impala. Dawn and Buffy were piled inside with all their worldly belongings stashed in the truck. Dixie had actually given them the vehicle as a gesture of her appreciation, and the casino manager was trailing behind them with a van he had donated to the cause.

Vi and Rona were in the casino van with the three newer Slayers—Marie, Karen, and Stephanie—who had gone to town earlier to buy some toiletries. The logistics of simply feeding, clothing, and grooming their large party reminded Buffy of the days before the big battle, when Potentials started coming to the Summerses' home from all over the world.

Between the two vehicles, they had enough transportation to the nearest airport. Then they would all head off to England. Giles had managed to get everyone fake passports. They excitedly felt like secret agents. They were getting far away from Sunnydale and Hellmouths.

But when Buffy and the others entered the motel lobby, she took one look at Giles waiting inside, and froze. He looked worried, and more pale than usual. "What happened?" she immediately asked.

Giles took off his glasses. "Remember the Hellmouth in Cleveland? Demonic activity in and around it is off the charts."

"The Watchers Council called," Andrew elaborated, standing beside Giles. "The Cleveland Hellmouth has gone supernova with evil." He nodded somberly. "The Watcher's exact words."

"Oh." Buffy nodded. "No England, then?"

Giles put his glasses back on. "No. The Council were quite clear that we're needed in Europe. There appear to be a preponderance of Slayers on the Continent."

"That means there are more Slayers in Europe than in America," Andrew translated.

"Don't get jacked up," Faith said, joining the conference. "We've got a plan B, B." She put her hands on her thighs and got to her feet. She looked at Vi, Rona, and the three new Slayers as they stood grouped behind Buffy. "Robin and I'll go to Cleveland. And we'll take Karen, Stephanie, and Marie with us. You and Kennedy go on to England."

"No," Buffy said. "Because . . ." She trailed off. "Because you're right." At Giles's look of surprise, she said, "They're going to need seasoned fighters."

"We don't need a lot of muscle," Buffy pointed out. "We're training new Slayers, is all. Giving them the manual that I never got and showing them how to live by the Girl Scout law."

Kennedy looked miffed. Faith looked over at her and said, "You may be needed in tea-town, Junior. There may be trouble. Take Willow and One-Eyed Jack, too, B."

Xander saluted Buffy. "One-Eyed Jack—that'd be me. In so many ways."

"Do I still get to go to England?" Andrew asked.

"But Cleveland . . . the Hellmouth," Vi said anxiously. "Shouldn't *both* the big guns be there?"

"They will be," Faith said airily. She grinned at Robin. "Give me everyone else and we'll shut that Hellmouth down so fast, those demons won't know which way to run."

"Am I going to the bad place?" Andrew whined.

"I'm thinking we can take the casino van to Cleveland," Faith added. "Give us some time to find out what's going on and wheels when we get there."

Buffy considered. "That works. We'll drive Dixie's car to the airport. It'll fit us all."

"The car seats . . . um *five*," Andrew murmured plaintively as he counted heads.

"Okay. We're good," Faith agreed. She turned to Robin. "Can

you tell Marie what's going on?" She turned back to Buffy with a crooked grin and said proudly, "He speaks French, even."

Buffy raised a brow. "A man of many talents."

Faith chuckled. "Mad skills, B."

"I am not hearing this," Xander murmured.

Giles crossed to the reception desk. "I'll call the airport."

"We'll load our gear into the van," Faith announced. "Saddle up, girls. We're back on the job!"

"It's a plan," Buffy announced. "We're good to go."

"But . . . going where?" Andrew pressed as he was swept along with the others.

EN ROUTE TO LONDON

With the mysterious fall of Sunnydale, airports were skittish; but after a short delay and Giles using his accent to charm the British Airways reservationist, they were on their way.

As they lifted up, Buffy and Dawn held hands tightly. Tears streamed down Dawn's cheeks; and Buffy's eyes welled. The Summers sisters were being wrenched away from everything they had known. Buffy had hoped to show Dawn the world. Maybe it would be different now. Maybe Dawnie would be safe.

"I wonder what the movie will be," Dawn said in a determinedly upbeat tone. "And if we'll get something good for dinner."

"On an airplane?" Buffy was skeptical. She glanced at Giles, who sat across from them with his eyes closed, wearing in-flight earphones. "A British airplane? Dawn, have you ever eaten British food?"

"I heard that," Giles informed them, opening one eye. Then he opened both eyes and gazed kindly at the sisters as he pulled the phones from his ears. "I'm quite sure things will go well in England. And Faith and the others will deal handily with the Cleveland . . . situation."

"You used to lie better," Dawn said.

Giles looked taken aback. "Not at all."

"He's right. His lying skills are unchanged. It's that *you're* older," Buffy told her.

Dawn smiled at them both and leaned back in her seat. She kept hold of Buffy's hand, and a surge of protective anxiety washed through Buffy. Also, grief.

Good-bye, she said.

To so much.

Giles shifted uncomfortably. The amount of leg room he had was abominable. His back was sore, and he was tired.

Like Buffy and Dawn, he was trying to put on a brave face, but the truth was, he was equally anxious about what was to come in England. He detested the new head of the Watchers Council. Lord Ambrose-Bellairs was an overbearing aristocrat who, Giles was certain, had thrown his money around to buy his position, just as his ancestors had purchased their noble rank. He would be another Quentin Travers, and Buffy would like him just as much as she had liked Quentin. That was to say, not one whit.

Giles partially agreed with Faith that they shouldn't get entangled with the Council again. But many new Slayers were approaching them, seeking help and advice. It seemed the wiser course, if not the pleasanter one, to become involved.

Alas.

Willow concentrated on the wards she had placed around the jet as she remembered what it had been like in England. Her coven sisters had been so kind to her, despite the fact that she had tried to end the world. She had learned so much, both magickally and emotionally. She had grieved, and mourned, and she had thought she was ready for a new love in her life.

She was so sorry that she'd been wrong.

Tara? she silently called. *Can you see me? Help me guard this plane, sweetie. Help me keep them safe.*

Kennedy sat four seats away from Willow. It was a welcome relief from the discomfort of being with her, yet not being *with* her. She would keep up her end of the bargain—she would be there for Willow—but she wouldn't torture herself if she could avoid it.

I'm a full-fledged Slayer now. The wonder of that had not worn off. *My life is different. I'm different. I'm strong. And I'll get through this. I'll get through anything.*

She smiled.

The flight was tedious, despite the fact that Xander hadn't seen the movie. Mostly he read the in-flight magazine over and over, and went shopping in the duty-free catalog. Not that he could afford to buy anything.

But someday, damn it, I'm going to own a pair of fake rock stereo speakers.

He dozed and dreamed. In his dream, he and Anya had gotten married after all, and she was carting around crates of pine-apples. He had no idea why, but she was supremely happy doing it.

When he awoke, he remembered that Anya was dead.

Andrew drummed his fingers on his tray table as he watched the young boy seated beside him totally blow the fifteenth level of Death Duelers. At last he could bear it no longer, and he said, "You need to get the Gem of Narthosis *first*. Then you can wipe out the Orcs in one fell swoop."

The boy raised a brow.

"Try it," Andrew encouraged him.

The young lad did so. "Blimey," he said, gazing at Andrew in wonder.

I think I'm going to like this strange new land, Andrew thought happily.

They landed. It was late.

There was fog so thick that it was like shower curtains. Everyone was tired; they didn't have much in the way of luggage—okay, a couple of carry-ons with toothpaste and extra underwear—but their passports had passed muster, and a guy was waiting for them in a limo.

Buffy let Giles deal with him, Brit to Brit, and she piled in with the others. They drove forever, and there was nothing to see.

Then they stopped. The driver opened the door, and everyone got out. A building rose in the fog; there were lights in arched windows that glowed through the mist like those paintings by Thomas Kinkade.

Then a large door crashed open and a voice trilled out, "Queen Buffy?"

"We're in England for sure," Andrew breathed.

Then there was a glow, as if from a flashlight.

"Welcome," a man's voice said. "Do come in, please."

"Sir Nigel?" Giles called out.

"Giles. So good of you to come. If you would be so kind . . ."

"It's all right," Giles said to Buffy.

I already don't like him, Buffy thought as she and Giles led the way into the Watchers Council Headquarters.

The reception room of the Headquarters reminded Willow of old-fashioned lithographs of gentlemen's clubs, cozy with leather seating and walls of books. There was even a poor stuffed tiger in the corner, and busts of women with wings on either side of the large, lit fireplace.

A uniformed butler served everyone tea and salmon pâté sandwiches while they spread out in the room.

The young girl who had called out to Buffy was named Belle, and Lord Ambrose-Bellairs was chastising her.

"That was rather forward of you, Belle," he remonstrated the young Slayer. He cleared his throat as he glanced in Buffy's direction. "We're rather old-school, Miss Summers."

Belle was standing at parade rest, facing the new head of the Watchers Council. Her blond hair was pulled up in a bun on top of her head, and she was wearing a green sweater and blue jeans. She reminded Willow of Tinkerbell.

Lord Ambrose-Bellairs—now *there* was a name to be reckoned with!—was surprisingly young and bald. Although he wore a black turtleneck sweater and wool trousers, and an unexpected earring, he sounded like a stuffy old fuddy-duddy British aristocrat.

Willow instinctively didn't like him.

"I'm sorry, sir," Belle said breathlessly. She glanced shyly at Buffy. "It's just, she's the Slayer, sir."

"*You're* a Slayer," he said. He smiled coolly at Buffy. "Not meaning any disrespect, of course."

"Of course." Buffy sounded like she didn't like him, either.

Belle's sweet shyness reminded Willow of Tara. She smiled encouragingly at her. Belle noticed, and her shoulders eased down a little.

Andrew took a bite of his little sandwich and said, "Yick, I mean, I guess I'm not so famished after all," then proceeded to eat every single cookie—*biscuit*—on the tea cart.

Dawn sipped aromatic tea in an overstuffed chair. Buffy surveyed the new surroundings, while Giles's curiosity kept him at the bookshelves. Xander shrugged and ate Andrew's discarded sandwich. And Kennedy warmed herself before the fire. The light played over her features; she was so lovely.

Willow's throat tightened with fresh grief.

Lord Ambrose-Bellairs turned to Belle the Vampire Slayer. "You may go."

Buffy frowned and said, "I don't think so."

The Watcher blinked and raised his brows. "I beg your pardon?"

"You don't say when she can and can't go," Buffy said evenly. "Those days are over. Watchers have one job: to *help* us, *not* to tell us what to do."

Willow was afraid Belle was going to keel right over from shock. Pouring a fresh cup of tea, she moved her hand through the steam and asked the goddess to add calming ethers. "Have some of this," she suggested, offering the cup to the young girl.

"Thank . . . thank you." Belle glanced nervously at her Watcher. But he was looking hard at Buffy. Buffy coolly held his gaze. Giles watched them, keeping his silence.

"I see," Lord Ambrose-Bellairs then said slowly.

"No. I don't think you do," Buffy retorted. "We quit the Council a long time ago. We closed the Hellmouth without any help from you. You made the First Slayer, but Willow here made *all* the Slayers. There's no monopoly on our power anymore. You are not in charge."

"Ms. Summers, you've certainly accomplished great deeds," Lord Ambrose-Bellairs said. "However, the closing of Sunnydale's Hellmouth consumed all your attention. More has been going on in the world. The activity at the Cleveland Hellmouth is unprecedented, and across the globe, young girls turned into instant Slayers have no idea what's happened to them. We of the Council have intervened as best we could to keep order. We feel . . ." He hesitated.

"Yes?" Giles interjected blandly. "What do the Council feel, Lord Ambrose-Bellairs?"

"Please, let's not stand on ceremony. Call me Sir Nigel."

Giles remained silent.

The man cleared his throat. "Very well. To put it bluntly, we're of the opinion that the . . . problem is the same as it ever was. That conditions overall have not vastly improved in the battle between good and evil."

"What?" Kennedy half-shouted as she turned from the fire.

"Are you loco?" Andrew cried. "Hel-*lo*? We kicked the First's butt!"

"Yeah," Kennedy said.

"Indeed. All the way to Cleveland, it appears," Sir Ambrose-Bellairs replied.

Willow was aware that Belle still hadn't taken a sip of her tea. Belle was too distracted, staring at Buffy with flustered admiration.

"Look," Xander said, stepping toward the center of the room, "let's have this little chat another time. Like, tomorrow. We're all very tired."

"Xander's quite right," Giles said, pushing up his glasses. "This isn't the proper time to discuss this. Everyone is exhausted. Tempers are short."

"Right." Sir Nigel rose. "We've prepared rooms for you. I'm sorry, but you'll have to double up. I apologize for any inconvenience—"

"Who am I sleeping with?" Andrew asked, raising his hand.

"We put you in with Mr. Harris," Sir Nigel told him.

Xander's shoulders sagged. "'Xander, Spike's moving in. Xander, Andrew is your roommate.' Why does God hate me?"

"God loves you," Dawn said stonily. "You're alive, aren't you?" She got up. "Where does Belle sleep?"

"With the other Slayers," the man replied. At their blank looks, he elaborated. "We have approximately a dozen *en situ.*"

"That means 'here,'" Andrew said helpfully.

"And they live, like, in a dorm?" Dawn asked.

The man looked distinctly uncomfortable. "There are some accommodations below the first floor—"

"The servants' quarters?" Giles asked, his voice rising. "Good God, you house Slayers there?"

"We're crowded here," Sir Nigel replied. "We have staff, and all the Watchers keep rooms—"

"Rooms, I presume, that are not belowstairs?" Giles asked.

Sir Nigel shrugged as if he had nothing to apologize for. "It's very ad hoc. We weren't expecting such an influx. If we had realized what you were about to do . . ."

"Oh sure, blame it on us," Andrew said, then swallowed and added, "Your Lordship, sir."

"This totally sucks," Kennedy groused. She glared at Sir Nigel. "Is that where you intend to put Buffy and me too? Because we're just Slayers?"

Sir Nigel shook his head. "Good heavens, no. You're . . . guests."

"We'll sort this out in the morning," Giles ventured. "Please, show us to our *quarters* and we'll reconvene at breakfast."

"Belle, would you please escort . . ." the Watcher began, then seemed to realize that asking a Slayer to play hostess would be poor form at this point. "Very well." Casually, he crossed the room with a sort of *come along, come along* gesture.

Willow whispered to Belle, "Drink your tea."

Flashing Willow a grateful smile, Belle put the cup to her lips.

Kennedy lingered at the doorway. Willow caught up to her and said, "I suppose we'll be sharing a room."

Kennedy nodded. "I suppose. It's okay, Willow. Don't worry."

Willow felt like crying. "I'm not worried."

Her girl—her *friend*—touched her cheek. "Good."

Breakfast didn't go all that well either.

It started out with cooked tomatoes and fish with their heads still on and their eyes staring, and went downhill from there.

Slayers had cooked the breakfast. Slayers had served it. The

Watchers Council treated their Slayers like servants, sending them out to kill things and then come home and do the chores. Buffy was incensed. It was like those books about the rich tormenting the poor she was supposed to have read for English Lit.

"Let me get this straight," Buffy said to Lord Ambrose-Windbag as he oddly scooted two granules of food onto his upside-down fork. "You did nothing to help us shut down the Hellmouth, so that puts you back in charge."

Giles looked up from devouring his disgusting fish. "Buffy, one must remember that the original Watchers Council were, ah, blown up. The new Council *have* been giving some direction to the Slayers they have located."

"Yes, turning them into scullery maids like our sweet little Cinder-bella," Andrew said, sadly shaking his head.

Everyone ignored him.

"However, the majority of Slayers are not coming to us," Sir Nigel said. "They're going to Italy."

There was a beat as everyone processed that. Then Buffy said, "Because the food and the weather are better?"

Sir Nigel gave her a little *oh that's so not funny* smirk and said, "No, because of the Immortal."

"Oh." Giles sat back in his chair. "Of course."

"The who?" Buffy asked. She glanced at Giles. "Is this some-one I'm *supposed* to know about?"

"Not precisely," Giles told her. "He's declared himself neutral in matters of good and evil. So although he's amazingly powerful, he's not relevant." He pushed up his glasses. "Or hasn't been, until now." He turned to Sir Nigel. "Why is he gathering Slayers?"

"*Au contraire,* old man," Sir Nigel said. "They are going to him of their own free will. Camping on his doorstep, as it were. He has a reputation, at least in Europe. . . ." He let his words trail off. "I must admit I'm rather surprised you never told your girl about him."

His girl? Buffy seethed.

"You see," Sir Nigel explained, "these poor girls have no idea what's happened to them. And the Immortal is known far and wide—except in America, apparently—as the greatest living expert on matters of the occult. And that is saying something, as he has lived for centuries. Millennia."

"Is he older than Yoda?" Andrew challenged.

Giles set down his fork and tapped his lips with his napkin. "Well, it seems clear that these new Slayers ought to come to London. Buffy can train them, and the new Council—of which I hope I may count myself a member—can provide some guidance."

Sir Nigel shook his head as he lifted his teacup to his lips. "Quite impossible."

Buffy was about to suggest a smack-down rather than let him forbid Giles a full seat on the Watchers Council Next Gen. But before she could go there, he continued: "We suggested that, but we can't seem to get them to leave Italy. We're not sure why. The Immortal's not keen on having them around either."

"Why not?" Willow asked.

Sir Nigel sighed and put down his tea cup. "We aren't certain. He's not an especially cooperative sort."

"That's accurate," Giles concurred.

"Then I'll have to go there and round them up," Buffy said.

"Yes, well." The man cleared his throat. "He specifically requested that you not do that."

"What?" She looked from him to Giles and back again. Giles shook his head to indicate that he, too, was at a loss.

"Something about you being a magnet for evil. He doesn't want the complications you represent."

Buffy rose. "I'm leaving, *now*. To get them."

"Perhaps we need a few days, Buffy," Giles offered. "We can learn more, and—"

"Remember Britney?" Buffy asked him. "Okay, she was a fraud, but when we thought she was all crazy because she was a Slayer, we bought it. Because it made sense. And if Slayers are winding up with some ancient magick guy who won't help them, and doesn't want *me* to help them—"

"There are other Slayers we need to help," Willow reminded her. "Slayers all over the world."

"Many of them en route to these premises," Sir Nigel reminded her.

"Yeah, Fawlty Towers, I get it," Buffy said. "We can't be everywhere at once. Giles, you stay here for the en route ones. I'll go get the other ones."

"Right," Giles said firmly.

"So." Buffy hoped Sir Nigel realized she was deliberately ignoring him. "I want Xander and Willow to come too. If I'm such an evil magnet, then I want some backup. Kennedy, I need you to stay and train the Slayers who are already here."

"Oh." Kennedy hesitated.

"It's okay," Willow said, avoiding Kennedy's gaze.

Buffy sensed something had changed between them, and she was sorry.

Andrew tapped his fingers on his plate. "Dawn, are you going to eat the rest of your bacon?"

"I also want Belle to come with us," Buffy added.

"Why on earth?" Sir Nigel asked, then shut down when she gave him her patented glare. "I'm not certain she would care to do that."

"Oh yes, I would!" came a cry from the entrance to the dining room. It was Belle, carrying a tray for clearing the breakfast things.

"Very well, if you wish to leave us, Belle." Sir Nigel sounded almost hurt.

"I do, sir!" she said happily. Then she covered her mouth. "What I meant, sir, was that I should like very much to accompany the queen, I mean Buffy, to Italy."

"Belle, we've been through this. You're a British subject. You already have a sovereign."

"Yes, sir," Belle replied, looking abashed. "Of course."

Wrong again, Buffy thought. *I may not be Belle's queen, but she doesn't live in England anymore. She lives in the Land of the Slayers.*

"I see I can't talk you out of this," Sir Nigel gritted. "I've got a private jet. We'll have it ready in approximately two hours. The Immortal has a landing strip near his villa, and—"

Buffy put her hand on Dawn's shoulder. "We're taking the train. We've never been to Europe."

Dawn beamed at her and smacked the back of Andrew's hand as he tried to pluck the strip of bacon off her plate.

Sir Nigel frowned at Buffy, then leaned across the table to address Giles. "Surely, given your concerns about 'backup,' and the increase in activity in Cleveland, they should take the jet."

"That might seem the wisest course," Giles replied. As the other man began to relax, he added, "However, it is not the course Buffy wishes to undertake."

"I'll protect you," Belle said to Buffy.

Buffy smiled at her and said, "I know you will."

CHAPTER SIX

The dumber people think you are,
the more surprised they're going to be when you kill them.
—William Clayton

ROME
THE VILLA BORGIA

She wants to kill the bull, Antonio thought. *She can't wait to kill something. Anything.* He watched as Ornella ran the stiletto along the quivering animal's flank. *I know the feeling. It is the Moon of Hermes, and death is the god's favorite message.*

Antonio patted the cell phone in his pocket and sent an invocation to the god. He checked his watch. Less than an hour to go. No one knew that he had initiated the rites at the party for Sabatino, the Milanese fashion designer. The first requirement for successful magicks tonight was wine. He had splashed Sabatino's champagne on the earth.

The second was sex. He smiled at Ornella.

The third, death.

That would come soon.

And then . . . if the stars favor us, we will do an amazing thing, my dead ancestors and I. . . .

Antonio Borgia crossed his arms and shivered with anticipation as he watched his lover taunting the bull. He felt invincible.

The blood rubies set in his cufflinks contained real blood. Wards and talismans sewn into his tux warded off curses from his many enemies. He had written spells in the blood of his sacrificial victims, one of whom had been the most feared and powerful wizard in Sicily.

For years, Antonio had kept the Sicilian's left hand to use as a Hand of Glory during his most important rituals. He was delighted when, one night, the Hand gave him the finger. He'd had to destroy it, of course, but it made such an amusing story.

Ornella knew few details of his sorcery. When they had become lovers six months ago, she had agreed not to ask questions about his "business," and she had remained true to her word. In return, she lived a life of ease and privilege as an international supermodel—a career she owed to Antonio's magicks.

Which she well knew, and appreciated. She had been a beautiful waitress in a terrible wine bar in the slums of Rome only six months ago. She had owned two dresses, a pair of jeans, and one pair of shoes.

Now she owned the fashion world.

Two weeks ago, her fortunes changed again. Without warning, Ornella became preternaturally strong. Her reflexes were sharpened. And as for her endurance, *Madonna* . . .

She thought he had enchanted her. He let her think it. He also warned her not to tell anyone. It would be their secret. . . .

But in truth he had no idea how it had happened.

Now, in his vineyard, he marveled afresh at the goddess his beautiful teenage lover had become. With her hair piled on her head, Ornella strode like sleek Diana, Roman goddess of the hunt, in the moonlight. He smelled night-blooming jasmine, and her spicy perfume.

Antonio was fascinated, and perhaps a little repulsed, by how eagerly she tortured the bull. As soon as she drew blood, etching a furrow in the heaving animal's side, something came alive in her:

an eagerness to dominate the creature, perhaps, or simply to torment it. He thought of the bull-baitings back in the day, when his illustrious ancestors had ruled Rome. Ornella would have been right at home, partaking in the gruesome blood sport. His mind moved backward further in history, to the famous bull-riders of Crete. From them had come the fables of minotaurs—and the tradition of Spanish bullfighting. Bulls were sacred to many people from many times.

"I am your mistress," Ornella told the bull. "Your queen!" She darted forward in the night, raising both hands over her head.

"Ornella, *cara,* no," he told her, holding up his hand. "Let me make magicks first. Then you can kill it as a sacrifice to the gods."

She raised a lush, dark brow. Everything about her was lush— her wavy, reddish-brown hair and eyebrows, her black, heavy eyelashes, and her full lips. In the highly elevated world of fashion, she was simply Ornella, one of the handful of women known by one name only. She was only nineteen to his twenty-eight years.

Such treasures must be jealously guarded. Antonio was worried about the looks he'd seen passing between Ornella and his master. Handsome, dashing, powerful, and, well, Immortal . . . how could a mere man compete with the lord of all Italy? With the acquisition of her incredible new powers, Antonio had no idea if Ornella still considered him, Antonio, to be worthy of her. Maybe she would set her sights on the Immortal himself.

But Antonio knew women well; he had to believe that he was still worthy of her, or she would sense his hesitation and leave him.

That was why he had spent several hours today at the spa owned by Wolfram & Hart Roma. The enchantresses there performed magicks to increase his allure and enhance his sexual prowess. They also cast a small glamour over him so that when Ornella looked at him she saw a more chiseled face than he actually possessed, more deep-set eyes, and a bigger chest. It was like having a little bit of plastic surgery, working out more than usual. Subtle changes, but effective.

They had cost a lot, but Antonio was happy to pay.

"I want to kill it now," she said. "I want its blood to spray all over my face, and this dress." Her eyes glittered; her chest heaved. She was amazingly turned on by the thought of her power.

He waved his hand indulgently. *"Va bene,"* he said. *"Mia cara, mia bellissima."*

She laughed and turned back to the bull, her smile widening. Then she lifted the hem of her gown and ripped it from ankle to hip. It was one of a kind, and had cost tons of euros. She was wearing nothing beneath it, a fact he had already verified an hour earlier at Sabatino's gala at the Colosseum. They had stolen away into the catacombs, giggling like naughty children, she with a bottle of champagne and he with a jug of common table wine slung over his shoulder. He had poured some of it on the earth and woven magicks over it.

They had made love in one of the tunnels housing the bones of fallen gladiators. She lay atop a stone slab said to contain the bones of Spartacus, leader of a Roman slave revolt in 133 BC. Spartacus outwitted the Roman legions for over two years, humiliating the consuls and generals, who had completely underestimated the might and cunning of the enslaved gladiator. Antonio could relate.

He served the Immortal.

"Vampires nest in these catacombs," he'd told her, and she'd thrown back her head and laughed.

"There's no such thing as vampires, 'Tonio." She put her arms around his neck. "But I'll bite you if you like."

"Maybe you've become a vampire," he replied, toying with her. "That would explain your strength."

"As well as my taste for champagne and caviar," she'd said, laughing. "But drinking human blood—that is disgusting."

He said nothing.

She didn't need to know all his secrets.

They kissed, deeply. She was so strong, she could snap his neck if she wanted to; he had no reason to assume she wished his death, but he had enemies. Water trickled in the distance; Antonio heard a muffled chuckle. He raised his head. A shape flitted in the darkness. A footstep . . . was that the flapping of wings?

She had noticed none of it. She whispered, "*Caro,* come back to Ornella," and he had given his full attention to his lover. *Madonna,* what bliss . . . far more amazing now than the first time, six lovely months before. And that had been so astonishing that he had bound her to him magickally, without her knowledge.

But bonds like that loosened with time; he had not rebound her, preferring to see if she would stay with him willingly. He might have to rethink that plan.

Now, back in the vineyard, Ornella's sword flashed as she raised it toward the sky. Then she darted toward the bull like quicksilver, bent deeply at the knees, and vaulted onto its back.

"Look what I can do! I am a superwoman!" she cried.

As she landed behind its head, the bull bellowed and waggled its horns, unsuccessfully trying to gore her bare thighs. Her throaty laughter filled the night air. She leaned to her left and hacked the restraining rope in two. The bull knew it was now free and took off with her on it, stampeding into the vineyard with a low, angry scream.

"Ornella!" Antonio shouted.

She answered with gales of laughter as she and the bull disappeared into the darkness. "Don't wait up!" she cried back to him.

He raised a hand in salute.

"Good riding, *cara*!" he called. With a sigh and a smile, he gestured in her direction, warding her with protective magicks. He was no poseur in the world of the arcane; he was a well-known and accomplished sorcerer. And now he was needed downstairs.

Antonio turned and walked toward his villa, feeling the clods of dirt through the paper-thin soles of his custom-made dress loafers. At the villa's main entrance, two of his minions bowed low in welcome. They were *monachetti,* Italian gnomes who usually inhabited caves and tunnels. Short and stubby, with curly black hair and black eyes and bulbous, amusing faces, he had found a nest of twenty living in an abandoned winery in Spoleto. They attacked him; he easily put them enthrall. Now they lived to serve him . . . or, on occasion, to die trying.

The two *monachetti* were dressed like monks in rough brown robes. They wore close-toed shoes, even in summer, for Antonio could not abide the sight of their hairy toes.

The taller one skittered ahead and wrapped both its misshapen hands around the large metal ring in the center of an ornately carved wooden door. Over the transom a stone carving of the danse macabre was featured in bold relief—Death leading skeletal dancers in a merry reel. The carved pediment was from the Middle Ages, when the House of Borgia ruled Rome. The arcane Kabbalistic symbols that warded the house and called down miseries on enemies of the Borgias were more recent, added during the Victorian Age.

The door opened, revealing the grand foyer of Antonio's baroque villa. His heels clicked on the squares of white-and-black marble that spread across the foyer and its majestic double staircase. The banisters were gold; the staircase was carpeted in burgundy.

An enormous gilt chandelier hung above his head. As he passed beneath it, it lit up and glowed with an unearthly splendor—as well it should, for it had been a gift from a grateful demon, a brother in sorcery named Ilconceptio. Antonio had arranged for Ilconceptio's twin brother Hilario to eat bad fish. Just a little poison, cunningly worked into the sauce at a small dinner party. Some rosemary, some tarragon . . . who could detect a drop of something else, something lethal?

Hilario died in agony, blood draining from his eyes, ears, and nose. His fortune went to his mistress.

And his mistress went to Ilconceptio.

She was devoted to Hilario, but a love spell took care of that. She soon forgot that he'd even existed. She was so devoted to Ilconceptio that if he ordered her to, she would kill herself to prove it.

Or kill anyone he told her to.

Mistresses, *monachetti* . . . such was sorcery Italian style. If he had to do the same to Ornella to keep her, he would.

Though Antonio had taken credit for the poison, he hadn't created it: It was a family recipe, and Antonio was about to visit the cook, deep in the dungeons of his villa. She was, truth be told, his secret weapon in the vicious *vendetti* that were also part of sorcery Italian style.

Her name was Lucrezia Borgia, his ancestress. She was born in 1480, to a Rodrigo Borgia, a power cardinal in the Church, and his mistress. Rodrigo became the most notorious Pope that Rome had ever seen, a depraved sexual despot. Her brother, Cesare, terrorized enemies and allies alike. His torture chambers were hells where prisoners screamed for death. Together, the men had advanced the family to the highest echelons of society by marrying Lucrezia first to the Ruler of Milan, then to a duke and, when the duke was murdered, to a prince.

Lucrezia's title was Mother of Poisons and Potions. She experimented on the prisoners in her father's dungeons, refining her potent and cruel potions.

Her brother Cesare was her lover. Now he was Antonio's mentor and guide. By following Cesare's counsel, Antonio rose in the ranks of the exalted being whom he served: the legendary Immortal, the most powerful man—if man he could be called—in all Italy.

The man who wants my woman . . .

Antonio snapped his fingers; a dozen of his little *monachetti* stepped from the shadows and faced him before an ebony bookcase containing Antonio's lesser volumes on the Black Arts.

Eleven of the twelve *monachetti* were holding golden chests about a meter long on each side. From inside the chests, things kicked and scrabbled.

Antonio's chief minion, grizzled, elderly Fata, bowed its head. Its arms were empty. It said, in a gruff and barely comprehensible voice, *"Buona sera, Signore."*

"And good evening to you," Antonio answered. "Is everything prepared?"

"Sì, signore," Fata replied. It turned around and reached for the spine of a leather-bound volume titled *Stregheria.* The book was a fake; it was actually a lever. As Fata tugged the spine, the bookcase slid to the left, revealing a barred, iron door.

Fata spoke in its native tongue—a strange guttural language— to the smallest minion in the ranks. The creature swallowed hard and approached the door. It handed Fata its golden box and splayed its hands against the door.

Antonio waited.

Nothing happened.

Then Antonio unfastened the top stud of his tuxedo shirt and found the gold chain around his neck. He lifted it over his head, revealing an old-fashioned black key. At its top, a skull gleamed, its eyes twin rubies. He handed the key to his little minion, who accepted it with a trembling hand.

The others watched on in fascination as their peer fitted the key into the lock, took a deep breath, and turned the key.

The door creaked open, causing several of the *monachetti* to startle. The little *monachetto* took another breath and crossed the threshold. *"Signore,* it is safe."

Antonio held out his hand for the key, which the little minion gave him. Antonio tousled the creature's hair, and the gnome's reaction made him think of a starving puppy grateful for scraps from the table of its master.

The *monachetto*'s task was not yet over; its job was to lead the others down the circular path of stone steps into the dungeon below. Antonio walked in the middle of the file, protected on either end.

As they descended, torches on either side flared to life. Skeletal hands held them high. Dead bones stirred; dead mouths sighed and moaned. The enemies of Antonio's family lay entombed in the walls, and they did not rest easy.

Antonio murmured an incantation of protection. These had been the torture dungeons of his family for centuries. Even he still tortured people—and things—upon occasion, but his visits to this place were generally of a far different and more productive nature.

And far more exciting.

At the bottom of the staircase there was another door, this one at least fifteen feet high. The anxious little minion moved aside as Antonio waved his hands before it, whispering in ancient Latin.

A ghostly form materialized. It was a monk, its face shrouded by a caul. It bowed low, then put its hand around an invisible latch and yanked on it.

Fresh sighs and whispers filled the chamber as the door opened.

Then the phantom monk reached into itself, near its chest, and pulled out a brilliant scarlet cloak embellished with black roses and skulls. It bent on one knee, offering the cloak to Antonio.

Antonio took it with a flourish. The cloak unfurled and settled around Antonio's shoulders. A hood magickally raised up from the back and covered his head.

As soon as Antonio was covered, the specter vanished.

Clad in his sorcerer's robe, Antonio snapped his fingers again, and the first six *monachetti* walked across the revealed threshold.

Antonio waited. Nothing happened to them. Satisfied that the dungeon had not been penetrated by any of his enemies, he entered. The remaining seven minions trailed in after him.

The chamber, a pentagram, was approximately the size of the grand foyer. It was made of the oldest stones in the villa, stones old even when the Immortal was young. The stones were stained with blood. From the ceiling hung thirteen black and silver hangings depicting hearts pierced through with thorns and daggers. The total effect reminded him of Carnival in Venice, a flurry of color and drama.

Directly in the center of the chamber stood the beating heart of his house, the altar on which he had made countless sacrifices. He was not the first Borgia to worship the dark gods, nor would he be the last—of that he was certain. The base of it was a Roman sarcophagus carved with the double faces of the god Janus. The top was the lid of a stone coffin said to have shut away the depraved Roman emperor, Caligula, who was buried alive.

Atop the altar was Antonio's most prized possession—a mirror. Its gilt frame was made of entwined roses, and skulls, and the letter *B*. The glass itself, clouded at the moment by the icy vapors wafting from the frame, was made of crystal stolen from the *atydion*—the sacred holy of holies—of Hermes himself.

The minions drew back. The mirror terrified them. They were willing to chance death when opening the dungeon's doors, but Antonio had never been able to conquer their fear of the mirror. He knew that each little gnome would rather die than get near it.

That was probably a healthy fear.

He turned to them and said kindly, "You may go."

Each one set down his gold box and scurried out the door. It shut behind the last one with a resounding clang, and Antonio was alone.

From a hidden compartment in the center of the sarcophagus, he extracted an enormous cauldron. It was the approximate shape and size of a baptismal font. Rubies and emeralds spelled out his family name: BORGIA.

He began to chant in Latin, gliding to each gold box and opening it with a flourish. What was inside . . . well, once upon a time he would have hesitated. The first time he had performed the act, he had gotten drunk afterward and hadn't slept for almost a week.

Now the sacrifices brought him pleasure.

He reached in and lifted up a sweet newborn boy, cradling it in his arms. Then he felt inside his scarlet robe for his sacrificial dagger, decorated with the same roses and skulls as the mirror frame.

He took the life with efficiency and flare, draining the warm, steaming blood into the cup. He would later feed the bodies to the hellhounds that guarded his perimeter.

With the blade of his dagger, he stirred the blood, then began to trace symbols on the crystal—ancient, powerful runes that summoned the forces of the Black Arts, and bent them to his will.

"My desire is to speak to my illustrious ancestors," he said in Latin. "Lucrezia and Cesare Borgia, I call upon you."

The blood moved of its own accord, shaping and reshaping the runes. They were made into the symbols of an ancient spell, one of the most powerful he had ever learned. If not performed properly, the awakened mirror would suck the life out of him.

"I call upon you," he repeated, shifting from Latin to Italian and back again.

Then they appeared: two skulls, bone-white and spectral, staring blankly out of the mirror. Then muscles stretched over the bones; cartilage filled out the nostrils; teeth appeared in the jaws.

Next came the eyes, gluey and white, then sparkling with color and life—at least in Cesare's case. One of Lucrezia's remained milky and scarred. Last was the hair. In Lucrezia's case, long and golden, topped with a diadem of rubies and gold; in Cesare's, dark and curling around his ears. He wore a mustache and a goatee. An enormous ruby hung from his left ear.

These were the Borgias of legend, members of a dynasty whose name had come to signify corruption. In their lifetimes, people had whispered that they were in league with the Devil; that they were vampires; that they were incestuous lovers.

Three out of three—fantastico . . .

The Borgias *were* vampires, and had been for seven hundred years. And for all but the first two of those years, they had been exiled in another dimension, unable to leave. Antonio didn't understand all the details, and the elder Borgias had never seen fit to clue him in. He hoped that, in time, they would divulge their secrets.

The mirror flickered. The Borgia siblings were as pale as chalk and, on occasion, their appearances would go negative, so that they looked like X-rays. It was an artifact of their being vampires, appearing to him through the medium of a magick mirror. After years of research and study he had successfully created the mirror only three short months ago. When Antonio had first contacted his otherworldly ancestors, they were astonished . . . and pleased.

Tonight was another step toward their ultimate plan. Would they succeed?

The Borgia vampires were terrifying, yet alluring. They were dressed in Renaissance clothing of black and silver, with black velvet mourning bands around their right biceps. They were a striking pair. Antonio was humbled by the sheer pleasure of being related to them.

Lucrezia smiled at Antonio and said, *"Buona sera, caro Antonio.* It's an auspicious night."

"The Moon of Hermes. A night when magicks are strong," Cesare added.

"Sì." A rush of excitement washed over Antonio. "One of the strongest moons of the year."

"A good night for our experiment," Lucrezia added.

The background behind the two Borgias snapped into sharp relief. They were seated in their great hall. Their twin thrones were gold, studded with more precious stones than Antonio had seen in one place, even counting the treasury of the Vatican. Each time he witnessed evidence of their wealth, his mind was boggled. His patrons were probably the richest denizens of half a dozen dimensions.

Lucrezia waved her slender jeweled fingers. "Shall we begin?"

From his pocket, Antonio pulled the enchanted cell phone he had created. It was concealed inside the latest cell phone style to hit Italy: very tiny, decorated in a soft metallic purple cheetah print. He held it up to the mirror and flicked it open.

"Ah," both Borgias said, and sighed.

Without taking her eyes from the cell phone, Lucrezia picked up a bell and rang it.

There was movement behind her throne. Then a leathery, reptilian figure dressed in a spangled robe similar to Antonio's approached. Large horns curled on its—his—head, which was crowned with a pointed cap. His golden eyes glowed at grotesque angles. He had no nose, and his mouth was pulled back in a rictus of a grin. His multitudes of teeth were tiny and sharp. His name was unpronounceable, but he was a wizard native to the dimension the Borgias had ruled since the 1400s. He bowed to Lucrezia and Cesare.

Lucrezia pointed to the mirror and spoke to the wizard in his native language. The wizard turned and regarded Antonio and the cell phone. He pulled a large rectangle of glass from his sleeve and put it before his face as he leaned forward, examining it as Antonio held it out for him. His eyes bulged in the refraction; it was a magnifying glass, but it also scanned for danger. Antonio was familiar with it. He had several of the antiques himself.

The wizard nodded and put away the glass. He bowed low

again to his master and mistress and spoke to them in his native language. They answered back.

Then, with a flourish, Cesare pulled an identical cell phone from his sleeve. It was a work of genius, Antonio had to admit. Aided with magicks beyond his ken, his ancestors had been able to duplicate the complicated workings of modern technology. The question remained: Would it work tonight? So far, they had had no luck. Magickal engineering had taken place on both sides of the mirror. Tonight, they would try again.

Lucrezia sighed hopefully, clasping her hands to her chest. Cesare smiled at her; they locked gazes, and Antonio watched them silently communicating. He didn't know if they actually used telepathy, or if their hundreds of years together had bonded them in ways he had yet to achieve, even with victims of his thralls.

"Would you begin?" the wizard asked Antonio in very old Italian, a form not spoken in Antonio's world since the days of the Inquisition. There were many occasions when Antonio couldn't understand what Cesare's and Lucrezia's minions were saying. The only reason he could converse as well as he could with his ancestors was that they had applied themselves to learning modern-day Italian.

As always, it startled him how brilliant they were.

"It may be that the problem will still be the depth of the chamber from the surface," Antonio reminded them. "I've magickally boosted the signal. . . ."

During the course of their experiments, both sides had made modifications, calculations. Antonio had been working feverishly so they could be ready for the Moon of Hermes. The vampires' wizard had done the same, following all the specifications Antonio communicated to him.

"Do it," Lucrezia hissed impatiently.

Antonio began to punch in the number, one of the most magickal in all of sorcery: 137-1113.

The three closed their eyes and invoked the dark god of the moon. *"We call upon Hermes, upon Pan, upon Lust and her brother, Death . . ."*

Antonio took a breath and hit the send button.

Nothing happened.

Failure again.

He was dashed; he saw the disappointment on Cesare's face, the anger on Lucrezia's. He couldn't read the wizard's expression. To him, the demonic face was always filled with fury.

Lucrezia swore in ancient Italian.

And then the cell phone in Cesare's hand rang.

It rang!

Their wizard took an eager step forward, but kept his distance as Cesare carefully depressed the connect button and put the phone to his ear. Lucrezia moved to his side, pressing her ear against his.

"Can you hear me now?" Antonio asked, though he knew they wouldn't know that was a line from a television commercial.

"Perfetto." Lucrezia grabbed the phone from her brother and moved away from the mirror. "Can you hear me now?"

"Sì," Antonio told her.

She moved out of frame. "Now?"

"Sì."

"Caro amore, divino, bello . . ." Lucrezia purred compliments into the phone. "Antonio, I am so proud of you. So proud."

"This extends your sphere of influence," Antonio crowed.

"Like the tape machine," Lucrezia said.

"Sì," Antonio said proudly.

They had learned an amazing thing: If Antonio set up a tape recorder, it would record Lucrezia and Cesare's voices through the mirror. Then, when he replayed the tape, some—but not all—of their chants and spoken spells would actually work in Antonio's dimension. Their influence was moving beyond the barrier of the magick mirror.

Cesare crossed to his sister and took the phone. "Let us give thanks," he said into it. The wizard hurried away, then returned with two jeweled, golden goblets on a gold tray. The vampires each took one and held them high. Antonio was prepared for the ritual. He reached into the cabinet and extracted a bottle of fine old grappa and a leaded goblet for himself. He poured, and the three toasted one another and sipped.

Antonio doubted his ancestors were drinking wine.

Then the three spilled the rest on the ground, for the gods.

Cesare set down his goblet and tapped a black cloth to his lips. A human servant approached, bowing and scraping, and carted both goblet and cloth away. Cesare ignored him, but he fascinated Antonio. The man was the descendant of one of the humans who had been brought to the hell dimension with Cesare and Lucrezia. What would it be like to trace your ancestry for seven hundred years, knowing that your family had once lived in a different dimension?

Cesare leaned back in his throne and crossed his ankle over his knee, unaware that he looked like a modern-day businessman conducting business on his phone.

"Now tell me," he asked, speaking into the phone although of course Antonio could also hear him through the mirror, "how are you faring with the Immortal?"

Antonio had known Cesare would ask. He always asked.

"He seems to be pleased with me," he replied. Then he hesitated.

Cesare noticed. "Yes? What is it?"

Antonio didn't trust his ancestors. He admired them, yes, and he wanted to be like them—in some ways. He had no desire to become a vampire. He wished to know why Ornella had become so inhumanly strong. But he didn't dare reveal her change to these two. Not until he understood it himself.

He seized on the other problem at hand. "I think the Immortal wants my woman. I could put her enthrall again, but . . . it's more interesting when she has her own mind about her."

Cesare and Lucrezia stared at him, then turned to each other and burst into gales of laughter. This time it was Cesare who lifted a bell from the little table at his elbow and rang it. An exquisite young girl glided into the mirror's view. She was clearly also one of the descendants of the original humans Cesare and Lucrezia had brought with them into their dimension. Through the centuries there had been some intermingling, but there was no hint of the demonic in her appearance. Dressed in an elaborate gown of black velvet and silver lace, her long black hair streamed down her back. She presented herself to Cesare, curtsying low, but daring to gaze up at him with rapture.

"This is Celina, my beloved," Cesare said, cupping her chin as he urged her to her feet. "I want you to understand something, Antonio. I truly love this exquisite young woman. I have sung her praises. I have forsaken other beds for hers."

"Except mine," Lucrezia put in, and the two chuckled fondly.

He stretched out his fingers. Celina placed her hand trustingly in his. Without rising from his throne, he guided her toward Lucrezia, who extracted a small jeweled vial from her cleavage. The demonic wizard at Lucrezia's side coolly offered a golden, jewel-encrusted goblet to his lady.

As Cesare set the cell phone on the arm of his throne, Lucrezia poured the glowing green contents of the vial into the goblet. It began to smoke. Lucrezia swirled it, an odd little smile playing across her face.

Celina drew back slightly, but Cesare's firm grip kept her rooted in place. *"No, no,"* she whimpered.

Lucrezia extended the smoking cup to her. The girl mutely

shook her head from side to side. Cesare wrapped his left hand around the back of Celina's neck, forcing her still. Celina's chest heaved. She began to moan.

Cesare looked at Antonio. "I love her," he emphasized. Then he let go of her hand and pried her mouth open, yanking back her head. Lucrezia rose from her throne, eager and aroused. The contents of the goblet began to sizzle. Celina's eyes grew huge as she stared at it; she struggled in Cesare's grasp as Lucrezia approached. He held her fast, tipping her head farther back as his sister dramatically raised the goblet into the air.

Antonio was fascinated by the sight. He gripped the phone with one hand and clutched the edge of the altar with the other, leaning forward, as if he could leap into the mirror. But he could only listen and observe, a voyeur to the spectacle.

Lucrezia tipped the goblet over Celina's mouth. And before Antonio could fully grasp what was happening, the liquid burned a hole from the inside of her mouth through the bottom of her jaw. Her screams of agony were impressive. Antonio had heard few that surpassed them. Celina's knees buckled as her arms jittered in an almost comical way.

Without delay, Lucrezia handed the now-empty goblet to the wizard and, from her sleeve, she produced a long, thin stiletto. She aimed it at the girl's throat, jabbing quickly. Then, in quick succession, she stabbed her again, in the hollow of her throat, and then over her heart. Blood began to stream out of the wounds. It was tinged with green, and it smoked. The girl writhed in Cesare's grasp as he sighed sadly, *"Ah, bella, carissima."*

With a long, low laugh, Lucrezia bent her knees and fastened her fangs over the girl's heart. The girl went rigid, her back arching. Tears spilled down Cesare's face as he wept. Lucrezia drank deeply. She held on to the girl's shoulders, enlarging the wound and burying her face in it. Then she drew back, showing her blood-soaked features first to Cesare, and then to Antonio.

Cesare dropped the girl to the floor. She was a corpse now, a ruin. The vampire wiped his eyes. His face was a study in grief as he went to the phone and picked it up. "I loved her," he said. Then he moved to Lucrezia's side. He cocked his head, then began licking her face. Antonio heard the slurping and thought of man-eating jungle cats sharing their kill.

"Then why . . . ?" Antonio asked, in part because he was expected to, and in part because he needed to know.

"Because I can love again," Cesare told him. "And so can you."

"But . . ." He could say nothing more, not without revealing Ornella's strange new powers. He was tempted to explain to them what had happened. And yet, something in his gut ordered him to remain silent.

Antonio was young, but many men serving in the court of the Immortal had not survived as long as he had. Magick and instinct had served him well.

"*Va bene,*" he said airily. "A lover can be replaced."

Lucrezia spoke directly to the mirror. "If you wish to remain in the Immortal's service, give him no reason to doubt you. If he wants your woman, let him have her. Don't put her enthrall. He'll sense it."

Cesare took a handkerchief from his robe and began methodically wiping his face.

"To take his place, you must be wily and strong," Lucrezia continued. "For now, give him no reason to doubt your loyalty."

"*Cara,* we are talking about Roman politics," Cesare remonstrated. "No one believes anyone is loyal."

"Let me rephrase," she suggested. She looked hard at Antonio. "You must present yourself in such a way that the Immortal believes you have tied your cart to his star. That you are utterly vulnerable to his remaining in power."

"I've been doing that," Antonio assured them. "I'll strike when he's the surest of me."

"But only when we can help you," Cesare reminded him. "We

want you to succeed, my dear nephew. A Borgia will rule Rome again: you."

"I'm grateful," he murmured, lowering his head.

Cesare's chuckle made the hair on the back of Antonio's neck stick straight up. *He killed a girl he was in love with. But he won't kill me. I'm their golden boy. And I'll do whatever I have to, to keep it that way.*

"Now," Cesare said, "let us try to call you."

Antonio told him the number. "I'll disconnect first."

Cesare punched in the numerical sequence and handed the device to Lucrezia.

Antonio's phone rang. Thrilled, he connected and put the phone to his ear.

"Your time is coming," Lucrezia's voice proclaimed through the phone. "The signs and portents point to it. We'll do everything we can to make your dreams a reality. Be daring and bold."

"We have faith in you," Cesare added, speaking to him directly through the mirror.

"Grazie. Mille grazie." Then Antonio glanced down at his Rolex and noted the time. "It's nearly sunrise," he said. "The Immortal has arranged for all the court sorcerers to greet the Dawn of Hermes with a ritual."

Lucrezia waved her hand in a gesture of dismissal. "Then go, *mio caro.* Give him no reason to doubt you. You need to remain close to him, as close as possible."

Antonio made a fist. "Then, when he least suspects it," he said, "we'll strike him down, and the destiny of the Borgias will be fulfilled."

Vampires and sorcerer smiled at one another.

After Cesare put the mirror away, most assuredly shutting off the other world's communication, Lucrezia turned to him and said, "What do you think he's hiding?"

"The possibilities are vast," Cesare replied. They nodded in unison like the wise old soulless vampires they had become. Cesare kissed the remarkable cell phone and handed it to Theodoro, their wizard. Theodoro wasn't his real name, but Cesare preferred it to his demonic one. Even after all this time he did not like the native language of this dimension. It was ugly. "Make a dozen more of these. If something happens to the first dozen you made, we'll have spares. And let's see if we can make some modifications of our own."

The wizard bowed low as he clutched the cell phone between his palms.

"And don't fail," Cesare added, looking down meaningfully at the smoking corpse of his former mistress.

The wizard's expression betrayed nothing, but he swiftly left the room.

"Soon we won't have to depend solely on Antonio anymore," Cesare told Lucrezia when they were once again alone.

"Not that he's a bad sort," she reminded him. "And he's the most direct descendant we have been able to find. He is our blood. But I know your thinking. We need spares."

"That's why Father and I married you off so many times," he said, and they both laughed again. "It's a pity that our son died."

That was so long ago, back when both of them still had beating hearts.

"It's fortunate that Father had other children. Of course, I had more lovers than the Pope Himself," she said wistfully. She opened her mouth as if kissing a lover, and half-closed her eyes in dreamy sensuality. She was uncommonly beautiful; the milky eye was the flaw that made her perfection believable.

"No one had more lovers than Father," he rejoined as he glided into her arms, "while he was alive. But you've outlived him by seven hundred years. Once we return to our dimension, you'll have more lovers than even you can manage."

She flashed her fangs at him. "Do you really think we'll find the Orb of Malfeo?"

"I do, Lucrezia, *cara amore*. With this new way of sending our spells back into our home dimension, I truly do."

"Then let's celebrate," she whispered, baring her neck. He ripped at her throat, and she gasped with pleasure.

"We will have Rome back," he murmured, muffled against her neck. "And we'll be rid of that bastard, the Immortal, once and for all."

Many pleasure-filled hours later, their wizard returned their cell phone. Lucrezia performed the requisite sacrifices while Cesare spoke the words of their finder's spell. Drenched in blood both demon and human, she looked on adoringly as Cesare once again conjured a glowing blue sphere of the world as it currently existed in Antonio's dimension. It rotated in three dimensions, moving slowly as he commanded the mystical forces to reveal the location of the orb.

They had performed this same ritual thousands of times, with no results. But tonight—

Cesare held the cell phone in a bloody hand and dialed Antonio's number.

Antonio answered on the first ring. *"Sì?"* he said breathlessly.

Cesare mouthed, "Abracadabra."

The sphere in the great hall of the Borgia vampires picked up speed, whirling and sparkling; then the blue hue lifted from it and shot into the phone. He smiled, wondering if it would emerge from Antonio's phone in the same form.

"It is I," Cesare announced. He paused, waiting to see if Antonio indicated that he saw magicks trailing from his phone. But he made no mention, and Cesare continued: "And I see that the phone works even when you are far away from the magick mirror."

"Sì," Antonio said proudly.

In the hall, the sphere glowed and spun. And then . . . a tiny pinprick of red beamed from one side of it.

Lucrezia gasped and grabbed Cesare's arm. He saw it as well, and it took him a moment to recover. At last, after seven hundred years of searching, their enhanced scrying spell had located the Orb of Malfeo. *I give thee thanks, Great Hermes,* Cesare said silently. *This was accomplished during your moon.* He waved his hand and flicked his fingers against the wall. The red light expanded and flowed against the wall of the great hall.

North America, Cesare noted.

He moved his hands again, requesting clarity from the god. As the red light became moving figures, Cesare narrowed his eyes. The figures were silhouettes, then blurry images, and then they clicked into distinct pictures. He saw untold numbers of demons and monsters: A Lindwurm. Raging Turok-Han. He knew, then, what he was seeing. "Tell me, Antonio, is there an active Hellmouth in Rome?" he asked neutrally.

"I don't think so, *signore,*" Antonio answered. "But there is one in Cleveland."

Cleveland is in North America.

"I see. *Grazie.*" He kept watching. He saw skyscrapers and Japanese cars. Girls strutted boldly down the streets, no chaperones in sight, in immodest clothing—*jeans, they were called, and belly shirts, wifebeaters*—that would have seen a woman sent to a convent in his day. He heard the jangle of discordant music emanating from a dark-haired girl's steel-colored boom box.

He smiled, vastly amused. Lucrezia was equally transported as she stared at the images. They had watched hours of television with Antonio, seen DVDs, and knew much about the ways of the modern world. *Yes, an American city for certain. West Huron is the name of the street. Good.*

"I don't think I need to tell you to guard your phone with your life," Cesare said to Antonio, somewhat distracted.

"Yes, of course," Antonio promised.

"Very well. Until next time." Cesare summarily disconnected.

Then he smiled brilliantly at Lucrezia and said, "The Orb of Malfeo. It's in the Hellmouth in Cleveland."

"Cesare!" she cried, overjoyed.

They both vamped and melted into each other, biting and tearing with abandon. After centuries of searching, after the yearning and hoping . . . it was too wonderful.

In ecstasy, they created a bloodbath.

CHAPTER SEVEN

We are born princes and the civilizing process makes us frogs.
—*Syrus*

ROME
ROMA TERMINI TRAIN STATION

"I don't like this," Buffy said to Xander and Willow as they trailed behind a dark-skinned man wearing a red turban and a black business suit.

The Immortal had sent a limousine to meet their train at the Roma Termini train station, which, Willow had dutifully reported from their guidebook, was the largest railway station in Europe. Translation: bustling and brimming with travelers. But the man in the turban had identified Buffy immediately, and told her that he was Mr. Bey, the Immortal's driver, "sent to bring you to His Excellency."

The only way the Immortal could have known which of the hundreds of trains they were on was through spies, or magicks, or both. As far as Buffy was concerned, the Immortal was either trying to intimidate her, or impress her.

He had her attention, at the very least.

At first she had refused the ride, citing security reasons. But Mr. Bey assured her that he himself was also an accomplished sorcerer, and he had personally overseen the thorough warding of their car against curses, spells, and "more mundane ways of ending your lives."

Still, Buffy demurred, saying, "We'll come for a visit once we're settled." Giles had arranged for rooms at the Roma Suprema Hotel.

"With all due respect, *Signorina* Summers, it doesn't work that way," the driver replied, deferentially inclining his head. "His Excellency the Immortal's palazzo is heavily warded. One enters by invitation only." He glanced up at her, and the ferocity on his face gave her pause. "Any attempt to visit him without his express permission would be regarded as an act of aggression."

Well, la-di-dah.

Buffy looked first at Xander, then Willow, then her sister and the new Slayer, Belle, all gazing back trustingly, waiting for her to make the best decision.

However, no pressure.

"Okay. We'll take the ride," Buffy announced.

Willow told the driver, "I'm going to do a little warding of my own on the limo, if you don't mind."

He bowed his head again. "As you wish."

With their luggage, which was pretty much none, they followed the driver through the winding station, a mixture of modern architecture and Old World touches—marble statues, an ornate gold clock—to a curb dominated by a black stretch limo just like in Hollywood. A second man in a turban, this one purple, stood beside the passenger door with his hands folded. As they approached, he gave a slight bow and reached for the door handle.

Buffy looked expectantly at Willow. The Wicca spread her arms and began to chant. A sparkling light passed over the stretch limo as if a giant invisible hand were sprinkling it with glitter. Willow lowered her arms. "I don't know, Buffy. I warded it as well as I can, but he might have used magicks I've never even heard of."

"I'll go in first," Belle volunteered. On the train, Belle had repeatedly stated her vow to protect the "Slayer Queen." Buffy was touched by Belle's offer, but of course she couldn't let her go all self-sacrificing.

Which brought up an interesting point about Slayage: For the first seven years of her life as a Slayer, Buffy's mandate was to step in and save people, no matter what. The Slayer was expendable. Live to fight another day? Not totally necessary. Because somewhere out there, she had a replacement—whether or not Faith was in the picture, because for so long, Faith didn't count. Now her replacements were all around her. Now she had a life and sister Slayers who cared about her. So . . . how did that affect the prime directive?

"No need, Belle," Buffy said, moving ahead of her group. "I've got seniority, so I'll take the first bullet." It was meant as a joke, but Belle looked stricken.

Before Buffy could explain that she was just kidding, Dawn caught up to Belle, tugged on her coat, and whispered something in her ear. Belle giggled. They were close in age, and they acted like they'd known each other all their lives. Buffy remembered how it was when she had first met Willow, and so big sister was glad Dawn had a friend. But Buffy was also wistful—Dawn was growing up. And that would mean growing away. So many changes, so fast. Not only was she not the only Slayer anymore, she was less and less the focal point of Dawn's life.

That's as it should be. That means I'm doing the job Mom began.

The driver opened the passenger door, and Buffy slid onto butter-soft black leather. The others piled in, arranging themselves against the large sofalike seats that formed a U. Directly across from Buffy, inside a black wood console that featured a flat-screen monitor and a vast array of what looked like fruit juices, coffee, and pastries, gleamed a huge crystal vase brimming with long-stem red roses.

Buffy plucked a white envelope from among the roses and opened it. She pulled out a white card and read: "Welcome to the Eternal City. The Immortal."

Belle said, "Those are American Beauty roses. My parents' garden."

Yeah, and they don't seem to grasp that their daughter has superpowers, Buffy thought as she studied the flowers. Belle had told her about her family. The family motto was "benign neglect."

"You know, receiving flowers is better than receiving someone's ear, or finger," Xander offered. "At least it shows he's got class. And he's not going all Brando on you."

"Yeah," Buffy said slowly. "Maybe." She repositioned the card among the flowers and sat back.

They pulled away from the station into bustling streets of skyscrapers—some quite modern, others looking like opera sets. Not that Buffy had seen much opera, but her mom used to receive brochures to season tickets for the Los Angeles and San Francisco opera companies.

We're in Europe, she thought giddily. *I thought I would die in Sunnydale. With any luck, I might not even die in Italy.*

"Can we eat the pastries?" Dawn asked. "What's Orangina?"

"It's quite good," Belle said. Her eyes glittered. "May we open it, Buffy?"

"Sure," she said.

Belle easily popped the cap off the bottle, which was shaped like a bud vase and was the old-fashioned kind that usually required a bottle opener. Dawn retrieved two glasses; she looked around and asked, "Does anyone else want some?"

"Sure," Willow replied, and Xander nodded.

Buffy shook her head as she settled back against the seat. Belle and Dawn got to work pouring and handing out the drinks. As Buffy watched the pleasant scene, her lids flickered; she yawned. She should stay on alert, but she could feel herself relaxing into drowsiness.

She heard Willow murmur softly, "Buffy?" Then, "Ssh, I think she's asleep."

"Brilliant," Belle whispered. "She deserves a rest."

And then Buffy dreamed:

Of a face, kinda doughy, a little cynical around the eyes. It was a man, wearing one of those retro-chic hats like Usher wore now. Very fifties, Hollywood Confidential. *No, not a man; it was that demon, the one with the bad clothes, the one I found in Giles's apartment after Spike's and Dru's attack in the library; when they killed Kendra and put Xander and Willow in the hospital.*

Whistler. The one who had said, "The more you live in this world, the more you see how apart from it you really are."

No, he never said that to me. I never heard him say that.

He said, "The faster you kill Angel, the easier it's gonna be on you."

So I did. I killed Angel when he went all evil and tried to end the world. I killed him even though Willow's spell had restored his soul, because that was the only way to save the world.

I rammed the sword through his chest, spilling his blood and sending him straight to hell. He looked so stunned . . .

And I killed Spike.

He was so grateful when I told him that only a Champion could wear the amulet, and then I gave it to him. And it drew down the light that set him on fire. . . .

"You always kill the one you love," Whistler said. "Ain't it a bitch?"

Then his face changed, morphing into a collection of chiseled, angled features set in flawless olive skin—a square jaw, long nose, a broad forehead. Heavy black brows, and large, deep-set brown eyes fringed with lashes . . .

He murmured, "But don't worry. You can't kill me. I can't die. I am Immortal."

Aghast, the Slayer blinked and looked quickly around.

"*Signorina* Summers?" the man with the incredible face asked gently.

Buffy frowned. "Who . . . ?"

She was sitting in an overstuffed crimson velvet chair, in the most beautiful room she had ever seen. It gleamed like a music box, all gold and crystal, mirrors and chandeliers bordered by wood painted with roses and cupids. The ceiling was painted too.

About twenty feet away, Dawn, Belle, Willow, and Xander were seated on matching red velvet couches facing a cheery fire. Their backs were to her, and they were chatting companionably. For a moment, Buffy was confused, thinking she was back in Sir Nigel's study in the Watchers Council headquarters in London.

She looked back at the man. He was dressed in a tux, and he was holding two crystal goblets of what looked like champagne. He seemed to be glowing as if from within, and his eyes, when they looked at her . . . she couldn't manage to look away.

He was the Immortal. She knew it without asking.

"What did you do to me?" she demanded.

He cocked his head, all big-eyed innocence. *"Scusi?"*

I was dreaming. But I don't remember coming here. I don't remember the drive, or getting out of the limo, or anything.

She squinted at him. "You blindsided me. Us. Made us sleep."

"Ah. Caught." He gazed at her with sudden understanding and inclined his head. "It's true, Miss Summers. I bewitched you. All of you." He waved his hand at the others. "However, they don't remember it. I gave all of you a false impression of the ride to my palazzo. But it doesn't appear to have worked on you."

She bristled. *"You knocked me out?* You bewitched me into dreaming . . . what I dreamed? You are really in troub—"

He leaned forward, intrigued. "You dreamed? What did you dream?"

"Something I prefer to keep to myself."

She rose abruptly, forcing him to take a step back, which he did with a grin. She caught a spicy whiff of subtle aftershave. Beneath the clothes, muscles shifted over long limbs.

Like the dream, the thought came unbidden: *The Immortal is a hottie.*

"So where are the Slayers?" she demanded, moving on. "And if you make it all spooky hard to find you, how do they find you?"

"Madonna," he said, touching his chest as he raised his brows. "You're all American efficiency, aren't you? Very well. Magic. I permit them to arrive here. But I certainly don't let them 'find me.'"

She pushed back her hair, wondering if her makeup had stayed on her face. Or if there was any drool anywhere . . . from the sleeping . . . not that she cared. Much.

"I'm hosting a dinner in your honor tonight," he said. "To celebrate your arrival. Fine food, dancing, music. I have an excellent chef. He cooked for the Doge, back when Venice had a Doge."

"We don't have time," Buffy snapped. *Whatever a Doge is.*

"To eat?" His smile widened. Before she could respond, he added, "I've invited all the Slayers. They're expecting to meet you."

He paused as if he thought thanks were due. She sighed. "What time?"

He beamed at her. Mr. Hottie Sunshine. "Nine o'clock for cocktails. Dinner's at ten."

"That's too late," she insisted. "We've been traveling and we're exhausted. Make it earlier."

He moved his shoulders the way only really rich people could, when informed that their plans might inconvenience someone else, and they really don't care. "Alas. All the preparations . . ."

"Can be changed," she said. "Just put everyone in a deep sleep and send them a memo in their dreams."

"I did not interfere with your dreams," he said, leaning toward her, his smile fading, as if all the fun of meeting was over and they were moving on to somewhere else. "But I could, if you would like."

"I would not. Like," she said, trying to clear her throat.

"Perhaps you will change your mind." He handed her a glass of champagne.

"Or you'll change it for me?" she asked, not smiling.

But his light smile returned and he held up a hand as if to say, *I surrender.* "That, I think, would be impossible." He clinked his champagne glass against hers. "Tell me, Slayer, were you dreaming about death?"

She was startled. "Stay out of my head."

He gazed at her over the rim of the glass as he sipped. "I would never *dream* of invading your privacy." When she didn't take the bait of his pun, he lifted a brow. "It's an easy call, assuming a Slayer is dreaming about *la morte.* Some Slayers have called it *bellamorte:* 'the beautiful death.' Sometimes it comes as a relief."

"Uh-huh." There was a pretty oval table topped with a mosaic of a man wearing a laurel wreath. Seeing no coaster, she set her glass down on it and said, "Will you call us a cab?"

"But where are you going?"

"To my hotel." She lifted her chin. "Funny thing. I've had a nice nap, and yet I'm still dog tired."

"I have rooms for you here. All of you. If you'd like to nap before dinner . . ." He moved his hand, and another turbaned man silently approached. "Mr. Aram will be happy to escort you to your suite. He'll draw you a bath as well." He gave her clothes a once-over. There was nothing wrong with her black sweater and trousers. At all. "And I have selected a number of dresses you might like to wear to dinner."

She was taken aback. "They . . . they probably wouldn't fit."

"They are your size," he told her as Mr. Aram hovered at a discreet distance. "Your shoes will fit as well."

"How do you know that?" she asked angrily. "Get it off some Slayer fansite?"

"I know a lot about you," he replied. He tilted his head as he gazed at her with frank admiration. "I know what you've been through." A smile spread across his face, and his eyes were . . . what was that word? Limpid. Weird word.

Good eyes.

Seductively he asked, "Would it be so terrible to enjoy a nice, hot bath, put on a pretty dress, and eat wonderful food?"

Okay, maybe not, Buffy thought as she reached for the rose-scented soap. Her hair was piled on top of her head; she was up to her neck in bubbles. There were candles everywhere.

The tub was marble, like the columns surrounding it, and the fixtures appeared to be gold. In reach of the tub, there was a fruit and cheese plate, more champagne, and mineral water. She finally convinced herself to leave the bath's warmth, and tried on a black satin bathrobe and matching scuffies. The scuffies were very welcome, like two matching hugs for her tired feet.

The rest of her suite was equally impressive. A canopy bed was swathed in rose-colored hangings, and behind it stood an actual stained-glass window of a knight in shining armor slaying a dragon. An incredible home-entertainment system faced the bed. To Buffy's left was a huge armoire carved out of dark wood.

And inside . . . *oh, my God.*

Clothes to die for. Well, not literally. Clothes like celebrities wear to the Oscars: a golden ballgown; a red slinky thing cut down to here; something simple, sleek, and jet-black.

He sure is going all out for someone he said he didn't want to meet. Typical filthy rich man overcompensating. Probably drives a really big car, too.

She was debating just putting back on her own clothes when Dawn and Belle bounded in. Dawn was wearing a blue-and-silver strapless gown that molded her torso, then fanned out in a bell shape. Her hair was pulled back in a French chignon held in place by a silver clip. She looked very pretty.

No. She looks beautiful. She's a beautiful young woman, not a pretty girl. She's growing up.

Hanging shyly behind, Belle was dressed in a clinging thirties-style gown of silver satin, with a silver-and-pearl camellia behind her loose flowing hair. Her vintage look reminded Buffy of her dream about Whistler, and she had a moment's pause. *Did I do wrong, bringing them both here?*

"Buffy! I'm a princess!" Dawn burbled. "Belle's a movie star. What are you going to wear?"

Buffy considered. She held out her original clothes. "Maybe these?"

Belle gaped, horrified, while Dawn scrunched up her nose. "Buffy, these *stink*!"

"Yeah, well. Then maybe not such a good idea." Buffy gestured to the rack of gowns. "You pick."

"The gold one," Belle suggested. "You'll be the gold, and I'll be the silver."

"And we'll wear them to the Bronze," Buffy joked. Belle didn't respond; of course not—she wouldn't know the Bronze.

"Wear the red one," Dawn urged her sister, tugging on the non-existent bodice. "It's extremely Jennifer Lopez."

"Then that's the one I *won't* wear." Buffy's hand moved back toward the gold one.

"Quite sexy," Belle agreed.

"Which one is the least sexy?" Buffy pressed.

"None!" Dawn said, laughing. "They're all va-va-va-voom." Belle laughed, too, and wiggled her hips.

"Excuse me?" Buffy said.

"That's what Xander said when he saw us," Dawn said, twirling in a circle. "That we're va-va-va-voom."

"I'm going to have a talk with him," Buffy said. "Where is he?"

"Outside," Dawn replied. "In the hall. He's wearing a tux."

"Quite distinguished, with the eye patch," Belle offered. Her cheeks were pink, and Buffy wondered if there was a little crush action going on. She remembered Dawn's crush on Xander. That now seemed so long ago.

"Yeah, with the eye patch he's really mysterious. Like a spy." Dawn waggled her eyebrows.

Buffy grinned and then brought her attention back to the wardrobe choices, feeling self-conscious and, truth to tell, a little old. "I don't know. All these dresses are so . . . much."

"Everything around here is so much," Dawn said as she sat on Buffy's bed. "What do you think his deal is? The Immortal, I mean."

"Yes," Belle said, tentatively touching the gold dress. "He's quite the enigmatic sort, isn't he? He tells you not to come here, yet he acts like you really *are* the Queen of the Slayers." She gazed in rapture at herself in the armoire's interior mirror. "Oh, I *am* a bit va-va-va voom."

"He's just throwing his weight around, trying to impress us," Buffy explained. "He tells us don't come, we come. So then he puts on airs like he's glad we're here. Guys like him are all an act."

"Yeah." Dawn pursed her lips together. "Manipulative Immortal guy." She bit her lower lip. "It's kind of working."

"Hard not to let it," Buffy admitted. "It's pretty much working on me, too. It's pissing me off."

"Quite understandable," Belle offered. "A man who gives us champagne and lovely gowns . . ."

"And puts a spell on us without our permission," Dawn reminded her. She smoothed her hair. "It could mean he's evil."

"He's probably in his room grinding his beautiful white teeth with fury that we're here." Buffy shook her head. "Those teeth have to be fake. They're so white. If he's so old, they should be all yellow . . . of course, Angel and Spike have . . . had nice teeth. . . ."

"Wow. You've put a lot of thought into this," Dawn said. "The whiteness of his teeth."

Buffy's face grew warm. "Not really."

Dawn pointed to the black dress. "Wear that. It's the classiest."

"Okay." Buffy reached for it.

"It'll be brilliant with the Immortal's tux," Belle said.

Buffy froze. "I'll wear the gold one," she said.

Buffy dressed quickly, and then she, Dawn, and Belle swept into the hall. Xander and Willow were waiting; when Xander saw her, he literally choked. Then he said, "Hi, I'm Xander. You are the goddess of Buffonia. You be my dinner partner, and I'll be your devoted fan."

"No. Be her deputy," Willow said, eyes twinkling mischievously. "Buffy, you look amazing."

So did Willow. She was wearing a slightly medieval dark green velvet gown with long sleeves, her hair loose over her shoulders. It reminded Buffy of something Tara would wear, and the thought made her sad.

"I'll also be your tour guide aboard the *H.M.S. Boris Karloff Movie*," Xander said as they began to walk down the hall, past rows of creepy oil portraits. "Anybody else suspect the Immortal is watching our every move through an eyehole in one of these things?"

"Oh, I'm sure he has Mr. Bey and Mr. Aram do the spying," Buffy told them authoritatively. "Right now, he himself is busy telling the cook how much sleeping potion to add to our soup."

Belle looked concerned. Xander gave her a wink and said, "See, this is the way that we alleviate tension. We talk about the things we're afraid of, and did I mention that the last time I wore a tux, I broke a woman's heart?"

They had just turned the corner of the hallway when Mr. Aram appeared, bowing low and saying, "I will escort you into dinner."

"Spy," Xander muttered under his breath, and everyone laughed—except Mr. Aram, who pretended not to notice.

They followed the man down marble floors and walls of whitewashed stone, lined with soft electric light and row upon row of framed pieces of art. Some were portraits and others were landscapes.

"Oh, my God, that's a da Vinci sketch," Willow murmured to Buffy. "I wonder if it's real. Do you think all these are originals?"

"Yes, *signorina,* they are," Mr. Aram replied, finally giving up the politeness of being deaf, and puffing up like a proud papa.

They climbed a flight of stairs, walked down another hallway, and then descended a flight of stairs. If Mr. Aram had been a cab-driver, Buffy would have suspected he was taking the scenic route so he could charge them extra money. Instead, perhaps he was taking them on the scenic route so his boss could show off his enormous bachelor pad.

Just about the time Buffy started wishing for hiking boots instead of four-inch heels, she inhaled the heavenly scent of freshly baked bread, and lots of garlic and rosemary. Her stomach almost rumbled, and her mouth watered.

They turned one last corner and faced a large wooden door. As if by magic, it opened for them, revealing a glittering crowd of perhaps two hundred people in tuxes and glittering gowns. Their attractive faces were illuminated by hundreds of candles. Men, women, young girls—it was like a picture in a glossy fashion magazine.

A hush fell over the room as all eyes fastened on Buffy. She stared back, and it was like one of those dreams where she had to sing in public naked. She narrowed her eyes suspiciously and found the Immortal, who was standing in front of a crowd of at least four dozen young girls, who were wearing everything from elaborate prom gowns to black leather jackets. A blonde with inch-long hair gaped openmouthed at her; beside the blonde, a dark-skinned girl with beaded cornrows burst into tears. Then a hazel-eyed girl peered from around the Immortal and squealed, "It's Buffy!"

Cheers erupted, joined by earsplitting, high-pitched shrieks that would have shaken the rafters, if there had been rafters. As it was, the ceiling just went up and up, and the enormous room clanged with sound.

"Buffy! Buffy the Vampire Slayer!"

"Wow," Xander said loudly.

"It's like you're a rock star," Dawn shouted into Buffy's ear.

A minute later—though it felt like hours—the Immortal walked up to Buffy, kissed her on both cheeks, and put his arm around her shoulders.

Then he turned and faced his guests. "My friends, young Slayers, I present to you . . . Buffy, Queen of the Slayers!"

The room erupted into louder cheers and higher-pitched squeals. The Slayers—so Buffy assumed—jumped up and down, clapping their hands and waving at her. More were crying than not. A petite Japanese-looking girl was holding something that looked like an autograph book and a pen; she waved them over her head when Buffy glanced her way. "Queen Buffy! Queen Buffy!" she cried.

The chant was taken up: *"Queen Buffy! Queen Buffy!"*

The cheering intensified; another half dozen girls broke down in sobs. The Japanese girl stumbled; a young woman with an auburn ponytail caught her, and they fell weeping into each other's arms.

"Long live the Queen!"

"I think this had better stop," Buffy muttered. She looked at Xander. "What do I say?"

He smiled crookedly. "How about, 'I am the great and powerful Buffy, don't look behind the curtain, form one line, and no shoving if you want to go back to Kansas'?"

"Sounds good," she replied. She raised her hands.

Immediately the room fell silent, except for one high-pitched voice that called out in accented English, "Buffy, we-a love-a you!"

The cheering started all over again. The Immortal applauded in rhythm like a cheerleader at the big game, ten seconds to go and the quarterback had the ball.

"Buf-fy! Buf-fy!"

It's gonna be a long night, Buffy thought.

CHAPTER EIGHT

Cry 'Havoc!' and let slip the dogs of war;
That this foul deed shall smell above the earth
With carrion men, groaning for burial.
—Julius Caesar, William Shakespeare

CLEVELAND

Devastation.

Disaster.

Payback.

"The Hellmouth is dead. Long live the Hellmouth," Robin breathed as they pulled the van over and stared at the mess that was Cleveland. He was driving, and had been at the wheel for hours. From the dying guy in the hospital to the well-seasoned kung fu–fightin' son of a Slayer, Robin Wood was back in the game.

Willow's magicks were that good.

Too bad she isn't here to patch up this town, Faith thought, stunned at the scene splayed out before them. *Or maybe not. Leaves more for us to do. I was going stir-crazy back in the desert after we mopped up those shapeshifters. Road trip made me nuts too. How many times can one girl ask, "Is there anything to fight yet?"*

She grinned like the warrior she was, more than ready to rumble. Itching to rumble. All she needed was a target and she was in the game, herself. Dude, she *was* the game.

"This, um, is bad," Rona said from the backseat.

Good call. Also, a matter of perspective.

Thick smoke clogged the sky as it boiled up from rows of burning buildings. Police cars were massed in an otherwise empty parking lot, their blue-and-reds flashing against the brick buildings. A clump of National Guardsmen pursued enough varieties of demons to make a demon U.N. as they galloped down the streets, throwing bricks through shop windows and diving in after loot.

Unobserved by the Guardsmen, a black-haired woman in jeans and a T-shirt that read GOD'S WOMAN clutched a baby in her arms as a towering, bruise-colored demon shambled after her. The demon menaced her with several arms and more tentacles, all of them extending like whipcords as it ran her to ground, barely missing her. The woman stumbled, whirling to face the monster, and began to scream.

And that, of course, was Faith's call to arms.

"I'm gone," Faith said, pushing open the door.

"Be careful," Robin called after her.

She snickered. *That guy is so hot, but he's not too bright. "Careful" is not the point of me.*

The woman's horror rooted her to the spot, a not uncommon reaction when someone faced down their worst nightmare. Faith punched the turbo. The demon's tentacles ended in talons; one more lurch and it would slice right through the woman's hands and dice the baby she was holding.

This was the downside of having something to fight: The presence of something hit-worthy usually also meant the presence of someone who might get hurt. Violence didn't occur in a vacuum. If someone was looking to destroy something, well, then, there was a destructee. As far as Faith was concerned, nobody had to be a victim when she was around.

She grabbed the shrieking woman's arm to get her attention, shouting into her face, "Yo, move it! See that van? Run to it!"

Faith darted in front of her, taking on the monster with an awesome side-kick. It didn't do much except give the woman a microsecond to pull herself together and obey Faith's order, and that was enough.

Faith whirled around and gave the monster another kick, this one a good sharp jolt to its chin. Then she grabbed hold of a tentacle extruding from its midsection and threw herself sideways to the ground. As the screeching creature tumbled toward her, she rolled over on her back, planted both boots against its face, and yanked hard on the tentacle. It ripped free with a totally gross *sllllurp*. Green goo—demon blood—cascaded from the wound and soaked Faith's shirt. She grimaced but smashed her fist inside the wound, feeling something coiled and pulsing and pulled on it.

What appeared to be a gelatinous cable appeared in her hand, green blood shooting from it. *Guts.* The demon howled and batted at her. She reached in and found more cable, and jerked that free too. She was covered from head to boot in goo; she kept her lips firmly pursed to avoid getting any of it in her mouth. Some flicked in her eye, though, and that pissed her off. She pummeled the thing mercilessly. It flailed at her for a couple of seconds. Then it went rigid and fell over backward.

Rock!

She wheeled around toward the van, then saw the looks of horror on the faces of the passengers—Vi, Rona, Marie, Stephanie, Karen, and Robin, who had leaped out of the van to get the woman. Chick was limping badly. The baby was shrieking.

Halfway down the block, a Humvee zoomed down the sidewalk and caromed off a row of mailboxes. It collided with a fire hydrant, slamming so hard that it knocked the hydrant askew. A column of water shot into the sky and Faith ducked beneath it, washing the demon blood off her body.

Soaked to the skin, she darted back to the van. Robin was half-carrying, half-dragging the hysterical woman and her baby toward the vehicle. Rona slid open the passenger door, and Robin helped her in.

Faith waved her hands. "Let's get out of here!"

Faces stared back at her as if they couldn't believe what they were seeing.

She frowned as she loped up to Robin and said, "What? I still got demon blood on me? It's not like we have to worry about the upholstery."

Then Robin grabbed her wrist and pointed past her, saying, "Faith, turn around."

She did so. Her eyes widened, and she said something not quite appropriate for prime time.

God, what is that?

A massive, rippling wall of crackling green flames or waves of energy rose above the burning buildings. Within the wall, an enormous face formed, its grotesque features elongating—a skull necklace; a triangle of glowing eyes; and yow, Gramma, what big black teeth it had! It appeared to be staring down at her like a panel in a comic book; the green shimmered and melted into brown, then purple, then orange, like an aurora borealis, only not pretty.

The face disappeared, to be replaced by another one. New guy looked vaguely familiar, with two human male faces jutting from a common neck.

The second image flickered out of view much faster than the first, to be replaced by a hooded figure, all skeleton and black robes, who was holding a black shiny cube with a green eye floating in it.

They heard distant explosions. Maybe the Guardsmen were shooting rocket launchers or hurtling grenades or something.

"Hey." Robin grabbed her elbow with his left hand, moving her forward as the other Slayers piled out of the van, forming a semicircle.

Faith took a step forward, leading the others—and realized that her feet were sticking to the asphalt. It was *melting*. Everyone glanced down anxiously at their shoes but it was harder to ignore the strange figure in the sky overhead.

And then the figure and its surrounding green flame vanished.

"What was *that*?" Vi shouted.

Faith looked at Robin. "No clue," he said.

"Let's go." She clapped her hands. "Everybody back in the van."

Robin glanced at the tires. "I'm thinking I might not be able to drive it out of the asphalt."

Three wicked explosions in rapid succession shook the earth, these far closer than the initial barrage that had greeted the figures.

There was also a lot of screaming. Faith pinpointed the source of the explosions: a brick building on the corner. She shouted, "Marie, Rona, Vi, with me!" and hauled.

Wrong. No hauling possible.

Faith's boots sank into the Play-Doh street; she felt as if she were wearing rubber buckets on her feet. The other Slayers were having just as difficult a time.

"Sacrée merde!" Marie cried.

You got that right, Frenchie.

They hobbled to the building. Flames burned in its adjacent alley; Faith slogged past the building to investigate.

The smoldering carcasses of three Harley-Davidsons lay in fetal positions. Their gas tanks explained the explosions.

From the prodigious numbers of fiery dark blue body parts, it appeared to Faith that the bikes had caught on fire; then demons got stuck in the super-sticky asphalt and couldn't retreat soon enough. Pieces of metal had blown everywhere, and demon arms, heads, and torsos still sizzled in patches of fires.

Faith said to Rona, "Nothing to see here, folks."

"Right." Rona wheeled around, yelling to the others, "Back the way we came!"

The other two Slayers nodded. Everyone struggled back to the van. Robin was busy gunning the engine, yet the sucker wasn't moving. The tires spun uselessly in the thick asphalt. T-shirt mom was huddled in the back of the van. Stephanie and Karen had their faces pressed to the windows, eyes huge. They were scared.

Seeing the others return, Robin popped open the front passenger door. Faith climbed in while Stephanie slid the side door open for the other three Slayers, who were complaining about their singed feet.

Robin tried to move the van again. To Faith's intense relief, the van lurched forward. It moved slowly, but it moved.

"Well, I think we can safely assume the Hellmouth is open for business," Robin said. "Where's the map?"

Faith retrieved the map from her back jeans pocket that the Watchers Council of Britain had e-mailed them via a cyber café in St. Louis, Missouri.

"Okay, here's West Huron," Faith said, tapping the map. She looked at a passing street sign to check her bearings. The van couldn't travel very fast along the soft asphalt, so she had plenty of time to read it. "The Hellmouth is about five miles to the east of us."

"Under a high school, like back home?" Rona asked.

"Worse. Under a club," Faith said. "Demons are gonna be wicked crazy. All that alcohol, girls with their belly rings and boobs hanging out. Wait." She grinned at Robin. "That *was* high school."

"Not on my watch," Robin retorted.

"Well yeah, it was," Faith said. Vi and Rona giggled. "I hear you were a good principal, though. Not that I've had all that much experience with principals. Well, not in the schoolroom." She chuckled. "On the other hand, I was in a couple of pretty nice offices . . . on some comfortable desks, yo . . ."

Robin shook his head as he pulled the corner of his mouth in a crooked smile. "You always try to shock me."

"I always seem to manage it." She put one leg up on the dash. "Don't I, Robin?"

"Oh, Faith," he murmured, "you're so young," and he returned his gaze to the street.

Outside the van, all they saw was chaos. Fires, smoke, cars, and buildings ablaze. People running, screaming. Monsters freely roaming the streets. No cop cars here, and no Guardsmen.

"It's the end of the world," their rescued passenger moaned. "My baby hasn't been baptized. She can't die until we find a priest."

"I thought they revised those rules," Rona ventured.

"Lady, she's not going to die at all," Faith barked at her as she stared at her reflection in the rearview mirror. "For God's sake."

"Easy," Robin cautioned her.

Faith crossed her arms and slumped down in her seat. "I can't stand wimpy chicks."

"If you were a mom, you'd see it differently," he replied. "It's not wimpiness. It's protectiveness."

"Easy for you to say. Your mother was a Slayer."

"What?" Rona leaned forward. "Are you kidding me?"

"Died in the line of duty," Faith confirmed. "Spike killed her."

"What?" all the other Slayers chorused.

Robin kept his own council. Trust Faith to drum up some drama. Tough gig, having a mother who was a Slayer. He used to hate her for dying when he was four. Hated Spike worse, for killing her.

Old days, old ways. The world was new.

"Mr. Wood, is that true?" Vi pressed.

"I'm Robin," he reminded Vi.

Then he hit the brakes—perhaps reflexively, since they weren't going very fast—and pointed through the windshield.

Where a city block had once stood, there was only a heap of bricks and wood, and a hole the size of Sunnydale High School. Rubble blazed and smoked, embers glowing on the perimeter of the sinkhole.

It was a hellhole—the location of the Hellmouth of Cleveland, an opening between this dimension and the hell dimensions spread across time and space.

Demons were pouring out of the abyss. There were half a dozen with mottled, leathery faces that looked like tanned cowhides, jostling others whose faces were bloody bones. Tentacles whipped; fangs flashed. In the center of it all, a huge Lindwurm, at least twenty feet long, reared on its hindquarters. Its belly was glowing, in preparation for spraying flame on everything in its path.

A winged dragon shot past the Lindwurm, screeching eerily as it flew into the night. Balls of fire pulsed in rapid succession from its mouth, like a fusillade of bullets.

Bring it on, Faith thought defiantly. *We can handle this. This is nothing.* Her heart was thundering, her blood pumping. Faith loved the battle. Faith lived for the battle. When it came to the physical stuff, she was total Valkyrie.

From the seat behind her, Rona whispered, "Oh, no. No. Oh, God."

"Faith?" Vi croaked, pointing to the left. "Faith, do you see it?"

Faith craned her neck to match Vi's line of sight.

Whoa.

Death as they knew it walked toward them: A lone Turok-Han emerged from the rubble. About seven feet tall, it was a nightmare of rictus glee and humpback bone, something a special-effects geek would invent for his nights playing dungeon games with his pimply assed buddies: *We'll make it ugly, then uglier, then even uglier. Bones with horsepower—oh yeah, a killer without an off switch. . . . No roll of the dice is gonna insure survival against this puppy. . . . We'll get it to kill all those snobby cheerleaders who won't date us. . . .*

The Turok-Han were the pure demon vampires who had killed over two dozen of the Slayers in the Sunnydale Hellmouth during the final battle. The only reason the Slayers had been able to defeat them was through Spike's intervention with the amulet. Otherwise, Faith and Buffy would be dead with all the rest.

We don't have an amulet now, Faith thought, her Slayer instincts ratcheting up to overdrive. *All we've got is half a dozen Slayers, a guy, a religious woman with a limp, and an unbaptized baby.* "Back the van up," Faith ordered Robin.

Not yet spotting the van, the Turok-Han turned his evil nightmare face in profile—a study in rigid hurt and fluid, eager pain—and hefted a war club over his head. Gesturing over his shoulder, he bellowed like a mindless animal.

Which was pretty much what he was.

"Robin, I said, back up," Faith repeated through clenched teeth. But she knew what he would say before he said it:

"I can't. The van's stuck."

In the melting asphalt, of course. Because without that terrible piece of bad luck, how would they deliver the viewers of the show to the commercial break?

I've seen enough girls die, Faith told the universe as she visually tracked the enemy. It hadn't spotted the van yet, and that was the only good thing about the scenario.

Maybe there was worse issuing from the Hellmouth—Lindwurm was nothing to sneeze at either—but the Turok-Han symbolized the fight they couldn't win. *I don't mind much dying—I've been living on overtime ever since Angel took me in and saved my soul—although Robin, well, there's that. He seems to think we could actually have a relationship, and that'd be something to see.*

But if it gets down to picking someone to take out, hey, my number was up a long time ago.

Then the Turok-Han spotted them. Its face cracked with what might pass as a smile, but hard to tell. Maybe it was a reflexive reaction to the promise of fresh, circulating blood.

"He's seen us." Rona said.

"No problem. One Turok-Han, six Slayers," Faith said. "Unbuckle your seat belts, girls. It's gonna be a crazy ride."

"What do we do, Faith?" Stephanie asked.

"We should run like hell," Karen muttered.

"Oh my God, please don't leave us," the mother pleaded. "I can't run. Or if you go, take my baby—"

"Will you shut up about dying?" Faith yelled at her. "Listen to me, Slayers. There's only one of him. We each killed Turok-Han in the battle, right? You've done this before. This is nothing new."

A second Turok-Han charged out of the sinkhole.

And a third.

And a fourth.

All racing toward the van.

"Non, non," Marie whimpered.

"What are they?" their passenger screamed. "Oh, my God, get us out of here!"

"Welcome to the Hellmouth," Robin said. He grabbed Faith's hand and kissed her knuckles. "If this is it . . . well, Faith—"

She swallowed. "Don't wimp out on me," she bit off.

Then she pushed open her door. "Everyone out of the van! *Now!*" she yelled.

"Cross! Block! Kick!" Belle yelled at the Slayers in training.

Only three days after the dinner, Buffy had organized the starstruck gaggle of Slayers into a training camp of sixty young warriors. And each day, *more* showed up.

The Immortal managed to house many of them in his vast compound, which was perched on a hill; the rest were living in such lavish tents that they might as well be permanent buildings. The tents were erected in a vast, bowl-like plain that extended for miles. On the opposite side of the palazzo was a thick forest. Plain and forest buffered his land from the busy city of Rome; and as it was heavily warded, the only people who saw it were those who possessed the proper magicks—and who knew how to use them.

The Slayers met every morning in the courtyard of the Immortal's palazzo. The ones who lived down in the tents joined the others for a lavish breakfast; when all that was cleared away, they began training.

Today, Buffy had put Belle in charge of a martial arts session, and the young Englishwoman was doing a fantastic job. The Slayers crossed their arms to block an oncoming blow and executed a fine whipkick.

"Rising sun!" Belle cried.

The Slayers were dressed in navy blue, red, or green warm-up outfits, in rows of six Slayers each. They looked like they were marching in the opening ceremonies for the Olympics. Buffy's outfit was black and very stylish. The Immortal had purchased the outfits; he had connections in Milan. He'd bought everyone lots of clothes, waving his hand all what*ever* when Buffy told him to keep a running tab. She'd get Sir Nigel to pay him back.

"Now, let's say your adversary is made of stone, or something equally dense," Belle said to the troops. She leaped into the air, then landed on one foot and snapkicked her heel into the straw dummy positioned in front of her.

The dummy toppled over. The Slayers applauded.

"Let's see you do it," Belle encouraged them, making karate fists as she walked up and down the rows.

They set to work, very aware that Buffy was watching them. The Slayers were totally hopping to, working their butts off to train and be as much like Queen Buffy as they possibly could. The idol worship had not worn off. But Buffy had only been in Italy for four days, so it could happen. The newbies had come from as far away as Russia and China, and other lands not known for their democratic forms of government. So maybe that explained their insistence upon treating her like their ruler. It was very embarrassing.

And to think how hard I lobbied for Homecoming Queen.

Other newly created Slayers were making their way to London. At her request, the Watchers Council had put out a "Message from Buffy" to go there and await further orders. That had slowed the arrival of Slayers to Italy, and put the pressure on England. Sir Nigel had purchased an old convent to house them all. Giles said it was very nice.

It had better be.

Her and Dawn's apartment was also very nice. It was located in a ritzy section of Rome. Trouble was, they spent hardly any time there. All the action was here, on the Immortal's compound. Willow and Xander had opted to stay in the Immortal's palazzo, both of them explaining that they wanted to keep a close watch on him. Buffy preferred having somewhere private to decompress. And to eat Italian ice cream and watch *L'eredità,* a really weird quiz show, like *Jeopardy!* only with lots more sound effects, including electric shocks.

Behind her, Mr. Aram called out, "Your Majesty?"

She turned. He Who Tiptoes stood at the top of the stone stairs leading to a Roman temple and, from there, to a side entrance into the palazzo. He showed her a silver tray, on which rested a light purple animal-print cell phone. Not what she thought the Immortal would pack, although he did seem to enjoy the fashion trends.

Let it be Giles, she thought as she headed for him. *With news from Cleveland.*

The last time they had heard from Robin, it was to tell them they'd arrived in the city limits, and the Hellmouth was spewing out demons left and right. There had been nothing since then.

Eagerly, she took the portable phone off the silver tray. She said to Mr. Aram, "Don't call me that again," as she put it to her ear. He inclined his head and tiptoed away.

"Giles, what have you heard?" she asked. She leaned against a low stone wall holding back a profusion of orange geraniums.

"Buffy. No word, I'm afraid," Giles replied. "But the Council have done some scrying magicks and they are able to say with certainty that at least one of our party is still alive in Cleveland. Possibly more."

One? Buffy clenched her fist, feeling helpless. Not her favorite emotion. "That's it. I'm going."

"No. We don't know what's happening there."

"That's not the way I work, and you know it." She held on to the phone and walked farther away from the training, climbing the steps toward the ruined Roman temple.

"These are different times," Giles said.

"Giles, it's an active Hellmouth." She leaned against a column. "We *do* know what's going on. Demons, monsters, total chaos. We sent half a dozen people to Cleveland to fight that. Those are not good odds."

"I understand that, Buffy," Giles said quietly. "But you don't have to be the one to go."

"But I—" She stopped. Someone was eavesdropping on the other side of the column. She frowned and bent around it to see who was there.

Oh, God. Not again.

It was one of the sorcerers on the Immortal's staff, a slimy young guy named Antonio who really thought he was all that. His anorexic supermodel girlfriend, Ornella, was with him, and they both drew back when they realized Buffy had busted them in the act of spying on her.

She palmed the phone in a reflexive gesture of privacy and hissed, "Do you *mind?*"

The two made little apology faces and drifted away.

"Buffy?" Giles queried. "Hello?"

"Sorry. I wasn't talking to you," she said into the phone.

"Kennedy's picked some Slayers to take. Quite green, of course. But perhaps a little more seasoned than your lot."

This was old territory. Kennedy wanted to go. Buffy was worried she had some death-wish thing going on, now that she and Willow had parted company. She said, "Kennedy is—"

"A Slayer, and a damn good one," Giles stated. "She's proved her mettle, Buffy. Give her a chance to take some of the load off your shoulders. You have family to think of."

An image of Dawn rose in her mind and she pushed it away, feeling guilty.

Dawn has support, if something happens to me. She's got Giles and now Belle.

But I'm her sister.

The Slayers are my sisters too.

This is where having more than one Slayer gets complicated. It makes the most sense for me to go to Cleveland. I'm the most qualified.

"What if something happens in Rome?" Giles asked, as if he were continuing her mental conversation. "We're still not certain of the Immortal. To be quite blunt, his enthusiasm for this training project is rather alarming. It's not his usual method of dealing with outside forces."

Buffy nodded even though she knew Giles couldn't see her. She had been thinking the same thing. But she hated staying behind.

"Buffy . . . ," Giles persisted.

"Tell her to get ready," she said, surrendering. "Sir Nigel's private jet gassed up?"

"Yes. I'll let you know when she takes off."

"Good."

"Buffy? This is the right thing to do."

"You're the Watcher," she shot back. Then she exhaled, pushing back a tendril that had escaped over her forehead, and said, "I'm sorry, Giles. I'm just cranky."

"Quite all right, and quite understandable." He paused. "The Immortal, how's that going?"

"What can I say? He loves to shop," Buffy muttered.

"Perhaps you two are soul mates," he tossed off.

"Ha. British humor is so peculiar. Ha."

"It's all the tea and fog. Makes me giddy. Cheery-bye."

"Bite me," she responded pleasantly. "Check in if you hear."

"Of course."

Buffy disconnected.

Kennedy's going. But I should go. It's where I'm needed most.

What was that saying I heard once? "The graveyards are full of indispensable people."

Yeah well, Mom is in a graveyard. Dawn doesn't need me there, too.

She put the phone in the pocket of her black workout clothes and headed back toward the practice area. The Slayers were punching the air and shouting, "Ho!" which actually made her smile a little.

"Scusi?" Antonio called after her. Ornella pranced beside him in a pair of ridiculously tight black leather pants and high heels. The way she was sinking into the grass, the Immortal ought to pay her for aerating the lawn.

Buffy really couldn't stand them. For one thing, Antonio hit on her whenever Ornella wasn't around. He had started in on her at the welcome dinner on the first night, saying things like, "Oh, you are called a Slayer? You are the queen of all these Slayers? How *fascinating.*" Like he was interviewing her on a talk show. And he had not let up since.

"What?" she bit off.

Antonio put his arm around Ornella. "I was just wondering—"

A branch snapped, drawing the attention of all three toward the sound. The Immortal stepped from the columns of the Roman temple. He was wearing laurel leaves in his hair, a toga bordered in gold, and leather sandals. His biceps and forearms were bare, and Buffy could see what happens if you work out forever.

"Antonio, the sorcerers are convening for the noon ritual," he said in English. "I believe you're needed?"

"Of course, sir." Antonio inclined his head. Ornella did the same. Then the two hurried toward the side entrance to the palazzo.

The Immortal made as if to kiss Buffy on both cheeks in the Italian style, but Buffy drew back.

He said, "Good morning, *cara*. You look troubled."

She certainly didn't trust him enough to share her problems with him. She back-burnered Cleveland for a moment, realizing that the people she wanted to discuss it with were Willow and Xander. Willow had asked to sit in on the noon ritual, and Xander had suggested that he coordinate the provisioning of the Slayer encampment with the Immortal's staff.

She headed back toward the training area to ask Belle to take over the rest of the session.

"Anything I can help with?" the Immortal asked. He fell into step beside her.

"I'm fine." She glanced toward the side entrance, which was closing after Ornella.

"You don't like them, do you?" he ventured, gesturing with his head toward Ornella and Antonio.

"No, actually." She raised her chin. "I pretty much don't."

He nodded as if he was making a mental note. "Why is that?"

"They're"—she moved her shoulders in a mock shudder—"shudder-making."

"Antonio is an . . . odd man." The Immortal made as if to take Buffy's elbow as she started down the last flight of steps, but he demurred. "He comes from a very old and magickal family. Have you heard of the Borgias?"

"Rings a bell," Buffy said, then made a face. "A very small bell. I wasn't much for history class."

"Stay here in Italy with me awhile," he said, chuckling. "I *am* history class." Then his smile faded, and he looked hard at her. "You *will* stay awhile?"

"You didn't even want me to come," she challenged. "Why the nice now?"

"At first, because I have manners." His skin glowed, and there were no lines around his big, clear, brown eyes.

He's been moisturizing for centuries.

"Now . . . I know you," he added, in his lilting Italian accent.

She blinked. "Oh, hah."

"I've been on the sidelines too long." He moved his shoulders and put his hands in his pockets, maybe going for boyish charm. "I've maintained my own interests, and I haven't dabbled in outside issues. Until now."

"So I'm an outside issue," Buffy said. "How flattering."

"You." He gave her face a slow reading. She wondered what he thought, mentally categorizing all her flaws. "You are a young woman of passion. You have dared to love fully, and your heart has been broken. At least . . . three times."

She folded her arms across her chest and tucked her chin in, gazing up at him through her lashes. "Are you reading my aura? Or maybe my yearbook?" she asked disdainfully.

His teeth were bright white. "You're a very defensive person. *Bene,* I can understand why. Your life has been very painful."

"I'm not a victim, if that's what you're trying to say."

"Not at all. You're a survivor. Surviving . . . can toughen one."

"Like an overcooked pot roast."

"Exactly." He began to reach for her, then waited a beat before he added, "Why don't you admit how attracted to me you are?"

Buffy's lips parted. "No," she said.

He held out his hand. She frowned and did not unfold like a lotus flower of passion or whatever he expected her to do. He was a walking, talking romance novel hero, and frankly, Buffy wasn't much of a reader.

"You have my phone," he reminded her.

"Yeah. Sorry." She fished in her pocket and handed it to him. He closed his fingers around hers, and okay, there definitely was electricity. A sharp tingling that was almost painful, like an electric shock. She felt it grab her spine and rattle her ribcage. Not pleasant, actually. Just extreme.

"Buffy," he began. He stared down at their clasped hands. He didn't let go. "Something's happening."

No way. He's coming on to me!

"Well," she began. "Static electricity, dry weather . . . although it looks like rain."

"In the world. Something's going on. I'm not sure what, yet. But it's evil."

"Oh. That. I mean . . . okay." She tried to clear her throat as she gave her hand a little jerk. He let her go. She put her hand in her pocket. "That would be new," she said wistfully. "Evil in the world."

He didn't lose patience. Patience was probably something he was good at. "The balance is off. You *do* know that The Powers That Be attempt to keep the two in balance? Good and evil?"

"I got the memo."

She decided to tell him a little. "When we closed the Sunnydale Hellmouth, the Cleveland one went into overtime," she said. "That's what I was on the phone about. I was talking to Giles. At the Council headquarters."

"I know." When she frowned, he said, "caller ID. I sent Mr. Aram to you with the phone. And, of course, I have my own magicians. We monitor the ebb and flow of evil in the world. Cleveland is crazy."

"Right." Then, remembering she was Joyce Summers's daughter, and that that meant some decent manners, she said, "You've been more than kind to us."

He inclined his head. "It's a pleasure." He slowed as they drew closer to the training field. "I want to talk to you."

She kept going. "You are talking to me."

He looked at the low wall behind them and perched on it. "I have vast occult resources here. My library is unparalleled. And I have numerous sorcerers and necromancers on staff."

"Like Antonio Borgia," Buffy said drily.

"If you want him gone, he is gone," the Immortal replied. At her look of surprise, he said, "I have lived a long time. I have good instincts. And to be honest, Antonio has . . . concerned me for some time. But not enough to do anything about him."

"However, if there's something I can do to make Italy more comfortable for you, I would terminate his employment without hesitation."

"Well, that's very . . . thoughtful. . . ." She shook her head. "We won't be here much longer. I'll be taking these Slayers to England. Just waiting to see if there are any stragglers on the way to your place."

He crossed his legs as if settling in for a chat. "Where will you house them?"

"We just got a convent." She gave him a wry smile. "I'm sure there's a joke there."

"How will you pay for their upkeep?" he persisted.

"Sir Nigel's loaded. And I suppose he's got friends. Maybe we'll open up a housekeeping service. With their superstrength, they could probably do two, three houses a day. There must be tons of dukes and duchesses over there who can't find good help."

"You could stay here. All of you. As my guests. We have plenty of messes for you to clean up right here in Italy."

Buffy's smile faded. "I was only kidding about the cleaning lady thing. I can't be bought. And neither can my Slayers."

"*Your* Slayers?" He looked from her to the field of Slayers and back again. "So you've accepted the crown?"

"I'm responsible for them," she said with asperity. "I came up with the plan to turn all the Potentials into Slayers. So, in that way, yes, they're my Slayers."

"Did you realize what you were doing?"

"I was averting the apocalypse in the only way I knew how." She recrossed her arms and started walking again. "Are you telling me you disapprove of my actions? Because I really don't care."

"*Cara,*" he reproved her gently as he shadowed her. "Such a temper. All I am saying is, I might be able to provide what you need right here in Roma."

She stopped. "Oh, really?"

"*Sì.*" He reached out and touched her hand. "It's cold and dreary in England, *bella bellissima.* Their food is terrible."

"And Sir Nigel's reputation precedes him. He's a terrible snob and he will never treat you as an equal. He will try to force the Slayers to follow his agenda. Why put them all at his disposal? Some can stay in England. And some can stay here. With us."

She narrowed her eyes. "'Us'? Do you have an agenda for 'us'?"

"Only this: I'll help you, if you permit it." He brushed a strand of hair out of her eyes. "You are your own woman, Buffy Summers. I would never presume otherwise."

Together they watched the Slayers training. Belle blew on a whistle around her neck just like a gym coach, and Buffy chuckled silently.

"You have to find the sweet spot, Haley," Belle was explaining, using martial arts jargon. "The breaking point. In your average demon, it's the center of the sternum."

"Or the neck," Buffy said quietly to herself, not wishing to interject herself back into the session.

Haley, a young girl with a braid of sandy brown hair down her back, half-raised her hand and said, "What about the neck?"

"Good girl," Buffy whispered.

The Immortal turned to her and said, "By the way, you're welcome to use my phone anytime. I'll get you one of your own. I didn't realize you didn't have one, or I would have remedied that already."

"A trendy purple animal-print job? Thanks," she said, and gave him a look. "I mean that."

"I know." He smiled. "And? It's the fashion."

"Thought so," she said, grinning at him.

"Hey," Dawn said, coming up from behind Buffy and the

Immortal. She was wearing pink jeans, a fuzzy pink sweater, matching leather shoes, and a pink shoulder bag with a black leather *D* emblazoned on the front.

"Perfection." The Immortal kissed his thumb and forefinger.

"Grazie," Dawn said merrily. She popped open her bag and fished out a black credit card. "It was a lot."

"It was nothing," he said, pulling out a fine leather cardholder and slipping the credit card into it.

They both looked at Buffy. "What?" Dawn said, sounding terribly guilty.

"You took his credit card and went shopping?" Buffy asked her sister.

"All over Rome," the Immortal answered for her. "With Mr. Aram."

"He's an awesome shopper," Dawn told him.

He grinned. "Isn't he? You should see the tooled black cowboy boots he talked me into. I'll wear them to dinner."

Dawn smiled nervously. "Great."

"Did you go by the school?" he asked.

She looked stricken. "Um . . ."

"School?" Buffy echoed. She looked from the Immortal to Dawn and back again. "Do I want to know this?"

"It's a private academy here in Rome. Very rigorous academics," the Immortal told her. "Exclusive."

"Expensive," Dawn added.

The Immortal waved his hand. "Please."

Dawn turned to her big sister. "It's an amazing school, Buffy. They have ballet and singing, and everyone takes Latin, and . . . math. There's lots of math."

"She has to go to school somewhere," the Immortal said innocently. *"No?"*

"No," Buffy shot back.

Dawn looked dashed. "See?" she said to the Immortal. "I told you she wouldn't let me."

"Now, wait just a minute," Buffy began, then sighed. "Let's talk about it at dinner."

Dawn clapped her hands. "Yay! I mean, okay." She smiled hopefully. "It's really near our apartment."

"At dinner," Buffy repeated.

Dawn reached up and kissed the Immortal on the cheek. *"Thank you."* Then she darted away.

Buffy sucked in her cheeks and bit her lower lip. "I'm so glad to know you don't have an agenda for us."

Before he could reply, she brushed past him.

"Belle," she said abruptly, "I'm leaving you in charge for now." *Xander will help me sort this out.*

The kitchen of the palazzo was as big as Buffy's entire house had been back in Sunnydale. Most of the staff were men, but there was one old lady dressed in black who was waving a wand over all the pots and pans and murmuring incantations. Buffy wondered if she was saying, "Poppies will make them sleep," like the Wicked Witch of the West did in *The Wizard of Oz.*

"Have you seen Xander?" Buffy asked the collective men and a couple of demons who stirred, chopped, and grated. No one spoke English, but one bisque-hued guy in a tall white hat and an apron that read KICK IT UP A NOTCH! gestured to a black door on the opposite side of the kitchen.

Buffy entered a huge library of cookbooks. Or maybe spell books. She crossed through it and opened another black door, feeling more like Alice in Wonderland than the Slayer.

After a few more doors, she found herself on the upper balcony of a vaulted room shaped like a pentagram. There were rows of leather theater seats, and a couple of piles of clothing were neatly folded on two of them. She recognized Willow's green sweater on one, and beside it, the Immortal's purple cell phone was resting atop a Roman toga. The overhead skylight was shaped like a crescent moon with cutouts of stars in rainbow-shimmering glass spiraling from the moon's lower horn.

The marble walls were covered with living vines that looked like mistletoe. And in the middle of a marble mosaic floor of Roman figures, an oak tree sprang from the tiles and spread its branches wide over the large five-pointed space.

She called out softly, "Xander?"

There was no answer. She waited a minute, then picked up the Immortal's phone. He had given her permission to use it. She dialed London.

Giles picked up immediately. "Yes?"

"Giles, I'm thinking I should—"

"Buffy, Faith is on the other line," he said, excited. "Let me try to put you on."

Her heart nearly leaped out of her chest. "Oh, my God! Do I have to push anything?" She stared at the cell phone.

"Yes, see the little button with the word 'flash' on it?"

"Italian phone," she said. "But there's something here with, like, a picture of a blinking light."

"Is there anyone around who—"

She pushed it. "Hello?" she said.

Her knees actually buckled when she heard Faith's breathy "Yo, B."

"Faith!" she cried. "Oh, God! You're alive!"

"Got that right," Faith quipped.

"Who else is alive?"

Faith's tone changed, becoming more somber. "We lost three, the new ones. Karen, Stephanie, and Marie. Robin's okay. Vi and Rona. That's it."

"What's happening?" Giles asked. "Can you describe the situation?"

"Basically, it sucks," Faith replied. "Nothing we can't handle.

We saw some weird projections the other day, or maybe they were real. These figures that grew. Lotta Turok-Han, and—"

"Can you describe them?" Giles said.

"Same as the ones we fought before," she replied. "Ugly mothers—"

"The weird projections, I mean. What did they look like?"

"Yo, you're breaking up," Faith replied, her voice overlaid with static.

"Faith?" Buffy and Giles said at the same time.

Just then, in the palazzo, a gong sounded. With the phone in her hand, Buffy craned her neck to look over the balcony.

In stately procession, about thirty sorcerers, all wearing red-spangled robes, hoods drawn over their heads and hiding their faces, entered the room.

"I have a magician here," Giles told Buffy. "I'm going to ask her to see if she can reconnect me with Faith."

"Okay. Reconnect me, too?" Buffy asked. "We should at least be able to tell her that Kennedy—"

She was startled to see Antonio rushing toward her in his street clothes, his face mottled with fury. He grabbed the phone out of her hand and said, "What the hell are you doing with my phone?"

She blinked at him. "*Your* phone? That's the Immortal's phone. It was on top of his toga."

"That's *my* toga," he said hotly, plucking it up by the boatneck collar and letting it fall open. Sure enough, the gold border design was different from the one the Immortal had been wearing.

"Oh." She moved her shoulders. "Sorry. Your phone looks just like his." She added, "Which is very . . . trendy." *In a scary way.*

"*Sì.* It's a fashionable look here in Italy," he said harshly as he began to put the phone in his trouser pocket.

"Wait," Buffy said. "I was just about to—"

The phone trilled. Buffy caught her breath as the man put it to his ear and said, *"Prego?"* He listened, then said something in Italian. After he disconnected, he slipped the phone back into his pocket.

"Listen," she said, "I was making a really important call. I have to use your phone again. Please."

"I can't," he said. "I'm sorry."

"Scusi?" came a voice from behind Buffy. She turned to see the Immortal. Looking extremely pissed, he held out his hand. "Give her that phone at once."

Antonio paled. "But sir—"

"If you wish to remain in my employ, you will give *Signorina* Summers your phone immediately."

The man did so. Buffy dialed Giles back.

His line buzzed with a busy signal.

"Thanks," she said. She flipped the phone shut and handed it back to Antonio.

Ignoring him, the Immortal said to Buffy, "We'll get you a phone as soon as the noon ritual is completed." He cocked his head. "Was that an important call?"

"Yes." She ran her hand through her hair. "Very important."

He glared at Antonio.

"Sir . . . ," Antonio tried again.

"Feel free to observe the ritual," the Immortal said to Buffy. To Antonio, he added, "You may go."

Antonio was a study in freaked out: His features were taut, and a vein pulsed in his forehead. Buffy totally got that; the Immortal was not someone she would want to piss off either. Without another word, Antonio plucked up his toga and left the balcony, going back the same way he had come, through a red door on the opposite side of the balcony.

"It was an important call that I didn't get to complete," she said. "May I use your phone?"

"Certainly." The Immortal reached in his pocket and handed her his phone. Amazing. It was identical in appearance to Antonio's. The trends in Italian guy phones were very odd. She could not see Xander bragging on his purple jungle phone, ever.

She said, "I'm going outside. Maybe I'll get better reception."

He waved his hand at it. The phone notably tingled in her hand. "You should get better reception now," he told her.

The gong sounded again, and the Immortal said, "That's my cue." Then he swept back the way he had come, through the same black door Buffy had used.

Her mind racing, her heart still pounding, Buffy hurried from the balcony, dialing Giles. "Anything?" she asked.

It was Sir Nigel, not Giles, who replied: "We said we would inform you of any developments," he said coldly. "Now please, leave this line clear and let us do our job."

Before she had a chance to say another word, he hung up on her.

CHAPTER NINE

Eat a third and drink a third and leave the remaining third of your stomach empty.
Then, when you get angry, there will be sufficient room for your rage.
—Babylonian Talmud

Antonio was furious. And frantic.

As he and Ornella returned to Antonio's villa, he raked his hair and glowered out the limo window at the rows of cypress pines lining his drive. They were ugly. Everything was ugly.

He wanted to kill something.

"It's that bitch Buffy's fault. She doesn't like us. So now he thinks he doesn't either," he muttered, smacking his fist into his open palm.

Antonio recalled the Immortal's speculative gaze on him amid the large circle of robed sorcerers. The Immortal was turning against him. It wasn't just the cell phone. It was a lot of things. But they boiled down to one source: Buffy Summers.

Ornella's mouth twisted. "All right, maybe he doesn't like us. But maybe he would like . . . us . . . better if he knew that I'm a Slayer like her."

He put his finger to his lips as he glanced at his chauffeur. The Lucite barrier separating the front of the car from the passenger section was up, but one never knew. . . .

She tossed her splendid hair. "I don't understand. Why keep it a secret? I would think the Immortal would be delighted to find out. I should be training with those girls every day, not skulking around pretending I'm just your girlfriend."

Uh-oh. Just his girlfriend?

"And another thing, Antonio." She pursed her lips. "You let me think my powers were a magickal gift from you. But you had nothing to do with it."

He raised his brows, trying to look amused, though in truth, his heart was pounding. Was she turning against him as well?

"I never said that. And I may very well have had something to do with it. Your Slayer abilities may have been latent, and I brought them out in you. We don't know precisely how it works."

Her answering laugh was cynical and harsh. "Oh, come on, 'Tonio. Don't take credit where it isn't due. You haven't answered my question. Why not tell him?"

It was coming to a head, then, her realization that she might be better off without a man who had a shaky position in the Immortal's household. It was time to show her that there was more to Antonio Borgia—a lot more—than being an on-staff sorcerer in the employ of the Immortal.

Maybe he had better put her enthrall again.

"All right." He caressed her lips with his curled fingertip, tracing the mouth he had kissed so often and so well. "Can you wait two hours? Then you'll have your answer."

She looked intrigued. "Tell me now."

He smiled at her and touched her hair, though in truth he would love to slap her face and tell her how lucky she was to be *just* his girlfriend. Ungrateful to her core. Had she forgotten all the wonderful things he had done for her? The career she had? The rival models he had gotten rid of?

"Give me two hours, *cara,* and I will tell you. Until then . . . you can amuse yourself, *no?*"

She shrugged petulantly. "I suppose."

The car rolled to a stop in front of his villa. They waited for the driver to help them out, Ornella first. She gazed across the lawn to the vineyard gate and sighed.

"You must get me another bull to kill," she told him.

"I'll get you something better," he promised her. "Now go on in. I have a lot of preparations to make for your surprise." He kissed her cheek, and then her lips.

She kissed him back, then entered his house without so much as looking back over her shoulder at him.

A very bad sign. She was detaching from him, too, just like the Immortal.

As soon as she was out of sight, Antonio clapped his hands. His gnomes the *monachetti* appeared. "We're going to the dungeon," he told them.

Lucrezia Borgia, Mother of Poisons and Potions, could not believe her eyes as she stared through the mirror at what Antonio had brought them.

Eagerly she gripped Cesare's heavily jeweled fingers. His grip was equally tight. His breathing was slow and measured, a sure sign of his excitement. Her brother—and lover—was nothing if not composed under pressure.

"You say that this woman is something called a 'Slayer,'" she said slowly, feigning ignorance, though in truth Lucrezia knew exactly what Antonio had with him tonight.

"Ornella," Antonio said, and gave her a little push forward. "Show them."

The exquisite woman was wearing very sexy exercise clothing. Her dark hair was pulled back, and she had on heavy makeup.

A fabulous creature, Lucrezia thought.

The woman lifted her sword as Antonio clapped his hands.

A roar echoed through the dungeon, audible to Lucrezia as she gazed through the magic mirror. Antonio's amusing *monachetti* dragged forward a fabulous red demon hobbled with chains. Chains draped his chest, and pulled his hands together in front of his body. The fierce creature was man-shaped, rippling with muscles, his only clothing a loincloth. He was enraged.

Lucrezia was enraptured.

"You are ready, *mia bella*?" Antonio asked the woman— Ornella.

"Let him go. I can't wait another second. I'm bursting," Ornella urged, never taking her gaze from her target.

Antonio nodded to the *monachetti*. Four of them crouched at the demon's ankles while two more climbed on top of twin towers of the same golden boxes in which Antonio usually kept his sacrifices. It was a task quite beyond the little men, and Lucrezia licked her lips in anticipation of a festive slaughter before the Slayer could intervene.

The demon growled. The poor little *monachetti* were trembling.

Then Ornella said, "Get out of the way!" and rushed the chained demon.

The *monachetti* leaped away and clumped behind Antonio, who cried, *"Cara, no!"*

She raised her sword over her head and hacked the demon's handcuffs in two. He made fists and rushed her; one, two! she cut off his hands. Green blood sprayed across the mirror, the walls, the floor, the Slayer.

The *monachetti* started screaming and scrabbling for the door.

As the demon raged and shrieked, Ornella planted the sword into his abdomen, squatted with her legs widely spread, and ripped him to his sternum.

His green heart fell out of his chest and landed on the floor with an unceremonious plop.

The demon fell backward against the stone floor.

Lucrezia closed her eyes and inhaled. She could almost smell the blood.

Not the blood of the demon.

Of the Slayer.

It had been seven hundred years since she had tasted Slayer's blood . . . but she had never forgotten its tangy, delicate bouquet, its heady thickness. . . . There was nothing in the world like the blood of a Slayer.

In any world. On any plane.

She gripped Cesare's hand until she drew blood. He did the same. They stood in ecstasy, tantalized almost beyond bearing.

Oh, I remember, I remember, Lucrezia thought, swaying.

Bloodied and beaten, once upon a time, a Slayer had languished in the Borgia dungeon. Seven hundred years ago.

And ever afterward, the vampire queen had dreamed of finding another.

ROME, 1503 AD

It was blackest night, and torchlight flared over the writhing figures of the mob as the peasants pushed and shrieked at the gates of the Borgia Palace. Their faces were distorted with hatred and bloodlust.

I would kill them all if I could, Lucrezia thought.

Slowly.

Malfeo, Dread Lord of Hell, whose eyes were like serpents, his nose like a desiccated skull's, his ears long and pointed and his teeth multitudinous, turned from the window.

Malfeo had first presented himself to the siblings during a rite they had performed in hopes of raising their aunt from the dead. It had been said that Cecelia Borgia was a witch, and they desired to learn the Craft from her. But Malfeo, a master vampire from a hell dimension, had materialized instead, in an infernal ball of fire that reeked of sulfur and damnation.

He had complimented them both on their occult skill, and regaled them with stories of his life. There were vampires in his world, and demonic beings who were not vampires. The demons served the vampires.

"Your world was meant to be the same," he told them. He had offered his protection . . . and changed them both. They were of his blood, and he was their sire.

Lucrezia and Cesare weren't certain if their earthly father knew that they were vampires. Though gossip swirled around them, he had never asked, and they had never told him. Malfeo became the center of their orbit in all things, and they loved him as they had never loved their father.

Now, as the peasants advanced, Malfeo's black cape whirled like a Gypsy dancer's as he embraced Lucrezia and said in thickly accented Italian: "*Cara,* this is the moment we have dreaded. This is no charade. They know how to kill you, and they will not leave until they run a stake through your heart."

She was terrified, and she reviled herself for being so careless. The fault was hers: She never should have drunk from the pretty little child she had found crying for its mother in the moonlit palace gardens last night. But the night was so beautiful, and the child, so fresh . . .

Afterward, her careless servants hadn't made the grave deep enough. A dog had dug up the little corpse and dragged it through the filthy streets until the brat's mother herself had discovered the pitiful wreck and run screaming to the parish priest.

With this careless misstep, she had unmasked both herself and Cesare. For years, rumors had circulated that the Borgia brother and sister were vampires, but no one could prove anything. A complicating factor was their father, the most powerful and feared Pope in the history of the Catholic Church. His edicts were obeyed as if issued by divine order. His enemies went missing, an act committed by Providence. Who would dare accuse the children of such a potentate of anything?

But the feared and hated Pope lay on his deathbed. He was not expected to live the night. His protective mantel had been snatched from their shoulders.

The gilded doors to Lucrezia's chamber flew open, and she and Malfeo turned to see Cesare burst in. His face was swollen, and his fine clothes were slashed. He was panting, and as he raced toward Lucrezia, he tumbled to the fine wool carpet laid over the marble floor.

"Mio amore!" she cried as she fell to her knees beside him. Lifting himself on his elbow, he wiped blood and sweat from his brow and put his hand against her cheek.

"You're alive," Cesare said. "They proclaimed on the streets that you were dead. They're parading a woman's head through the streets. I couldn't get close enough to see it. I was so afraid that it was you, *cara.*" He was panting hard with every word. "I ran here like a madman. Some peasants saw me. They're dead," he assured her.

"Is help coming?" she asked, her fingers probing the grievous wounds on her brother's forehead. "Our father—"

"There will be no help from the Vatican," he groaned. "Our dear father, Rodrigo Borgia, is dead."

She caught her breath. Then she rose to her feet, tottered for a moment, and raised her fists toward the ceiling. "Damn him! Damn him to hell for dying now!"

She bared her teeth and grabbed up handfuls of her curly blond hair, spittle foaming at the corners of her mouth. Then she vamped, fully.

The guards posted at her door shrank back.

"Father, you stupid bastard!" she shrieked in Italian. "You stupid, weak, moronic—"

"Easy, *cara mia, bella mia,*" Cesare urged her, slowly getting to his feet. He gripped his shoulder; his hand came away dripping with blood. "We must plan. The palazzo is surrounded."

Malfeo glided toward them. He put his arm on Rodrigo's shoulder and drew the back of his leathery hand across Lucrezia's cheek.

"My children," he said to them both, "your cause here is lost."

"You can't mean that, can't say that," Cesare spat. "You are our patron. You have smashed our opposition before. You're far more powerful than this rabble."

Malfeo clenched his jaw, his teeth extending over his lips. "This time, the citizens of Rome are too powerful in their anger, even for me." He dipped his head. "The time has come to leave this dimension, if only for a brief season." He held up one long, bony finger. "Once your detractors have turned to dust, you may return."

"It will be sooner than that," Lucrezia hissed. "I'll have them poisoned. I'll burn down their houses. I'll lay waste to all of Rome!"

Something rocketed through the window and crashed into the fine wool carpet on the marble floor. Cesare grabbed Lucrezia and flung her to the floor, covering her with his body. She screamed, more in fury than fear.

The carpet ignited. Fire shot across the room as if someone had laid out a trail of gunpowder.

"Guards!" Lucrezia shrieked. "Put that out!"

The men in Borgia livery—silver and black—raced out the door, their shoes clattering on the marble, and she realized they were probably not coming back.

Another projectile shot through the window, flinging shards in all directions. A long, jagged piece of glass pirouetted through the air, then tumbled and lodged in Lucrezia's eye. The pain shot to her brain; it left her speechless as she sank to the floor, writhing and gasping.

"Ah, my poor girl," Malfeo said softly, moving to her side. He held her still and yanked out the shard. Blood dripped from the end.

"I . . . will . . . not . . . go," she rasped, grabbing on to his wrist as she covered the bloody socket. She knew she was a vampire. She knew she would heal. But the pain was horrible. "Rome is mine. It is mine."

"It will be yours, but for now, you must leave." Malfeo cocked his head. "You have been so faithful to me, Lucrezia. You have given me sacrifices. You have entertained me. You have loved me." He bent down and kissed her on the lips. "Now listen to me. You must do as I say."

She flung her arms around his neck and clung to him, seeking his demonic strength, his comforting presence. She adored him beyond all reasoning, and she had never needed him more than in this moment.

"We must obey Malfeo," Cesare told his sister. "It is our last hope."

"Hope dies within me here, now," she whispered, pressing her palm against her damaged eye. It would heal, but she did not know if her heart would ever heal. To be forced out of her home . . . out of her very dimension . . .

I must trust Malfeo now, Lucrezia realized as her brother clasped her hand and patted her bloody cheek. *He is my love. He is my sire.*

The fire leaped from the carpet, to the tapestries hanging on the walls: fine portraits of Borgia princes and dukes; depictions of the Great Hunt; Lucrezia herself, as the Goddess Venus, rising from the sea foam. The smoke and heat devoured them with as much relish as Lucrezia had devoured the young child whose death had brought all this misery upon them.

"They will think you perished in the flames," Malfeo advised them.

"In a way, they will be correct," Lucrezia said. At last she surrendered to her fate.

"Come desiderate, mio bello Padrino," she murmured. "Your will be done. It is time." She heaved a heavy sob.

"No tears," Malfeo said. "Your eye has weeped enough for one night." He chuckled at his own humor. "Stand close, my children."

Lucrezia and Cesare huddled against him. He spread his arms; his cape fell like cauls over their faces. Lucrezia was fainting from pain; she heard a strange noise, like singing. Her body erupted into searing heat; then ice water spilled into her veins. For a moment she panicked, thinking he had poisoned her.

She pulled the cape from her face, to see the fiery room shimmering around her; the columns of her bed of state stretched and pulled; the walls bent. The room began to whirl. She felt horribly nauseated; she could look no longer.

White light shot in all directions as she tumbled and fell through a tunnel of moonlight brilliance. She went numb from head to toe. There was a tremendous explosion, followed by a second, and then a third. She was plummeting at an unimaginable speed, as if someone had tossed her out of the window of the tallest tower in their family palazzo—

It will not end here. I will not end, she vowed. Then she closed her eyes as she lost consciousness.

And when she awoke, she was in her exquisite chamber, in her bed of state.

Startled, she sat up. There was her carpet, undamaged. Her window, intact. The tapestries unsinged, hanging from the walls.

I dreamed, she thought.

Then a form moved to her right in the bed, and Malfeo pushed the covers off himself. He grinned up at her. *"Bella,"* he said. "Welcome to my world."

On the other side of Malfeo, Cesare's head popped up. He grinned at Lucrezia.

"Is it not wonderful?"

And it had been. Malfeo loved them, and re-created their Roman palace down to the tiniest detail. For two years, they presided over a fabulous court assembled for them by Malfeo. During that dreadful night of the escape, he had also transported over six hundred humans to serve Lucrezia and Cesare. At first, they had devoured many of them, until they developed a taste for the demon blood of

Malfeo's race. Human blood became a rare delicacy; to insure a steady supply, they matched up appropriate couples and forced them to breed.

But after two years, Lucrezia grew homesick. She began to languish. She stopped feeding, and would spend hours at the window that was so like the window the mob had destroyed back in Rome, looking out on an alien landscape.

Then one day Malfeo presented her with a wonderful *regalo*—a fantastic gift. It was an orb.

"With this globe, you may travel to your home dimension of your own will," he told her. "You will not need my aid."

As she reached for it, he held it out of her reach, staying her with his finger.

"You must listen, impatient one. This first time, we will go together, you and Cesare and I. This teleportation orb has power that quickly fades. Your visits must be brief, and they must be made when the moon is full. The moon will magnify its power."

So they had used the orb. Malfeo held it, and chanted in his native language. Lucrezia listened carefully, and watched every gesture he made.

They returned to Rome in the dead of night. It was not the happy homecoming she had anticipated. Her palace lay in ruins, and the ground was sewn with salt. The streets were filthy. The people were ragged and thin.

Rome needed the firm hand of the Borgias. The death of her father the Pope had brought misery and despair. It was obvious to Lucrezia that only through the resurrection of their house could Rome sparkle and shine as in the old days. She dreamed of returning in glory, with troops and magicks so strong, no one could stop her.

She made it her blood vow.

The next full moon, she took the orb out of its carved ebony box.

It glowed in her hand; she willed herself to Rome, and in the next instant she whirled into existence on a bridge festooned with gold ribbons and rosettes. A group of revelers in elaborate costumes and gilded masks jostled her as they capered past, pouring wine into one another's mouths. She circled around; as she caught hold of the bridge, she stared at the reflection of the full moon on the water. From there, she lifted her gaze.

She was thunderstruck.

The exquisite arches and ornaments of the Doge's Palace glittered in moonlight and torchlight. Hundreds of figures in fancy dress laughed and paraded in the courtyard.

But the Doge's Palace is in Venice!

She had accidentally transported herself to the wrong city, during the festive season of Carnival.

Her first impulse was to return to Malfeo's dimension immediately. But the night beckoned. The humans were fresh and beautiful, glittering like butterflies. How she had missed this liveliness, this gaiety. This variety.

With great care, she slipped the orb into the pocket of her cloak. Patting it anxiously, she moved among the celebrants, gazing at their throats. The scent of blood saturated the air.

"Signorina?" came a voice, in the distinctive Venetian dialect she had always thought so provincial. Now it was the sweetest sound she had ever heard.

He was young, and virile. He wore a cloak, a mask, and a feathered hat. In his right hand he carried a goblet of wine, which sloshed over the rim as he bowed deeply.

"Your mask is terrifying," he said jovially. And it was only then that she realized she wore her vampire visage.

I will take this man, and then I'll go.

Bloodlust overtook her.

"Come with me," she whispered seductively, grabbing his hand.

She raced with him across the bridge and down the stone steps that led to the canal below. Partygoers lay together, groaning with carnal appetite; no one would notice what she was doing to him.

He chuckled softly as she pushed him against the wall. He took a drink of wine, leaned back his head, and closed his eyes in eager anticipation of what he thought she was going to do.

What a perfect lamb.

While his eyes were closed, Lucrezia opened her mouth and buried her fangs in this neck.

The blood! She was delirious with the flavor. It was hot and young. She sucked hard, harder—

The man's resistance slackened, and he grew limp in her arms like a babe—

Until someone yanked her away from him, grabbing her by the cloak and tossing her backward.

Lucrezia caught herself as she tottered at the water's edge. Her attacker was a young girl with bright red hair cut short like a boy's. Her eyes were huge; she was frightened, but resolute.

The vampire queen laughed as she wiped the man's savory blood from her mouth. The other revelers had taken note and were scurrying away into the darkness, her dazed paramour gasping, *"Strega!"*—witch—as if a word could possibly wound her.

They faced each other, she and the girl. Lucrezia hissed at her adversary and lunged at her without giving the girl time to react.

But react, she did. The girl met Lucrezia head-on.

They knocked heads. Lucrezia's vision blurred; she saw masonry, mud, black water. And then the girl was on her, hitting her. She grabbed the fastening on Lucrezia's cloak—

The orb!

Lucrezia batted the girl's fists and pushed her off. She got to her feet and grabbed up the cloak, yanking the orb out of her pocket. She intoned the words Malfeo had chanted, praying to the dark gods that this time she'd gotten them right.

The orb shimmered in her grasp. She flashed the girl a triumphant look and braced herself for teleportation.

Just as a light shot from the orb and expanded into a sphere of brilliant, blinding white, the girl threw her arms around Lucrezia.

As if from far away, a man shouted, "Gabriella! No!"

Then all sound was swallowed as Lucrezia and the girl blasted through a tunnel of light in their deadly embrace, and landed tumbling on the floor of the palace. The girl drew back her fist and punched Lucrezia in the face.

Lucrezia howled as the girl was jerked backward. Malfeo had hold of her arms, and he gripped her tightly as he yelled at Lucrezia, "Get up!"

Cesare was there too; he drew his sword, preparing to run the girl through.

Lucrezia cried, "No! Stop! I want her."

The girl was not killed. Instead, she was dragged off to the dungeon and chained to the wall. She pulled herself free. She was beaten and rechained.

She pulled herself free yet again. She nearly destroyed her cell, until Lucrezia had it fortified; had her lashed; and withheld food and water from her for nearly a week. The girl began to babble; she said she was Gabriella the Vampire Slayer; she kept calling for Mario, who was apparently her "Watching One." She was chosen to fight evil; she was something of an avenging angel, or a saint.

When she was positive the girl could not resist, Lucrezia drank of her.

How to describe her blood? *Divino,* truly. Of the gods. Of heaven, and above heaven.

Lucrezia lay in a daze for an entire night, staring at the ceiling as she felt the blood of this Slayer filling the place where her soul had once been. She was a demon now; she had no need for her soul.

But she must have more of this blood. So she would drink from her until she was almost dead, then stop and allow her to recuperate.

During the weeks that the girl regained her strength, Lucrezia used the orb to travel back to her dimension, seeking "Mario," looking for another like Gabriella. She always came back empty-handed.

Malfeo inquired as well, and eventually they learned that there was no other like this Slayer. She was unique, the only girl in all the world who possessed this blood.

"I wish it were otherwise, my dear," Malfeo told her sadly as he loved and caressed her. "But she's the only one."

So Lucrezia continued the cycle of feeding, letting her rest, and feeding again.

"Why stop there?" Cesare asked her one fine evening as she drank from Gabriella's wrist. The girl was unconscious. "Why not breed her with another human and get her pregnant? Perhaps you'll get a baby Slayer."

Lucrezia hesitated. Women die in childbirth.

"But what I'll do is make myself like her," Lucrezia decided as she and Cesare made a night of bleeding her. Gabriella had been starved for days, and Lucrezia had drugged her just in case. She was so strong. They had brought silk pillows to lounge on in her cell. As a troubadour sang, they nibbled and drank from the unconscious girl.

She pulled Gabriella's arm from her brother's lips and drank. "I will become a Slayer."

She lay back in a delirious languor. "I am the Mother of Poisons and Potions. I will extract the essence of her Slayer gift and imbue myself with it."

He looked thoughtful. "She appears to be some sort of goddess, I think." He trailed his fingertip down Lucrezia's shoulder. "If you manage it, I'll be the brother of a goddess."

But Gabriella tricked me, Lucrezia thought now as she stared through the mirror at Antonio's Slayer girlfriend. *She pretended to be weak so I would let down my guard.*

Four courtiers helped her get the orb. They escaped together. . . .

And Malfeo went after them, to get her back and retrieve the orb. For, like the Slayer, there was only one orb.

He went to get it, and he never came back . . . and Cesare and I swore vengeance on the one who killed him. . . .

She roused herself, aware that Antonio and Ornella were waiting for her to say something.

"We are delighted to meet you," Lucrezia said to Ornella, as Cesare inclined his head in agreement. Antonio looked on, beaming. As well he should. What a prize.

"The feeling is mutual, *Madonna* Borgia," Ornella replied, her face bright and eager. Her eyes shone. She was far too thin, but perhaps that was the fashion these days. Antonio was emaciated as well.

"Antonio said he had a surprise for me, but I never dreamed I would meet Lucrezia and Cesare Borgia."

"But as we agreed, it is our secret," Lucrezia said silkily. "Cesare and I aren't ready to reveal ourselves to the world. We would deal very harshly with anyone who violated our privacy. I hope you understand."

The girl was properly cowed. *"Sì, Signora."*

"Our physical natures are such that we must remain in this dimension," Cesare told her. It was true. They couldn't leave without the Orb. Antonio had been coached to go along with whatever they told the girl. And they had threatened him with the withdrawal of their patronage if he told her they were vampires.

"We have been separated from our beloved Roma all this time. Imagine our delight when a direct descendant of ours contacted us with his impressive sorcery." He beamed at Antonio, who preened.

"Let me be blunt, *Signorina,*" Cesare continued. "We wish to see Antonio assume his rightful place as leader of the Roman magickal community. Back in our time, the Immortal was a horrible despot."

"Yes," Lucrezia said, sighing. "He was responsible for exiling us to this place."

Cesare's brows lifted, anxious that she not say too much, but

Lucrezia knew what she was doing. Very slowly she would lay the groundwork that would insure Ornella's dedication to their cause.

"The Immortal is not to be trusted." She lowered her gaze. "I was once . . . his beloved." She gazed up at the lovely young girl. "But he cast me aside and forced us into this alternate dimension. He never stays with a woman for very long. This Buffy? A month, if she's lucky." She let a tear slide down her cheek.

Ornella was very young, very thin, very beautiful, and very gullible. She laced her fingers through Antonio's. Antonio had told his ancestors something of the girl's past—a child of the slums raised to great heights. Lucrezia was certain the waif was already calculating what her fate might become if she left Antonio for the Immortal. Now she had new information, and something to consider: If the Great One left her high and dry, and Antonio was lost to her because she abandoned him . . . she might easily wind up in the gutter again. That she was beautiful and wealthy and had contacts throughout the world of fashion would not figure into her decision-making process.

It was always so much easier to manipulate people with low self-esteem.

"I-I would never trust him," Ornella assured her. "But how can we protect Antonio from him? Buffy Summers has set him against us."

"We have a plan," Lucrezia said. "We want you to listen to it very carefully."

"You don't have to do anything you don't want to," Cesare assured her. "But I'm certain that you wouldn't mind very much becoming a queen."

"A . . . queen?" Ornella echoed, stunned.

"Queen of the Slayers," Cesare told her.

"But, Buffy . . . ," she began, glancing uncertainly at Antonio.

"Buffy serves the Immortal," Cesare said. "She will force those girls to do the Immortal's bidding. A travesty. And after he dumps her? What will become of those girls?"

"But if *you* were queen . . . ," Lucrezia suggested. She moved her shoulders like a cat. "How much better it would be. For so many."

Ornella took that in. Antonio slid his arm around her waist. She turned to him and said, "I have never much liked the Immortal, you know? He's not a very nice person."

We have her, Lucrezia rejoiced. Cesare's quick glance in her direction communicated the same thing.

"We want a Borgia on the Immortal's throne," Cesare reiterated. "We'll reward those who help us with our dream."

Which Borgia that would be, might be open to interpretation. And as for the destruction of the Immortal:

Lucrezia had waited day and night for Malfeo's return. Pacing, wondering if the Slayer had harmed him. Fearing for him, making sacrifices to every dark god she could imagine; pouring over books in search of finding spells, teleportation magicks, something, anything, to bring Malfeo to her, or she to him.

Then word came in the form of an attempt to take over Malfeo's throne: The master vampire was dead, at the hands of a minion of the Immortal.

For trespassing. *They hadn't given Malfeo a chance to explain his presence, nor even to withdraw from the protected territory. They had hacked him to pieces and dumped them in a sewer.*

"Your patron is gone! His throne belongs to me! And there is no one to protect you interlopers!" shouted the demon king Jacario at the head of his attacking army.

Jacario had badly miscalculated. Since their transplant to Malfeo's dimension, the Borgias had not sat idly by, depending on Malfeo to protect them from jealous enemies. They had secured a court of their own, granting the favors they had the ability to give, and promising better ones if they were ever in a position to do so. Sex, money, and politics were the same in one dimension as another.

By daybreak, Jacario's head dripped from a pike, and the kingdom belonged to Lucrezia and Cesare, the bereft foster children of Malfeo. From that day to the present, they wore nothing but black, and they swore a blood vendetta against the Immortal and all who served him.

As far as they were concerned, Buffy Summers served him. Ergo, she must die at his side.

She told Ornella none of this. Nor Antonio. They had no reason to know, at the moment.

Ornella said, "Whatever I can do to help Antonio, I will do."

"There's my lovely girl," Lucrezia murmured, reaching out as if to caress Ornella's cheek. Ornella moved forward as if yearning for the contact.

"We need to go now," Antonio said, putting his arm around Ornella. "It's been quite a night, eh, *bella?*"

"Oh, Antonio, so soon?" Ornella murmured, looking disappointed. She smiled at Lucrezia. "There's so much I want to ask you. So much to talk about."

"We'll meet again soon," Cesare assured her. "We have many things to discuss, we four, do we not?"

"*Sì, sì,* we do," she enthused.

"*Ciao,*" Cesare said, kissing his fingertips.

She giggled and did the same.

The leave-taking rapidly became tiresome, but Lucrezia and Cesare remained polite and warm.

Lucrezia raced into Cesare's arms as soon as Antonio and Ornella left the chamber, and began kissing him in a frenzy of joy.

"Hundreds of Slayers! Perhaps thousands! I will have Slayer's blood again!" she cried. "I will have all I can possibly dream from now until the end of the world. I will have Slayers to experiment on, Slayers to breed . . ."

She danced in the throne room. "I will finally become a Slayer myself!"

Cesare watched his sister with affection. He knew she didn't realize that her eye had never properly healed from the piercing by the flying shard of glass back in Rome. It was milky and missing the iris. Yet she believed herself to be beautiful, and he would not disabuse her of that belief.

To him, she *was* beautiful.

And so was her lust, and her ambition.

"We will retrieve Malfeo's orb, and we will retake Rome," he said, "and *you* will be the Queen of the Slayers!"

CHAPTER TEN

*In a moment, in the twinkling of an eye, at the last trump: for the trumpet shall
sound, and the dead shall be raised incorruptible, and we shall be changed.*
—I Corinthians 15:52

ROME, ONE MONTH LATER

The world was falling apart. Volcanoes erupted beneath the seas;
tsunamis raced across the floodplains of Japan. Storms raged all
over the globe: Hurricanes hit the islands of Hawaii and the coast of
poor Florida, again. Elsewhere, the temperature currents of the
world's oceans dropped, and it began to snow.

Hail fell in Tahiti.

Italy was not spared. Water and ice rushed over the canals of
Venice and flooded the lower floors of buildings. The Doge's
Palace was awash in sewage and thick, black mud. Birds flocked,
separated, flew in crazy circles. In Rome, wild winds stripped the
trees of leaves, and rain and sleet poured down like buckets of ice
water.

Global warming, the experts said. Except that it was cold
everywhere. Both Giles and the Immortal explained that it had to do
with the currents growing warmer, which moved warm air to places
it should not be; and the alteration of the ozone layer reached the
ice caps, which began to melt.

More simply put, it was end-of-the-world weather. The Watchers Council declared that the unexplained phenomena were not so much anomalies of nature as supernatural disasters. Demonic activity was up all over the world. Vampires boldly hunted in packs. People were dying in clusters that suggested Hellmouths yet undiscovered; and centers of evil where the forces of darkness were gathering.

Buffy found herself thinking about her fungus analogy: how the evil of the Hellmouth may have spread tentacles far beyond the environs of Sunnydale. Maybe there were more Hellmouths than the Watchers Council had ever dreamed; and all those Hellmouths and hellholes were connected; maybe evil had conduits throughout the world, through which dark magicks flowed, nourishing everything of the bad while choking out the good. Like weeds and roses.

Now, from her position beneath the skeletal embrace of storm-whipped chestnut trees, Buffy shielded her eyes against the dull nickel sun as snowflakes fluttered down in waves. Her heart jackhammered. The enemy could be anywhere, and the enemy was wily. A few more stupid moves, and her side was going to sustain more casualties than she could count in Italian . . . and she and Dawn had been studying Italian for almost a month. It was still not her favorite subject, but she did know that *settantotto* was the word for seventy-eight.

Beside her, Chani the Vampire Slayer, wearing a modified Indian sari over her winter leggings and down jacket, hissed, froze in her tracks, lifted a crossbow, and took aim.

"No!" Buffy whispered sotto voce, but before she could stop her, Chani released the bolt. *Bawang!* It shot from the bow like a grenade.

"Ow! Ow, ow, ow!" Xander screamed.

He dropped from the tree he'd been hiding in—no mean feat, as there were no leaves to conceal him—clutching his butt as he tumbled into a snowdrift. "She killed me!" he cried. "I am dead in my ass!"

Buffy whipped out her cell phone and dialed the non-com number as she headed toward Xander. "Magician!" she announced. "Soldier down!"

"On my way!" the voice on the other line assured her.

Buffy disconnected. "Chani, war *games*," she reminded the newest of the newer Slayers as she reached Xander, who was lying gasping in the snow. "*Exercises*. Pretend."

Chani spoke anxiously in Hindi. Then she wrapped her face in her veil and took off running.

A woman in a spangled set of scrubs raced toward them. She carried a black bag; she skidded to a halt beside Xander, opened the bag, and produced a packet of herbs. "Roll over," she said to Xander.

"What women are always saying to me," Xander grinned, complying. "However, no dignity left."

His pants were covered in blood, and the bolt stuck straight out of his left, er, cheek.

"Bull's-eye," Buffy said gravely.

"Okay, there was a shred. Now shredded," Xander managed.

The magician fwopped on some latex gloves. She held the herbs just above the arrow's impact.

"Abracadabra, heal thrice, thrice, thrice," she intoned in heavily accented English. Then she switched to Latin. The packet of herbs began to glow, and she moved it very slowly over Xander's wound. Blue energy flowed from the herbs to the injury, which was bleeding profusely. After a few seconds, the bleeding stopped.

She tugged gently on the bolt.

"Can-a you feel?" she asked him.

"Nope."

The magician reached in her bag and pulled out a small sphere. She waved it around, then she nodded at Buffy.

"You can-a pull?" she asked.

"Sure." Buffy wrapped her fingers around the bolt and gave a sharp yank. Xander didn't react.

A different shade of blue sparkles emanated from the sphere as the magician tapped the area. Then she nodded and smiled shyly at Buffy as she put her supplies back in her back and peeled off her gloves into a plastic bag.

"All better," she announced.

"Grazie," Xander said. "And let's forget . . . this ever happened."

"Prego." Her cheeks warmed as she got to her feet. "Bless you, Your Majesty Buffy," she murmured.

"Don't call me that," Buffy said. But there really wasn't much use in asking anymore. "Xand?"

"Feelin' no pain," he slurred. "However, just a tad bit stoned."

"Okay. Rest for a while." She shielded her eyes. "Chani?"

The slight Indian Slayer slunk out from the trees and presented herself to her queen, head lowered, sniffling.

Buffy tapped the crossbow. "Remember? Keep your weapons unloaded. No bolts. We are just practicing. Prac-ti-cing."

Chani sighed heavily and shook her head as if to say, *I don't understand.*

"Xander, after you come around . . . and get fresh pants . . . work with her."

"No," Xander pleaded. "Scary girl. You can work with . . ." His eyes fluttered shut, and he began to snore.

"I'll get a gurney," the medic told Buffy. "He'll be fine."

"Thanks," Buffy said.

"Of course, Your Majesty."

Grrr. Argh.

Buffy moved on, bounding through the snowy forest. Belle was the captain of the Red Team. Buffy's Slayers were the Blues. The Blues' mission was to find Red's flag and steal it. It was a combination game and training exercise, part skill booster and part morale booster.

Morale was becoming a problem. Everyone was worried about the world in general, and the Slayers kept hearing bad things about

Cleveland in particular. A month ago, Kennedy arrived to confirm that it had been Turok-Han that were responsible for the deaths of the three young Slayers. There had also been a civilian with a baby, but they'd made it to safety and were somewhere in Missouri now.

Of the twenty reinforcements who had shown up with Kennedy, only two were still alive. Twenty more reinforcements had been sent.

Seventeen of those were dead.

It was colder in Cleveland than in Rome. And as for England . . . forget it. Ice and snow were piled everywhere. Andrew called Buffy now and then just to whine.

"Wear a sweater," she told him.

"I do. I have. But it's so cold and depressing. I'm a Californian. I need my ultraviolet or I get depressed. And . . . and all they eat is *fish.*"

"Pretend it's sushi," she retorted, exasperated.

"It's sushi with heads," he said. "All I eat here is pizza. Can't I come to Italy? They have better pizza there."

Training took on new importance. Everyone realized they could be sent to the Hellmouth next. Some were eager to go.

And some were mad as hell at Buffy that she had put them in this predicament.

"I didn't ask to be a Slayer!" one sour teenager from Florida had flung at her, and left. Buffy had no idea where she went.

Others followed. Sacred duty, yada yada—the speech was lost on these girls. It had been lost on Buffy at first too. But Buffy had been forced to be the Slayer, anyway. These guys? Not so much. So far, there had been three dozen deserters from Italy and nineteen from England. Sir Nigel was gloating at the disparity.

Buffy had no idea what would happen to the ones who had left. For all she knew, they might start robbing banks.

But for now . . . war games.

She leaped over a tree trunk, landing on the far side of a

poorly concealed hole covered over with tree branches. *Sloppy,* she thought.

"Ca-*woo*!" It was her side's signal call for identification: Approach and be recognized.

"Ca-woo!" Buffy called back, trotting forward. She was thirty or forty yards from one of Blue's secret encampments. Water, food, and recon—a chance to check in with Belle via cell phone, decide when to call it a day. All good.

She jogged around a tree; and then another; and ran smack into a pair of track shoes dangling in front of her face.

She leaped back and looked up.

No. Oh, God, no.

Her name was Sandra, and she was a former ballerina from Barcelona. She had not wanted to stay; she had begged to leave, three days ago. She told Willow she wanted to go back to Spain and resume her ballet career, which would be phenomenal now that she could leap higher than the top of the scenery. Sandra had been too ashamed to tell Buffy, so she had asked Willow to do it for her.

Of course Buffy wanted the new Slayers to have the choice about whether to train and accept the life of a Slayer. But she had insisted on talking to Sandra herself. Buffy considered each girl who left a personal failure—not their failure, but hers.

So she had tried to explain that being chosen meant being special, different.

"But I am a ballerina," Sandra had replied in heavily accented English. "That is special enough."

And then she left. I failed her. I didn't make her safe.

Wind blew through the tree branches, making Sandra sway.

On TV, hanged dead people don't look very terrible.

In real life . . . Buffy retched.

Then she straightened and clambered up the tree. She shimmied out to the rope and yanked the knot apart with her fists, gathering up the two ends like the reins of a horse. The top of Sandra's head hung down; she was wearing a black jacket like Chani's, another gift from the Immortal. There would be no more gifts for Sandra.

Buffy knew the joy of physical agility, the sheer pleasure of training your body and having it do what you wanted. Buffy wondered what it would be like to be a ballerina with the ability to dance like a goddess, then to have that gift replaced with the mandate to battle vampires and demons.

She wondered if Sandra had parents who should be contacted. Or a little sister. Or a priest.

"I'm sorry," Buffy said. "I never wanted this. . . ." She trailed off helplessly. Of course she never wanted this.

I had to save the world.

With great care, she guided the rope along the branch as she made her way back to the trunk. She climbed downward, allowing the body to gently touch the ground. As if on cue, it began to snow. The flakes drifted onto Sandra's inert body, sprawled on the hard earth.

Buffy got down and trudged to Sandra's side. The frigid air rippled through the dark hair, death's skeletal caress. Aching, Buffy touched her cheek. She folded Sandra's arms over her chest and prepared to carry her to camp.

Something crackled beneath the girl's jacket. Buffy unzipped it.

Around Sandra's neck was a leather thong; and hanging from it was a piece of unlined writing paper. Something was written on it in far more Italian than Buffy could understand.

This is the fate of those who follow Buffy Summers, the so-called "Queen of the Slayers." She forced this power upon you and now expects you to fight her battles. Come and join me, and I will give you sanctuary. We will make the world warm and safe again.

—Regina of the Slayers

"That's really what it says? And no mention of irony that 'warm and safe' actually means hanging dead from a tree?" Buffy asked Giles on the speakerphone. Willow had scanned in the message and e-mailed it to the Watchers Council. Giles—or someone like him—had received it back on the mothership in England, and translated it. Buffy still didn't fully trust the Immortal, so she had not taken it to him.

To get the results via phone, they had convened in Willow's room in the Immortal's palazzo. Willow had the best room; it was decorated with a mural of a forest, and her canopy bed was hung with flowered green velvet. The Immortal had recently bought Willow an entire new computer system and given her his word that he wouldn't snoop. No one had believed him. She warded her room constantly but no one knew if it was doing any good.

"That's what it says. Much like the others we've received." That was Sir Nigel. "And as we've discussed, *Regina* is the Italian word for 'queen.'"

"As we've discussed," Xander said pointedly. "We got it."

There had been other notes from this Queen of the Slayers, recruiting Slayers to her side of a fight she seemed intent on waging against Buffy. As if there weren't enough problems to contend with—Cleveland and the wrongness of the world in general. There was no doubt in Buffy's mind that this "Queen" was taking advantage of the chaos to make a bid for power.

Stupid Queen.

"But this is the first time we've seen a recruitment poster around the neck of a dead Slayer," Xander ventured. "I'm thinking escalation."

Willow wrapped her embroidered wine-colored sweater around herself and scooted further down in her chair. She looked scared and sad, yet resolute.

Buffy knew the feeling. And she was grateful that Willow was on her side.

"You're quite correct," Sir Nigel said. "First, we had reports of Slayers being recruited by this so-called Queen. Next, of being pursued and forced to swear allegiance to her. Now, an actual assassination seems to have occurred. Perhaps the poor girl was trying to escape."

"She was escaping. She was going back to Spain," Buffy murmured. "She didn't want to be a Slayer."

"We made her a Slayer," Willow said softly.

"And then Queen Regina killed her because she was a Slayer," Xander added.

Anger and guilt boiled in Buffy. "Because she was a Slayer on my side. Only she wasn't. She didn't want to be on anybody's side." She went to Willow and put her hand on her shoulder. "You only gave the power to all the Potentials because I asked you to."

Willow's shoulders were rounded, her head lowered. She said nothing.

"There was no other choice at the time," Xander insisted. "If the Hellmouth had fallen, the rest of the world would have fallen too."

"Angel was in Los Angeles," Buffy reminded them. "He would have held the line. Maybe."

"You're missing the point of what I'm saying," Sir Nigel cut in, sounding frustrated. "I'm suggesting that Sandra had been taken captive by the other queen, and was trying to escape from *her,* not you."

"Count me chastened about my life-threatening point-missing," Xander muttered under his breath.

Sir Nigel was not finished. "That's our belief, at any rate: that Sandra was captured as she was attempting to go home. Which means that the rogue queen is either nearby, or that her lieutenants have infiltrated your ranks."

"That's not good," Xander offered.

Everyone took a moment to process the lack of goodness.

"Infiltration," Willow said slowly. "Spies?"

"Traitors," Xander replied. "Also not good."

"We need to find out who they are," Xander said. "Doesn't the Immortal have spells for this kind of thing?"

"Let's leave him out of this as much as possible," Sir Nigel ventured. "We still don't know what his agenda is."

Buffy couldn't disagree there.

"We need to round up all the Slayers we can locate, Giles," she said. "Their lives may depend on it."

"I thought that was already what we were doing," Sir Nigel interrupted.

"We need to step it up," Buffy informed him, taking back the conversation. "It's one thing if Regina wants to have her own adoring Slayer groupies. It's another if she's going to start killing them off. We made those girls Slayers. We have a duty to protect them."

"We're agreed on that," Sir Nigel said.

Then Giles cleared his throat in time-honored Giles style and said, "Buffy, we have something more to discuss."

"Mr. Giles, I really don't think we ought to bring up anything else for the nonce," Sir Nigel cut in.

"Thinking that's probably exactly what we ought to be discussing, then," Xander said. Buffy and Willow both nodded at him.

"Well, it seems there's a price on your head," Giles said. Willow's eyes grew huge. "We assume Regina's offering the reward, but there are an awful lot of demons angry with you at the moment. More angry than usual, I should say. It's not the first time they've been angry, of course. But the Hellmouth—"

"It's standard operating procedure for there to be a reward for bagging me," Buffy replied. "Hence, no big."

"And on the heads of Willow, Xander, Faith, Kennedy, and . . . and myself," Giles continued. There was an awkward shuffle, a muffled whisper.

"You're leaving something out," Buffy accused him.

"And on your sister, Dawn," Sir Nigel informed her. "Particularly, and specifically."

"On Dawnie?" Willow whispered incredulously.

Xander moved to Buffy and cupped a hand around her shoulder as if to help her absorb the shock. There were no words for the emotion that gutpunched her. She stared at the speakerphone as if it were a demon she had never encountered before, and had no idea how to kill.

"Wh-who could do such a thing?" Willow asked, taking Buffy's hand and squeezing it.

"Someone who wanted Buffy to be very distracted," Sir Nigel replied.

There was silence in Willow's room, and on the other end of the phone. Buffy's heart raced; her mind kicked into overdrive. Despite the weirdness of the world, Dawn had started the expensive private school with all the math; she loved shopping with Mr. Aram on the Immortal's mega-unlimited plastic and she was even cooking with the Immortal's Doge-pleasing chef. She was blossoming in Italy, loving her sister being around 24/7.

No.

Buffy balled her fists and raised her chin. "What's the plan to protect all of you?"

"We have one," Giles said quickly. "It's rather . . . it may not be what you would approve of."

"Tell me. Whatever I have to do to make sure Dawn is safe, I'll do."

"And Willow," Xander interrupted.

"And Xander and you, Giles," Willow added.

"We propose sending some Watchers to Africa," Sir Nigel said.

The three friends traded looks. "Because that stuffed tiger in your living room is getting a little moth-eaten?" Xander quipped.

"I noticed that too," Willow said, not smiling.

Sir Nigel ignored them. "This whole trouble began when the

powers of the Slayer were given indiscriminately to Potentials all over the world. We are thinking that we would send some of our people to the cave in Africa where the three Shadow Men appeared to Buffy. There, perhaps, we can learn more about the essence of that power."

Willow scooted back up in her chair as Xander raised his brows and said, "Whoa."

Buffy folded her arms and began to pace. " 'Our people?' Oh, you mean the guys who chained down the Primitive and forced the demon into her, then became the Watchers Council? Those people?"

"Her name is Senaya," Willow said gently. "The Primitive. The First Slayer."

But Sir Nigel was on a roll. "You've been quite forthcoming in the past, and we appreciated your description of your encounters with the Prim—Senaya—and the Shadow Men."

Buffy said nothing. She was waiting for the other shoe to drop.

Sir Nigel did not disappoint.

"Using a skilled negotiator, we're hopeful that we can persuade the Shadow Men to share all the details with us: precisely which demon was used, how the essence was transferred into Senaya, and how it has been handed down from Slayer to Slayer. Then we can harness that power—"

"Control it," Buffy cut in. "Take it back and put us Slayers under your thumb."

"I warned you, Mr. Giles, did I not?" Sir Nigel said huffily. "I told you this would be her reaction."

Buffy leaned forward and spoke loudly into the speakerphone. "Giles, you can't have agreed to this. Have you been replaced with your evil twin?"

Giles made no reply.

"Now, as you are the one who has spoken directly to the Shadow Men," Sir Nigel continued, "we would appreciate your telling us precisely how you managed it."

Willow frowned. "But Gi—" She closed her mouth and looked at Buffy in confusion. Then the lightbulb went on.

Giles *knew* how Buffy had contacted the Shadow Men. She had shown him Robin's magick lantern shadowcaster from his mother's emergency kit of Slayage items. He knew about the spell Willow had cast to bring Buffy back.

He knew all this, but he was not telling Sir Nigel that he knew.

He was going through the motions so that Buffy and company would know what Sir Nigel and his cronies were planning.

He was warning them.

She decided to play along. "We're already in a heap of trouble," she objected. "I don't want to endanger the Slayers any more than they already are. Why on earth should I let the Watchers go . . ." She trailed off as Xander cleared his throat and raised his hand.

"Not a Watcher, can't be a Slayer," Xander said, also getting what was going on. "So I'm pretty much a good candidate for this job."

"Me too," Willow added. Since, of course, she had performed the spell that had brought Buffy back.

"I can't be hearing this correctly," Sir Nigel said.

Turning from the phone, Buffy mimicked writing on a piece of paper. Willow picked up a small notepad next to her computer and handed Buffy a pen with a fuzzy pink feather top. It reminded Buffy of high school, and she was momentarily thrown at the realization that they had all changed drastically since then.

We'll talk after I hang up, she wrote.

"We're going to get back to you," Buffy said into the phone.

Sir Nigel was not done. "I must warn you, we have sorcerers on staff here and—"

"Are you threatening me, Sir Nigel?" Buffy asked sharply. Icy anger washed through her veins. She really didn't like this guy. He was a control freak, and he wasn't even hiding the fact that he wanted the Council to take charge again, just like in the bad days.

"Of course, not," he retorted. "What purpose would that serve?"

"Oh, I don't know." A beat. "Your purpose?"

"We're on the same side, Miss Summers," he said.

"That's good to hear, Lord Ambrose-Bellairs. I gotta go now. Giles? I'll catch you later."

"Very good, Buffy," Giles replied.

She disconnected and turned to her two most trusted lieutenants.

"I want to go on record here," Xander said. "Sir Nigel? Pretty much hate 'im."

"I second that," Willow said, raising her hand.

Xander was on a roll. "Have you noticed that he talks like Quentin Travers? He's got to be forty years younger than Quentin Travers. They both speak Evil British Arisotcratese."

"Couldn't agree more," Buffy said. "Now listen. Two things. The shadowcaster device was destroyed in Sunnydale; and Willow, you need to stay here. No Africa for you. The Immortal has more magick users around here than we have Slayers, and if he turns on us, I'm *so* gonna need someone with black eyes. Plus, if we have trouble getting Xander back, you'll need to be here to coordinate the exchange."

"That's not a specious argument," Willow conceded.

"Plus, it's true," Buffy asserted.

Willow brightened. "But hey, good news. When I knew we were headed for the big battle, I boxed up a lot of the good stuff and shipped it to myself in England. To Giles's country home. Which he knew, and arranged for some of the coven members to sign for the packages and store them in his basement."

"Wow, Will, way to go," Xander complimented her. "I wish I'd thought ahead like that. Remember my old skateboard? Sucked into the pit of hell." He looked very sad.

"I could have saved Mr. Pointy and Mr. Gordo," Buffy said, sighing mournfully.

Willow was sad for them both. Then she said, "Maybe Giles has already shipped the shadowcaster to us. Maybe the call was his method of alerting us that it's on the way."

"The plot is thickening," Xander said.

Willow took the pen and paper from Buffy and started making a list. At the top was #1: *SHADOWCASTER, En Route?*

She looked up from the pad. "Remember when we did this last time, that demon popped through the portal when you went to see the Shadow Men? We have to be ready to fight something weird when we send Xander through."

"We've got lots of Slayers to fight weird things," Buffy pointed out. "Unless some of them are spies or traitors." She looked at Willow. "Can you do some kind of magicks to weed out the ones with shaky loyalties?"

"Like, read their minds?" Willow queried, looking uncomfortable.

"Unless you'd rather have one of them kill Dawn for money," Xander said flatly.

"Okay." Willow chewed her lower lip and wrote on her list, *Loyalty Detection Spell.*

Buffy frowned. "And even if they are loyal, I don't want a bunch of 'em yakking to the Immortal or Mr. Tiptoes about what we're up to. We're going to have to figure out how to explain to them that they've gotta keep this to themselves."

Xander creased her forehead as he said archly, "What? Spill, and risk the displeasure of Queen Buffy? You underestimate the cult of personality. Your cult. You're still Number One with the rank and file, Buff. Whether you want to be or not."

Buffy exhaled. "And here I thought I'd have time to compete on *American Idol* once I shared my power."

Willow gave Buffy a weak half-smile. "It does seem like now that we have really strong Slayers, they need an even stronger leader."

"Which affords you many exciting opportunities for personal growth," Xander pointed out. "You could probably benefit by taking a few leadership training seminars, preferably in warm climates. Which you could then write off your taxes, so double bonus."

"To pay taxes, I need an income," Buffy replied, then anxiously added, "right? I don't have to pay taxes if I don't make any money?"

"Only in the most socialist nations," Xander assured her. He slapped his hands together. "I'll get dressed for desert duty and you can brief me on how to deal with the Shadow Men, okay? I seem to recall there was some hitting involved."

"Yes. And sticks," Buffy said. "They pounded the ground with sticks."

"I used to do that too. When I was five," Xander said, nodding to himself. "Also, there was that whole crazy jackhammer thing when I was in construction. Worked better than sticks."

"Jackhammers are never magickal," Willow opined.

"They are if you're trying to get through eight feet of Sheetrock," Xander shot back. "Hey, there's a thought for a money-making venture. We open Slayer Construction." He spread his hands as if he were reading a sign. "We get it done really fast, and we don't wear butt-crack pants."

"It has a certain flare. Not," Buffy said drily.

"However, I'll look fine in butt-crack pants," Xander continued. "Thanks to the medicmage. Wanna see my lack of crossbow scar?"

"Pass," both girls said in unison.

Willow moved to the dresser about twelve miles across the room and began pulling out pretty gift boxes and a locked metal container.

"I'm going to make you some talismans. And a spellsphere. It's something new for me," she added proudly. "I read about it in the Immortal's library. He has the most amazing holdings."

"Which is what?" Xander asked. "Not the holdings, because I have a sneaking suspicion that that means books. The spell-sphere."

"Oh, it's really cool," Willow said, grinning. "I record a spell; then, when you're ready to use it, you activate it."

"Cool," Xander said. "It's like TiVo for magick."

"Exactly." Willow looked excited. Buffy had to smile. Willow loved the magick. Now that the Wicca had broken the good/evil barrier on its use, she was able to enjoy it again.

There was a knock on Willow's door. Willow glanced at the others before she went to open it. Buffy stood posed for defense, just in case, and Xander drew close.

Mr. Aram appeared before Willow with an air-freight parcel in his arms. It was a large, cumbersome package, and his arms were looped around it. "This came for you, miss."

"Thank you," she said, reaching for it. Before she could take it from him, Buffy collected it. It wasn't that heavy, but then, she was a Slayer, so heavy was a relative term. She gazed at the address label, which was upside down: RG, WC.

Rupert Giles, Watchers Council. We have a winner!

"Would the three of you care for some refreshment?" Mr. Aram asked, looking from Willow to Xander and Buffy. "Your Majesty?"

"How about some sandwiches?" Buffy told him.

"And some trail mix," Xander told him. "And a couple of sports bottles of water. Also, maybe? Some beef jerky? Oh, and some barbecue potato chips?"

The man's polite, blank expression did not change. He was probably used to getting all kinds of strange requests from the Immortal.

"Very good," he said. He bowed in Buffy's direction. "Your Maj—"

"We've talked about this," she reminded him.

"Buffy," he corrected.

"Very good," she said, and he bowed again, and shut the door.

"Well, he gets an A in servant but a B for effort, 'cuz of the recurring 'Your Majesty' thing," Xander said. "Tell me that's from Giles, Willow. 'Cuz that would just be cool."

"It is," Willow said, walking with Buffy to the bed, where Buffy set it down. She added, "I'll need scissors."

Buffy reached over, hooked her fingertips under the flap, and ripped as if the cardboard were tissue paper. Much with the bubble wrap and layers and layers of protective Styrofoam, and then . . .

"*Viola, chicas,*" Xander said.

It was the shadowcaster, a circular ring of distressed metal. Also in the box, the figures that attached to it, of the three Shadow Men and the girl in chains: Senaya, and the men who had forced the demon into her, creating the First Slayer.

Then, at the bottom, lay the large book written in ancient Sumerian they had also found in Nikki Wood's Slayage bag; it was the owner's manual for the shadowcaster. The words had changed into English as the spell progressed.

"Rock, Giles," Xander said, whistling appreciatively. "He's got such a great sense of timing, he should be a novel writer."

"Or a trapeze artist," Willow murmured. She lifted the shadowcaster and examined it. "It looks ready to go."

"Then let's go too," Xander urged.

"We'll wait for the food, and we'll get a few Slayers in on this gig in case a really bad demon drops out of the portal," Buffy said. She thought a moment. "Do you think we should call Faith and Robin and clue them in?"

"Let's call but be sneaky, like Giles was," Willow ventured. "I still can't guarantee that our conversations are staying private."

"It's getting harder and harder to talk to her," Buffy observed. "Because of the interference, I mean. Not 'cause she's Faith."

"Mystical energies making it harder," Willow said. "Remember when the power went out in Sunnydale? Hoping that doesn't happen to them."

"The Watchers Council isn't wrong," Xander said. "Things are askew, and getting more so."

"Yes." Buffy picked back up the original thread. "So, we eat, you go to mystical-portal Africa, you see what you can find out."

"Roger, dodger." Xander looked pleased. "It's nice to be back in the game," he said. "Not much for a one-eyed sidekick to do around here."

"I'm glad you're here, Xand. I'm always glad," Buffy replied warmly.

"I know." He smiled at her. "And I'm always here. It's a whole big 'Yay, Xander's here' thing. Except soon I'll be there."

"Soon you'll be there," Buffy affirmed.

She picked up Willow's phone. "I'll give Faith a call, talk in general terms. She's smart; she'll know something's up."

"And not up with people," Xander said, then shrugged when Buffy and Willow just stared at him. "Never mind. Long story."

Buffy gave him a puzzled, crooked grin and punched in Faith's number.

CHAPTER ELEVEN

Death sucks.
—Elizabeth Engstrom

Haley the Vampire Slayer crept through the dark forest. Her arms were badly scratched, and the stitches in the deep cut across her forehead itched.

A owl hooted.

Haley hooted back.

Two figures in long black robes stepped from the underbrush. One was taller. Both wore elaborate Venetian Carnival masks that concealed their faces. But she knew who they were, and she dropped to one knee and lowered her head. "Your Majesty Regina," she said reverently.

"What on earth happened to you, young one?" Regina demanded, placing her hands on Haley's shoulders and bidding her rise. "What terrible ordeal did Buffy put you through?"

Haley's eyes welled as she melted under the kindness of these two. "Buffy arranged for us to meet in secret in the dungeon of the Immortal's palace. She and Xander Harris and Willow Rosenberg were there. They had a round thing with puppets on it. The witch spoke magickal words; it began to spin. There was a shimmering flash, and Xander disappeared inside it. Then a demon dropped out of the ceiling!" She touched her forehead. "Buffy made us fight it."

Buffy had also sworn the four Slayers she had enlisted for "demon duty" to secrecy. As far as Haley knew, she was the only one of those four to violate Buffy's trust.

For a good cause, she reminded herself. *Regina wants to help us. Buffy just wants to use us.*

"Oh, poor *cara,*" Regina murmured, reaching out a gentle hand to caress Haley's cheek.

Haley had met Regina and the man she called "my consort" two weeks ago, when she had decided to run away. She was tired of the training, tired of being a Slayer, and she was terribly homesick. She was only fourteen and she had lived on an American military base with her parents in Germany when her powers had come to her.

Regina had found her about three kilometers from the Immortal's palazzo. Haley had read about him in a Potential chat room; she'd tried to find him on her own. But she had gotten terribly lost, and she was thirsty and hungry. Regina had explained that the Immortal kept the location of his compound private with wards and spells. But then he had changed his mind and allowed the young and inexperienced new Slayers to find his compound.

"There's so much subterfuge," Regina had gone on to explain. "They don't take the welfare of you Slayers into account while they're concocting any of their private schemes."

She had gone on to explain that although Buffy talked a lot about fighting the forces of evil, the truth was that she had become a power-mad tyrant who regretted sharing her power with others.

"She wants all the power back," Regina had explained. "And the only way to do that is to keep all of you under her thumb. You've seen how she treats you all. Like inferiors."

"Yes," Haley had agreed.

The consort said, "If you run, she won't stop looking for you until she finds you. And then she'll make you pay for your disobedience—"

"But I have dedicated my life to stopping her," Regina cut in. "You're in a unique position to help me."

And so Haley had become Regina's spy.

When she finished telling her about the spell and the demon, Regina turned to her consort and said, "We need to talk to Lucrezia and Cesare about this."

"Hush!" he hissed, and Haley was shocked by the imperious tone of his voice. Then he turned to Haley and said, "You have done well, little one. Return to the palazzo now. Use this." He put a finder's sphere in her hand. He gave her a fresh one every time she met with them. It would help her find her way back to the palazzo. It had become more difficult to locate it. Lately he had resumed warding his territory with a vengeance.

"Thank you. So much," Haley said. She knelt, brought the hem of Regina's black-velvet cloak to her lips, and kissed it.

"Do you have the old finder's sphere?" he prodded.

She nodded, fishing in the pocket of her coat. "Here," she said. "There are more of us than there used to be," she said. "More Slayers who want to join you. Just say the word. . . ."

"Soon, *bella*. But not yet," Regina said, stroking her cheek. "We'll let you know when the time comes."

"We won't fail you," she said earnestly. "I promise you."

"*Bene, bene,* that's wonderful." Regina bent down and kissed the wound on her forehead. "You will heal more quickly now. But you must return immediately, before you are missed."

Haley smiled up at them both, then turned and headed in the direction she had come.

Antonio and Ornella waited until the little Slayer had disappeared back into the forest before they removed their masks. Antonio opened his palm, revealing the finder's sphere that she had obligingly returned to them, as she had the five others he had given her. Of course they weren't simply finder's spheres; while in her possession, they acted as low-level surveillance devices. They were extremely weak; anything too substantial would be detected by the Immortal's skilled warding capabilities. Indeed, two of the five hadn't been able to pick up anything due to the pervasive magickal fields cloaking the Immortal's compound.

But they had been able to capture some precious phone numbers. And the news of Africa was interesting, although neither was sure what to make of it.

The kiss on the forehead was part of a spell that would prevent Willow Rosenberg from learning that Haley had been disloyal to Buffy.

"Let's go see if we caught anything in our magickal web this time," he told Ornella.

The two melted into the forest, and made for his villa.

CLEVELAND

It was ten at night, day forty-two on the Hellmouth. Faith had a board in her left hand and a rusty hammer in her right. There was some blood and other matter on the business end of the hammer, a souvenir from whacking a zombie over the head. They liked the graveyard three stories below, and Faith had come to understand that the schtick about being the only one in her generation to fight the demons, vampires, and forces of darkness was just a euphemism for evil. Now there were daylight forces only Slayers could stop. And far too many of them.

There were cuts and bruises on Faith's face and arms. She was always wounded. Everyone was either injured or dead. Today had been a great day; no fatalities on their side.

Lots, on the other side.

She was preparing to nail the board across the broken sill, which let in cold air from the storm outside. Snow was gathering on the ledge. Except for the pesky draft, it was toasty warm in the room, which had once been a youth club for young Catholics.

Robin and Faith had lit the furnace, and part of every patrol was bringing back heating oil. The place was in need of repairs, with some very dangerously loose boards in the floor and a lot of grimy, cracked windows.

Along with the seven additional Slayers currently working the Cleveland detail, Robin, Kennedy, and Faith had holed up in a church. Vi and Rona were in charge of the newbies. Three of them were out patrolling, and four were sleeping. Robin, Kennedy, and Faith had taken the earlier patrol detail. The Hellmouth was active 24/7. The Slayers had to be too.

But with the strangely harsh weather, and the rise in demonic activity, most of the human inhabitants of Cleveland had evacuated the city. That made the Slayers' job easier, if anything about this job could be said to be easy. It was easier to run the demons to ground if there weren't any civilians to look out for. But the problem was, there were so many demons. They streamed out of the Hellmouth like Red Sox fans after a game.

I'm beginning to think this mission is a lost cause, Faith thought. *Not that I'm the kind of chick who runs. But I am the kind of chick who calls it like I see it. We're here to hold this Hellmouth, but it just doesn't love us that way.*

"Robin, Kennedy," Faith said, pointing out the window of their third-story headquarters. "Check it out. They're ba-ack."

Thrown against the sky, the freak show had returned. The snow cast three king-size shapes in silhouette; it was like watching a drive-in movie as the three gesticulated at one another, and it would appear they were having a lively argument.

They were usually arguing.

Faith and Robin had told the Watchers Council about the apparitions. The consensus back in Merry Olde was that these were evil gods intent on taking advantage of the current chaos to do mischief. Giles was especially concerned about Janus, and told Faith he would discuss his appearance with Ethan Rayne. But Giles wasn't certain that Ethan was still in custody. Although the U.S. government insisted that they still had him, they weren't certain where they had put him.

"It shouldn't be too difficult to research a containment spell," Giles told her. "Janus is a very old god, and there's a lot of literature on him. The Council will make it a high priority."

But so far, the Council had done squat about the occasional shadow-puppet shows that Janus and his two friends put on. This was the fifth time they had appeared in the skies over the city, and despite numerous attempts to exorcise him or something, the Watchers had obviously been unable to pull it off.

No surprise there. God, those guys are useless.

Coming up beside Faith, Kennedy made as if to wave out the window. "Hi, Janus! Hi, Kali! Yo, Death, how's it hanging?"

From across the room, Robin looked up from repacking the first aid kit and said, "I still don't think that's Kali. She's off, somehow. It'd be nice if the Council could get us some more information on those guys. Why we keep seeing them. They're obviously unaware of the effect. Is it astral projection?"

"I think the Hellmouth's got a holodeck," Kennedy insisted.

Faith snorted. "It'd be nice if the Council could get their heads out of their a—"

Robin's phone rang in the pocket of Faith's black leather pants, where it lived. "Giles or Buffy?" she asked Kennedy and Robin. "Or Andrew, to whine about how Buffy doesn't care about him anymore?"

"My money's on Sir Nigel," Robin replied, probably just to needle her.

It worked, a little. Faith made a face at him as she lifted the phone to her ear. "'Cuz he's just our favorite loser. Yo."

"Faith?" came a hissing voice, as if from far away. Then it started murmuring in what had to be Latin, or she wasn't a lapsed Catholic. It sounded creepy, evil . . . it made her skin crawl.

And yet, she couldn't disconnect.

She scowled. "Are you a phone solicitor?"

Robin looked at her. She kept listening, unable to stop. He made eye contact, mouthed, "Who?" but she found she couldn't speak. She was riveted to the spot, and her hand was frozen to the phone.

"Heus ut meus lacuna. Permissum vestri substantia adeo mihi."

"Faith?" Robin said, rising from the couch.

Kennedy joined him, her dark eyes narrowing. "What's going on?"

She reached Faith first; she grabbed the phone away from her and put it to her own ear.

Shaking her head as if to clear it, Faith cried, "No!" She wrenched the phone out of Kennedy's hand, yanked the window open, and tossed the phone out the window, hard. Pieces of glass dislodged from the window and clunked in the snowdrift on the broken sill.

Robin and Kennedy leaned out the window. The three watched the phone sail down toward the graveyard, well illuminated to guard against things trying to break into the church.

"Someone was chanting at me," Faith informed them as she smoothed back her hair. "Casting a spell to, I dunno, *heus ut meus lacuna.*"

"That translates as 'harken to my word.'" Robin scrutinized her. "Any of those words stick?"

She tossed her head. "No way." She looked at Kennedy. "But seriously, thanks, junior."

"You're welcome," Kennedy said.

"Who did it sound like?" Robin persisted. "Was it a human voice, or a demon? Did it have an accent?"

"I don't know. I can't remember." Faith frowned. "I hope I'm not possessed or something. Do I look possessed to you?" She paused. "It knew my name."

"That's not good," Robin ventured. He absently ran his fingers over the long cut on the back of his hand. "I'll get another phone out. We should call Buffy right away."

As he turned, Kennedy caught her breath and pointed out the window. "Oh. My. God."

As the three looked on, the figures of Janus and his backup dancers stretched into distortions of their already-distorted shapes, then pulled into thin, glowing ribbons of iridescent blue that arched against the starry sky. The ribbons thinned into gossamer strands that bent against the starlight like laser beams.

The strands aimed downward, and shot into the cell phone Faith had thrown into the graveyard.

Kennedy and Robin jerked in surprise. Kennedy said, "Whoa," and then Robin raced across the room for the door that led to the hall, and to the stairs.

As one, and without hesitation, Faith and Kennedy jumped out the window, landing in the soft earth and grass of the graveyard. Kennedy fell harder; Faith got up first and raced to the phone.

She picked it up, although she very carefully kept it out of listening range, and examined it. "You guys?" she said loudly, shaking the phone.

"Maybe you should rub it. Like a genie's lamp," Kennedy suggested as she got to her feet and jogged up beside Faith.

Faith turned the phone this way and that. "Not sure I want them to come back out," she said. "Unless they promise to grant me three wishes."

Robin loped from the front porch of the church into the graveyard. Faith grinned at him over her shoulder and said, "What do you say, Robin? Want me to rub it?"

"I don't want you to touch it," he said, extending his hand and pointing to the ground. "Put it back down. It's already tried to put the mojo on you."

Faith shrugged. "And then? If some demon happens by? Or if

someone says the right spell and those guys pop out ten feet from our front door?"

"Maybe we should throw it into the Hellmouth," Kennedy suggested.

"Maybe that's where they've been trying to go," Faith argued. "If we do that, we might be, I dunno, pouring gasoline on the fire."

Just then, Rona appeared on the front porch with a portable phone in her hand. "Guys? It's Buffy. She wants to talk to Faith."

"Are you sure?" Robin asked.

Rona looked confused. "Well, she said she wants to."

"I'll take it," Faith said. As she brushed past Robin, she said, "If I wig out, hit me with a shovel or something."

Rona walked toward her to hand her the phone. Faith said, "Everyone okay?"

Rona nodded. "They're asleep. Charmante took a bad fall today. She kind of passed out."

"Watch for signs of a concussion," Faith advised. She put the phone to her ear. "B," she said, "gotta warn you. Someone just called here and tried to put a spell on me. Then the three weird guys we told you about zapped into the phone."

"Oh." *Buffy at a loss. Here's a first.* "This phone?"

"No. Robin's. So we're trying to decide what to do with it. 'Cuz it's, like, magickally radioactive—you know what I mean?"

"Yes. Willow," she said away from the phone, "get on an extension, okay?"

"Hey." That was Willow.

"Before we get back to that, I have to tell you something," Buffy interrupted. "Xander's gone out of town. To visit an old, old friend of ours."

"I just love twenty questions," Faith snapped.

"Which we are playing because funny things have been happening to the phones," Buffy snapped back. "I, for one, have been calling you for hours and this is the first time I've gotten through."

"Point taken. So this old friend Xander went to see. His name start with an A?"

"No. This is a female. Someone who has a lot in common with you. And me. And Kennedy. But not with Willow. Or Giles."

The Primitive? "Numero Uno?" Faith guessed.

"Yes."

"Why?" Faith was intrigued. She hadn't realized they could go visit the First Slayer again. "Is it warm there?" she added, only half-facetiously.

"Because some other people were thinking about visiting her," Buffy replied. "We figured we'd better get there first."

"Those other people those guys you and I don't like so much?" Faith quizzed her. "Those crazy lookie-loo's?"

"Those would be the ones," Buffy replied.

Crap. "Okay."

"But we're getting there first. So far, it's all good."

"Check." Faith felt a little better. "You'll keep me posted?"

"I will. How you guys doing?"

"It's like Sunnydale with snow. We're doing okay. We've got the stuff, B." *I am such an awesome liar.*

"I know you do, Faith. Giles still thinks we'd better try to hold Cleveland. What do you think?"

"Um, thinking that over," Faith admitted.

"Okay. You let me know if it's pointless."

"I never pull my punches with you, B."

"Yeah, but I still beat you. Now here's Willow."

"Okay. All ears," Faith said, her gaze on the cell phone lying in the snow. *That is one weird mother. . . .*

And then Kennedy cried, "Oh God, Faith!"

Faith turned and said something far more graphic.

A horde of Turok-Han were charging into the graveyard.

IN THE BORGIA HELL DIMENSION

Propped upright beside Lucrezia in their heavily draped bed of state, Cesare frowned at her as he set down his enchanted cell phone. He tapped it as if he were spanking it.

He was terribly disappointed.

"I think she discarded the phone," he told his sister. "I didn't even have a chance to recite the entire spell."

"So it didn't work," she said petulantly. "You were unable to put Faith enthrall. And now we've lost her phone number."

"Antonio will get the new one. And we'll get it from him," Cesare assured her. Antonio was a very resourceful lad. Of course. He was a Borgia.

They also had the Immortal's number, but Cesare was wary of using it. He figured the Immortal had even more sophisticated surveillance magicks than they did. To even dial his number might be enough to alert him to their presence.

Tonight they had decided to call Faith, put her enthrall, and send her to retrieve Malfeo's orb in the Hellmouth. The ancient Latin that Cesare had been speaking to her would certainly have worked, if he had had enough time to complete the spell.

He said to her, "Don't worry, *cara*. We'll find someone to bewitch and retrieve the orb for us. Faith has many subordinates with her."

She crossed her arms over her chest. "But it has to be a Slayer. No one else will survive going into the Hellmouth."

"We could cast about for a demon there," he suggested. "Or simply dial random cell phone numbers until someone answers, put them enthrall, and send them to the Hellmouth. It wouldn't matter if a dozen died. Or a hundred. After a while, someone might get through."

She held up a finger. "But every spell costs, Cesare. You know that. We must pay the dark forces with a proper sacrifice to make our spells work. If we have to bewitch a hundred beings to achieve the retrieval, we have to pay for a hundred spells with sacrifices."

"True. But perhaps we could create a spell in such a way that the person who answered the phone would also serve as a sacrifice. That would pay the gods in their favorite coin."

"Blood," she said. "Death."

Then, without warning, the phone exploded. Bits of metal and fragments of metal shot in all directions. Tatters of blanket sprung into the air like flying snakes. Several pieces of debris lodged in Lucrezia's face, and she screamed.

Cesare threw himself across her.

"I'm hurt," she whimpered. "I'm hurt, I'm hurt!"

"Oh, *cara*," he soothed. *"Cara mia, bella . . ."* He plucked a piece of metal from her cheek.

She sniffled; then she inhaled sharply—a purely reflexive maneuver, since vampires didn't breathe—and pointed toward the foot of their bed.

"Cesare, *look*."

He followed her line of sight.

A sphere of blue rotated several feet above the floor. It was a representation of Antonio's world.

The center of the sphere glowed black. As the two vampires watched, holding each other, the black became purple, then black again. It wobbled, grew, collapsed, then expanded again.

Then, against the wall of their chamber, two images shot from the blackness, framed in jittering blue energy: a fabulous demon with three eyes and a necklace of skulls, and a cauled figure with a staff. They were thrown in bold relief, moving and speaking to each other, clearly unaware that Lucrezia and Cesare could see them.

What have we here? Cesare wondered, his glance ticking from the figures to Lucrezia. He raised his brows, questioning her: *Do you know what's going on?* Her eyes were wide as she shook her head in wonder.

A voice echoed throughout the room. It took Cesare a moment to realize that it was speaking English.

"We continue to have difficulties. You promised a solution. Perhaps you're not capable of leading us to victory."

"I agree with E'o." This was a different voice, apparently belonging to the cauled figure, judging by the body language of the other two as they turned to it.

E'o. I must research that name, Cesare told himself, taking mental notes. His mind was racing. He had no idea what was going on; who these entities were; and how . . .

My spell. It summoned them here! It didn't work on Faith, but it worked on them!

"Lucrezia," he whispered softly. But she didn't appear to hear him. She was gazing in utter amazement at the figures.

Then a third shadow flared onto the wall. It was not as distinct as the other two; hence, its owner had greater power to conceal itself.

It has two heads. It is Janus!

Unsure if he was doing the right thing, Cesare murmured his spell again: *"Heus ut meus lacuna. Permissum vestri substantia adeo mihi."*

There was a rush as if of wind; and then the two-headed form of the great god Janus appeared more distinctly on the wall. Tall, and stately, and brimming with power. A god to be reckoned with.

Bargained with.

Lucrezia sank to her knees and lowered her head.

Cesare kept his composure, but he was nearly as thrilled as the day Malfeo had appeared to them. Janus was an old god belonging to Rome herself. Like any self-respecting sorcerer of his times, he knew how to invoke the ancient deities.

Rising up on his knees on his bed of state, he bowed forward, placing his hands on the damask bedspread, and spoke in ancient Latin:

"Janus, evoco vestram animam. Exaudi meam causam. Carpe noctem pro consilio vestro. Veni, appare et nobis monstra quod est infinita potestas."

At once the shadow of the great two-headed Lord of Gates threw his arms into the air and shouted from his two mouths, "Who summons me?" The sound echoed off the walls. A piece of plaster dislodged from the ceiling and crashed onto the foot of the bed.

Cesare repeated the invocation.

The room quaked. The bed swayed back and forth like a ship at sea; fissures appeared in the walls and they broke apart. The floor cracked; one section pushed up over the other. The bed canted crazily.

Cesare spoke the incantation a third time, holding Lucrezia close as the explosions rocked the foundations of their palace. The bed crashed through the floor, landing unceremoniously in the subterranean grotto where they held their revels. Lucrezia and Cesare were submerged; he fought with the bedclothes as he gathered her up and swam with her in his arms toward the rocky stairs below the waterline.

A pair of enormous feet greeted them. Cesare raised his head to stare up through the gaping hole of the ruined floor as the two-headed god Janus turned the elder of his faces toward Cesare.

"Who are you, and why have you summoned me here?" he boomed.

Then the two figures they had seen took form beside him, gazing down into the grotto. One was three-eyed, with multiple rows of black teeth and skulls around the neck; and breasts and womanish hips. The third was Death himself.

"Before I rip you to shreds," the great two-headed god bellowed at Cesare, "tell me who you are and why you summoned me."

"Why he summoned *us,*" the three-eyed goddess corrected.

"It's something of a story," Cesare said, his English rusty. One learned many things in the course of seven centuries of life, including how to speak foreign languages. Learning English had been a practical move: there were many wonderful and powerful spells designed to be conjured in English.

"Not too long of a story," Cesare added quickly, as Janus crossed his arms over his chest and shifted his weight impatiently. "You see, we are . . . this is a demon dimension, and we rule here. We had thought to . . . harass one of the Slayers with a spell."

"Buffy?" Janus queried, his voice betraying his excitement.

"All of them, in truth," Lucrezia interjected. Cesare had not heard her speak English in years, and it was a delightful surprise. "Faith was our quarry tonight. But we are sworn enemies of all the Slayers. And as Buffy is their leader, we hate her most of all."

"Then you are our friends," the skeletal, robed figure announced.

"Yes," said the Kali-like female. "'The enemies of my enemies are my friends.'" She looked around. "But why are we here?"

"If you would be patient, they would tell us," the robed one hissed at her.

"We were attempting a spell on Faith, and we somehow inadvertently brought you here. Perhaps because of the proximity of the Hellmouth . . ."

Where my orb lies, Cesare thought with sudden, hopeful clarity. *And gods such as these would be able to retrieve it. . . .*

"*What?*" Janus demanded, uncrossing his arms. "You dared use a spell to call *me*—"

"To bring us to a place where I, for one, feel quite at home," said the skeletal figure.

The three-eyed female looked around at their surroundings, and gazed down at her body. "I feel no pain. I am exerting no effort to remain here." She smiled at Cesare. "I rather like it here."

Her smile was terrifying.

IN THE RUINS OF POMPEII, ITALY

The city of Pompeii was a tomb, and its inhabitants were laid out for all to see. An unsettling tableau of plaster statues frozen in time, their arms outstretched, on their knees or lying on their sides, mouths pulled back in shouts or contracted in gasps, revealed the last struggles of people who had suffocated during the eruption of Mount Vesuvius in AD 79. The original people had been thoroughly coated with toxic dust, which killed them. Then the corpses had decomposed inside the mantles of ash, leaving shells of hardened material that had lain undisturbed for centuries. In the 1930s, archaeologists had come up with the idea to pour plaster into "vacancies" buried in the ground. The silent figures were all over Pompeii, a testament to the full-scale death of a city.

"They had no chance to get away," the Immortal murmured. "They died trying to escape. Some could have been saved, but they simply couldn't accept that the end had come."

"I've always been pretty good at dying," Buffy said. "It's the living part that's tricky."

They had traveled from Rome to Pompeii in the Immortal's limo. He had had to assure Buffy that Dawn would be well looked after.

"As long as she remains on the palazzo grounds, I can guarantee her safety," the Immortal promised her. "My compound is the most heavily warded piece of real estate in Europe."

So, for the time being, no more apartment. And Dawn was not loving the fact that she wasn't going to school right now. Mr. Aram and Mr. Bey both stood guard over her, and Dawn was chafing under her restrictions. As many times as she had been in danger, it was still difficult for the little sister of the Slayer to comprehend her own mortality.

Her black gloved hands in the pockets of her black pea coat, Buffy stood beside the Immortal as they viewed the Garden of Fugitives. A family group had died there: father, mother, children.

"This little one had no chance either," he added as they walked on to a row of glass cases. He stood before the effigy of a dog and he bowed his head, as if he was praying.

Buffy read the sign. The poor creature had been chained to a post, and the descending volcano ash had smothered him. "Poor puppy," she said plaintively.

"His name was Socrates," the Immortal said, tapping the glass as if to awaken the dog. "An admirable philosopher, and an equally admirable dog."

She looked askance at him. "How do you know that?"

He said nothing.

The Immortal walked with Buffy down the fine stoned streets of the ancient city of Pompeii. Their boots echoed off the walkway, reverberating against the brick walls. The sound reminded her of many other hollow tombs she had entered, visiting death—or, in some cases, bringing it.

Wind whipped his dark, curly hair, and snow flurries fluttered on his shoulders. He smelled of sandalwood, and his face was sad as he quietly began to speak again.

"Many fled, and would have lived if they had not sought shelter to wait out the clouds of hot ash tumbling to the ground. But they lingered too near, stayed too long because they couldn't bear to part from their homes and possessions. Or to wait for a loved one. They couldn't fathom that they truly had to leave."

He raised his eyeline to the horizon.

"Romans in that time were very big on predicting the future. But no one realized that day that they were going to die."

In the distance, Mount Vesuvius rose from banks of snow clouds. Smoke and steam bubbled from the still-active volcano. Seismologists were looking closely at steadily increasing pressure inside the cone, and at the strange readings deeper in the earth.

"Look at the phantoms of chaos around you," the Immortal said. "Look how fast death came upon them. The screams, the terror. Perhaps some of them wouldn't have perished if they had had a Slayer among them. Or many Slayers." His eyes took on a far-away look.

"You were there," Buffy said slowly. "You saw it happen."

How old is he?

"I have been present at many catastrophes," he agreed, turning to gaze at her. "And many times—I admit it—I stood by and observed, a voyeur to pain." He frowned, as if seeing things she couldn't . . . and had no desire to. She saw enough pain.

She couldn't imagine him acting like such a coward.

"This time, I must involve myself."

She frowned up at him. "Why? What's changed?"

He cupped her cheek. She felt the warmth of his hand. "I have never had a family," he said softly, his voice barely a whisper. "I have never had what you have. Close friends, loved ones . . ."

"You have to be a friend to have one." She aimed for lightness, but her voice cracked a little. What was happening to her? She had thought he was hot, sure, but this . . . this *feeling* . . . tenderness, closeness, intimacy.

I have said good-bye too many times. There are others I love . . .
. . . and can't have. . . .
I don't trust him. None of us do.

"Buffy." He trailed his fingers down to the angle of her chin. "I know you're grieving. Death visits me often. But she never stays."

She managed a smile. "She might if you put out some milk and cookies. Works on Santa."

He chuckled. "You bear your burdens well. But you deflect attention from yourself with your banter."

"Are you compiling a dossier on me for the FBI?"

"See what I mean?" He looped a strand of hair around her ear.

"I don't mean to be rude, but you pretty much comment on everything I do or say. It makes me . . . itchy."

"It's because I'm interested in you," he said frankly.

"Who isn't? Some people want to kill me, some people want me to be their queen." She looked askance at him. "You're really rich, right? You wouldn't just, you know, turn me in for the ransom?"

He actually guffawed. "Let's go back to the palazzo," he said.

Back to business. Buffy nodded, hoping for a good report from Xander. He'd been teleported to East Africa, and no one knew what had gone awry. He was near Lake Malawi, apparently known for its lovely *mbuna* fish. Problem was, Buffy didn't know the location of the cave where she'd met the Shadow Men. So she didn't know if Xander was close to the target zone or halfway across the continent.

She and four other Slayers had killed the demon that blasted through the portal in exchange for Xander. They had saved the body for Willow to use for the spell to bring him back. But the portal would not open for them to put it in. They had brought a freezer into the chamber to keep it in. It made a noisy hum.

She and Willow were trying to decide if they should attempt to bring Xander back through, have him fly home, or just wait to see if they could figure out what went wrong. If anything.

But the thought of him out there and unprotected made her very, very nervous.

I wonder if I asked for some real help, what the Immortal would do? she thought as they walked slowly back to his limo.

Was it time to put him to the test?

CHAPTER TWELVE

Death does not concern us, because as long as we exist, death is not here.
And when it does come, we no longer exist.
—Epicurus

EAST AFRICA
NEAR LAKE MAWALI

Xander in Africa. *I think that was a movie title. Oh, wait. Maybe that was* Xander in a Holding Pattern in Africa.

He gazed around at the Internet café where he had camped out for the last three days and nights, at least in African standard time. It was made of wood and some kind of thatching, and a group called Common Rotation was blaring on some speakers. He bobbed along as he typed on the Mac. The group was damn rockin', and he made a note to check iTunes for some of their cuts when he wasn't paying $12,394.47 a microsecond for connect time.

This journey had started with such promise. In the Immortal's palazzo, the shadowcaster had started spinning and the portal had opened, and Xander primed himself to meet the three Shadow Men, whom he'd privately named Gold, Frankincense, and Myrrh. Instead, he'd been dropped at the outskirts of a little village called Tanganyika. There were about three dozen round houses, which appeared to be made of adobe or something like it, topped with thatch umbrella-roofs. There was also a tiny restaurant and a gift shop. No other "tourists" had come through since he had arrived. Everything was covered with dust. The hundred or so villagers wore a mixture of colorful native garb and the Gap, and his appearance was cause for polite but mild curiosity.

When he realized that the restaurant had a small anteroom with a WiFi connection (the Internet café), he slapped down his credit card and crossed his fingers. Sometimes the magick works . . . the cute girl at the counter, named Angela, nodded and told him in accented English to log in at the Mac next to a pot of pungent herb tea.

Where they got the power for all this, he had no idea.

He checked in with Buffy and Willow, who told him to stay put until they researched why he hadn't gone to the cave. So he hung around, wishing for something to do besides running up charges on the PC and memorizing every item for sale in the gift shop. Angela told him he could send a live cichlid, which was a kind of fish, anywhere in the world for a very low price. On a lark, he sent a little yellow *mbuna* to Andrew, in London. Maybe it would help stem the whining.

Then, a little while ago, Willow had sent him some directions that included walking alone into the desert "by light of day." She also told him she wasn't positive it was going to work.

"I've got this thing I have to go to," he told Angela as he handed her back his teacup and powered off the computer. Back in Italy, before he'd gone through the portal, Willow had given him a bunch of talismans. He opened his shirt and began relooping them over his clothes like Hawaiian leis. Angela watched, saying nothing. He had no idea if she knew who he really was and why he was there.

"Good luck," she said in her sexy African accent. "Come back soon."

"Check." He gave her a jaunty wink, realizing that was stupid because, well, with the one eye it probably looked like a facial tick, and he wished he could erase it. *No such luck.*

Feeling less than dashing, he left the hut. He was wearing the clothes he had left Rome in, supplied, he assumed, by the Immortal: a Foreign Legion–style hat, with a drape thing that went down to his shoulders. Also, a khaki shirt and long pants and hiking boots. And his talismans, which were a jingle-jangling-jingling.

He stood for a moment and murmured, *"Je te touche."* He had no idea why he was supposed to say it, but Willow had e-mailed him very explicit directions on how to pronounce it.

He waited a moment, and then he felt something brush the back of his hand. The hair on the back of his head stood up. *Is it a ghost?*

The sensation came again, and he had the distinct impression that he should turn left. He walked straight ahead, then hesitated, and started to go right. The ghostly caress touched his hand again. He went right.

Okay. I've got an escort service, he thought.

Within an hour it was blazing hot—no global warming problems here to make it cold! Behind his sunglasses, his eyes were having trouble differentiating the blinding sand from the blinding sunshine. He was covered with sweat, which was good. That meant he was hydrated.

He stopped again. The sky was white; the sand blinding. He felt dizzy.

But this time, there was no ghostly caress of his hand.

"Hello?" he called. *"Mademoiselle* ghost?"

Nothing.

Wondering now if someone played a funny trick on Buffy's plucky one-eyed buddy . . .

He trudged on most trudgingly. A cooling wind began to blow, and that was nice.

The space in front of Xander began to shimmer like a mirage. He saw outcroppings of rock, and a dark oblong. The image blurred, losing contrast, then snapped into sharp relief.

It was a cave.

Hope it's the right one.

His boots crunched on the sand like fingers in cornstarch, and he took another sip of water before he secured the cap and stuck it in his pack.

He fingered the bunch of magickal talismans that clanged and jangled—some were metal, some bone; there were even a few feathers. In addition to protection, they were supposed to boost his signal when summoning the Shadow Men.

But this . . . is the pièce de résistance. . . .

He walked slowly toward the front of the cave, reaching into his shirt pocket and drawing out a small wooden ball.

The cave opening was surprisingly chilly. No one had prepared him for that. He shivered as he pried the top half of the ball from the bottom half.

Buffy's voice poured out:

"Shadow Men, I summon you. Speak to my follower, Xander. Appear before him. Grant him his wish."

"Okay, you hear that, guys?" Xander asked uncertainly as he walked into the cave. "Are we good? 'Cuz I'm in the cave. Xander has entered the building."

It was cool inside, and dark, and Xander could see nothing as he moved forward. He was pretty wigged, but he was Xander, and he did things like this even when he was wigged. Maybe he didn't have magickal abilities, and maybe he wasn't super strong, but he gave what he had.

The chill air wicked the perspiration off his face. He shivered. Then he saw the flickering light of a torch, and a figure half-crouched beside it. That crazy hair, the face paint . . . it was Senaya, the First Slayer.

Probably even better than the Shadow Men, if she and I can communicate. But God, is she scary.

Freaked, Xander held up a hand. *"Gort, baringa,"* he blurted, seized with a sudden giddy hysteria. It was a line of dialogue from one of his favorite movies, *The Day the Earth Stood Still.* He knew right now was probably not the best time to try to be funny but he was just so damn nervous, he couldn't make himself shut up. *"Klaatu barada nicto."*

Senaya stared at him as if she were about to spring forward like a cheetah, rip off his head, and stomp on it. She was one fierce-looking chick.

"Hey, Senaya, whaddup?" he said, waving awkwardly at her. "I come in peace for all mankind."

"Shadow Men," she replied in a gravelly, garbled voice, and charged straight for him with her spear in her hands and murder in her eyes.

When Buffy and the Immortal returned from Pompeii, Willow, dressed in a fuzzy maroon sweater, sweatpants, and scuffies, met them and said, "Giles called. He wants to talk to you."

Buffy looked pointedly at the Immortal, who inclined his head and said, "I have calls to return as well."

Willow raised her brows as the two friends watched him walk away. "Whoa, Buffy, there is sparkage," she said.

Buffy sighed. "I don't know."

"Yes. There is. I could practically see it." She grinned; Buffy's cheeks warmed, and she waved her hand as if to erase the conversation.

"I cast some spells and then I refigured the trajectory coordinates for the teleportation to the cave," Willow told her excitedly. "I sent Xander off this morning and I think I've got him pointed in the right direction."

Coordinates, Buffy thought. *I feel like we're on* Star Trek. She asked the Wicca, "What went wrong when we sent him through? Why did he end up in a village with souvenir *mbuna* fish?"

Willow raised a skeptical red eyebrow. "If I told you, would you understand?"

"Doubtful," Buffy admitted.

Willow scrunched up her nose and said, "Well, I kind of think I pronounced a couple of the words wrong. See, it starts out in ancient Sumerian and then it switches to English . . . and I winged it a little on the Sumerian. Assyrian, I'm there. But Sumerian . . . Dawn actually speaks it better than I do. We probably should have called her in."

Buffy's nod was noncommittal. She was feeling very protective of Dawn these days. But Willow had a point.

"It's no big," Buffy assured her, although it kind of really was.

Nor was Willow buying it; but they went together into the room Buffy used when she stayed at the palazzo. Willow sat on the bed while Buffy dialed the Watchers Council. She kicked off her scuffies and dangled her stocking feet over the side of the bed.

Sir Nigel answered the phone, and when Buffy asked to speak to Giles, he said, "I'll put you on speakerphone."

Buffy gritted her teeth. On the speakerphone, thereby affording them no privacy. Buffy figured he would object to the lack of it if there was a reason he needed it, so she let it go. "Giles?"

"I'm here."

"Okay. You called. What's up?" she asked.

"There's a bit of a problem in Los Angeles," Sir Nigel said offhandedly. "A rogue Slayer."

Willow stirred uneasily. Buffy cocked her head. "Rogue as in Regina?"

"Rogue as in quite mad," Sir Nigel stated flatly. "She was locked in an asylum for at least half a decade. She seems to have escaped, and she's gone on a rampage. Her name is Dana."

"Rampage?" Buffy asked. "As in . . . ?"

"Killing innocent people. Brutally," Sir Nigel said.

Willow and Buffy exchanged looks.

"Angel can find her for us," Buffy ventured, but as she spoke, she realized that that would have already occurred to Giles.

"No, we shouldn't go to Angel," Sir Nigel interrupted. "We've had some reports, Buffy. Angel's tenure at Wolfram and Hart has finally corrupted him. He's become one of their lieutenants, and we're advising you to steer clear."

Buffy blinked. "We're talking about Angel, right? Not Angelus."

"I fear . . . though he hasn't lost his soul, he is once again treading into murky territory, ethically and psychically," Giles said unhappily.

"And you . . . weren't going to mention this to me?" Buffy asked him, her voice rising.

"You've had a lot of other things to deal with," Giles reminded her. "Much as I hate to say it, Buffy, we're better off working alone."

"But . . ."

She looked at Willow, who drew her knees up under her chin. "It's pretty intense at Wolfram and Hart," Willow quietly told her. "There's evil everywhere. Hard not to pick up the vibe. I was starting to feel pretty cranky by the time I left."

"If you really think we should fetch this Dana, we should send one of our own," Sir Nigel said. "A Watcher—"

"No," Buffy insisted. She glanced around the room.

"I'll go," a voice piped up on the speakerphone. "I would love to go to L.A. For the cause, I mean."

"Andrew?" Buffy said. "You?"

"Why not me? I'm a valuable member of the team now. I was a deputy in the high desert."

Willow winced, stifling laughter.

"She's quite insane. Highly dangerous," Giles said.

"Um, okay, because I did deal with the First/Warren, you know. Not crazy, but I had a lot of alternate viewpoints to deal with. So I have some job experience for this kind of mission."

"Very well," Giles said. "Buffy, are you in agreement?"

She was a bit at a loss for a better solution. "Sure," she said.

"Really?" Andrew squealed. "Because, oh my God, I will finally get something decent to *eat*! That is to say, I accept the assignment. I won't let you down." He paused. "Shall I go pack?"

"That would be a splendid idea," Giles replied.

"It would be? Or it is?" Andrew asked.

"It is. I'm speaking . . . British," Giles said rather tiredly.

"Okay. Cool. This is Andrew, over and out, Buffy."

"Okay." Buffy smiled faintly. "Over and out, Andrew."

"*Wait.* What about my cichlid? Rupert, will you take care of Bobba Fett while I'm gone?" Andrew asked.

Sir Nigel said, "We'll assign a Slayer. . . ." Then he trailed off as if he had realized he wasn't being very swift with doling out more chores to Slayers within earshot of Buffy.

"I'll take care of it," Giles cut in. "And don't call me Rupert."

"*He.* BF is a he-*mbuna*," Andrew informed him. "Okay, packing now. Are there any messages for Angel?"

Buffy cleared her throat. "Tell him things are fine here. We're having a good time here in Rome."

She wasn't sure if Andrew knew about the prices on their heads, and she figured that was not something he should be talking about in the evil law firm of Wolfram & Hart. The people— and other things—who worked there might get ideas about cashing in.

Also, it would probably be wise to keep all their worries to themselves. W&H worked for the forces of darkness; they didn't need to know that the Slayers and the Watchers Council were in anything but great shape.

"Everything is good," she underscored. "Weather's freaky, but that's no big deal. Okay?"

"Check. And? If there are any new developments, you'll keep me in the loop, right?"

"Absolutely," Buffy assured him.

"Okay. Cheery-bye!"

There was a moment of silence. Then Giles spoke again.

"We've had more reports about Regina, Buffy. It appears that more Slayers are joining her ranks. She's making them all sorts of promises—none of which she can keep, of course. Which leads us to conclude that she's about to set some plan in motion. She'll use them to her own ends, and then, when it's over, she won't need them anymore."

"We believe she plans to move against you head-on, and soon," Sir Nigel said. "We want you to be prepared."

"Okay. On it," Buffy replied tersely.

"That's all for now," Giles said. "Any word from Xander?"

"No." She didn't want to talk about what Willow had told her in front of Sir Nigel, and that pissed her off all over again. "Has Faith checked in?"

"No." It had been four days since they'd heard from her.

"You guys have any recon data on her and the others?" Buffy asked him.

"All indications point to increased activity in and around the Hellmouth," Sir Nigel informed her, without a trace of emotion. "Still, one would expect a phone call from one of the key players."

"News flash, Sir Nigel? They're not down there *playing*. And another thing? It's really hard to punch in those pesky long-distance numbers when you're fighting for your life."

Sir Nigel vaulted onto his high horse. "Buffy, really, sarcasm—"

"Is highly warranted," Giles interrupted. "Buffy," he said, "we'll let you know the moment we hear something."

"Thank you, Giles. So much," Buffy replied.

They disconnected. She rubbed her forehead and said to Willow, "Wanna play anywhere but Cleveland?"

"Yeah. I'm in Sunnydale, with the First," Willow said firmly. She swallowed and said resolutely, "They're okay, and you really shouldn't even think of going there anymore."

"Really kind of have to, Will," Buffy said. "All the time."

"I know. These are the times when I wish I had some magicks to make it all better." Willow slid off the bed and stepped back into her slippers. "I'm hungry. Let's go to the kitchen and steal biscotti. We need to stay fed and as relaxed as possible, and biscotti works on both levels."

Wise Willow. "You got it."

They left Buffy's room and started down the hall, when Mr. Aram came rushing toward them. His face was chalk-white, and he was trembling. The Immortal followed close behind, his face clouded.

"Your Majesty," he said. Then he faltered. He turned to the Immortal as if for support.

The Immortal moved around him and put his arms on Buffy's shoulders. "It's your sister."

"Oh, my God, what?" Buffy said as Willow grabbed her hand.

"I found her on the floor," Mr. Aram said. "Unconscious."

"She appears to be in a coma," the Immortal filled in. His voice was steady, but his eyes were hooded, anxious. "We think it's magickal in nature."

"What?" Buffy could barely make sense out of what they were saying. "She . . . *what*?"

The Immortal took her arm, saying, "She's been rushed to the palazzo infirmary."

Buffy broke into a run. The Immortal kept pace. Willow scooted up to walk abreast of them as they hurried through a maze of corridors into a room similar to the one where the sorcerers convened to do their noon ritual. It reminded Buffy of Pompeii with its bright marble columns, its friezes of gods and goddesses, and its drapes of white linen and people in togas surrounding a large bed, in which Dawn lay.

A pure white wool blanket had been pulled up to her chin. Her skin was like alabaster. She was like one of the figures in the Garden of Fugitives. Mr. Bey stood guard beside her. When he saw Buffy and the Immortal, he swallowed hard, but said nothing. His concern for Dawn was evident in his features, in the pain in his eyes.

"Dawn," Buffy murmured, kneeling beside her. She took Dawn's hands in hers, rubbing them, warming them. Dawn didn't move, didn't blink. "Can you hear me?"

Buffy began to panic. It was too much like finding her mother.

She forgot how to breathe. Her sister. Her little sister . . . someone had done this. Someone had attacked her, hurt her. . . .

I can't. I can't see this. I can't stand this.

Willow squeezed her shoulder. And then Buffy remembered who she was: Joyce Summers's daughter. Dawn's big sister. She didn't have the luxury of panic.

"Who did this?" she choked out. She glared at the Immortal. "You said no one could hurt her if she stayed in your palace. That your wards would stop any threat."

He nodded seriously. "I stand by those words. Mr. Aram," he said, as the man wiped his eyes, "tell me again what happened. Did you take her somewhere? Did she leave the compound at any time?"

"No, *Signore*," Mr. Aram said firmly. "We were playing pool. And watching MTV. We had root beer and, how you say, Cheez Doodles. She wanted Cheetos. I left to get them and when I came back, she was on the floor."

"Were there signs of a struggle? Did she eat anything poisonous?" Buffy demanded. "What are you doing for her? Do you even have real doctors?"

At a signal from Mr. Aram, a man in scrubs, standing across the room with a chart in his hand, crossed to Buffy. He bobbed his head and said, "Your Maj . . . *Signorina* Summers. I am Alfredo Costa, senior physician in the employ of His Excellency. I assure you that I am a fully licensed medical doctor."

"At the Immortal's request, I am putting together a full team of Oriental Medicine doctors, homeopaths, psychic healers, sorcerers, and magicians from all over the world. We have already begun researching her case, and we will not rest until we have a full diagnosis and have embarked on a cure."

"Thank you," she said feelingly.

The Immortal stepped forward. "In addition, revered religious leaders with whom I am in contact have already begun to pray for her. And for you."

"You ask them to look into the weather?" she snapped. "That working out?"

"Buffy," Willow murmured.

The Immortal took her rebuke in stride. He said to Mr. Aram, "Have all the sorcerers convene for a healing ritual in one hour."

He turned to Buffy. "We'll find out what's wrong with her, and we'll cure her. I swear this to you."

She silently nodded, too upset to speak further. Then the Immortal drew her into his arms and held her. Behind her, Willow said, "I'll start researching."

"Thank you," Buffy said, as she pulled out of the Immortal's embrace, her gaze never wavering from Dawn's face.

I died for you. I'll do it again, if it will save you.

Numb, Willow watched the sorcerers' ritual from the balcony. It was strangely beautiful; the robed sorcerers performed a sort of dance to drumming and ethereal flute music. Antonio Borgia was among them—he had not been fired, because Buffy suggested that now was not the time to create enemies. The Immortal had complimented Willow's friend on her political astuteness, and Antonio had settled down. He had stopped stalking her. Now, during the ritual, he gazed up sadly at Willow, performing the intricate motions of the sorcerer's dance, and she wondered if she and Buffy had misjudged him.

She didn't like him much, either.

Then his supermodel girlfriend Ornella joined her on the balcony. She gave Willow a bouquet of baby roses and a covered ceramic pot. Willow opened the lid. It was minestrone.

Ornella looked shy and embarrassed and murmured, "This is an old family recipe. My *nona* swore by it."

Despite efforts to contain the information, news of Dawn's illness spread throughout the palazzo. Little Belle was distraught, and Buffy invited her to sit with her at Dawn's bedside.

Two hours later, Giles arrived via Sir Nigel's private jet. He had brought a crate of arcana and books, which he presented to Willow. She was grateful for the chance to help.

"I'll get to work," she told him, then began to break down. He held her, but she waved him away, saying, "Go to Buffy. She needs you."

Giles raced to the infirmary.

Out of breath, he stood for a moment on the threshold, collecting himself, and observing the hustle and bustle of so many different sorts of healers. The Roman temple style of the room made sense, when one considered the Immortal's origins. Passing through the room of white columns and stark linen draperies, men in turbans conferred with one another as a woman sat at a small table and gazed into a crystal ball. Standard medical diagnostic machines were mingled with the more arcane equipment of several different magickal traditions: baskets of runes, a lacquer cylinder of joss sticks, and three heaps of animal bones. The thrum of activity in the room was enough to wake the dead.

But it did not wake Dawn. She lay still and pale, looking not so much like a living, breathing girl as an effigy. Her sister sat beside her bed, wiping tears as they fell. Buffy was wan and looked rather fragile. He remembered her just before the battle of Sunnydale, when she had rallied her troops. How frightened she had been, her face puffy from the beatings the First had inflicted on her through its incarnations, her lips swollen and bloody. And yet, she had molded those girls into Slayers. Ever time she had been hit, she had come back swinging harder.

It was the lot of the Slayer.

I'm so sorry, he told her silently. *I had so hoped it would be over for you. Or at least easier.*

Then she turned and saw him. Her lips parted; she half-rose. And he saw in her face a flicker of hope, and perhaps a little relief. Quentin Travers had once said that Giles felt a father's love for his Slayer, and he had been right.

"Buffy," he said as he put his arms around her. He said gently into her ear, "Everyone is doing everything they possibly can."

She nodded to indicate that she had heard him. Then, against his chest, she said hoarsely, "It's like she's made of stone or something." She pulled herself away from him, turned, and grabbed up Dawn's hand and closed it in her fist. "Please, Dawn, *please* answer me!"

"The fairy tale of Sleeping Beauty is based on mystical fact," Giles murmured. "Snow White as well." He blinked. "Mystical poisonings, psychic comas . . . I understand Cordelia is still in a coma in Los Angeles."

"Yes, they're looking into all that. . . ." Buffy trailed off. Her heart thudded arthymically in her chest. "I keep wondering why the Immortal's magicks didn't prevent it, if he's in league with my enemies."

Giles took off his glasses and wiped his forehead. He had a wretched headache. "It wouldn't seem to make sense, would it? He's been quite generous with funds and living accommodations. Unless this has all been a long, drawn-out plan on his part to isolate you, then cause you harm. But there have been innumerable opportunities for him to act before now."

"I don't know whom to trust," she said wretchedly. She flashed him a guilty look. "I don't like the Watchers Council, Giles."

"Nor do I. I'm not sure I'll be going back to London, once we've resolved this crisis."

"Rome is nice," she told him. She started to cry again, then shook her head and took a deep, steadying breath. "Tell me what to do."

He gestured to Dawn. "Talk to her. It's my understanding that people in comas are often quite aware of their surroundings. Your voice would be a comfort, I'm sure."

Buffy nodded and sat back down. She picked up Dawn's hand and said sweetly, "Dawnie? I love you. I'm here."

Giles swallowed down his emotion as he stood behind Buffy, his hand on her shoulder.

But in his heart, he vowed, *I will kill whoever did this. I'm capable of it, and I'll do it.*

In her room, Willow looked up from the books. Her eyes were blurry; her back hurt. She was getting nowhere.

She wound through the palazzo to the two-story, five-sided room, standing on the mosaic heart of the god Hermes as she tried to recall the steps of the sorcerer's dance.

"Oh, Goddess," she wept as she sank to her knees. "Hecate, Queen of Witches, I implore you, save Dawn. Restore her to health. Oh . . . Dawnie."

She lowered her head and cried. Dawn was the closest thing she had to a daughter in this world. She had already lost Tara; she couldn't bear to lose another beloved woman. She couldn't. She just couldn't.

"Tara," she whispered. "Tara, appear to me. I am so lost . . . oh please, I need someone right now. I need *you*. It's Dawnie. Our Dawn. Oh Goddess, Tara, what will I do if she . . . everything is falling apart. We're in trouble."

She buried her face in her hands. The sobs came hard, wracking her body.

In the magick chamber, sighs whispered among the columns. The vines on the walls stirred as if they longed to climb down and hold the bereft woman.

Willow's sobs mingled with the sibilant, sympathetic magicks. Her agony rebounded off the mosaic floor, the overhanging balcony.

She stretched onto the floor, lying prostrate, begging the Goddess, "Please, oh please."

But evil answered, and struck her down. Willow sank into a poisoned stupor.

CHAPTER THIRTEEN

Avoiding danger is no safer in the long run than outright exposure.
The fearful are caught as often as the bold.
—Helen Keller

CLEVELAND
THE HELLMOUTH

Lisa Peterson's phone started ringing, and she jerked so hard, the half-frozen hot dog on the end of her fork dislodged and fell to the filth-encrusted floor.

She shouted an expletive and grabbed the phone. She couldn't imagine who was calling, couldn't fathom what they would want. But the phone hadn't rung in weeks, and each time she had dialed a number—for her parents in Florida, for her sister in Oregon, for 911—an electronic voice had informed her that there was no service at this time.

As far as she knew, she was the sole inhabitant of the West Huron Street Arms, once a low-rent apartment building, now her temporary hideout. Every night, when darkness fell, she scrambled into a new building and lay in the dark, her heart thundering, wondering if tonight they would find her and kill her.

Just as they—monsters from nightmares, demons from horror movies—had killed all the others.

Have they been looking for me? she wondered anxiously as she listened to the phone ring. *Is this a trap?*

Part of her was terrified to answer it. But another part thought, *It would almost be nice if it was them.*

And if they found me.

And if it was finally all over.

But there was that spark of self-preservation, that part of whatever she was at her deepest human level that wanted to stay alive. That part wanted to struggle on, even if it meant living like a wild animal, afraid of every shadow that moved. Lying in the dark and listening to someone screaming for help, then stop screaming.

Sometimes the sounds of the killing were more than she could stand. Then she would cover her ears and—

"Hello?" she said as she put the phone to her ear.

"Heus ut meus lacuna. Permissum vestri substantia adeo mihi."

Her eyes narrowed. She said, "What?"

The voice went on, speaking in a foreign language that was somehow soothing, somehow what she needed to hear. She kept listening. And listening.

After a time, the voice made sense to her. The words filled her mind. They said:

Go outside. Go down to the Hellmouth. Go inside the crater. Look for a shining blue orb. Retrieve it. Call me back when you have it. You will know the number. Call it.

The voice repeated the same words over and over, like a taped message. Maybe it *was* a taped message.

She moved through the dark. Her boot came down on the lost hot dog, squishing it. It felt like stepping on a rodent.

I shouldn't go outside, she thought, but the words of the caller were louder than her own words. Part of her was screaming at her to *stop! Stop now!*

But the rest of her crossed the pitch-black room and fumbled for the door.

She found the knob and turned it. The door wouldn't open. She remembered that she had turned the dead bolt. She clicked it back.

She opened the door and stepped into the hall.

The corridor reeked of the dead.

She trudged past pockets of terrible odors—the familiar stench of decomposition. Something squeaked and skittered away into the darkness.

She paid it no heed.

She was on the twelfth floor. The elevator was to the left. The stairs were to the right.

She took the stairs.

Her boots clanged on the metal. No one came to investigate. She kept descending, even though her quads began to ache. Sweat formed on her forehead, even though the air was frigid.

She reached the bottom floor of the building. She walked forward.

The front entry door had been ripped off its hinges. It had not been like that when she had crept into the building just before sundown.

She walked outside. The sidewalk gleamed with snow, which reflected the moonlight.

Across the street, a building was burning. Part of her longed to move closer to the warmth.

The rest of her listened to the voice in her head, which told her to keep walking straight down the street.

Her breath was puffs of steam; her body shivered violently. Her hand still held the cell phone to her ear, even though the speaker had disconnected.

She walked like a zombie.

Dead woman walking.

IN THE BORGIA HELL DIMENSION

"Antonio, Ornella, I have wonderful news," Lucrezia said to the couple, who spoke directly to her through the magick mirror. "The signs and portents indicate that the grand battle is close at hand. Victory is all but assured."

And if you believe that, you will believe that my father was the most chaste and unambitious of all the Popes who ever sat on the throne of Peter. . . .

Antonio wasn't on the same page, exactly. She could see it in his eyes. But the Slayer beside him was.

For now, that was enough.

"What shall we do?" Ornella asked excitedly.

Cesare slipped his arm through Lucezia's as he answered: "Continue to gather Slayers to your cause, lovely 'Regina.' Antonio, we have new magicks for you, which will keep you from harm when it comes time to make your play against the Immortal."

"You mean, when we attack the Immortal with my army," Ornella said, her eyes shining. She gripped Antonio's arm as she leaned close to the mirror.

"*Sì*, that is precisely what I mean," Lucrezia replied.

Antonio nodded thoughtfully. "We need more magick users on our side."

Lucrezia grinned at him. "We have made valuable contacts in your dimension, thanks to the technology you've given us." She tapped her cell phone. "They're responding to our call to arms. So many wish the Slayer ill. And now, Dawn Summers lies in a magickal coma, and her sister is already mourning her as one dead."

"A pity," Ornella murmured. "She is so pretty." Then she burst into a flurry of giggles. "This is so thrilling, *Madonna* Lucrezia! I never dreamed I would be a queen."

"It is thrilling." Cesare strode up beside Lucrezia and put his arm around her. "Soon you will rule Rome, children. It will be our greatest happiness."

"And you?" Antonio asked tentatively. "What will you do?"

"Ah." Lucrezia sighed. "In the vast libraries of the Immortal, and with his staff of sorcerers, it would be wonderful if one day you could find a way to bring us to your dimension. But if not . . . remember, we have a *vendetta* with him. Though we have lived in this dimension for centuries, we are still Romans, with hot blood and hearts that demand vengeance."

"Defeating him through you will satisfy our honor. That would be sufficient."

"Of course," Antonio murmured. He looked at his watch. "I must return to the palazzo. The Immortal has scheduled another healing ceremony." He inhaled slowly. "It's nerve-racking being there. I wish he had fired me. It would make it easier to escape detection."

"But he didn't. We have warded your mind, and those of all who toil in secret for our side. We work with what we have, *sì*?" Lucrezia reminded him.

Ornella smiled at her and kissed Antonio's cheek. *"Sì,"* she said pleasantly.

After the two had left, Janus, Shri-Urth, and E'o entered the throne room, which had been repaired. The Legion of Three had stabilized their physical manifestations so that they were the approximate height of the two Borgia vampires. Yet they retained the original forms in which they had first appeared to the vampires.

"Antonio and Ornella suspect nothing," Cesare said to Janus.

"Their stupidity astonishes me," Janus answered, and Lucrezia sighed wistfully.

"If we had another Borgia, we would use him. Or her. But Antonio is it."

Shri-Urth glided forwarded. "So my curse has worked. The Slayer's sister is dying."

"I salute you," Lucrezia replied. "We knew nothing of her life as a ball of energy, a key for the hellgod Glory to use to enter this dimension. It's fascinating."

"As a result, Dawn Summers the mortal is tied to this earth in mystical ways not even the Immortal can understand," Shri-Urth told her. "As god of an underworld, it is a simple matter for me to bring infection and pestilence to her. Now that we have a place from which to operate, I'll spread plague and disease over the world, until there are so few humans left, they won't be able to defend themselves."

E'o's eyes drifted toward the surface of her face as she said, "Vampires, you promised to find a means to allow us to enter their world with ease and to stay there as long as we wished. When will you accomplish it?"

"We are nearly there," Cesare told her.

Her brother's smile did not falter, but after all their centuries together, Lucrezia knew when he was upset. Now was one of those times. She shared his unease. These three hellgods planned to take over their home dimension. There would be no Borgia on the Immortal's throne. There would be no Borgias anywhere on Earth.

The forces of evil were raging against the forces of good—the Slayers—and they would have revenge for the destruction of the Sunnydale Hellmouth. They would not rest until mankind was wiped from the face of the planet.

We had such simple dreams. We would have been happy with Rome. Now we ourselves have been invaded. They are promising to extend our territory in return for our cooperation, but we really have no guarantees.

Perhaps if we throw our lot in with Buffy . . .

Too late for that. This is the thread of our fate now. We have woven our cloth too tightly to untangle ourselves now.

"The plan is this, then," Janus said. "Antonio and Ornella will weaken the forces of Buffy Summers and the Immortal by engaging them in battle. Once each side has decimated the other, we will come through, wipe up, and take over."

"Yes," Shri-Urth said. "That is the plan."

Janus was quite proud of his speech. His English had improved immensely. He wondered if E'o had noticed. And if she liked it. Now and then he detected a flicker of interest. He had been quite the lover back in ancient Greece. These past few centuries, not so much.

"We are the Legion of Three," E'o proclaimed. "We declare war here and now on every man, woman, and child unfortunate enough to live."

"Let the Games begin!" Janus shouted. His voice shook the columns of the room.

"Indeed," Lucrezia said, morphing into her vampire face. She grabbed Cesare's hand. He squeezed hers. They stood together smiling.

And trembling.

"Meanwhile, I have learned why they sent Xander Harris to Africa," E'o announced. "The secret of the Slayer's power lies in a cave guarded by Watchers and a Slayer."

"How do you know that?" Lucrezia blurted, astonished.

"Others have heard of our successes," E'o told them proudly. "Alliances are forming among leaders of hell dimensions, who in the past would have rather suffered eternal torment than cooperate with one another."

"But that was before Buffy destroyed the Sunnydale Hellmouth. Now, they are happy to provide information and support to the Legion of Three."

"Your power and influence are to be envied," Cesare said carefully.

"But not to be coveted, vampire," Janus boomed. "You cannot hope to challenge us. You know that, don't you? Work for us, and we will reward you with vast territories to rule over. Go against us, and you will plead for the true death."

Cesare waved a hand. "We are Borgias, my lord. Pragmatic. We will aid you. Be assured of our loyalty."

Janus snorted. "There is no such thing."

Cesare thought, *I couldn't have said that better myself.*

CLEVELAND

The battle against the Turok-Han in the graveyard lasted all night. Faith and Robin fought side by side, two halves of a well-oiled killing machine. She lunged, he staked; she stabbed, he beheaded. It was a macabre ballet, overseen by stars and a moon that cared not at all that demons and Slayers were dying.

When the sun came up, the Turok-Han that were still alive burst into flame and exploded. It was an emotional moment of déjà vu. Panting, staggering, Faith thought of Sunnydale and bowed her head for a moment, remembering the fallen. Including her old smoking buddy, Spike.

Kennedy, Vi, and Rona made it through the battle of the Turok-Han. Charmante didn't. Three others did—Sally, Brianna, and someone, was it Kim?—and they silently buried the dead. Faith was chagrined to realize that she didn't know the names of the others who had died. There were so many now, cycling through.

They had looked to Faith for words. She had a few, but she wasn't sure she believed them.

"There are other, better places," she said. "And that's where Slayers go when they die in battle."

Then Rona picked up a clod of dirt and snow and crumbled it in her hand. Vi did the same. They sprinkled it over the earth. Kennedy whispered, "We'll see you again."

Now, days later, Faith stared down from the church window at the sad little mounds buried under snow. Robin was still in bed. He was retrying all the cell phones that had belonged to the deceased. They weren't even going near the "Aladdin" phone, as they were calling the possessed one. They had buried it in snow as well.

"Still blocked," he said, putting it on the nightstand.

All the phones in town were blocked. All the computers. No one could call in, and no one could call out. They were cut off from Buffy and Giles both.

Faith knew it wasn't an accident. Things were heating up. The forces of darkness were putting on the pressure. What was gonna happen when things really blew?

"Come here," Robin said, and Faith did. Though she was dressed in a black turtleneck and black leather pants, she was cold. Robin was warm.

He kissed her; she kissed back. Her passion rose. . . .

And then he said, "I know you're scared. I am too."

She stiffened in his arms and pulled slightly away. "I'm a Slayer. I don't do fear."

"Yes. We all do fear, even Slayers," he replied.

She smirked. "Maybe Blondie. Maybe those guys. Not me."

He wrapped his hand around the small of her back. "Faith, don't try to bs me. My mama was a Slayer. I know the drill."

"Then you know I have to keep it together," she shot back. "Those girls . . . they look at my face to see how things are going. Like I'm an airline pilot, you know? I walk through the cabin, say, 'No sweat. It's just a little turbulence,' they breathe easier. I say, 'I don't know how to fly this thing,' they'll panic."

Just then there was a knock on the door. Robin pulled the covers up to his chin as Faith crossed to the door.

It was Rona. "We're ready to patrol," she said.

"We'll be right there," Faith replied.

They assembled in the foyer of the church, where the little fonts for holy water were dry, and the Slayers had added a hell of a lot of crucifixes. Faith glanced at a framed picture of Saint Jude, patron saint of lost causes, and thought, *Little help here?*

Kennedy came down the stairs with a satchel over her chest. It was full of stakes and a few assorted weapons they had boosted from nearby stores. All the businesses were shut down. Cleveland was a ghost town.

Except, now and then, they found people to save, or people they wished they could have saved, so . . . patrol.

Faith said, "Let's move out."

She went out first, raising her hand and looking up and down the street. The others waited for her signal. She gave it, and they emerged from the church.

"Damn, it's cold," Rona muttered.

They were about three blocks from the church when Faith heard the roar of motorcycles.

"What the hell?" Robin said, shading his hand and straining to see.

Kennedy, Rona, and the others turned in the direction of the sound. One of them—Denise?—moved up for a closer look.

A dozen or more demons on motorcycles roared around the corner. They looked like lizards and they wore full biker gear: leather vests and pants and boots.

And they had guns.

"Get back to base!" Faith shouted.

Denise put her hands to her mouth and started to cry. It happened: Slayer fought Turok-Han and lived; fought way too many regular vampires against too few Slayers and lived; fought an overwhelming number of demons and won . . . and then, she could couldn't fight anymore.

"Pull it together, Slayer!" Kennedy shouted at her, jerking on her arm.

The demon in the lead started shooting. The Slayer beside Denise jerked hard and collapsed to the pavement. Kennedy ran forward and grabbed her up.

"Move it!" Faith shouted.

Another shot rang out. A barrage of them. Vi screamed and grabbed her arm.

The demons roared up; the closest one began swinging a chain over its head; and even though Faith hurtled herself like a rocket at Denise, she was too slow. The demon's chain whipped around Denise's neck and yanked her off her feet.

As Faith hit the pavement, Denise was dragged just out of reach. By the time Faith got to her feet, the demon had roared all the way up the street. He got off his bike and stomped on her, and Faith prayed for her death.

The bikes each hung a U and roared back toward Faith and the others. From their vest, they pulled bottles lit with burning rags and aimed them at Faith's group.

"Molotov cocktails," Robin shouted. "Move it!"

Rather than lead the demons to the church, he and Faith herded the others back into the graveyard, to the brick wall behind it. Faith leaped to the top and gave Robin a hand up; then together they gestured for the others to jump up too.

One, two, three . . . the motorcycle demons raced into the graveyard, kicking up huge piles of dust caused by the destruction of the Turok-Han. The girls raced for the wall, Vi, Rona, and Kennedy herding the others as if they were on a cattle drive. Each took a hand of another Slayer and half-ran, half-dragged them along.

Rona was up first. Faith shouted at her, "Go on!" as she and Robin helped each Slayer scale the wall.

They rained down onto the other side like paratroopers leaping from a plane. The combined weight of eight people broke through a weakness in the earth, and everybody screamed as they plummeted into the darkness.

Faith and Robin jumped in after them.

Faith's heels hit concrete and splashed in shallow standing water. Her jacket elbow scraped cinderblock. It was a tunnel. Amazingly enough, a dim electric light flickered in a caged sconce, revealing the way forward.

Faith shouted, "Move it!" as she glanced anxiously over her shoulder. She didn't know if Chain Guy and his posse were on their way after them, but there was no reason to linger and find out.

The boots of the Slayers clattered on the cement and kicked up the stale water as she harried them along, pushing them hard, threatening them with what the demon had done to Denise. *You don't hurry up, they could do that to you.*

But maybe that wasn't the way to go. The girls' eyes were

glazed; they lurched forward almost mindless with fear, reminding Faith more of calves in a slaughterhouse than proud Amazon warriors. Time was never on her side. Except for Vi, Rona, and Kennedy, no one lasted down here long enough to get battle-hardened, just shell-shocked. A few training sessions in London and they were on their way down here.

Once they got here, they died.

We never have enough Slayers. We're always outnumbered. The Hellmouth just keeps spewing out demons. And it's getting worse.

But with the cessation of communications, it could be that there would be no more reinforcements. For all she knew, Buffy and Giles had given the Cleveland contingent up for dead—and decided the Cleveland Hellmouth wasn't a high priority item.

Buffy wouldn't do that, Faith thought as she stopped to give Rona a hand up. Rona had tried and had fallen hard. *We suffered and died to close Sunnydale. Cleveland's got to be shut down too.*

"Up! Up!" she shouted.

Rona scrabbled to her feet, gave her a nod, and grabbed hold of Sally, propelling her along. Brianna and the Slayer whose name Faith couldn't remember kept up, knees pumping, mouths clenched with exertion.

They kept running, running; there was a fork up ahead, and Robin, slightly ahead of her, looked at her and yelled, "Which way?"

"Left!" she said, not because she had any thought that left was the way to go, but because she was the leader and someone had to decide.

So everyone forked left, and left again, and after a long way of going straight, Faith told them to go right.

And that was a huge mistake.

Because the hole in the wall that she thought was an entrance into another part of the service tunnel was actually an entrance into an enormous cavern, about a hundred feet above a floor of fire, smoke, and steam.

She tumbled through first, and fell approximately twenty feet, landing on a two-foot-wide outcropping of rock. Before she could shout a warning, the others plummeted down after her. Vi almost overshot, but Faith grabbed her by the wrist and dragged her backward, accidentally slamming her back against the rock wall.

Soon everybody was grouped on the little overhang, and no one looked happy to be there. Vi was bleeding; others were white-faced and shaken.

Below, flames shot from a pit that fell away into blackness. Above, the space above them was clotted with smoke and steam. It was like being inside a volcano . . . or so Faith assumed, never having actually been in one. But it was hot and steamy, the way hell was *supposed* to be. The Hellmouth back in Sunnydale had been kind of a letdown in that respect.

There were demons everywhere, and monsters that weren't demons but also weren't things you found in zoos. It was like a Who's Who of the bad: Another Lindwurm wafted through the billowy steam; six trolls waddled around like they were looking for something to kill, eat, or both; there was even a quartet of Malaysian vampires, the kind that hopped. A Sirtharth Demon, which was tall and brown and looked pretty much like a crazed dead evergreen tree, lumbered away from the jaws of the Hellmouth, tentacles undulating from beneath its base.

More demons climbed out of a fissure spewing a noxious-looking gas the color of fresh blood. Vampires in full bat-face came next. She mentally urged them to move on toward a ruined section of the cavern, where there would still be some daylight to make them explode. She assumed she was seeing the opposite side of the collapsed section of the Hellmouth that she and the others had faced that first day when the streets had melted . . . and Slayers had died horribly.

So far, no one seemed to have noticed the group of human beings as they clung to the outcropping.

The noise in the Hellmouth cavern was deafening: monsters roaring, demonic weaponry and armor clanking. Bad guys everywhere, shouting. Evil beings were often very noisy. It was all a big power thing with them—like the way smokers who had something to prove often lit up in places where it was illegal.

Like Faith herself used to do.

Faith glanced back up at the hole as the last of the Slayers popped out onto the overhang. *Grace. Her name is Grace.*

"Looks like the biker demons aren't coming. I'm thinking we should go back in and take that other fork," Faith said loudly in Robin's ear. "It's safer than wading into this. I'll go first, to make sure it's safe."

He nodded. "You got it," he yelled back. Then he bent down and made a handhold for her. She was positioning her boot over his palm when Vi tugged on her jacket with a bloody hand and pointed across the cavern.

What the hell?

Directly across from them a lone girl, who looked about sixteen, was painstakingly making her way up the rock face. Her jeans and jacket had been half-torn off her body; her purple hair was matted, and she was filthy and covered with blood. She appeared dazed, looking straight ahead as she stumbled over piles of rubble and large boulders that had fallen on top of one another. The rocks were canted upward, so that she was ascending them like a staircase that led nowhere that Faith could see. She was using her right hand to guide herself along. In her left, cradled against her chest, a small blue sphere shimmered and glowed.

She moved like a robot, completely oblivious to the enormous blue demon mooking around in the rubble about fifty feet below her. It had just caught sight of her; with a roar that sounded a lot like *"Fe, fi, fo, fum, I'm so wicked hungry!"* it began clamboring up the side of the cavern, wielding a thick, nail-studded club over its head.

"Hey!" Faith cried, cupping her hands around her mouth. "Look out!"

Vi joined in, then Rona and Kennedy, and they all began yelling at the girl at the top of their lungs.

Which—naturally—attracted the attention of the demons coming out of the fissure.

Dozens of demon heads lifted in the direction of the shouting.

Dozens of demon mouths roared. Weapons flashed. Fangs glistened.

And all the other monsters headed for Faith and Company with fury in their eyes.

Faith turned to Kennedy and Robin. "Get the Slayers out of here," she ordered her, gesturing to the hole.

Kennedy nodded, and Robin yelled, "Okay! Let's move it! Back the way we came! Vi, you with me?"

"Hell, yes," Vi said, nodding.

"Good. You tell me if you need my help."

"I will," Vi promised.

Satisfied that the Slayers would be safe, Faith turned back, visually tracing a path from where she stood to the girl with the glowball. To her left there was another outcropping about ten feet away—an easy broad jump for a Slayer. Faith was about to go for it when Kennedy tapped her shoulder.

"Let me get her," she said, her dark eyes large and serious. There were bruises and cuts along her hairline. Kennedy had seen a lot of action. "The Slayers will do better if you lead them back."

"She's right," Robin concurred. "Let her do it, Faith."

Faith nodded. "Okay. Go!"

Kennedy scooted around her and ran to the very edge of the ledge. Then she squatted low and pushed forward off her heels, swinging her arms forward to give herself some momentum.

She flew through the air and landed well, got her balance, and straightened. She didn't look over her shoulder to see how her sister Slayers and Robin were faring; that was no longer her mission. The strange girl on the other side of the cavern was.

The blue demon was gaining on the girl; Kennedy propelled herself forward, finding handholds and toeholds as she raced along the cavern wall. "Hey!" she shouted. "Behind you!"

The girl kept trudging forward.

Then the demon vaulted into the air, as if it had jumped on a catapult. It landed just a couple of feet behind its quarry; it brought its club down hard as Kennedy cried, "No! Move!"

The club missed her, shattering a boulder beside her left ankle instead. The pieces of stone rolled under the demon's feet, like marbles; it lost traction, stumbled, and fell. It rolled sideways, its large bulk impeding its recovery to a standing position.

But Kennedy knew the demon would eventually get back up. It was only a matter of time before it got to the girl, who had no reaction to the attempt on her life. It was clear that she was under some kind of spell.

Kennedy scrabbled on, losing purchase more times than she could count, straining to close the distance as she made her way around the circumference of the cavern. Her hands were bleeding. She didn't care. She was making good headway; and she might actually save the girl's life. Moving as fast as a gazelle was a rush; saving a life was even better.

God, it feels good to be this strong. But I have to go faster. I have to.

Last rock, last dip, she had a clear path toward the girl. Kennedy waved her hand, urging her to step out of the way because she didn't want to lose any of her momentum. But the girl's eyes remained glazed and unfocused. The small sphere was shimmering an iridescent blue—and was she on a *phone*? Sure enough, the girl had just pulled a cell phone from her jeans pocket, and was placing it against her ear.

Won't work down here, Kennedy thought, but that was not the issue at hand.

She tucked in her head and raced for her as fast as she could, just as the demon regained its footing and charged her from behind. The girl kept walking. Kennedy kept going. So did the demon.

God, what if we squash her?

She tried to come up with a strategy for her two objectives: get the girl, kill the demon—whichever way it worked best. All she could come up with was what she did next: She shot out a fist and hit the girl full in the face, then pushed her to the dirt as her knees buckled. Next, Kennedy performed a low squat, hopped over her inert body, and slammed both her heels into the demon's eyes.

It bellowed in agony, dropping its club and cupping its hands over the sockets. Green demon blood streamed down its face.

Screaming with rage, it staggered left, right—and Kennedy grabbed its arm, giving it a hefty swing and sending it shooting out into space, toward the floor of the cavern.

"Got you," she said to the limp, purple-haired chick as she scooped her up in her arms. Her face was so bloody, it was difficult to make out her features, but her eyes were definitely closed. And her chest was definitely moving. So, still alive.

Kennedy turned to check her most likely exit—the hole she'd dropped out of, on the other side of the cavern. The Slayers and Robin were gone, but the cavern ledge was crawling with demons, some of whom turned and saw her. They bolted for the outcropping to the left, hooting and shouting. Some of them were so mentally deficient that they simply stepped onto thin air, just like Coyote in a *Roadrunner* cartoon.

Others, however, knew how to jump; they reached the ledge and began racing the obstacle course to reach her.

To her right, demons rushed up the rocky incline the same way Big Blue had come. She looked around, down, up.

No way out but through.

She said to the girl, "Sorry. I'm going to have to put you down because I have to fight these guys. But I'm going to try my best to get you out of here."

Still carrying her, she jogged backward as fast as she could, searching for the most protected area to lay her down. Then something smacked against the back of her head. She jerked her head; then saw that it was a piece of nylon rope, the end of which was looped around itself repeatedly, creating a thick ball.

She looked up. The rope swayed as if someone was trying to get her attention. She grabbed hold and gave it a quick jerk.

It moved lower.

Kennedy hoisted the woman over her shoulder firefighter-style. Then she hopped onto the ball with both feet at the same time. She hoped that whoever had hold of the other end of the rope had taken the total amount of weight into account when they'd jury-rigged this escape.

If it is an escape. For all I know, it's those biker demons, going fishing. . . .

Just as the rope began to rise, the first wave of demons to her right reached her; one grabbed her ankle. Kennedy took her other foot off the ball and brought her heel down hard on the demon's fingers. It roared and let go of her. Another lunged for her; she bent her legs backward, then swung them forward, knocking his arm out of the way.

Suddenly she was hoisted faster, and soon she was rising very swiftly . . . into thick smoke.

What happened?

She looked down, to see that the smoke was rising from the fissure and the cavern was rapidly filling with it. She took a deep breath and shut her eyes. It was bad, but she had been through bad before.

Then it was worse. She began to gag. It took everything in her not to cough; she knew she wouldn't be able to stop herself from inhaling. The pressure in her chest was getting worse . . . and worse. . . .

The weight of the unconscious girl was lifted from her; she kept her eyes shut and coughed deep in her throat, clenching her jaw shut. Just a few more seconds and she would either be home free or home fried. . . .

Hands gripped her and yanked her up and out of the smoke, laying her on the ground. She coughed hard; someone draped a wet cloth over her face.

As soon as she had pulled herself together, she wiped her nose with the cloth and let someone help her up to her feet. It was Faith. Her boss looked winded, but otherwise okay.

"Where is she?" Kennedy asked, panting. "Where's the girl?"

Faith ticked her head to the left. Kennedy looked past her. Then she saw.

She was lying on the ground, and Robin was giving her CPR. The snow beneath her was stained with red. Vi and Rona were on the ground beside him, watching him, Rona's hands on the girl's chest. Vi's arm was in a sling.

"Okay now, compress," Robin told Rona. She placed her hands on the girl's torso and pushed downward.

"C'mon, c'mon," Rona muttered.

"You got it done," Faith said to Kennedy. She moved her head in the direction of the girl. "No matter what happens now, your part was good."

"I know," Kennedy replied. "It's just . . . God, Faith, she was on the *phone*. What the hell was going on in her head?"

Faith moved beside Robin and started rummaging through the girl's pockets. "We may have more phone evil," she said to him.

"Compress," he said to Vi, then frowned as he processed what Faith had said. "Phone evil as in possessed phones?"

"Not sure. No phone now," Faith reported. "She must have dropped it."

"But we have this," Vi announced, showing Kennedy the glowing blue sphere, which she had cupped in her good hand. "Did the phone turn into a crystal ball?"

Kennedy stared at it. She said, "No. She had that in her other hand. What is it?"

"No idea," Faith muttered. "Not sure if we should hang on to it either. It might be possessed, like the other cell phone that those things went into. In fact"—she held out her hand—"I'll take it, Vi. If anybody gets, like, radioactive from holding it, it should be me."

"Actually? Rather you stuck around, Faith," Kennedy murmured, holding out her hand for the sphere. "So would the others, I bet."

"Hey, you got some clout around her, girlfriend," Faith said, putting both hands around the globe. "You trained the Potentials for the big battle, saved a few butts."

Yeah, and called Chloe a maggot . . . and then she hung herself. . . . The First took the credit, but I so do not want to be the leader if something happens to Faith.

"I'll keep it," Faith insisted.

"You're the boss," Kennedy replied, aiming for casual, but something in her tone caught Faith's attention.

Watching the efforts to resuscitate the girl, Kennedy's mind ranged back in time to the last time she had seen Willow. *Be well, my girl,* she thought anxiously. *Be safe.*

"Let's call it," Robin said sadly, jerking Kennedy back to the moment.

As she watched in silence, he took the wet towel she had been given, and draped it over the girl's face.

The other Slayers shifted in dazed defeat. Someone began to cry.

He looked up at Kennedy and said, "It's not your fault."

Her heart thudded dully. She hurt all over. She was frozen.

"I know," she said again as a single teardrop slid down her cheek, hot as a brand.

CHAPTER FOURTEEN

Empty-handed I entered
the world
Barefoot I leave it.
My coming, my going—
Two simple happenings
That got entangled.
—Kozan Ichikyo

AFRICA
THE CAVE OF THE SHADOW MEN

Okay, thinking that the Shadow Men are evil, Xander thought as Senaya charged past him at them. *Or that La Primitiva just really doesn't like them.*

But as he watched, she lowered her spear and rammed it into a demon that was bursting from the sand beneath Xander's feet. It was a hideous thing, mottled chocolately-brown, rot-green, and gray. Its face was elongated, and two bone-colored tusks jutted from its lower lip.

Senaya took another step forward and jammed the spear in deeper. The creature started bellowing, grabbing the spear with taloned hands, and then exploded. Not as tidily as when a vampire dusted, however: This guy really just exploded.

She jerked the spear out of the rib cage and stabbed it into the ground, eww, to clean it off. Then she shouted something Xander couldn't understand, but what he guessed was, *Look the hell out!* and he darted sideways.

Another demon burst through the sand, lunging at him. This one was just as ugly as its cousin, and Senaya dispatched it just as easily. Then she turned her spear upside down and began rhythmically stabbing the sandy floor with it. Jab, jab, jab, *wooohah*! An underground explosion signaled that she'd stabbed another rot-monster. She grabbed Xander's hand and dragged him behind herself as she continued to stab the ground. Explosions kept happening, lifting Xander off his feet. It was like running through a minefield.

She pulled him down a steep incline. They raced into some kind of chamber; there he saw the three Shadow Men, grouped in a tight circle. Each one was holding one of the famous sticks. They looked less than thrilled to see him . . . or maybe they were having a bad day. One of them had a red turbanish hat; and one had a black headgarb, kind of like a bandanna; and the third's porridge was just right . . . plus he had a sort of brownish-plaid hat that was the most stylish of the three.

Senaya flung Xander toward the three men. He stumbled and rolled across the sand. A hand shot up from the ground and glommed on to his left ankle. He shrieked. The black-bandanna Shadow Man lifted his stick up with both hands and drove it down, hard.

Wooohah! Another sand zombie exploded.

The Shadow Men circled Xander, raising and lowering their sticks. The things under the sand tried to grab them; now Senaya got into the act, stabbing anything that moved while Xander sat in the mush pot and Winken, Blinken, and Nod played Duck, Duck, Goose, circling him and circling him, vultures on parade. . . .

Xander remembered the spell sphere, which he had put back in his pocket. He took it out again, showing it to the Shadow Men as he opened it, and Buffy's voice came out again, asking them—in English—to help her loyal follower.

They circled him and circled him; he felt like he was in a 747 over Los Angeles International Airport waiting to land, only that was backward because then he would be the one going around in circles. *Ground control to Private Harris.*

They began to drone in woo-woo speak, none of which made sense; he grew dizzy and wondered if it was the content of their words or the way they were speaking that was giving him a steady dose of Sominex. Buffy had told him this part; had explained they would surround him and start to go all walkabout, except this was Africa, not Australia; and that even if they spoke in another language, he would eventually be able to understand them.

Not so far, Xander thought, growing woozier still. *Maybe that's only for Slayers . . . or for Buffy. . . .*

And then . . . magick.

He *could* understand them. Every mother's syllable.

He just didn't like what they were saying.

What you seek, cannot be had, Plaid Guy said, only not with his mouth. With his mind.

"Are you sure you know what I'm looking for?" Xander asked.

You cannot have it.

The ground kind of shifted; then another very ugly demon burst from the ground, teeth clacking at Xander until Senaya dove forward and stabbed it. It exploded with not much fanfare, and Xander blurted, "Thanks."

Senaya ranged around, spear tilted downward like someone spear fishing. The Shadow Men barely noticed as they continued to circle Xander.

Okay, I'm adaptable, Xander thought. "And what is that which I seek?" he asked aloud. "Besides the name of the guy who makes your hats? Because they are really nice."

You seek the means to stop the end of the world, Red Turban Guy replied.

"Whoa. Didn't see that coming," Xander blurted. "Actually, here to find out if you can help us with the secret of the Slayers' power, and—"

Ka-blam! And another desert demon bit the dust! Senaya

glanced fiercely at Xander, and he thought it might be her version of a smile. Hard to tell, though, really.

I just had a terrible thought. She's mostly demon. That probably means she wants me.

It is too late, Black Bandanna added.

"Why? Is she married?" Xander asked.

Because your kind will die. All of you.

As if on cue, dozens of demons burst up from the ground and flew at Xander and the Shadow Men; jaws clacked and finger bones sliced and it *hurt* and they were all over Xander, rolling with him in the sand, and then rolling him *under* the sand as they began to drag him underground. Sand poured into his mouth, his ears, and eyes. He clamped his lids and his mouth shut; but it was too little too late. He felt the sand closing over his head.

Then *bam! bam! bam!* just like Emeril in the kitchen, the demons began exploding. Xander kept his eyes closed; belatedly— and with a rush of panic—he realized that he couldn't get them open. The pressure of the sand had grown too great.

Oh God, I'm gonna die.

The pressure lessened; he was being lifted up, up . . . and then flopped over on his stomach as someone pounded on his back. He coughed hard, and then he climbed to his feet, a little wobbly.

Red Turban had two sticks in his hands; he handed one to Xander and, with the other, executed a truly amazing U-turn and stabbed a demon in the gut. The thing exploded; and as his stick was released, Red Turban jabbed it backward, penetrating another demon.

He looked over at Xander as if to say, *Got it?*

Xander did get it. His military training, acquired one magickal Halloween, was suddenly enhanced to include not only mental memories of weaponry and training, but physical ones. His body had never performed this kind of hand-to-hand combat before, but now it remembered moves Xander had never actually executed.

And he was on fire! G.I. Joe fire! It was like every little boy's soldier dream as Xander plowed through the bad guys. Senaya stood shoulder-to-shoulder with him, and she was total aggression. Her lips were pulled back; her eyes were practically shooting flames. This was one Slayer who had an entire jungle in her tank, not just one measly tiger.

And the weird thing was, it was catching. Xander started fighting like he had never fought before. He moved faster than he could think; he reacted with speed he didn't know he had. Forward, lunge, attack; forward, kick-kick-kick, thrust; forward . . . forward . . . dude, he had the quads and the triceps! He was a machine!

They were beating them back. The Shadow Men flanked him and Senaya, and they were whirling their sticks around like batons or, maybe more accurately, like lawnmower blades. It was Indiana Jones and the Cave of Exploding Evil; it was Arnold and Angelina Jolie, together again; it was Charlie's Angels and . . . hey . . .

It was the Slayers at the Sunnydale Hellmouth, and he was there, 100 percent times infinity.

Hacking and slashing, he could feel power and strength coursing through his body. He was dealing death, and it was such a frickin' rush; he was in the game, so deep and so forever, and God, he had never felt so alive in his life as when he was here, now, a *man* and a full-on participant and someone who was winning, damn it. After all the losses and the deaths and

Anya

he was winning.

And suddenly he was on his butt, and Red Turban was whacking him over the head—not too hard, and shouting in his head, *Stop!*

Panting crazily, Xander blinked at him. The merest smile flashed over the man's features.

They are all gone, the man said to Xander's brains.

Xander looked around, and nearly lost every bit of beef jerky he had devoured. There were demon body parts everywhere, slimy and green, and they were steaming. The smell was unbelievable . . . unless one had shared living space with Spike, back when he had been too depressed to shower.

"We did it," Xander said.

No, Red Turban replied.

"Ya-huh." Xander gestured. "Do you see anybody digging through the sand? I think not."

Then Senaya crabwalked toward him and put her face right up against his. When he looked into her eyes, he wasn't sure who was home. But it was not some nice girl who was gonna pack his lunch in the mornings.

It's not enough, Senaya declared in her gravely voice.

Plaid Guy stepped forward. *There is not enough good in the world to counteract the overabundance of evil. More evil entities have come forth across the dimensions to exact revenge for the Slayer's victory. They have overwhelmed the balance.*

This dimension is beginning to fall apart.

"But we'll figure out how to stop them," Xander argued. He looked at the four somber faces. "Right?" He grinned. "I got the mojo now."

There are too many, Plaid Guy insisted.

"So that's it?" Xander asked, feeling peckish. "I came all the way here and fought like a superhero to be told that there are too many?"

Black Bandanna took center stage. *The world will fall to the forces of darkness. That is foreseen.*

But it will happen faster if the Legion of Three succeeds in entering this dimension.

"You're not getting confused with the Evil Troika, are you?" he asked hopefully. "Warren, Andrew, and Jonathan? Because—"

Janus, Shri-Urth, and E'o. Hellgods.

Xander wasn't happy. "Hellgods generally more evil than evil nerds. Or rather, more effectively evil."

Ancient evil . . . and the sworn enemy of Buffy and all her followers.

"Not to worry," Xander said, worrying. "Buffy's made of tough stuff." His mouth dropped open. *I've known Buffy for almost nine years and I've never thought of saying that before. And it rhymes and everything. Thank God I thought of it before the world ended.*

The three Shadow Men glanced at one another, as if maybe they were debating on if they should say anything more. Then Plaid Guy intoned, *Sooner or later, she will die.*

"Yeah, but not anytime soon. Maybe when she's, like, a hundred and three, and she's finally graduating from college—"

Very soon, Red Turban cut in.

There is no chance, Plaid Guy said.

"Damn it! Stop saying that!" Xander yelled. "Buffy is not going to die!"

Looking puzzled, the three Shadow Men glanced at one another. Then Black Bandanna said to Xander, *We aren't speaking of Buffy. We are speaking of her sister, Dawn. She is dying.*

Xander gaped at them for a full minute before he could speak again. *"What?"*

She was the Key. She was energy, and now she has been transformed. But she is still energy. And all the energy of this time and place has been irrevocably altered. She will die.

Without another word, the three Shadow Men disappeared. Two of the three sticks disappeared. The other, he held in his hand as he stood in the Cave of the Secret and blinked at the carnage . . . and the hopelessness. . . .

Senaya hissed at him, "They . . . speak . . . truth."

"That's wrong," Xander insisted. "You're wrong."

"Dying. Now."

Her crazy, wild face flashed in negative contrast, and then she vanished.

"No!" he shouted. "No way!"

He rammed the stick down hard.

And suddenly he was in the cave no longer. He was standing in a vast, formless space where gray extended beneath him, around him, over him. It was like being inside a world of stainless steel. He had the stick, and he had himself, but the rest of the world was a flat, matte expanse of nothingness.

"Hello?" he said softly. He took a step forward. "Is anyone here?"

He turned around, and when he turned back, he wasn't certain where exactly he had been before. He took another step, and halted. With absolutely no landmarks to go by, he was completely bewildered as to where he was and where he was going.

Then, on impulse, he said, *"Je te touche."*

Something shimmered in front of him, a shape that wafted like a gossamer silver. It was about five feet tall, and he thought he saw a head, and arms . . .

It's a ghost. I know there are places between dimensions where the dead walk. They're called Ghost Roads.

Have I died?

The shape blurred forward and seemed to touch his hand, but he couldn't be sure. He didn't actually feel it. Like the words of the voiceless Shadow Men, he didn't sense the solid pressure of a touch. He experienced it indirectly.

But the shape drew back, enticing him forward. He took two steps in its direction, and it moved backward again. And again. It was leading him.

A horrible wailing shattered the silence. Xander jumped, startled. The shape wobbled backward, backward, urging him forward.

The wailing increased in volume . . . and in proximity.

It was right behind Xander.

He turned and saw a skeleton warrior riding a skeleton horse. The warrior wore a horned helmet, and black leather armor. In one bony hand it held a long, gleaming sword. In the other, it clutched the reins of its phantom mount. The horse whinnied. Fire spouted from its nostrils, and as it galloped over the gray, sparks shot from its hooves.

As the rider galloped toward Xander, another appeared behind it. And another, to its right. A fourth to its left. Three more.

Six.

Xander ran for all he was worth. The shimmering blur urged him on; he nearly heard a voice, but not quite. He somehow knew that he could trust it, and that it was trying to lead him to safety.

And what other choice did he have?

Xander felt the heat of the horse's breath at the back of his neck; smelled singed hair—his; smelled the stench of decay. He ran, wishing he could recapture his Berserker mode back in the cave. But he was just Xander, who was very tired and very scared; and who had no idea what the hell he was doing here, or anywhere, when the world was supposedly ending and his Dawnie was sick, and—

"*No!*" he cried, as the horse reared and the warrior raised up off his saddle, twisting to the right as he brought the sword in a semi-circle toward Xander's head.

"*No!*" he cried again as he parried with the stick. The skeleton's sword bounced off the stick as if it were made of iron, not wood—hell, as if it were a light saber—but his balance was thrown off, and Xander fell to the ground in a ball, covering his head.

"Xander," someone said.

He blinked, looking around. The nightmare warrior was gone. The stick was clutched in his hand. His head pounded; the throbbing grew more intense as he looked up in the direction of the voice. A shimmering, semispherical shape wobbled and bobbed like a huge bubble or a balloon smeared with Vaseline. No wait, a balloon and his eyes were smeared with Vaseline.

He was very woozy; with a trembling hand he raked his fingers through his hair, only to feel something sticky. He lowered his arm, looked; red blood—his—and green blood—demon's—coated his fingers. He wondered how badly he'd been hurt. Had he been struck, or was this an injury from the fall?

The form snapped into focus, and he caught his breath.

It was Tara. Her hair and clothes were glowing, and very white, like Gandalf; her skin had an amazing, pearlescent luster unlike anything he had ever seen before, especially on someone who was dead.

"Tara," he whispered.

"Don't be afraid," she said; and Xander had a sudden, vivid memory of the time he had gone to Sunday school with his cousin up in San Francisco. It had been near Christmas, and the nun, who had a face like a potato, had told them that, in the Bible, whenever angels appeared, the first words out of their mouths were "Fear not." And he and his cousin had decided then and there that Gabriel and Company must be really ugly, if that was what they said instead of "hello."

But Tara was beautiful.

"You're an angel," he breathed.

In the distance, another wail pierced the gray. Tara jerked, glanced in its direction, and said, "Xander, listen. There's not much time. Dawn is sick."

"I know. The boys told me," he said bitterly as he rubbed his head again. He was so dizzy. "They also told me there's no cure."

Tara shook her head. "There is. It's called the Death Orchid."

Yes! Everything that was him was happy. "Divine intervention so rocks," he told her. "Tell me how to get one."

Tara looked very earnest. "There's only one, Xander. In all the world."

"They always say that," Xander shot back. "But there's always a backup. Princess Leia, all those other Immortals on *Highlander*—"

"After the orchid is picked, then Willow must—"

A third wail rolled over the two of them. Using the stick, Xander hoisted himself to his feet and held it like a quarterstaff. He turned slowly in a circle, preparing for an attack. "Go on," he urged her. "Willow must—"

Her gaze darted past him as she scanned the area. She was not looking very relaxed.

"She has to take it to the Golden One. He can transform it. Xander, they're coming." Her voice was urgent. "I can't protect you."

She pointed, and Xander turned. With a rush of wind and a terrible wail, the skeleton warrior burst into existence again, about a hundred yards behind Xander. Only this time he had brought a lot of friends—more armed skeletons on horseback, stretching as far as Xander could see. Maybe hundreds.

He said quickly, "Keep talking. I'll do the fighting. Talk really fast."

The wind blew harder; the gray darkened to slate. Bone-glowing like moons, skeletons charged toward him. Lances appeared in their fists. And flaming swords, very Revelations.

The hooves of the skeleton horses thundered, drowning out Tara's words as she—

Disappeared? No!

"Tara?" Xander called. "You still here?"

There was no answer.

He was alone.

He said something that was not so nice, and then he took a deep breath.

The slate lowered to black, and he could see nothing.

"Xander to Tara, Xander to Tara . . . come in, Tara," he said anxiously.

If she heard him, he didn't know it.

Engulfed in darkness, Xander focused on his other senses. The noise of the approaching army was bad; the smell was worse. Then, fireballs burst like miniature explosions around him, and he saw what was coming at him: hundreds of grinning skulls on horseback; arms swinging weaponry of all kinds; banners with death's heads on them. The horses were all breathing fire, some of the skeletons were on fire; no one seemed to mind.

Horrible shrieks vomited out of them, sounds so hideous that Xander's knees buckled. He gripped the stick, wishing it were a rocket launcher; actually, wishing it were a thousand rocket launchers, manned by really beefy soldiers, or maybe angels, yeah beefy angels—

The nightmare warriors galloped toward him. Horse hooves shook the ground. The shrieks were ungodly. A trickle of sweat dotted Xander's temple. He held the stick tightly, aware that he was facing his own death.

Been here before, he told himself. *Lived through it. Can't die this time either. I have information the good guys need.*

Bargaining here, with God or anybody who'll listen. Preferably not Satan, but . . .

One of the warriors broke formation and cantered ahead of the others. Flames danced in its eye sockets—*neat trick; maybe I can do that sometime, like for a party or on a date; wanna see my eye socket start on fire?—*

Oh, my God, I'm going to die—

He gripped the stick in both his fists and held it chest-level. The warrior's eyes glinted and gleamed; its jaws clacked open and shut, open and shut, in time to the rhythm of its horse's gait.

Xander swallowed and held the stick in front of himself.

The skeleton raised its flaming sword and leaned out of its saddle, intent on hacking Xander to bits.

And Xander shouted, "No!" and ran toward it, instead of waiting like a condemned man for his executioner; he ran as fast as he could and the monster shrieked at him; its horse spewed flame at him, singeing his arm. But Xander kept running.

Then somehow the stick shifted in his grasp, as if someone

invisible were tugging on it. It raised about a foot as he held it, as if offering it to the skeleton to grasp.

The creature grinned evilly at Xander and brought the sword down.

Been here . . . Xander thought anxiously.

And then the skeleton's flaming sword hacked the stick in two.

Before Xander had a chance to react, the blackness roared and shuddered around him. Something like singing filled his head, and he was pushed away by invisible hands as the sword arced down again. The horse reared, and the warrior screamed in frustration. Flames shot from every part of its body, and rider and mount exploded.

A strange blue light filtered through Xander's surroundings, and he saw girls forming all around him, charging toward the skeletal army. He recognized one—it was Lucy Hanover, whom he had met years before. She had been a Slayer during the Civil War. There was a Chinese girl in brocade clothes; a Slayer in Victorian garb.

"Hey, baby," said a dark-skinned woman in bell-bottoms, a blouse with billowing sleeves, and an Afro. Xander stared; he had seen a picture of Robin Wood's mother: Slayer Nikki Wood.

"Hey," he managed, as they ran toward the army. "Do you . . . do you have . . ." He was having trouble talking and running at the same time. "Have you got a message you want me to take to Robin?"

"No, baby. I'm here for you," she told him. "We're gonna save your ass so you can save the world."

Hope flared inside him. "But the Shadow Men—"

"They're just men, sugar." She winked at him. "We're Slayers."

The front line of Slayers engaged the army. Swords flashed; crossbows twanged. Ghostly Slayers fell; more rushed forward to take their place. Nikki grabbed his arm and turned him to the right. He stumbled over his own feet and she righted him, dragging him along. She gave him an amused look and said, "Can't keep up?"

He didn't reply. It was obvious that he couldn't.

She ran so fast, he was almost flying like a kite behind her. He could hear the sounds of battle behind them; the clash of metal and the shrieks of the skeletons.

Ahead, a square of red light hung in the blue, jittering like a neon sign about to burn out. It was a door; and standing in front of it were two figures. One was Tara, and the other one opened her arms. . . .

"Oh, my God," Xander gasped.

It was Anya, his dear, dead Anya. She was dressed all in white; she gleamed with the same luster as Tara.

"This is a gift," Nikki Wood said to him.

She stopped and he drifted forward, as if in a dream.

Anya moved from the door and approached him. Her lips touched his. Warm, and soft. Her arms slid under his; her body pressed against him. God, she felt so good; she smelled so good; she—

—moved through him.

He whirled around.

She was gone.

"No, please," he cried out. "Anya, come back!"

All he saw was the battle; one of the Slayers—a blonde, like Buffy—turned her head and shouted, "Go through the door! We can't hold them forever!"

Tara reached her hand around a brass knob and opened the door. She beckoned him forward.

"Xander, remember the Death Orchid. And there's an orb. Faith has to get it to Buffy."

He tried to stay focused. He tried not to turn his head and search for Anya.

"Orchid. Orb." He shook his head. "What orb?"

"Faith has it. Buffy needs it." Her eyes widened as she looked past him. "It's what they want. Hurry!"

He glanced over his shoulder. The skeletons were overwhelming the Slayers, trampling them as they pushed ahead, racing straight for Xander. As the Slayers fell, more appeared to take their places—millennia of Chosen Ones, all dead, all fighting to help him save the world—

But the Shadow Men said—

"They're just men," Tara reminded him. "Remember the orb, Xander."

The door was open now; and bright white light emanated from it. Xander could see nothing as he reached the threshold.

Then Tara took his wrist, gazed at him, and kissed him. "Take that to Willow," she said. "Give it to her."

"I will," he told her.

"The Goddess be with you." Then she gestured for him to cross over.

He took a breath, took a step . . .

. . . and found himself tumbling in the chamber in the palazzo that he had left.

He looked down, to see Buffy in the chamber alone, dozing. Her eyes shot open and she jumped to her feet, shouting, "Xander!" as he fell.

She caught him and lowered him to his feet. She said, "You okay?"

He nodded; she crossed to what looked like a freezer, threw open the door, and dragged out a frozen, hairy, very ugly demon. She hefted it upward; he watched its trajectory and saw that an ellipse of white light spun like a lasso in the center of the ceiling. The frozen demon sailed into it, and immediately disappeared.

The ellipse winked out of existence.

"Whoa," Xander murmured.

Buffy smiled at him. "Welcome home."

He said, "I've got information. You need it. It's about Dawn and the end of the world. And I have to kiss Willow."

Buffy stared at him for a beat. Then she said, "All right."

• • •

When Xander and Buffy marched into the Immortal's library, Giles looked up from the stacks of books, took off his glasses, and exhaled with relief. "Thank God you're here," he said.

Xander gave him a quick grin. "Words I never thought I'd hear you say."

Giles let that pass. "Did you learn anything from the Shadow Men?"

"Can I have a glass of water?" he asked, looking around. "And maybe a chair?"

Buffy crossed and tugged on a bell rope while Giles pulled out his own chair for Xander, then got another for himself. The Immortal's library was enormous, with shelves that extended the height of the room, at least fifteen feet. Long ebony tables contrasted with black-and-white marble floors. A collection of some twenty globes of the world were scattered about the room; da Vinci sketches dotted the few spots on the walls that weren't entirely covered with books.

Mr. Aram appeared. He saw Xander and one brow raised; otherwise, he betrayed no emotion.

"Please bring Xander some water," Buffy said.

"Um, and a roast beef sandwich and some Cheez Doodles, three Sprites, and if you have any candy bars . . ." Xander amended.

"Of course." Mr. Aram inclined his head and withdrew.

"How's Dawn?" Xander asked.

Buffy's shoulders sagged. "Not good," she told him, lowering her gaze to the floor. "We can't find a cure. We can't find anything. . . . But how do you know about this? Did Senaya tell you?"

"Jumping ahead," he told her. "There's an orchid. And Tara told me about it. So, not jumping ahead." When Buffy and Giles exchanged astonished looks, he raised a hand and said, "I really did see her. It's called a Death Orchid. Also, there's a globe. No, an orb. Faith has it. You need it."

"*Tara* told you this? That's extraordinary," Giles mused. "Was she in the cave of the Shadow Men?"

"No. I got out of there and I saw her afterward. These skeleton warriors were after me and I broke one of the Shadow Men's sticks. I think it belonged to Plaid Guy. Anyway, hundreds of Slayers showed up and fought them while Robin's mom took me to the portal and Tara kissed me. Plus telling me the stuff about the orb and the orchid."

He rose. "I'll tell you more later. But right now, I have to kiss Willow for Tara."

Giles and Buffy shifted uncomfortably. Then Giles said, "You . . . don't know about Willow. Something happened while you were gone."

Xander blinked. "What? What happened to Willow?"

Buffy took his hand and held it, staring hard into his face as she said, "She's gone into a coma, too, and we can't revive her."

Xander paled. "That must be why I have to kiss her."

He rose and headed for the door. "Tell Mr. Aram to bring my food to Willow's room, okay?"

"Only, she's not in her room," Buffy said. "She's in the infirmary. With Dawn. We'll take you there."

Xander nodded as they left the library and rushed down the corridor. Xander was so exhausted, he could barely walk straight. But fresh adrenaline was pumping into his body.

"Did the Shadow Men tell you anything?" Giles asked Xander.

Xander nodded, frowning. "They said there's too much evil in the world, so the world is going to end. That all we can do is slow it down, but it is going to happen. There's something called the Legion of Three."

"The Legion of Three wouldn't be the Shadow Men, would it?" Buffy asked. "There are three Shadow Men."

"I think the Shadow Men ceased to exist, but don't quote me on that. On the Legion of Three, the Shadow Men gave me names. One of them was Janus. The other one was something like Shree Earth, and the other Io, like the moon."

Buffy smiled faintly. "Behold the knowledge."

Giles pushed up his glasses. "Janus, Shree Earth, Io. The Legion of Three. I'll get right on it."

"And they said the world was going to end. An Apocalypse," Buffy pressed.

"Tara was more optimistic, though." Xander turned to Giles. "Did you know she'd become an angel?"

"A higher being, I'd venture," he said. He was bemused.

"She looked great," Xander told him.

"The infirmary's this way," he said, steering Xander to the right.

They walked into the columned room. Xander slowed, taking in the healers, the machines . . . and the two beds surrounded by white drapes. Willow was lying to the right, and Dawn to the left.

He swept to Willow's side, took a moment to gaze down on she whose Barbies he had stolen when they were little kids, and whispered, "Okay, Sleeping Beauty, time to wake up."

He bent over and kissed her.

Nothing happened.

CHAPTER FIFTEEN

Love takes hostages.
—Neil Gaiman

Buffy walked with the Immortal in the gardens of his palazzo. Marble statues of Roman goddesses lined a walk sheltered from the cold by drooping arches of chestnut trees.

He was wearing a long black robe and a pair of boots, and he looked like one of the portraits that lined his hallways. He looked more at home in the outfit than in his regular clothes, and she remembered back to when she and Willow had bagged one of the Watcher's Journals to check out the old-timey clothes the girls of Angel's day had worn. She had been such a girl then, innocent and, well, rather superficial.

Today she felt positively ancient, perhaps as ancient as he.

"Faith has something that you need," he said slowly. "But you are unwilling to tell me what it is."

"Yes. And I need to tell her to bring it here. But I can't get through to her. All the circuits are, like, jammed."

"I'll put my staff on it," he promised. He stopped walking and turned to her, putting his hands on both her shoulders. "You should have come to me sooner with this."

She gazed steadily at him. "I do things my way." *And that's why I haven't told you about Janus, or Shree Earth, or Io. I'm still not sure enough about you.* Maybe because she was feeling a little defensive, she added, "Your staff find out anything about the Death Orchid yet?" That, she had told him about. She needed his help. If he managed to come though with useful information, she might trust him a little further.

"No," he said regretfully. "Not yet."

She said, "I'm going to sit with Dawn awhile."

"I'll walk with you."

"No." She softened her refusal with a little smile. "I need to be alone. So much is going on."

"None of it resolved," he finished for her.

"Right."

It was midnight, and Faith was caught in a nightmare. Kakistos had captured her Watcher, and he was tearing her to pieces . . . and the pieces were screams. . . .

A shrill melody pierced the agony; Faith jerked upright beside Robin as she processed—*cell phone*!

Another melody, and another . . . and she realized that all the cell phones they had lifted off dead Slayers and dead people and looted from closed stores, stored in a box beside the window—they were all ringing at once.

Robin murmured, "Oh, my God!"

The two bounded out of bed and rushed to the cell phones. Then, as they stood over the box, Robin looked at her and said, "What if this is a trap?"

"Hell, I don't know," she said, reaching out her hand and fanning it over the ringing phones, trying to decide which one to pick up. She felt like those people in movies who are about to snip the wires connected to the bomb: *red wire, blue wire? Eenie meenie . . .*

She took a breath and grabbed one.

Robin grabbed one too.

"Hello?" they said at the same time.

"Faith?" It was Buffy.

"I've got Giles," Robin announced to Faith.

"Yo, B," Faith said. "What's the what?"

"Faith, thank God," Buffy breathed. "We've been trying to reach you forever."

"Tell me about it," Faith drawled. She brushed her hair away from her face. Her hand was shaking. Robin had gone to the bed to sit back down.

"Yeah, it's been pretty grim down here," he was saying into his phone. "Yeah, the Hellmouth. It doesn't appear to be a concerted effort like Sunnydale. Just . . . chaos. They're not getting past the city limits, as far as we can tell."

"Faith," Buffy said, "do you have some kind of glowing ball?"

A huge wave of relief washed over Faith. If it had been real, it would have started at the Jersey Shore and flooded Boston Common.

"I do," she said. "I have a glowing ball."

"Okay, you need to bring it to us. Bring the Slayers in. We'll get the Hellmouth shut some other way. Do you understand? Come to Italy. We're sending the Watchers Council jet."

"How soon?" Faith asked her.

"Okay," Robin said to Giles. He looked at Faith. "Watchers Council jet is in the air, Faith. As soon as it lands, we're out of here." His eyes glittered. "All of us."

Faith closed her eyes. She thought of Saint Jude downstairs in the church lobby and thought, *Okay, so maybe you were there after all.*

As Willow's body lay in a coma, her soul struggled to be free. There was too much sorrow, too much death. She was terrified. She looked down to see utter destruction; she looked down to see the world ending.

It won't matter what we do . . . we will fail.

She flew through space and time locked in nightmare; she saw death in the faces of those she loved. She saw the end.

And then . . .

. . . the Goddess whispered, *"I have answered your prayers, Willow."*

Someone's lips touched hers.

Contact.

Connection.

Love, here, in this world; love that rooted her to the earth.

There is a perfect love; it is a force in the world. It is shared, given, received; it moves from heart to heart.

It can never die.

And it can heal.

Willow's soul flew back into her body; she no longer drifted. She dreamed. She slept.

And when she awoke, it was to find that someone was lifting her in her arms, and carrying her with great gentleness from the infirmary.

It was a tremendous effort, but Willow opened her eyes.

A most beloved one walked with her in her arms. It was not Tara, but it was someone Tara gave Willow the ability to love.

With a kiss.

"Kennedy," she whispered, clinging to her. "Are you really here?"

Kennedy didn't smile as she replied: "Giles and Buffy called us. They sent a jet and got us out." She gazed down at the witch in her arms. "I told you I would be with you, Willow. I said you wouldn't have to go through anything else alone, ever again."

"I meant it."

Willow started crying again, but these were tears of hope. Of release. The love that she shared with Tara was with her always; and

Tara had moved to a place where she knew that she was Willow's, and Willow was hers, forever.

But that love was not selfish. That love did not want Willow to be alone.

That love was multidimensional, and encompassed Kennedy.

The Slayer carried Willow to her room, and lay her down, and arranged the covers around her. Then she got up to leave, and Willow held out a hand. "Please," she breathed, "please don't go, Kennedy."

The dark-haired Slayer turned back to Willow. "I'm tired," she said gently. "I've been fighting hard in Cleveland, and there was a lot of turbulence on the flight. I'm about to drop."

Willow raised herself on her elbow. "Then sleep," she murmured, pulling back the blankets to make a space beside herself.

Kennedy hesitated, exhaling, and gazed with longing at Willow. "If I touch you, Willow . . ."

"Touch me," Willow whispered. "Kennedy, please, touch me. I've been in hell." Tears rolled down her cheeks.

Kennedy nodded.

"Me too."

When Buffy later knocked softly on Willow's door, it was Kennedy who answered. She was wearing the green bedspread, and her shoulders were bare. Buffy smiled faintly, and Kennedy positively beamed.

"How is she?" Buffy asked.

"Back in business," Kennedy replied, unable to conceal a mischievous grin.

"Do you think she's well enough to go to South America? There's something there that Dawn needs very badly. A special orchid that might cure her."

"I'm well enough," came a sleepy voice.

"Then I'll be going too," Kennedy announced.

Haley crept through the forest near the Immortal's compound. She had brought another Slayer with her. Her name was Concetta, and she was ready to meet Regina and her consort. Concetta was Italian, and she looked kind of like Kennedy, the Slayer who had arrived with Faith, some other Slayers, and a hot older man named Robin.

Haley hooted like an owl. An owl hooted back.

Stepping from the trees, Regina and her consort appeared in their fancy masks and robes. Concetta murmured, *"Madonna,"* which Haley understood was the way Italians said, "Wow."

The two Slayers approached, and knelt.

"This is Concetta," Haley announced, her head bowed.

"Welcome, lovely one." Regina drew them up to their feet and embraced them both.

"Mille grazie," Concetta said fervently.

"My wonderful subjects," she said. "Our magicks have revealed that our enemies are going to South America. There is an orchid there that they seek, and they must not have it."

"Then they won't," Haley replied fervently. "Tell us what to do."

"My good and faithful servant," Regina said warmly. "Very well. I am sending one of you to the Amazon rain forest. You will have a very important mission."

"I'll go," Haley said proudly. "Tell me what it is."

Regina touched Haley's cheek with cold fingers. *"Brava,* Haley," she said. "I knew I could count on you. *Bene,* you must kill Willow, the false queen's witch, before she can harvest the Death Orchid."

Kill Willow? Haley had not been prepared for that. Willow was very powerful. Also, she had been very kind to her. After she had sent Xander through the portal, and the fierce demon had come through, the four Slayers and Buffy had fought it. Haley had been wounded, and Willow had healed her, smiling gently and saying, "All better now."

"Well?" Regina asked, her voice rising. "Can you do that? Can you obey your Queen and trust that what she does, she does for the good of all?"

Haley raised her chin and said, "Consider it done."

"Wait," Concetta protested, knitting her brows. "Why just one of us? Why not an army?"

Regina's consort turned his masked face in her direction. "A wise question. I am impressed."

Haley flushed. She had been expected to follow Regina's orders. And not only had Concetta questioned them, she was being praised for it.

"The answer is simple," the consort replied. "There will be other Slayers on the mission. Not many, however. This is a covert operation. We want to escape detection." His masked head dipped half an inch as he spoke directly to Haley's friend. "But you are new to us, Concetta. You must prove yourself before we allow you on such an important mission."

"If you let me go, I'll prove myself," Concetta argued.

"Patience." Regina laid her hands on Concetta's shoulders. "'Tonio is right. . . ." He cleared his throat, and she trailed off. "There's plenty to do. We have a bold plan, my girls. There's wild work to be done, in my name."

"In your name," Haley said, lowering her head.

And his, she thought.

'Tonio.

IN THE BORGIA HELL DIMENSION

E'o was furious.

"You said you would kill the little keychild," she flung at Shri-Urth. "You said her death was assured."

Shri-Urth's caul hid his features; his voice was placid as he answered, "She is tied to the earth. She will sicken and die. Orchids and holy men will only postpone the inevitable. Besides, what does it matter?"

"It matters because you were wrong," E'o retorted. She looked from Shri-Urth to Janus, who was seated on Cesare Borgia's throne, one leg slung over an armrest.

Her eyes rose to the surface as Lucrezia Borgia swept into the room. The vampire queen's gaze lingered on Janus, and then she smiled at the other two members of the Legion of Three and said, "You summoned me?"

"How soon before your magicks allow us to remain in the other dimension?" Janus asked her.

"Very soon. We're preparing Antonio to wage war on Buffy and the Immortal. Once they're weakened, we'll sweep through."

"Thank you, my daughter," Janus said graciously.

Lucrezia bowed, and turned to go.

"And what if she's lying? What if she's wrong?" E'o asked hotly, indifferent to the fact that Lucrezia could hear her.

Lucrezia turned around and waited for the answer.

"Then we'll kill her," Janus replied, winking at Lucrezia as if the prospect of her death was nothing more than a big joke.

She threw back her head and said boldly, "I'm not lying, and I'm not wrong." She paused and added, "You'll need such as I when you take over their dimension. If you'd reconsider and allow Cesare and me to serve you there—"

"Never!" E'o snapped. "Be glad we'll allow you to live at all."

"Lucrezia," Janus placated, "we'll give you many dimensions to rule over. Be satisfied with that."

"As you wish." She lowered her head, turned, and—this time— left the room.

THE AMAZON RAIN FOREST

Green Hell.

That was what the rain forest was called, by people who had been in it. The nigh-impenetrable canopy of acacias, philodendrons, ferns, and bromeliads never ended; there was no solid earth, only veiny networks of streams and freshets crossing one another and crisscrossing again. Green Hell stank of rot, and the waters moved as huge snakes called anacondas and caimans, which were crocodiles, lurked beneath the surface, hungry and lethal. Jaguars and ocelots roamed at night, eager for the taste of monkey or peccary.

Poison-dart frogs, skittering down the towering acacias, exuded the same poison the indigenous people used to kill their enemies with poison darts they blew from hollow pipes.

"Maybe Sunnydale wasn't so bad after all," Kennedy said as she, Buffy, and Willow crept through the vines and dense undergrowth. Their hiking boots sloshed through the water. Their T-shirts were soaked through with sweat.

The Death Orchid lived in Green Hell. That was what Giles and the Immortal's staff of sorcerers had discovered. There was only one blossom once a century, on one tree. Willow was armed with spells to find it, and Buffy knew that if anyone could make them work, it was Willow.

Faith and Robin had wanted to accompany the band to the Amazon, but someone had to stay and protect Dawn. It had taken everything Buffy had to leave Dawn's side, but Giles was with her, and Buffy knew that if they didn't find the Death Orchid, Dawn might never wake up. That had made her decision a little clearer, if not easy.

Seemed she was always making the tough decisions.

Vi, Rona, and Belle protectively escorted Willow as the group trudged forward. They were agog at the marvels of the rain forest. *Become a Slayer, see the world.*

It was raining again; the dense canopy of leaves cloying as the Slayers brought down machetes to hack a path through the choking jungle. Layer upon layer greeted them at every turn. Doggedly the Slayers hacked the vines and tree branches; everything was so saturated with water that nothing broke cleanly; it was as if every tree, every bush, every fern were made of rubber.

Monkeys chattered and scrabbled overhead. Large pods fell like bombs. Through it all, Buffy couldn't shake the feeling that they were being watched. Whoever had cast a spell on Dawn must know about the Death Orchid. Buffy prayed they hadn't already retrieved it.

Behind Buffy, someone started swearing in German. Buffy didn't speak German, but she could tell the speaker was losing her cool. Some of the Slayers with them were young, untried. In any other circumstance, trekking through this terrible place would be too much to ask.

But Dawn was dying.

Thunder rolled. The sky broke open, and rain cascaded without warning. The Slayers cried out; the rain pelted them, hard. Some tried to take refuge beneath the *Honey, I Shrunk the Kids*–size leaves, some longer than the girls who huddled beneath them.

Great, Buffy thought. She looked at Belle, who appeared to be weary to death; like she wanted to slide down in the muck, hang her head between her legs, and cry.

But she kept going.

Buffy moved up to the little Brit and put her hand on her arm in a comforting gesture. She said, "We'll find it. Then we'll get the hell out of here."

"Buffy, I think we're near," Willow said as she waved her hands in the air and a blue glow enveloped a large tree about ten feet ahead of them. It towered above the others. Something white attached to the trunk was enveloped in a darker field of blue.

"I think that's it," the Wicca added, awe-stricken.

Buffy nodded. "I'll climb up."

Beneath the staccato of the rain, there was a strange, sibilant hiss. Slayer and Wicca jumped. Buffy took Belle's hand, then moved forward to Willow and guided them toward the undergrowth. Buffy's boot slid on a smashed mushroom, slimy and fragmented.

There was another hiss. Belle's eyes widened as her body spasmed. "Buffy, I've been hit," she slurred.

Her eyes rolled back in her head, and she sank bonelessly to the ground. She flopped backward as Buffy moved to catch her. Her eyes remained open although the oversize raindrops fell on her face, hard as stones.

"Kennedy!" Buffy shouted, covering her eyes with her palm. "Protect Willow!"

Then the forest went insane.

Shadowy figures dropped down from the trees, lurching after retreating Slayers as the girls gave in to their survival instinct to flee. One of them landed scant feet from Buffy; she stared up at it as she realized she could actually see through it, see it shifting and moving like a vibration as it disturbed its surroundings.

It looked at her.

As if moving in a strobe light, it advanced, ratchet-jerking in a steady, machinelike pace. Thunder rolled over the other Slayers' screams. She grabbed Belle under the arms and tried to move backward. She was slipping and sliding; the thing was coming for her.

Vi appeared, charging behind it, her fist around a wicked huge machete. She squatted, pushing up through her insteps, to rise into the air. She raised her hands above her head and, as she descended, brought the tip of the knife down hard into the back of the creature's neck.

It bellowed in words, in a language Buffy didn't understand. Vi followed its line of descent as it collapsed, stabbing it repeatedly, the knife making a thick sucking sound.

The trees were disgorging more of the things; Buffy felt the impact as one landed about a foot away from her.

Then something pierced her chest with a sharp sting.

The forest wobbled, green on green on green; the rain slowed until she could see each droplet, then accelerated until she could see nothing but black lines of water. The trees bent and swayed.

Then Kennedy was shaking her. A nimbus of green light crackled like ball lightning behind her.

Buffy's eyelids fluttered. There was movement everywhere, but she couldn't follow it. She squinted, gasping at what she saw: a figure, hanging from the tree, hanging by her neck, the rain plastering her hair to her head. She had no face. . . .

Twisting in the rain . . .

All around her there was terrible screaming. She saw more faceless girls; she saw blood, all around her; she was drowning in blood.

Hands were on her, dragging her through the blood; Kennedy was yelling at her, "Help me, damn you!"

A wind whipped up as Kennedy finished moving Buffy to safety, laying her beside Willow and Belle. The other two were breathing, but something was wrong with them. *Poison darts?*

Vi and Rona were still alive, still fighting.

Everyone else . . . slaughtered.

The wind became a gale, whipping huge elephant-eared leaves in her way. Vines shook at her like fists. Roots shaped like men barred her way as she tried to see, tried to figure out what to do next.

Beside her, Belle slipped and slid in the mud. Kennedy bent down to help her up.

Her feet lost purchase as she slid down an embankment. Tumbling and shouting, Kennedy soared over the edge and down, deep down, into a rush river, tumbling and brackish and whitewater fast.

She managed to take a breath before she shot below the surface.

In her mind, she carried the image of Willow.

Willow was all she saw, all she knew.

As the dead Slayers hung in the rain, Haley buried her face in her hands and sobbed. It was horrible, hideous . . . she had had no idea it would be like this. She knew some of these girls, had trained with them.

Now she had watched their slaughter by the monsters in the forest: bizarre demons that lived in the trees and could become invisible as they tore the faces off their victims. Slayers—like she herself—who had learned how to use poison dart guns and had shot Buffy and the others.

Buffy would have sent our sister Slayers to die in Cleveland, she reminded herself. *She had to be stopped.*

But what of the others, who had been so brutally slaughtered. Buffy had let Slayers leave and go home. She had never threatened anyone, never done anything like this to anyone. . . .

She fingered the vial in the pocket of her khaki pants. It was the antidote for the poison darts with which Buffy and Willow had been shot. Without the antidote, they had minutes to live. Their muscles would freeze up, and they would be unable to breathe.

Unless she acted.

If I'm caught . . . She looked up at the faceless Slayer hanging from the trees. She knew the Slayers under her command were searching for her right now.

She thought of Regina and all that she had promised: safety, and the world back the way it had been.

If this was the price for that . . .

With a shaking hand, she pulled the vial from her pants and ran to Buffy.

She knelt beside the Slayer Queen she had betrayed, parted her lips, and poured the antidote into her mouth.

LOS ANGELES

Andrew sat in his hotel room with his Watchers Council satchel on the table, munching some microwave popcorn he'd bagged from the break room at Wolfram & Hart. He was taking some downtime. *Stargate SG-1* was on; he had made contact with Angel and—

"Yes, Mr. Giles!" he cried into the phone as Giles picked up.

"You'll never guess what! Guess who's here and alive and all in one piece!"

"Dana?" Giles queried on the other end of the line.

"Dana?"

"The Slayer you were sent to retrieve?" Giles prodded.

"Oh yes, that's going very well," Andrew assured him, although whoa, crazy Slayer, very scary. "No, it's—"

And then he realized that he couldn't tell Mr. Giles that Spike was alive. Because Mr. Giles would tell Buffy. And Spike didn't want Buffy to know. He had specifically asked Andrew not to tell her. And when you've ridden the road with a man . . . who is a vampire . . . you don't spill his guts. So to speak.

Oops.

"It's Janice Burchette!" he announced, in a moment of pure genius . . . and, okay, a fib.

"I beg your pardon? Who is Janice Burchette?"

"Mr. Giles, don't you *know*? She was Nabrun Leids in *Episode IV: A New Hope.*"

"How remiss of me not to have remembered that."

"Yes. I saw her at Whole Foods. The one in Woodland Hills." Without missing a beat, he added, "How's Bobba Fett?"

"What?"

Panic rose in Andrew's voice. "My *mbuna*? You are taking care of him?"

"Your . . . fish. Is fine."

"Thank God. Oh, I've been beside myself." Andrew thought longingly of Bobba Fett, then tossed some more popcorn into his mouth.

"Listen, Andrew, we're still quite anxious about Angel's current situation. All you need to do is retrieve Dana and get out of there. If he asks questions about what everyone is up to—"

"Taken care of," Andrew assured the Watcher. "I said Willow and Kennedy are relaxing in Rio. And okay, I did mention that

Xander's in Africa, but Angel was hardly listening to me. I mean, not that he doesn't listen to me, but—"

"No need to prevaricate," Giles said. "The less said, the better."

Andrew lost track for a moment as, on the TV screen, Col. O'Neill took a tumble into what appeared to be the ruins of some kind of ritual chamber.

"I missed something," he murmured.

". . . We're not happy that he's working through Wolfram and Hart, and—"

"Right," Andrew said, frowning at the screen, trying to remember if there had been mention of a ritual chamber earlier in the show. Or maybe on the commercials. It was sort of left field.

"We're sending some backup Slayers to you. Just collect Dana and get out of there, good?"

"Sure, Mr. Giles," Andrew said. "I am on the mission."

"God help us all."

"What?" Now there was a shadow on the wall of the ritual chamber. It looked very sinister. . . .

"Andrew, call me back when you've more to report. Aside from sightings of starlets."

"I will," Andrew promised. *Except I won't be mentioning Spike. I honor the code of the Brotherhood of . . . Us.*

Giles hung up.

Andrew turned up the volume and settled back with his popcorn. "Look out," he told Col. O'Neill. "Something's going to get you."

THE AMAZON

Lying in mud, Buffy awoke with a start. Her head pounded, and water dribbled off the tall, overhanging leaves above her.

She looked over to see Haley the Vampire Slayer with Belle's head in her lap. She was pouring something into Belle's mouth.

"Where . . . how did you get here?" she asked fuzzily.

"Buffy?" Willow murmured. She lay on the other side of Buffy; she was rubbing her face and trying to get up. Buffy looked back at Haley. Belle moaned as Haley helped her to a sitting position.

"Are we back in Italy?" Belle asked. "You weren't with us on the trek."

It became clear at once: Haley was on the other side. The attacking side.

"What did you make us drink?" Buffy demanded, jumping to her feet as she looked up at the tree. The blue glow was gone.

But the Death Orchid was still there. She could see the white blossom.

Haley jumped anxiously away, crying, "An antidote, I swear! Please, Buffy, get the orchid. Quickly! They're looking for you. You only have a few minutes before they figure out what I've done. In fact . . ." She looked over her shoulder and screamed.

Three Slayers not of Buffy's party were headed toward them. One was tall and dark; the other two were small and blond, like sisters.

"Willow!" she shouted. "Hold them!"

Willow spread open her arms and recited something familiar in Latin as Haley ducked behind her. The three Slayers attacked, but a force field stood between them and Buffy's party. They pushed against it, pounding as the magick barrier rippled.

"Haley, you are dead!" one of them shouted. "When we tell Regina what you've done—"

Buffy raced toward the tree, finding a machete in the mud and grabbing it up. She hacked and slashed like a banshee as Willow yelled, "Hurry, Buffy, I can't last. I'm still weak."

Buffy reached the foot of the tree. She craned her neck and stared at the white Death Orchid, so very far away. She was dizzy and weak.

That didn't matter.

She grabbed a hanging vine and hacked it free. Then she yanked off her hiking boots and socks and tied the vine around her ankles. She grabbed onto two low-lying branches, and hopped onto the trunk. She inched her feet upward.

So far, so good. But she was terribly dizzy.

"Belle!" Willow shouted. "Where are you going?"

The Slayer wondered briefly what was going on. Then she filled her mind with thoughts of her sister.

And then she hauled.

Coming back . . . coming back . . . Kennedy spewed river water. Choking, she coughed hard, then pushed up on her knees.

Belle the Vampire Slayer flung herself around Kennedy and cried, "You're alive!"

Kennedy was sprawled on a riverbank, and she smelled awful. The little Slayer embracing her was sopping wet. "You fished me out," she guessed, as Belle nodded. "How did you know where to find me?"

"I don't know," Belle said. "I just did. But we have to get back to Buffy. Right now. She's retrieving the Death Orchid, and Willow's magick barrier is weakening and . . ."

"Okay," Kennedy said.

But they were met en route by Buffy and company. Buffy had a big white flower in her hand and she shouted, "Back to camp! Now!"

Kennedy ran all the way through the jungle, back to camp. She helped Willow, who was unsteady. They were shrouded by Willow's magicks as the treacherous Slayers and their accompanying demons searched for them.

Buffy signaled the pilot of the two seaplanes that had brought them in. Vi, Rona, Kennedy, Belle, Buffy, Willow, and Haley got in the plane and took off for Rio, where the Watchers Council's jet was waiting for them. Willow held the precious orchid in the special case that Giles had created for it with the help of the Immortal's magicians.

The evil Slayers were left behind, still searching for them. They were left in the rain forest to fend for themselves.

Once they were in the air, Haley confessed all: about Regina, and the spheres, and Concetta . . . and all of it.

"Let's just throw her overboard," Kennedy growled. Haley looked terrified.

"Please, I'm so sorry! I . . . I thought it was Buffy's fault that we were dying. Cleveland . . . I didn't want to go there." Her eyes welled.

"Save it," Buffy said coldly. "Tell us more about Regina and this consort of hers."

"I told you all I know. I never saw their faces. I only met them in the forest." She choked back a sob. "Please don't kill me."

"You have to give us something more," Buffy persisted.

"I . . ." She hesitated, her eyes widening as something dawned on her.

"What?" Belle asked. "Tell Buffy everything, Haley."

"She called him something." She thought a moment. "'Tonio. She called him 'Tonio."

"Short for Antonio," Willow supplied. "Could it be Antonio Borgia, Buffy?"

Buffy narrowed her eyes. "I never liked him."

CHAPTER SIXTEEN

O nobly-born, that which is called death hath now come. Thou art departing from this world, but thou art not the only one; [death] cometh to all. Do not cling, in fondness and weakness, to this life. Even though thou clingest out of weakness, thou hast not the power to remain here.
—Tibetan Book of the Dead

TİBET

Seated on a simple thatched mat on a dais, the Golden One smiled at Willow as she dipped her head to the stone floor of the plain, unadorned temple and opened the case containing the Death Orchid.

"You have done well, young witch," he said.

"Thank you, Great Master," Willow replied humbly.

He wasn't really golden, although he was dressed in a golden robe and wearing a small pillbox-style hat of gold cloth. He was a very old, very wise sorcerer, and he had agreed to help Willow cure Dawn. Kennedy and Belle sat a little ways behind her. Vi and Rona had returned to Italy with Buffy, to deal with the expected confrontation. A quick phone call to the Immortal had revealed that Antonio Borgia had not been seen for days. His fashion model girlfriend, Ornella, had disappeared as well. They had searched his villa, discovering a chamber beneath it that had recently been filled with concrete, just like the Initiative complex so very long ago, when Buffy had been with Riley.

The Immortal's sorcerers searched for the fugitives, with no success. Willow wondered if his magicks were all that powerful if he couldn't manage to locate a former employee and his girlfriend. Her own magicks had failed as well, but her mind was on other things.

The orchid, and Dawn.

Giles reported that there was no change in Dawn's condition. Although she was no better, at least she hadn't gotten any worse.

"I will begin to work on this," the Golden One told Willow as he reached for the box. She rose and handed it up to him. His smile was beatific, and Willow felt renewed simply by being in his presence. "You should rest, you and your comrades. I'll need you later," he added as she began to protest. "We have prepared rooms for you. I'll have you guarded. You'll be safe."

He clapped his hands. A gong sounded. After a few seconds, the door in the back of the temple opened. Willow turned around to look; from their places on the floor, Belle and Kennedy looked as well.

A lone figure stood backlit in the doorway.

Willow caught her breath. Though she could not make out his features, she knew in a second who it was. "Oz," she murmured.

His eyes widened as he strode forward into the temple, bowing low to the Golden One, keeping his gaze on Willow. The sorcerer smiled and said, "You know each other?"

"Old . . . friends," Willow told him, rushing toward Oz.

"Then I'll leave you to catch up." The old man rose from his haunches and left the room. Oz bowed. Willow followed suit.

"Oz!" Willow cried.

He moved to hug her, then stopped, taking in the two other women, and said, "Um, hi."

Belle held out her hand. "How do you do? My name is Belle the Vampire Slayer," she said proudly.

"I'm Oz," Oz replied, shaking hands with her. He said to

Willow, "We heard about the power-sharing thing. That's pretty intense."

"Yeah, we did it." Her cheeks warmed as she flushed with pride. "Kennedy and I."

"Hey, nice work," Oz said to Kennedy.

"Thanks." She stuck out her hand. Oz took it, and they shook. Then Kennedy said to Belle, "We should leave these guys alone." At Willow's glance, she added, "It's okay, Willow. I know you have a lot to talk about." She sounded a little shaken, but kept a smile in place.

"Some of the guys are waiting to take you to your rooms," Oz said to Kennedy.

"Thanks. I'm beat," Kennedy said; to Willow, "We'll bed down. You two visit."

"Thanks," Willow said feelingly.

"But who is he?" Belle asked sotto voce as the two walked away.

"I'll explain," Kennedy replied.

They left by the back door, Kennedy shutting it behind them both.

"Oz, your hair is red. Like mine," Willow said. Then she melted into his arms and leaned her head against his shoulder. He held her for a long time. She sniffled a little, overtaxed with exhaustion and emotion.

He reached into his jeans pocket and handed her a little square of red cloth.

"Is this a handkerchief?" she asked him, unfolding it.

He gave her a patented Oz grin. "It is now."

"What are you doing here?" she asked, wiping her nose.

"We live here. We guard the Golden One and his monks in exchange for room and board."

"We?"

"Bunch of guys. Like me."

"Werewolves?"

"Yeah. There's ten of us. We're a pretty tight pack." He smiled faintly. "Remember how I was working on controlling my wolf side? The Golden One's helped with that. We still change, but we stay in control. It's quite a breakthrough."

"That's great!" she cried, giving him an impulsive hug. "I'm so happy for you, Oz."

"Thanks."

"Who do you guard him from?" she asked.

He shrugged. "At first it was just local demons out to make a name for themselves. But the Golden One has been warning us that something big is on the way. Says it's not just for his own sake that he has to live. Since he's good, he's needed in the world to counter-balance the evil."

"That jibes with what we heard from Xander."

"Xander. How is he?"

"One-eyed," she said sadly. "Bad guys."

"That's awful," Oz said.

"Yes. It is. But he's doing pretty good. He just got back from Africa."

He took her hand and led her outside. They walked down a path and over a river, on a wooden bridge that led to a small island clustered with wooden huts.

"We live here," he said. "I go down into the village every few weeks. They have an Internet connection." He grinned at her. "I have lots of downloaded music. You've heard of Ghost of the Robot? Awesome group. Seem to have disbanded, though."

She smiled fondly and said, "Can we go in your hut and talk?"

"Is that okay with your girlfriend?" He paused. "What happened to Tara?"

Willow looked stricken. "I have to tell you something. Someone killed Tara and, um, I went evil and tried to destroy the world." She pursed her lips and raised her brows. "I thought you should know."

"Do that often?" he asked.

"Just the once."

He smiled. "I used to do it once a month."

"You didn't go evil. Just wolfy."

"Thanks," he said softly.

"Xander saw Tara in Africa. Like a vision."

"Sorry it wasn't you?" he asked.

"I saw her when I gave all the Potentials their power. It was incredible."

Then he stopped before a hut painted with white stars and a full yellow moon, and pulled down a black metal latch. It swung open, and Oz gestured for Willow to step inside.

It was plain, but homey: what looked to be a futon bed on a wooden pallet; a brazier, in which coals were glowing, warming the hut. A bookcase of adobelike bricks and boards lined one wall. *A Treasury of Lycanthropy* abutted *The Ten-Minute Manager.*

On the wall beside the bookcase hung several framed photographs: Oz playing with Dingoes Ate My Baby; Oz with Xander, Willow, and Buffy. Then three of Willow alone—two smiling, one very pensive.

To the left of the photographs, positioned just above an acoustic guitar, an amazing pencil sketch had been carefully matted and framed. It was an incredible likeness of her, and she thought to herself, *Wow, I look so . . . beautiful.*

Oz walked up beside her. "I'd like to take credit for that, but Angel drew it."

She bobbed her head. "But you framed it."

"I did." He gestured toward it. "Museum quality. Acid-free matting. I hauled it up here in a really big backpack."

"I'm guessing there's no Mrs. Oz Werewolf," she murmured.

"No. But I'm okay with that." A beat, and then, "What about you?"

"No Mrs. Willow Witch, but I'm good too." She crossed to his bed and sat cross-legged on it. "Let's catch up. Tell me what your life is like."

"It's really good, Willow." He sat across from her. "Never thought I'd end up in Tibet guarding a holy man. Life takes some twists and turns."

"Tell me how you got here," she said.

They talked all night, strolling outside beneath a crescent moon. Willow felt at peace for the first time in a long time. She was still worried about Dawn, and Regina, and the Legion of Three, but it was as if she were in some sort of protective bubble, kind of like the force field she had erected between Buffy's group and the bad Slayers—whom they had left in the rain forest. Buffy hadn't known what else to do with them.

Willow thought back to the shapeshifters in the desert. Buffy had had so much trouble killing them; she had to be convinced that they were inhuman. She had the same problem with Regina's Slayers, even though, as Buffy, she, and the others had walked away, one of them had shouted, "Our queen will rescue us and we will slaughter all of you!"

A few days passed. The moon would be up soon; Oz and his guys would do the wolf thing. Kennedy slept with Willow, and it was good. Belle had her own hut, but she was smitten with one of Oz's werewolves, a young Thai man named Somtow.

The Golden One announced that he had distilled the essence of the Death Orchid into a potion. He suggested that Willow try astral-projecting Dawn to Tibet so that he and Willow could administer it to her without having to transport the unconscious girl from Rome.

"I myself cannot do it," he informed her. "You and she are intimates, but I carry no part of her in my soul. You do."

Willow performed rites and rituals, both in her own tradition and those of the Golden One. She enlisted Belle and Kennedy, teaching them how to breathe, and to visualize and connect. She toiled long hours; and on the night before the full moon, she begged Hecate for success.

But Willow failed. She said to Oz, "Something's surrounding her, preventing my magicks from succeeding."

She consulted with the Immortal's sorcerers, and the next day they gleaned the answer: The protective barriers they had erected around Dawn to keep out bad magicks were acting as a magickal dampening field for long-distance magicks of any kind.

"You'll have to bring the potion to Rome," Giles concluded. "There appears to be no other way."

Willow discussed the situation with the Golden One, and he asked to meet with her and Oz. Kennedy was edgy about being excluded, but said nothing as Willow left her side.

They met in the afternoon of the night of the full moon. In a few hours, Oz and his guys would transform into werewolves. In his golden robe and his pillbox hat, the Golden One sat on his dais, legs crossed one over the other like a Buddha. Oz and Willow sat below him on the simple mat, legs tucked underneath them.

Werewolf and witch bowed low. The Golden One bowed back. It was a mutual gesture of respect . . . and affection, for Willow had grown to care for the brilliant old sorcerer.

Each sipped tea brought by a monk in a saffron robe. Then the Golden One got down to business.

He said, "A single Death Orchid provides essence for only one dose of restorative potion. Another Dead Orchid will not be ready for harvesting for one hundred years."

"So if Willow tries to take the potion to Rome and something happens . . . ," Oz said, trailing off. He looked at Willow. "Two Slayers aren't enough protection."

The Golden One nodded. Then he said, "But we are presented with a dilemma, my young friends. As you have already learned, there is not enough good in this dimension to keep it from falling to the forces of evil. Therefore, we must protect any person or entity who represents a repository of good."

Oz got it. He said, "We can't afford to lose you."

The sorcerer dipped his head. "Although I have no fear of death, and would gladly give my life to save Buffy's sister, we cannot afford the luxury of the destruction of more good."

"It would be a catastrophe," Willow said.

The Golden One continued. "I believe we should request more Slayers, to accompany the potion to the Rome. Oz and his men must remain here to guard me."

"Time is of the essence," Willow said. "Can we afford to wait for other Slayers to get here?"

"We must," the Golden One said. "The effects of the imbalance are already affecting this dimension."

"The weather. The flood and earthquakes," Willow filled in.

"Yes, and it will continue to get worse until this dimension becomes uninhabitable for humans," the Golden One said. He gestured to the temple walls. "Places where good is especially strong will serve as sanctuaries for a time, but then the evil in the world will overcome them as well."

The Golden One closed his eyes and said, "Once a certain degree of disharmony is reached, the fabric of our reality will begin to deteriorate rapidly, unless a solution to the problem is found."

"Hope is a good thing," Willow said.

His smile was almost lazy as he opened his eyes and beamed at her. "Hope is a good thing." He looked first at Oz, and then at Willow. "Do you agree with this decision?"

They both nodded. Willow said, "I need to contact Buffy and tell her to send some Slayers. The Watchers Council has a private jet. They can probably fly them here."

"I'll take you into the village tomorrow so you can use the Net connect," Oz said. "We don't have time now. It's late."

The meeting over, Oz and Willow walked back to Willow's

hut. Kennedy and Belle were inside, playing Chinese checkers.

"Hey," Oz said, poking in his head as Willow went into the small enclosure.

"I'm winning," Belle announced merrily as Kennedy grinned at her.

"You're winning *now*. You lost the first three games."

Oz smiled fondly, then shut the door behind himself.

Willow explained the situation to the girls, and both brightened at the prospect not only of the arrival of more Slayers, but of finally having a mission.

"I'll go into the village with Oz tomorrow," Willow concluded.

The sky lowered. The moon came out, and the wolves began to howl. Belle left, and Kennedy went with her.

Willow put on her wine-colored fleece pajamas and crawled into bed. She pulled the thick natural-fabric duvet over herself and closed her eyes. *I'll miss Oz,* she thought as she drifted off to sleep.

She was awakened by a loud crash. Bolting upright, she heard a horrible roar, followed by another. The dirt floor was breaking up; the entire hut was rocking. "Belle! Kennedy!" she cried, pushing open the door.

She dashed outside, to find the two Slayers racing ahead in the moonlight. Though she was unable to match their pace, she followed, huffing and wheezing in her bare feet through the snow.

As she crested the small rise before the row of huts, towering piles of ash filled the space where the Golden One's temple had stood. Several outbuildings were blazing like infernos.

"Wha-what?" she asked, confused, pushing back her hair as something hairy and large flashed past her. A werewolf. "Oz!" she cried. She waved her arms at the Slayers. "Belle! Kennedy!"

She stumbled toward the towers of ash. A werewolf bounded into a haystack-shape of smoldering embers, then took off yelping, smoke rising from his singed hide.

More hairy shapes raced past her. She looked around for the Golden One, or his monks; for Belle or Kennedy.

From the opposite direction, Belle darted toward her, the moon bathing her in moonlight. She had on a long T-shirt and a pair of leggings, and socks.

The ground behind Willow rumbled; hot breath wafted against her hip as a wounded werewolf cantered past her. Blood poured from the creature's gut; then it began to morph into the young man Belle had been hanging out with.

As his features became clear, Belle started screaming, "Somtow! Oh, my God!" and dropped to her knees in a panic, throwing her arms around him.

At the same time, Kennedy burst out of one of the outbuildings. Her nightgown flapped around her knees, and the hem was sooty and spotted with blood.

She saw Willow and Belle and dashed toward them. She held a golden flask in her hand topped with a jeweled stopper.

"Let's get the hell out of here!" she cried, grabbing Willow's wrist. "I've got the potion."

Willow hesitated. "What about the Golden One?"

"Dead. All his monks, too." Kennedy looked at Belle, who was sobbing hard. "Get up, Slayer. *Now.*"

"But he's . . . he's—"

"We have to go," Kennedy insisted, her voice gentler.

Wiping her face with the back of her hand, Belle gently laid her head on top of Somtow's. Kennedy gave her a hand up. Then she and Kennedy each took one of Willow's wrists and they hustled her away from the massive funeral pyre.

Snow tumbled from the sky.

The ground roared like a raging creature, and a fissure erupted to Belle's left, throwing the three to the snowy ground.

Another crack burst open, and Willow cried out as Kennedy began to fall in. She got to her knees and yanked on Kennedy's wrists;

in a flash, Belle dropped beside her and caught hold, pulling as well.

They hoisted Kennedy up and out of danger, and as the earth shook again, the three cautiously rose.

"What's happening?" Belle asked.

"It's the disharmony from the Golden One's death!" Willow yelled, clutching the flask to her chest. "We have to get this to Buffy right away."

As they turned to run, werewolves dashed toward them. Willow counted eight. The lead werewolf loped up to her and put his muzzle against her outstretched hand.

"Oz?" she said.

The wolf's eyes glittered at her. He lowered his muzzle, raised it again. The other werewolves grouped up behind him, as if awaiting his commands.

Pursued by explosions as the cracks burst open, humans and werewolves ran into the night.

ROME

Mission accomplished.

Willow, Kennedy, and Oz stood together on the stone steps overlooking the training field, proud that they had managed to bring the elixir to Dawn. The Golden One's death weighed heavily on Oz and the seven werewolves who had accompanied him, but they had agreed as a pack to offer their services to Buffy.

They moved into some of the tents on the same plain where many of the Slayers were housed. Generators and magicks warmed the tents and the caves, and everyone settled in. There was a lot of flirting, some hooking up.

Belle mourned for Somtow, and slowly moved on.

Now Dawn smiled at Buffy as Mr. Aram and Mr. Bey walked her up and down the Slayer's training field. A magician led the way, invoking the ancient gods of medicine to strengthen and heal the Queen's sister.

Andrew and a retinue of Slayers had returned with Dana, who was so damaged emotionally, no one was sure if she would be able to make the road back. Andrew didn't share many details of the adventure, preferring to appear mysterious. Buffy started to ask him about Angel, but Andrew held up a cautioning hand and said, "These are things that the Slayer of the Vampyres need not concern herself with."

"He's quite right," Giles told Buffy. "Which I realize is astonishing, yet there it is."

I told Angel myself that I need time, Buffy thought sadly.

And now, weeks later, she wondered if that still held true.

"Are you ready?" the Immortal asked Buffy. He was dressed like a stylish Italian man ready to go out for the evening. Which was what he was.

Buffy nodded. Dawn had finally persuaded her big sister to take the Immortal up on his invitation to go dancing.

With the help of his sorcerers, the Immortal had managed to shift the weather in Rome, protecting not only the tents and the caves but the Eternal City within a magickal bubble. It would last perhaps a few days at most, but it had vastly improved the Slayers' morale . . . and Buffy's, too, she had to admit.

But nothing on earth could have made her happier than seeing her sister making so much progress after having nearly died a few months before.

It was a sweet moment, an interlude. Then everything came crashing down. The bubble burst, literally.

Mount Vesuvius erupted. Lava shot into the air, devouring a heavy snow and rushing; the world was fire and ice as thousands, then hundreds of thousands, fled Rome, and then Italy.

Global earthquakes spared none of the continents; whole cities fell into huge cracks in the earth. Governments demanded answers; scientists fumbled, unable to explain what was happening.

"It's gone past global warming," one noted British meterologist said during an interview on TV. His eyes were enormous behind his glasses. "It's as if the core of the earth is superheating. No, that's not it either. It's . . . cataclysmic."

Hurricanes whipped seacoasts; monsoons drenched Asia. Snow blanketed every continent, heralding a new ice age.

"Is it Cleveland?" Faith asked Giles, Robin standing beside her. They all were meeting in the Immortal's library—some habits never die. Buffy lounged in the doorway with her arms crossed, feeling antsy and impatient. "Because if it is, we can go back there."

"No, you can't," Giles told her, pushing up his glasses. "It's too dangerous."

Faith smirked at him. "Excuse me? Slayer here. Nothing is too dangerous."

"That's your pride talking, not your common sense," Giles snapped.

"Don't have a lot of common sense," Faith replied, not at all insulted. "Tell him, Robin." She shifted her weight as Robin remained silent. "Look, we're Slayers. We're going stir-crazy. It's not our way to stand around picking our butt . . . noses while the world goes to hell."

"Nevertheless," Giles replied.

Buffy uncrossed her arms and left the room. She had heard enough. She agreed with Faith, but what were they supposed to do?

She checked in on Dawn, who was asleep. In the magick chamber, the Immortal's magicians were dancing a spell, Willow among them. Kennedy and Oz were watching.

Buffy said to Oz, "Are your guys good with sticking around?"

He nodded. "I'm going down there now, and tell them about this meeting."

"I'll go too," Kennedy said.

At that moment, Willow left the dancing magicians and came over to them. She said, "What's up?"

"Giles wants everyone to stay here. Says Cleveland is out for now."

Willow exhaled, looking relieved. She took Kennedy's hand and said, "I'm glad, to be honest."

"Me too," Kennedy replied softly. "Oz is going down to talk to the guys. I figured it might be time to check in with the Slayers down there. Want to come?"

"Sure," Willow said. "Let me get out of my robes and into something warm."

The three took their leave of Buffy. Buffy was glad for the friendship among them—old lovers finding new ways to love each other—and smiled as they walked down the hall and out of sight.

Then she took her cell phone out of her pocket and dialed a number she had rarely used. It was Wolfram & Hart in Los Angeles.

Her heart pounded as she waited for her connection.

And waited.

There was only dead air. Then her phone disconnected.

She tried again. And again.

Stymied, she stared down at her phone. Then she had an idea; she called the Italy phone directory. "Wolfram and Hart, Rome headquarters," she said.

In a second her phone rang, and she was connected. "Buffy? Buffy Summers? The Vampire Slayer?" replied a woman's deep, throaty voice. "But this is such an honor!"

"Well . . . thanks," Buffy said, a bit taken aback. "I have a request. I can't seem to get through to Los Angeles. I thought about speaking to Angel about—"

"Ah! Angel! He and Spike were such darlings when they were here!" the woman gushed. "We gave them such a fantastic sendoff. Stylish jackets." The woman made a kissing sound. "They both looked so beautiful!"

"*Spike?*" She couldn't have heard her correctly.

"Oh, yes, I love him! He is so brooding, so fantastic with his hair and his long coat! Half of Wolfram and Hart Roma is in love with him!" She sighed. "The other half, of course, is in love with Angel! I myself am torn, because they are both such beautiful men!"

For a moment Buffy couldn't think. Her mind was spinning. *Spike is alive?*

"Spike . . . died," she said finally. "In Sunnydale."

"Oh, but no! That was a temporary condition! As it is so often, *sí*? We've heard of all his daring adventures! He's like a pirate! We were so glad that Wolfram and Hart Los Angeles was able to reattach his arms after that crazy Slayer cut them off!" She made a spitting sound. "We shall speak of her no more."

"Crazy Slayer . . . *Dana?*"

She leaned against the wall, too shaky to stand. Why hadn't he contacted her? Hadn't told her . . . She had grieved. . . .

She tried to make it make sense. "They were . . . *here.*"

"*Sì, sì,* you didn't know? They went to the club, looking for you."

Buffy was incredulous. *"They did?"*

"Angel said something about going to your apartment. That your friend Andrew was staying there as well? I said nothing in reply, of course. I didn't realize you had leased your own place. I wish you had come to us. We have wonderful apartments! They are simply to die for!"

"What?"

Just then, Andrew sauntered down the hall. He was wearing a turtleneck sweater, a pair of black pants, and what appeared to be a smoking jacket. He gave her a little wave.

"Andrew was in my apartment?" she said into the phone.

He paled and tried to hang a U. Buffy clutched the phone in one hand and grabbed him with the other.

"If he is planning to stay, perhaps we could interest him in a villa. They are so reasonable, so beautiful—"

"Hold on," Buffy said heatedly. She pulled the phone away.

"Andrew, Wolfram and Hart Roma tells me that Angel and Spike were also in *my apartment*."

Andrew blanched.

"I'll be in touch," Buffy told the woman.

"Delightful! Anything we can do for you, Buffy, we are so delighted to do!"

"I can explain," Andrew murmured as she disconnected the phone and stuffed it in her pocket. "The Immortal paid me a lot of money to keep them from bothering you while they were here to retrieve some head or something. Plus, I got to go out with supermodels. So I did it."

"I can't believe you!" she shouted at him.

"You should. Believe me." He nodded like a bobblehead. "But also, well, that's *amore*. He organized this whole wacky scheme just for you, because he was jealous. He wanted you to forget about them." He made a face. "I'm sorry."

"You. Are. So. Busted," she flung at him. *And so is the Immortal.*

"Why, there he is now!" Andrew exclaimed, sagging with relief.

The Immortal walked up to her, ducking his head like a mischievous boy. "Don't blame him. It's true. I was jealous."

"That's just incredible," Buffy said indignantly, although she couldn't hide the warmth in her cheeks. "And very wrong."

"It's simply . . ." He sighed and cupped her chin. She jerked her head out of his grasp. "I am Italian," he finished.

"He finds you very attractive," Andrew said dreamily, smiling at her. "I was trying to give love a little helping hand."

"Oh, you're both too much," she said. She glared at The Immortal. "That was really underhanded."

"All's fair in love and war."

"What if they had information for us?" she said. She crossed to a brass coatrack of jackets and coats, installed because of the intense cold, and grabbed her down jacket. She began to slide her arms into it.

"Where are you going?" he asked.

"For a walk." She zipped up the zipper and pulled the hood over her hair. Then she yanked out the gloves in her pocket and crammed them on her hands.

He made a face, then pulled open the drawer of a credenza opposite the row of outerwear and pulled out a bundle of small colorful tubes. "Use these glowsticks if you need light. You break them, and they glow," he told her. Then he leaned forward and brushed his lips against hers. "And forgive me?"

"I'll think about it," she bit off. She took the tubes from him and stuffed them in her pocket.

"Think about this as well." He kissed her again, more warmly.

Buffy said nothing, only left him and Andrew in the hall and jogged outside to the grounds of the palazzo. The snow made a blanket; the air was chill.

She felt claustrophobic as she traversed the training field. The temple ruins were heaped with snow. Despite the fact that the Immortal's grounds were vast, she didn't want to be there. She thought of Angel and Spike—what had they been doing here? She had been so upset, she hadn't asked—and moved into the forest, reaching with a gloved hand for a glowstick and broke it, giving herself light.

She ran, trying to burn off some nervous energy.

Spike. He's alive. And he didn't let me know. He never called, never came for me . . .

. . . until now. And he came here with Angel. They're working together at Wolfram and Hart. What does that mean? Does he still have his soul? Does Angel?

The question rooted her to the spot.

The trees were more like frozen columns, snow piled so high that Buffy could barely make out the sticklike canopies of branches. The sky was white; the earth, bone-colored.

When the glowstick began to dim, Buffy reached into her jacket and pulled out another. Then she saw a shape weaving in the drifts ahead of her.

She caught up to it. It was a half-frozen figure in a parka and a ski mask, which stopped when Buffy came toward it. It started to turn, then stopped, and a gloved hand reached up and tore off the mask.

Buffy recognized her. She was a Slayer who had gone missing months ago. Buffy pushed distracting thoughts of Spike and Angel to the back of her mind and gave the dark-haired, distressed Slayer her full attention.

"I'm Concetta Caprio," she said, falling to her knees. "*Mia Regina,* my queen, I deserted you and our sisters, and I am so sorry. They are crazy. They mean to let demons into our world."

"What are you talking about?" Buffy demanded, pulling her to her feet. Seeing the girl's fear, she pushed: "You were looking for me. You found me." She had a flash of realization. "That means they're not far from here."

Concetta's tears sparkled on her cheeks. Her dark eyes were like whorls of storm in the white snow. "Don't make me take you there. Please, get me back to the palazzo and I'll tell you everything."

Buffy hesitated. She knew very well that this could be a trap. For all she knew, the girl had some sort of magickal weapon that would blow the compound to kingdom come. Or maybe Antonio and Ornella assumed she would force the Slayer to take her back to their hideout . . . which is just what she wanted.

"I say we drag her back to their secret headquarters," said a voice behind her. It was Faith, wearing a parka like hers, hood covering her dark hair.

"You followed me?" Buffy asked.

"As backup, is all. Plus, all that talking made me feel like putting my fist through a wall. Saw you book, decided to leave too." She grinned. "Choice is easier now, huh? Two of us to fight our way out once we have a parley with the bad guys?"

Buffy nodded. She turned to Concetta and said, "Let's go."

"No, no!" Concetta begged. But her reaction seemed forced. By the look Faith gave Buffy, the dark Slayer held the same opinion.

So, a trap. That's okay. I went with the Anointed One to see the Master, and that turned out all right.

Except for the part where I died. . . .

"Bring it on," Faith murmured to Buffy.

The two Slayers flanked Concetta, who said, "Please, don't make me do it!"

You are never gonna get an Oscar, Faith wanted to tell her. But she said nothing as Concetta launched herself into a very bad acting job. Buffy wasn't biting either.

Concetta wailed as they forced her back the way they had come. They wove through the frozen forest.

Buffy said to Faith, "Spike and Angel were here. In Rome."

Faith was incredulous. "Spike?"

Buffy nodded. "He lived through it somehow, Faith."

"Heaven kicked him out too, huh?" Faith said, smirking.

"I wasn't kicked out. Willow pulled me out." She took a breath. "The same thing must have happened to Spike."

"Willow didn't mention it," Faith said, then shrugged to let Buffy know she was kidding. "Wolfram and Hart, they have a lot of mojo, could reanimate just about anybody, including this one guy I swear fell asleep while I was—"

"*Faith.* Get serious. Spike is alive."

Faith cocked her head. "And you like him best, eh, Blondie? Angel's out of the running?"

"This is not the time—"

"There's never been a better time," Faith countered. "B, the world is seriously in trouble. If Spike's good, then doesn't that help with the balance?"

She blinked. "I guess . . . he's been accounted for."

"Guess so."

"They were in Italy," Buffy added.

Faith's lips parted. "Get out. And they didn't stop by?"

"They didn't know where we were," Buffy said through her teeth. She told Faith the whole story.

"What a jerk," Faith said. "I don't care if they're immortal or vampires or what, men are just so amazingly—" Her words were cut off as she, Buffy, and Concetta suddenly plummeted through the air—

"Trap!" Buffy cried.

—into an underground vault made of stone.

Buffy and Faith landed on their feet while Concetta tucked and rolled onto the floor. Torchlight flickered over rotund, orclike demons in chain mail armed with axes and swords.

"Nicely done," said a woman's voice in heavily accented English. Then she spoke in Italian, and the demon guards parted down the center, moving to either side of the chamber.

They revealed Ornella, dressed all in black leather, seated on a throne. Concetta got to her feet and dipped a curtsy to Ornella before positioning herself on Ornella's right, trying to look all smug but, actually, not so sure of herself.

No surprise there, thought Faith. She glanced at Buffy, who likewise stood grim-faced and ready for the next predictable trick.

"So what's the what, *Regina*?" Faith said to Ornella. "We're here. What do you want?"

Evil Chick Queen pinched her perfect supermodel features in a less than workable version of a triumphant smile. "I didn't think Concetta would be able to fool you."

Concetta shifted, frowning, but said nothing as Faith spoke again. "Yeah? So?"

"So . . . I have an offer to make." She crossed her legs. "Antonio thinks that we have organized our Slayer army to go against you and the Immortal so we can take over Italy and rule this dimension.

He thinks the strange weather is a result of magicks performed on our behalf."

"Magicks that will end when our rule is established."

"Magicks performed by . . . ?" Buffy said. Faith knew she was scanning the chamber, looking for avenues of escape, while she was talking to Ornella. She knew it because while she was listening to Ornella and Buffy, she was doing the same thing.

"By his ancestors, Cesare and Lucrezia Borgia. He's wrong. It's a lie." She shook her head as if she couldn't believe how stupid he was. "There is a trio of hellgods more powerful than the Borgias could ever dream of being."

"That would be Janus, Shree-Earth, and Io," Buffy said.

Ornella raised a brow. "You know of them. Your pronunciation of their names is incorrect, but you're close."

"Not so good with the languages. Especially villain-ese," Buffy retorted. Faith grinned.

"This world is being brought to its knees. There's no need for a battle between us. It would be a—how does one say—suicide mission." She extended her hand. Great acrylics. "Join me now. Bring the Slayers in and they will all be spared."

"Because the Trio needs Slayers for future battles," Faith said.

"Precisely." She smiled at them, then shrugged. "But what battles can there be for us? This world is finished."

"Battles in other dimensions," Buffy said. "Are you as stupid as you are evil? Hellgods won't be content with just our dimension."

Ornella's eyes glittered as she laughed. "They want this dimension because of you, Buffy. Because you closed the Hellmouth. They want all human beings to die because you're a human being."

"That would be you, too," Buffy said.

"Yeah, and so what are they waiting for?" Faith piped up. "What's holding them back if they're so hot to trot?"

Buffy looked at Faith. "Glory couldn't just waltz right in and take what she wanted," she said. "She needed a key." Her eyes widened. "Oh, my god, Faith. We have something they don't. Something they need."

Faith thought hard. *The sphere we got off that girl?*

"Great minds thinking alike?" Buffy asked her.

"I'd say," Faith replied.

At that moment, part of the wall moved. It was a door, and Antonio Borgia pushed it open, stomping across the threshold.

"Ornella!" he cried. "What is this?"

Then he spoke in rapid Italian. Faith had no idea what he was saying, but she guessed he hadn't known about this little meeting. The so-called Queen of the Slayers looked as guilty as if he had caught her in bed with another power-hungry madman intent on destroying the world.

She replied; they began to argue. Faith gave Buffy a questioning look, and Slaysistah nodded.

Time to rumble!

In complete synch, she and Buffy each grabbed the nearest demon guard, disarmed him, and disemboweled him. Faith bagged an ax; Buffy got a sword.

They started swinging. No one hacked like Faith and Buffy, together again. Heads flew, guts spewed. It was like being inside a horror movie, only it wasn't horrible at all, as far as Faith was concerned.

Concetta tried to get in the way; Faith was so pissed off at her that she hacked her jacket right off her body, grabbing the pieces as the girl freaked out.

"Faith! Come on!" Buffy shouted as she cleared a path to the door.

It was so easy, it was almost disappointing.

They bounded out the door and up a spiral of stairs cut into stone. A few horned demons appeared, but not as many as Faith would have expected.

Up, up, and out . . . to a field of snow covered with dead and dying demons of various shapes and sizes. Green blood soaked into the white. On seeing the Slayers, the dying ones tried to rally, raising up on elbows or just grunting and moving their hooves like slowly dying really ugly pigs.

Slayers 1 and 2 didn't bother with any of them.

"Let's go," Buffy said, and they sailed into the freezing snowstorm, with no clue how to get back to the palazzo. Then she glanced down at the shredded jacket Faith was holding and said, "What's that?"

"Temper tantrum," Faith replied, but as she glanced down, she saw that something was glowing through the fabric. Faith felt with her hand in a pocket and pulled out a small sphere.

"That's a direction finder," Buffy said. "Common magickal object; I think they get them at the magickal drugstore. Willow makes them. Maybe Concetta got one from Ornella to lead her to us. Maybe it'll show us the way back to the palazzo."

"Maybe so," Faith replied. "If we even really need help."

Then, as the first flank of demon guards from the underground chamber clambered out, Faith and Buffy dashed into the snowstorm. Something like lightning crackled above them, and the earth shifted and shook.

The sphere glowed like a compass as Faith held it out in front of herself. By the time they successfully reached the forest of snow, the sky was turning red, sections sparkling with dazzling colors. Large figures raised against the kaleidoscope, shadow puppets enacting a macabre performance.

"This happened in Cleveland," Faith yelled as gale forces picked up. "Only, not so flashy. Just snow, but the big figures were there. It's the Legion of Three."

So that's what they look like. Creepy.

"I think they get projected into our dimension like shadows. Or cutouts over a flashlight," Faith went on. "I'm not sure they're aware we can see them."

"Stuff like this happened when Glory nearly won. The sky melting and all like this," Buffy said.

She took a breath. "Faith, I think we should contact Angel. Do *you* think Wolfram and Hart has gotten to him?"

Faith adjusted her hood over her head, tucking in all the errant strands of dark hair. "All I know, Buffy, is that when everyone else gave up on me, couldn't see any good in me, Angel still believed in me. It's hard for me not to believe in him."

"What about Spike?" Buffy asked, grabbing on to a tree trunk as the earth rumbled beneath her boots. "I know Spike. I know he's good."

"Then we need to get a hold of them," Faith said. "As soon as we get back. Because we need some help, B."

Using the finding sphere, they managed to get back to the palazzo. Buffy was half-frozen. Her hands and feet hurt.

As they pushed open the front door, Mr. Aram rushed toward them. "Would you care for some hot tea?" he asked solicitously.

"I would care for a phone," Buffy replied.

"Where's Giles?" Faith asked, glancing around. Ignoring Mr. Aram, she said, "We have to talk to Giles about the you-know-what. Make sure it doesn't wind up in the wrong hands."

"Too late, *cara*," said the Immortal as he stepped forward from the shadows, all dark and handsome and very sad.

He pointed to Buffy and Faith and said, "Seize them."

CHAPTER SEVENTEEN

It was not death, for I stood up,
And all the dead lie down.
—Emily Dickinson

Dozens of hooded guys—sorcerers and rotund, overmuscled demons—rushed from doorways and hallways. As they surrounded the two Slayers, Buffy shouted at the Immortal, "You're a bad guy!"

The Immortal's minions closed in on them. She and Faith fought hard, and well: Between them they felled at least twenty of the Immortal's henchmen before they were subdued. Buffy was cuffed with something that felt magickal; it tingled with energy that burned her, and she couldn't break free.

"I am not so much a bad guy as a practical guy," he replied, running his hand down her cheek. "I saw and heard everything in your meeting with Ornella, Buffy. The glowsticks in your pocket were scrying devices. I thought perhaps you were on your way to a meeting of some kind."

"I was right. Once I understood that Ornella was dealing with Lucrezia behind Antonio's back, I figured out the puzzle. I also knew you'd easily escape her. Unfortunately, I contacted Antonio a little too late. No matter. Here you are."

"You set me up!" she cried, jerking her head free of his caress.

He shook his head. "Not on purpose. We were at an impasse."

"'We' were at an impasse? So 'we' spied on us?" Faith flung at him. "Don't think *we're* on the same team, bro."

"If you had trusted me, I could have helped," the Immortal insisted. "As it stands now, I must protect myself."

He nodded at one of the hooded, robed guys holding on to Faith. The guy did something, and Faith groaned and slumped. "Faith! You killed her!" Buffy shouted, struggling again to free herself.

The Immortal pointed to the robed man, who showed Buffy a syringe in his hand. "Drugged, only. So we can present her to the Legion of Three. And you as well, *cara*."

He folded his arms across his chest, walking slowly as he inspected his captives. "I have just finished contacting them. I will give them the real Queen of the Slayers—after I bring them through to this dimension with the sphere Faith brought you from Cleveland. I've finally pieced together what it is, thanks to your meeting with Ornella and Antonio. It is actually called the Orb of Malfeo, did you know that?"

"I really don't care," Buffy said, fighting to free herself.

"Of course you do."

She seethed. "Just . . . how can you do this? I thought you had decided to be good."

For a moment he looked sad. Then he moved his shoulders and sighed philosophically. "You're so young."

"And you're old enough to know better," she retorted.

He held out a hand as if to say *humor me*. "Let me tell you a few things. Antonio Borgia's ancestors, Lucrezia and Cesare, are vampires. Lucrezia is interested in distilling the essence that is in your blood, that makes you a Slayer. The Legion of Three is interested as well. I will give them a legion of Slayers to experiment on. The ones who have rallied to your side, and the ones who have fallen in with Ornella and Antonio."

"So they'll spare you?" she asked snidely. "I can't believe you think they'll honor any promise they made to you."

He barely blinked. "In return, I will rule over another dimension. This one will become uninhabitable to anyone and anything except pure demons." He smiled. "They wish to retain my services. As I am someone who is more than human, they find me valuable. Like you, *bella bellissima*."

He flicked his wrist. "Take her to my dungeon," he told her guard.

As the demon began to drag her away, Buffy shouted, "I have such bad taste in men!"

She fought and kicked; then something pricked her arm. Needle, like Faith. Her eyes rolled back in her head, and she was out.

"Slayer," came the voice.

It was Whistler again, appearing to her as he had in the limo. Same retro clothes, kind of pudgy, make that—

"Doughy, huh?" He narrowed his eyes as he gazed down at her. "I guess I am. Behind on my Jazzercize." He squatted; she realized she was lying on a cold, hard floor; her eyes were closed, and she was asleep. Prophetic dreams were part of the Slayer accessory kit.

Whistler dangled his hands between his legs and cocked his head.

"Listen, kid, remember when I fished Angel out of the gutter after he went all remorse-crazy, took him to L.A., showed you to him? That was when he decided to devote himself to helping you. Remember when I came to you before you sent him to hell? That was another intervention."

"So is this."

She shifted in her sleep, listening.

"The Powers That Be are not ready for this world to be given back to the demons. They're gonna mix it up again." He nodded at her. "They're gonna help you."

Buffy murmured, but could not quite wake up.

"Now, what I'm going to show you is probably going to mess

you up," Whistler said. "But you gotta see it, like Scrooge with the three ghosts before he buys everybody a nice turkey dinner. And then . . . we'll see what happens next."

Still silent, Buffy stirred.

He snapped his fingers. "Now, come with me. Stay asleep, but come with me. Quick."

Buffy felt herself floating; she pulled out of her body and looked down on it. She was unconscious, and heavily chained. There were bruises on her face from battling to get out of Ornella's meet-and-beat and her capture by the Immortal.

Then she turned and looked at Whistler, who was standing just outside her cell. A human-shaped being stood beside him, shorter than Whistler, bathed in blazing white light that shot off in all directions. It shimmered and pulsed; she could make out no features, but she felt deep in her soul that it was someone—or something—that was good.

"Who is that?" Buffy asked Whistler.

His answering smile was mysterious. "Can't say, yet." He gestured for her to join him and the luminous being.

Like a ghost, she passed through the bars of her cell. "Can't, or won't?" she asked.

The being remained silent. Whistler said, "You've always been so impatient. Now come on."

The three glided down a hall. Buffy couldn't feel the stones beneath her feet. Nor the air, which must have been very cold.

"Hey, did I die again?" she asked Whistler.

"Nope. Not yet, anyway." He grinned at her.

"Ha. Ha."

The dungeon was vast and dim, illuminated only by a handful of weak electric lights. Towering bluish-hued demon guards in armor patrolled in front of the rows of cells. They were heavily armed, axes slung over their shoulders, sheathed swords hanging from leather belts.

They didn't notice Whistler, his glowing buddy, or her.

After about half a minute of walking, Whistler and the being stopped in front of a cell and Whistler gestured with his head for her to look inside.

Xander was sprawled on the stone floor, his right wrist shackled to a loop in the floor. His face was bloody.

"Stay focused," Whistler reminded her as she doubled her fists.

Farther on, Faith had been thrown into a larger cell with Robin. Faith was limp, her knees buckled, as she hung from cuffs bolted into the wall. Robin's hands were cuffed around a painted black metal post in the center of the cell.

Down another row of cells to the left, Vi and Rona lay side by side, each heavily bound with chains and ropes. Rona was lying in a shallow dip in the floor pooled with foul water.

She must be freezing, Buffy thought; she knew then that the Immortal was not at all sorry about what was happening. The bruises, he might have been able to rationalize as injuries sustained in battle. But his cavalier lack of concern about their comfort spoke volumes, and they weren't books on manners.

Next to that cell, Giles and Andrew were cuffed with their hands over their heads, sitting up against a damp stone wall. They were both slumped forward, unconscious.

Giles! Buffy called, but she knew he couldn't hear her.

If she had been angry about Rona's predicament, what she saw next boiled her blood. Two cells had been skipped, and were empty; but in the third one, which was parallel with Giles and Andrew, Belle had been chained standing up, like Faith. Dawn lay unconscious at her feet, her hand lying on Belle's boot—as if, at the last, she had either tried to free the little English Slayer, to comfort her, or to be comforted by her.

Dawn, who had been near death not too long ago, thrown into a cell in a track suit, her sweet face sporting a bruise . . .

"Your sister's not dead. But she's gonna be if you don't kick it up a notch," Whistler told her. "Okay, this part of the show is over."

Buffy floated through the low ceiling and then the floor and ceiling of the room above her, and the room after that; there were people everywhere, going about their nightly duties—a man polishing the marble floor in the room where Buffy had first met all the Slayers; the chef with the Emeril apron, seated with a glass of wine, reading a cookbook.

She, Whistler, and the nameless light-person soared through the air, through the snow and a tunnel of brilliant white light. Heartbeats like drums thundered in her ears.

Whistler sighed. "Now I need to give you some setup, girlfriend. Prepare you for what you're about to see. 'Cuz it ain't pretty."

"Listen hard. Angel and his homies have gone up against Wolfram and Hart. He's got a guy named Gunn on his side, only Gunn's got about five seconds left to live. Remember Wesley? He's dead. He had a girlfriend, but she's been destroyed by this hellgod living inside her body. Hellgod's name is Illyria. And your boy, Spike. He's there too."

Buffy said, "When did Spike come back?"

"Doesn't matter right now. When I say 'gone up against Wolfram and Hart,' I don't mean Angel and Sipke are suing them. They're fighting them, Buffy. In a rainy alley. With a couple of swords. And Wolfram and Hart's got demons and monsters and hellbeasts and dragons."

"They'll die," Buffy said. "Unless we help them. I'll get the Slayers and—"

"Don't wake up," Whistler admonished her. "You wake up, this won't work." He took a breath. "Okay. Right this minute, as we speak—well, as I speak and you listen—Angel, Spike, Gunn, and Illyria are in an alley. They're facing down a whole hell's worth of evil creatures—there's even a dragon, Angel wants it bad, gotta love the symbolism—and they know that they can't win this one."

No.

Back in the cell, the lids of Buffy's eyes flickered as her heart burst into a mad counterpoint. She began to thrash. Buffy was aware of it, it feeling like an echo against her consciousness.

"Don't panic," Whistler said to floating Buffy. "Don't, Slayer. Keep it together. There is nothing you can do to change this."

That's not true that's not true, no, oh God, no—

"I love them, too, well, for all of me being a metro hetero-sexual. I love 'em, Buffy. But this is not about them. Or you. This is about *the world.*"

The glowing shape lowered its head as Whistler raised a hand and said, "Look at them down there. Look."

And she saw them, about a hundred feet below on the ground in the pouring rain: Angel, Spike, a dark man who was bleeding, and a woman with blue hair. Angel was drawing a sword; Spike stood beside him.

Facing them . . . hell and worse. Demons, monsters, ogres, trolls; lesser vampires and Turok-Han—all the forces of darkness that she, the Chosen One, had promised to slay—surrounded by bil-lowing black smoke, flames . . . and a horrible stench, one Buffy knew well: the smothering odor of death, the foul breath of the Hellmouth as it opened its maw.

The four Champions stood poised for battle. The odds were unbelievable, and yet they prepared as if the fate of the world depended on defying those odds. The blue woman and the dying man were strangers to Buffy, but she would do anything, give any-thing, to save them.

This cannot be happening. This is a bad dream.

Angel's face was grim and determined. As Buffy's heart pounded, she gazed down on him in a moment that stretched back through time, to their first moment together; their first kiss; the night of her seventeenth birthday; and when he left. . . .

Spike's gaze was hard, but his eyes glinted with battle lust. Her heart broke for him. They had fought so hard not to love, she and he; and then, fought hard to love . . . and for love, he had died for her; for them all, his soul blazing within him. He had died. . . .

He can't die again. I won't let him. I will end this.

The dragon launched into the air as the hordes charged.

"Angel!" Buffy shouted. "Spike!"

They didn't look up. They were bracing for the onslaught.

Her throat tightened; she took a breath and lingered long on Angel's face, on Spike's. A million memories washed through her. Tears splashed through the air; one landed on Angel's shoulder, but he didn't notice it. Another, on Spike's hair.

The demons converged on them—

—and Whistler said, "Here's the deal. Look at those odds. They didn't come here to defeat the forces of darkness. They are facing certain death, wouldn't you say?"

The demons were almost on them. The dragon opened its mouth and gouted flame.

Over the roar, Whistler continued, "They came here to do what's right. To fight, no matter what. To do good. To *be* good.

"That's what a Champion is. That's what you are, Slayer."

As the demons raced up to them, Angel and Spike did not flinch; they did not so much as step back—

Angel! Spike! I must be dreaming this. I have to be dreaming this.

"Let me help them," Buffy begged.

He sadly shook his head. "You can't, kid. And I'm not going to make you see what happens next."

"Please."

Buffy wept. Bitter, harsh tears stung her face and dripped into her soul like pellets of acid. What she saw . . . it was not real. It didn't mean anything. It couldn't be true.

The luminous being beside Whistler opened its arms. The arms extended, became something like wings, or veils; the veils extended across the sky, covering the black rain with white. Buffy blinked . . .

. . . and she was somewhere else. Somewhere warm, and safe.

I've been here before.

And she was not alone.

To her right: *Angel.*

To her left: *Spike.*

Themselves, and yet . . . not themselves. When she looked at each of them in turn, she saw them, but not with her eyes.

She saw them with her heart.

Felt them with her soul.

Champions. The words came into her mind. She had no idea who spoke them. She wasn't even certain that she heard them.

She simply knew them.

She extended her hand. Spike took it.

Angel took her other hand.

Then the glowing figure took Spike's and Angel's free hands, completing the circle.

Buffy floated in love, and honor, and it was no longer about earthly yearnings and joys and despairs. It was not about choices.

It was about soul mates.

There are other, better places for those who do good.

There are other, better ways to love.

She saw Angel's eyes. And Spike's smile. Tears glistened on her cheeks as Angel and Spike both became bathed in white light, and their features gradually faded, until his eyes and his smile were only a memory. Both of them took on the mantle of the same blinding white light as the shimmering being; when she looked down at her body, she saw that she, too, had become luminous, ethereal.

Then her body seemed to lose its shape altogether; to flow, and to merge, joining with Angel, Spike, and the other being. She lost sense of herself; she gained awareness, briefly, of them; and then, they were . . .

. . . in a place where there was only love.

I love you.

I love you.

I love you.

I am you.

Her heart swelled, and she knew she would be with them again.

And again.

And again.

Then something new filled her soul, and her spirit; she was more than she had ever been. She was beyond the Slayer. She was not only herself.

She was *we.*

Then she was returned. She was flesh and blood again. Buffy again.

Spike, Angel, Whistler, and the glowing figure had disappeared. And she was back in her world, facing her battle, without them.

It is the battle, she realized. *The final battle. It started while I was gone.*

Getting her bearings, she floated through the snow-filled sky above the Immortal's mountain complex. His sprawling palazzo and vast, manicured grounds spread below her like a fairy kingdom, but the ground on which it extended was shaking and jittering apart. Sections pushed up. The Roman statues tucked among the trees toppled over, one after another, reminding her of the frozen dead of Pompeii.

Below, on the bowl-shaped plain, the Slayers who had called her Queen raced between their tents, which were falling down. Wind whipped at them as they lugged weapons—spears, axes, swords, crossbows—and massed into long rows.

At the foot of the hill, three figures struggled to maintain their balance as they inspected the Slayer army: Willow, Kennedy, and Oz. Buffy realized only then that she had not found them among the prisoners in the dungeon.

Of course! They left the palazzo just before I did!

Maintaining her balance by holding on to a spear planted into the ground, Kennedy was wearing a gold chest plate and a battle helmet with a red plume over a thick black sweater and black jeans. She looked amazing, like a true Amazon, someone who could inspire and command. Beside her, her arms outstretched, Willow conjured a fireball, its orange glow shading her long black-and-maroon dress and flowing sleeves with washes of warmth. Her black cape flared in the wind like wings.

Oz was dressed in a heavy jacket and gloves, but his head was bare. As the earth rumbled and shook, he raised a hand.

Seven young men joined the Slayers. Oz's werewolves.

Kennedy pulled the spear from the ground and unfurled a banner attached to its shaft. It was her name: BUFFY, topped with a crown.

Argh! No! Buffy protested. *I am not a queen.*

The entire assembly raised their arms and cheered. Then, like one living creature, they turned around and faced the other way. Bodies shifted, weapons glinted. The very air trembled.

Beyond the plain, bordered by more hills, stood a second army. Young girls dressed in battle gear of silver and black stared down Kennedy's troops. They held the weapons of Slayers—axes, swords, crossbows.

Towering behind them on a black-shrouded dais twenty feet in the air, Ornella stood in a long black coat and black fur hat, flanked by a very familiar figure.

Buffy seethed.

It was the Immortal, wearing his long ebony robes. In black-gloved hands he held the orb that Faith and Robin had brought back from Cleveland. The sphere that would let in three hellgods to destroy the world.

The Immortal held the sphere above his head. Though she was hundreds of feet away from him, Buffy heard his words as he threw back his head and began to speak:

"Janus, evoco vestram animam. Exaudi meam causam. Carpe noctem pro consilio vestro. Veni, appare et nobis monstra quod est infinita potestas."

The sphere began to glow a deep, rich blue.

He spoke again:

"Janus, evoco vestram animam. Exaudi meam causam. Carpe noctem pro consilio vestro. Veni, appare et nobis monstra quod est infinita potestas!"

Flares of blue energy shot from the sphere. As if in response, lightning crackled across the distressed sky. It traveled down the jagged clouds, heating the falling snow until it was steam, which boiled and rose into the sky.

All the Slayers glanced up anxiously. Willow closed her eyes and murmured words, and the fireball that had hovered between her hands flew through the wind and steam toward the Immortal.

As the flames got close to the sphere, they winked out.

Willow tried again. Again.

The sphere continued to spew flares of energy while the lightning joined it until, at last, a portal shimmered in the air, very close to where Buffy floated. It was covered over with a floating curtain of dark blue light, and things moved inside like creatures caught in amber.

Buffy squinted. There were two vampires in full vamp mode, a male and a female. Behind them . . . demons with heads like skulls.

And behind them, the Legion of Three. Ethan Rayne's two-faced god, Janus; the one that looked like Kali, the destroyer goddess; and one that looked like Death.

The dark light began to fade; the vampires moved closer to the portal.

They're coming through, Buffy realized.

On the field below, the Immortal shouted, "For the world! Attack!"

Kennedy yelled, "For Queen Buffy!"

The two armies swarmed toward each other. Spears extended, axes raised; girls too young to go to prom and girls who should be in college; and young women; they all raced at one another, shrieking like banshees. Faces white with fear; faces contorted with hatred.

The first flank engaged, and Slayer gouged Slayer. One of Ornella's black-clad warriors stabbed one of Kennedy's—no, Buffy's—Slayers in the chest with a sword. The wounded girl gasped and toppled to her knees as the other Slayer placed her boot on the girl's shoulder and yanked out her sword.

A file of Buffy's Slayers stopped running and took aim with their crossbows. They let fly a volley of bolts, which arched despite the wind and lodged into the bodies of the enemy.

And then the two vampires stepped from the crackling portal. They floated as if on an invisible staircase from the portal to the dais, where each embraced Ornella.

Buffy noted the startled glances of some of Ornella's Slayers as they realized vampires had just joined their side. But the chaos overlaid their surprise, and they rejoined the fray.

The sky went dark. The moon rose.

Oz wolfed immediately. So did his pack. It was an unexpected bonus; Buffy knew they could stay in control. Now they could battle as superstrong werewolves, not just superstrong guys.

But she was so wrong.

Oz and his pack were slathering, mindless. Snarling and howling, they attacked Buffy's Slayers.

Buffy looked to see a row of red-robed sorcerers who had moved to stand in front of the Immortal's dais. They were dancing and dipping, performing a spell. As far as Buffy could tell, they had enchanted Oz's pack and taken away their self-control. Her allies had become her enemies, through no will of their own.

In a fury, one of the werewolves lunged at Willow; she recoiled and brought up a magickal barrier. It smacked against it, but barely noticed as it flew at her again.

The plain ran with blood as Slayers fell beneath one another's weapons. The savagery was terrible.

Buffy's helplessness, more so.

"You're Slayers! You're sisters!" she shouted, but no one could hear her. No one could see her.

The werewolves howled; the wind became a gale. Blood splattered.

Then the Immortal's palazzo exploded.

"Dawn!" Buffy screamed.

At once, she plummeted toward the enormous columns shooting through the air; and chunks of marble as big as cars; and pieces of furniture and pieces of bodies. Fire spouted upward, and steam. She heard screams; a dog barking. Wolves howling.

Down she fell; and then—

—she felt strangely . . . calm.

A warmth suffused her, moving from the top of her head through her face, into her chest and spreading out through her abdomen. She felt as if she were glowing inside.

Then Buffy the Vampire Slayer opened her eyes. She was in her cell, in the dungeon, which was vibrating apart. Beneath her back, the floor split in two; before the earth could swallow her, she yanked her left wrist free and rolled to the side. She tried to pull her other wrist free, but the bolt had been driven more deeply into the stone floor. She gave it another yank.

Then the edge of a sword came crashing down on the chain attaching her handcuff to the bolt, and broke it.

Buffy glanced up to the bearer of the sword.

It was a child of maybe four. A little girl, she was swathed in white light, wearing a simple white long-sleeved dress that touched the floor. She was glowing from every pore of her body. Her platinum hair was tinged with a halo.

She had eyes just like Angel's: dark and serious, with a hint of golden warmth.

And a smile like Spike's—when he really, genuinely smiled, a slightly crooked grin with a hint of the boy he must have once been.

The sword she held in both hands, its point tipped to the

ground, was the same one she had seen Angel raise to fight the dragon.

"Who . . . ?" she asked, but the little girl put a hand to her lips and very solemnly handed her the sword. Silently, Buffy took it and slowly rose.

The girl reached out her arms, and Buffy wonderingly picked her up with her free arm. The girl scrambled from Buffy's embrace onto her shoulders and placed her palms over the crown of Buffy's head.

Strength poured through Buffy as if someone had transfused it into her veins. As the glow washed throughout her body, she felt renewed, invincible, stronger than anyone or anything. She felt as if she could conquer the world.

She felt like a Slayer.

A fierce euphoria shot through her—followed by a more powerful sensation: a surge of hope.

The stone floor swayed and buckled, but Buffy walked effortlessly over it. The cell door fell open as she approached.

The little girl's palms remained on her hair.

A demon guard coated in marble dust spotted her, and roared an alarm. Lightning fast, she ran him through. He dropped.

The next one came, and the next. But no more; the others panicked as another explosion ripped through the dungeon.

The stones beneath Buffy's boots grew warm.

Then hot.

She ran into Xander's cell and touched the sword to the shackle around his right wrist. His chains fell away; he opened his eye. The blood on his face disappeared.

"Buffy," he breathed, reaching out a hand. Then he grimaced and scrabbled up, away from the hot stone.

Together they ran down the alley, to Faith and Robin. As she touched the sword to Faith's chains and gathered her up, she said to Xander, "Go get Dawn."

He nodded and left.

"He doesn't see you, does he?" she said to the little girl. But the child said nothing.

Faith stumbled, reviving, then rushed past Buffy to help Robin up. She said, "What's going on?" She glanced around at the crumbling cell, then down at the hot floor.

"No time to explain now," Buffy replied. She didn't really understand it herself.

Xander arrived with Dawn and Belle, and Dawn raced into Buffy's arms. The five dashed into the other two cells and freed Giles and Andrew, then Vi and Rona. No one noticed the little girl.

The palazzo shook again, massive sections ripping apart. The black-and-white floor tiles cascaded through gaping holes in the dungeon ceiling. Water rushed down the side of the wall, hitting the floor and turning to steam.

"This way!" Buffy shouted as she spied a flight of stone steps. She led the group up, holding Dawn's hand protectively as Belle shepherded her from behind. The little girl rode Buffy's shoulders, as light as gossamer.

She's an angel, Buffy thought, holding her steady as she reached the top of the stairs.

For a brief moment she froze, astounded by the devastation before her. The palazzo was gone. There were no walls—nothing but pieces of weathered stone and pocked marble half-buried in melting snow. Pockets of steam blew from large holes. Weeds whipped in the wind. It was a ruin, and it did not look as if it had been inhabited for centuries.

She bounded forward to let the others up: Dawn and Belle, Vi and Rona. Giles and Andrew, who murmured, "Wow, it's like the Death Star after Luke drops the payload in the laundry chute."

As Faith reached the top of the stairs, she yelled, "B, lava down below! Rising fast!"

"Lava? No way," Dawn said.

"Way!" Xander asserted, popping his head up. He was the last one; he shouted, "Grab me!"

Buffy rushed forward and yanked him up. She glanced past his feet to see liquid orange and scarlet bubbling and smoking.

"It is lava," she said. "Let's go! Xander, Giles, take care of Dawn!"

The Slayers raced ahead—Buffy, Faith, Belle, Vi, and Rona. Giles and Xander flanked Dawn.

Andrew cried, "What about me? What should I do? Where are we going?"

The sky was falling.

The stars were winking out, one by one; as Willow drew down the moon, she braced herself for oblivion.

The Shadow Men were right, she thought. *We're outnumbered.*

The plain was awash with blood. Slayers pitted against Slayers battled as the real enemy—Ornella, the Immortal, the two vampires and their minions, and the three hellgods—watched from the sidelines. Willow understood their strategy: Weaken the side of good, and then swoop in and pick off what was left.

Unless the end of the world took care of that for them . . .

Reality was beginning to warp and shift; strange faces and stranger places superimposing over this reality. The signs and portents of the death of the world were clear to those who knew how to read them.

The Immortal knew how; as Willow watched, he conjured another portal with the sphere. It wobbled beside him on the dais; just before he stepped inside it, he turned and waved at Willow. He handed the sphere to Janus.

Then he was gone.

Hopefully, forever.

Then one of Ornella's Slayers blew on a horn and a large contingent of her Slayers retreated. Headed by a Slayer with dark hair, they raced toward the dais as Ornella beckoned them. Janus waved his hand over the sphere, and another portal formed.

The dark-haired Slayer led them into the portal. They went without hesitation. Then the two vampires followed after.

Willow's eyes teared with exhaustion and despair. None of her magicks were helping; as reality tore apart, fewer and fewer worked. It was the end, really and finally and truly.

Tara, will I see you? she wondered.

Kennedy was down with the others, fighting the hopeless fight. Most of the werewolves had been killed, to prevent them from attacking the good Slayers. She had managed to divert Oz long enough to place him in a magickal containment cube, but the power was shorting out, and soon he would be free. The cube was less than ten feet away, and Willow had picked up a crossbow.

If he attacked her, she would kill him.

"Oh, Oz," she said aloud, mournful and exhausted.

The feral werewolf bared his teeth at her, then threw back his head and howled.

Then Willow suddenly felt an odd sensation of warmth, and even a glimmer of . . . hope?

Startled, she turned.

"Buffy!" she cried, waving her arms.

Above her, on the top of the hill, stood Buffy and the others: Faith, Robin, Giles, Andrew, Dawn, Vi, Rona, and little Belle. A little girl was sitting on Buffy's shoulders, but when Willow looked at her, she saw Angel and Spike in her features.

The nine warriors charged down the hill; and Willow saw shadowshapes moving with them: four. One was . . .

Angel? And Spike?

"I feel them," Buffy said to the little girl. "They're here. The four. Angel, Spike, Gunn, and Illyria." She knew them, knew their histories.

Knew they were here to help her win.

The little girl kept her hands on Buffy's hair, and Buffy bounded down the hill and past Willow. She raced onto the field of battle and flew past the battling Slayers. The black-clad Slayers tried to stop her, but no one could touch her.

She kept running until Janus, Shri-Urth, and E'o saw her.

I know who they are.

The Legion of Three gathered, conferred; then they stretched out their hands as energy poured out of them—interdimensional evil took shape as slathering demons, monsters, hellhounds, all of them racing toward Buffy.

She did not stop, did not slacken. She knew that the little girl on her shoulders was what would tip the balance; there was now more good in the world than there had been, when the Shadow Men had made their dire prediction: This little shining soul was new, created from the valor and self-sacrifice of Champions who loved Buffy, and loved good.

The monsters came at her. She took a breath and thought of her mother; she thought of everyone who had fought and died at her side, and for her sake; and for others. Good would always prevail. Good was always stronger than evil.

Hope, a force that could annihilate despair, and cruelty and ambition.

Buffy held the sword out in front of herself as they came at her; and she knew, in that moment, the exhilaration Angel had felt when the dragon swooped down on him; and Spike's fierce joy as he prepared to give his life, again.

The little girl on her shoulders whispered, "Good-bye," and Buffy knew she was about to die.

The sword glowed.

The monsters came.

The world . . .

EPILOGUE

Buffy lay alone on the field of battle. The wind blew through her hair. Something heavy pressed against her chest.

She heard weeping.

Slowly she opened her eyes to find Dawn falling to her knees beside her. The hilt of Angel's sword crossed her heart.

"Buffy!" her little sister screamed. "Xander! She's alive!"

Dawn threw her arms around her, moving the sword away as Buffy tried to sit up. Xander ran toward them. Andrew trailed behind, shouting and cheering, "She's alive! She's alive!" as if he were the mad scientist Dr. Frankenstein.

Beyond the quartet, on the plain, a large pile of sticks had been built. Giles stood beside it with a torch in his hand. Belle, Vi, and Rona stood beside him, arranging more sticks at the base. They turned, looked, and began to run toward Buffy.

Then Faith loped over. She was a nightmare, covered in blood, and the sword in her fist dripped with gore.

Faith's eyes met Buffy's. She said simply, "Some of them wouldn't surrender, Buffy."

Buffy choked on her horror. After a few moments, she found her voice. "*You* killed . . . Slayers? Girls?"

"Had to," Faith said simply. With an expression of disgust, she dropped the sword.

"I . . . couldn't," Kennedy told her, approaching with a crossbow. "There were a few who still refused, Faith. I let them go."

"They'll retaliate," Faith said. "Find others, re-form an army . . ."

"But not today," Kennedy said gently.

Oz approached then, said, "Hey," and smiled at Buffy.

"Hey," she replied.

He said to Faith, "I found Ornella. One of my guys messed her up pretty bad. She killed Antonio after Buffy and Faith came to visit."

"Good riddance," Faith spat.

"Buffy." It was Giles, walking slowly toward her. He still carried the torch. He looked from the tower of sticks to the torch, to her. "We thought . . ."

She realized then that they had arranged her clothes around her, and had placed her folded hands over the sword. The tower of sticks was her funeral pyre.

"We saw . . ." Dawn's throat was too tight to speak.

"We saw you die," Giles said.

The crown of Buffy's head tingled. She reached up.

The little girl was not there.

Angel didn't die, she realized. *Spike . . .*

She broke down. The long nightmare was over; the grieving, unnecessary. As she sobbed out her exhaustion and her relief, the others held her.

The ones who loved her held her.

Hope filled every fiber of her being.

"I love you," she said to them as they crowded around her, laughing and crying, rejoicing in the amazement that they were all here, and all was well.

Andrew blinked. "Even me?"

"Even you."

She walked toward her pyre then, and she saw that they had planted the banner with the crown in the sand beside it. She yanked the pennant off the staff and began to shred the tattered fabric.

"No queens," she gritted, as Kennedy and Willow came up to her.

"Sorry about that," Kennedy said. "We knew it would piss you off. But Ornella was doing that whole 'Queen' bit, and we had to make sure our girls knew which side they were on."

"We almost used a happy face," Willow added. Then she said to Kennedy, "I need a minute with Buffy."

Kennedy nodded and walked back toward the others.

Willow took Buffy's hands in hers. "I saw her," she said. "Your child."

Buffy swallowed hard. "I think you were the only one who could."

"Magick user," Willow said, "Plus, I had an ascended moment when we did the Slayer spell. When I saw Tara." She took a breath. "Your little girl was beautiful."

"She was theirs. And mine," Buffy said wonderingly. "We gave her life, and she tipped the balance. Our daughter saved the world."

"Because of her, there was more good in the world than evil. There still is," Willow said.

"For now."

"For now," Willow agreed. "Maybe she'll come back someday. Maybe Spike and Angel will too."

She touched Buffy's cheek, and then she gave her dearest friend some space.

Buffy the Vampire Slayer raised her face to the dawn.

She was different, again. Not the same as all the other Slayers. Again.

She touched her lower abdomen, closed her eyes, and communed with heroes.

She said to them, *I will see you again.*

> He like a comet seemed,
> But wild and glad and free,
> And all through Heaven, I dreamed,
> Rushed madly up to me.
> —"A Heterodoxy," Lord Dunsany

ABOUT THE AUTHOR

Bestselling author **Nancy Holder** has published sixty books and more than two hundred short stories. She has received four Bram Stoker Awards for fiction from the Horror Writers Association, and her books have been translated into more than two dozen languages. A graduate of the University of California at San Diego, Nancy is currently a writing teacher at the school. She lives in San Diego with her daughter, Belle, and their growing assortment of pets. Please visit her at www.nancyholder.com.

As many as 1 in 3 Americans
who have HIV... don't know it.

TAKE CONTROL.
KNOW YOUR STATUS.
GET TESTED.

To learn more about HIV testing,
or get a free guide to HIV and
other sexually transmitted diseases:

www.knowhivaids.org
1-866-344-KNOW